Dogged Pursuit

A Veronica Kildare K-9 Mystery

TRACY CARTER

Cover Design by Jeffrey Zamaiko of JJ Zamaiko Photography
Author Photograph by Paul R. Carter

Print ISBN 978-1-66783-454-2
eBook ISBN 978-1-66783-455-9

FIRST EDITION: 2022
Printed in the United States of America

CHAPTER 1

O n very rare occasions such as this one, where my fingers have passed the point of numbness and gusting winds pelt me with freezing rain, I think longingly of my former life as a legal assistant, with a nice, cozy indoor job. Then I remember how that life ended in shocking violence, fear, and heartache, and how much safer I feel now, in Colorado, and my longing dissipates rapidly. I just hope the scent trail my dog has been following for the last two frigid hours isn't dissipating at the same rate.

"Pay attention, Veronica. Shari is counting on us," I tell myself sternly while focusing on my four-year-old Chesapeake Bay Retriever. Leda sniffs the air repeatedly to hone in on the scent which is her job and continues trailing. Trailing is basically a dog following a specific person's scent pattern wherever it has wafted, either on the ground or in the air, as opposed to following a particular set of tracks (tracking). Leda's tail is up and her whole body radiates intensity. This is today's mission and she loves it. As Leda hesitates briefly at a trail intersection in the Boulder County Open Space area where we are working, I call her back with one quick word, grab the plastic baggie containing the scent article (a red bandanna fished from a Jeep) and open the baggie for Leda to get another good sniff of the target's scent. When Leda is actively sniffing, she breathes in and out over one hundred and fifty times a minute. She looks up at me with her serious, almost yellow eyes (which alarm many people unfamiliar with Chessies) and turns abruptly back to business. I reinforce the Find command—even though she's definitely got it—while tugging my rain hat down lower on my forehead in a vain effort to stay just a tiny bit dry.

"Of course, this has to be one of the 30 days a year it's not sunny in Boulder," offers Sgt. Tim Donovan of the Boulder County Sheriff's Office, who is following Leda and me as support while we track Shari Wright ever upward in the trail system below the famed Flatirons. I murmur agreement to Tim knowing he won't be offended by my single-minded focus on my dog. We actually met through his wife, Sylvia, who took me under her wing when I joined the same yoga class last year. Tim and I have worked together several times now in similar lost person situations after his department called me in as an independent resource. Tim, Sylvia, and their four ebullient teenage daughters have rapidly established themselves as part of my extended family over the past year. He never seems to mind the quiet time he gets when working a situation with me. Having two sets of twins makes for an interesting dynamic in the Donovan household! I am only 30 but feel so much older than his bubbly, friendly girls. And small talk is definitely not my strong point any longer.

From what I learned during our Thursday morning briefing after the Sheriff's Office called me at 11:00 a.m., Shari is a typical Colorado mountain kid, loves hiking and snowboarding, and waitresses while she attends university. Her friends became alarmed when she did not return from an early afternoon hike the day before, and oddly, no texts or photos were sent by Shari to any of her friends during the hike. Unfortunately, no one was sure which of Boulder County's 40,000+ Open Space acres accessible to the public she had chosen to visit and it took some time to locate her ancient Jeep tucked away on street parking access near the Greenbriar Connector. Her cell phone appears to be turned off. Modern technology is a great locator, until it isn't. Now we are going old school with a trailing dog. Here's how.

A human body contains approximately 60 trillion cells. Every day, about 50 million dead cells drop off this human body. This is the scent that Leda is following primarily in the air and occasionally on the ground. Leda's body language is all positive as she surges steadily forward at the end of her 16-foot long line made of ½" wide supple webbing. Now is a good time to tell you, I am obsessive about my dog's safety. My line is shorter than those used by many trainers, as I worry constantly about Leda surprising a bear around a blind corner while she's intently working—just like the mama and two cubs we saw shoving berries into their mouths by a creek during our morning run a few months ago. Luckily for us, the bears were so intoxicated by the luscious fruit that my dog and I skidded to a halt and backed quietly up the hill without drawing any attention. Thank God for obedience lessons and a rock-solid recall.

Leda appears locked in, following Shari's scent trail up the muddy Lower Big Bluestem Trail and then the Upper Big Bluestem Trail, for a short jaunt on the Mesa Trail and then onto the Shadow Canyon Trail. The wet weather is helping us in some regards by keeping the trail largely vacant of hikers, and the scent relatively fresh—although presumably at least 18-24 hours old by now. A dog has 200 million scent receptors in its nose, distributed among the plentiful folds located there. In contrast, a human has at most a mere 5-20 million wedged in a space the size of a nickel way back in their nose. I'm betting on my dog. "Good girl, Leda. Find," I urge her on quietly while wiggling my fingers in their gloves for a little warmth, and feeling the cold trickle of persistent rain dripping down the back of my neck.

"Looks like she was headed toward Bear Peak, maybe, after those last few turns on the trail, and her friends said she likes hikes with vistas. You get the great view of the mountains to the west from there," I say to Tim while half turning my head so he can hear from behind me.

"If so," he replies, "I'm afraid she's gotten into trouble. That's normally just a good long day hike for someone in Shari's condition and the weather was fine yesterday afternoon." Tim keys his shoulder radio with a few brief words to alert the EMTs trailing us hopefully up into the mountains with

3

our latest supposition. We pass by the monoliths called Devil's Thumb and the Maiden, usually popular with rock climbers, but not on this raw day. Most of the surrounding rocks are seasonally closed due to wildlife but the Maiden is always open. It's unusual to see the majestic spires of rock without their customary background draping of impressively blue sky, but rather with this flat, pewter-colored scene looming behind them. The Maiden is renowned for its descent featuring a 120-foot free-hanging rappel to a narrow, open saddle named the Crow's Nest. And before you ask, I have not had the pleasure. Not afraid of heights, but not inclined to dangle on a rope.

"Since you guys called me in right away after her vehicle was found, the trail seems pretty decent for Leda and easier for her to follow without dozens of searchers having trampled all over the Open Space."

Tim gives a wry chuckle. "We heard you last year after you found that poor, elderly lady with dementia who had wandered away from her care facility. Leda did a phenomenal job on that trail even though they made it tough on you with all the prior searching and blundering around by the care facility personnel." I nod briskly to that comment and keep my eyes on Leda's wet, but still curly-haired spine. I am just amazed that, within a few years of my leaving Ohio as a heartbroken and devastated shell of my former self, my life has been totally restructured around dog training, thus allowing me to find a sense of purpose again in my new community.

Up and up we climb, battling the driving rain, tenacious wind, and slick footing—until Leda pulls strongly on her line and abruptly veers right off the trail, angling up a side hill and toward a cleft in the canyon wall. Her ears are up and she's sniffing the air energetically. Tim rips off a piece of pink surveyor's tape to mark the spot where we leave the trail for those coming behind us. The dogs and I have hiked this trail several times and never noticed this obscure cleft in the rock before. All the miles of running and snowshoeing to stay in shape for situations like this one are certainly coming in handy. As it is, my legs are getting a bit weary, but we need to find Shari.

"I wonder why Shari deviated from the trail here. The way to the peak is clearly marked," Tim speculates. We follow Leda carefully picking our way over and around jagged rocks—many of them deceptively slippery after the overnight and morning showers. The scree field on our right looks like an enraged giant has smashed thousands of bowling balls and dashed them down the hillside in a fit of pique. The wind intensifies and the sky looks increasingly angrier and more ominous. Leda does agility training two or three times a week with me and it all pays off whenever she has to clamber over any obstacle for her job. On the other hand, I feel I could move a lot more quickly if not encased in full head to toe rain gear.

"Well, maybe she had to pee, or was looking at fall foliage—or was trying to photograph a bird or wildlife," Tim finishes my sentence. Leda's pace has picked up as she presses forward into her harness literally dragging me across the rugged terrain. I'm almost holding my breath, thinking to myself, please... please let her be okay. Leda makes a sharp right turn around a massive boulder in the shadow of Bear Peak and immediately her locate barks ring out in excitement. Three sharp barks—just like she was taught. Tim and I hasten forward, rounding the behemoth rock, and find a pale and lifeless Shari prone on the ground. He immediately calls her name and reaching for her wrist, checks her pulse.

Tim calls out to me. "Veronica, she's alive!" We share a quick, pleased grin before he immediately starts to assess her condition. A massive purplish bruise darkens the side of Shari's face and her ankle is bent at a decidedly unnatural and nausea-inducing angle. Tim gets on his radio calling forward the rescue team, which has been moving stoically up the mountain behind us for several hours as we tracked Shari. They will hustle up here quickly with a stretcher, and more importantly, their medical knowledge. Shari is worryingly still, but her chest *is* moving ever so slightly. Tim has pulled a Mylar thermal blanket out of his pack and tucked it around Shari.

As the medics arrive breathing hard, but all hustle and efficiency, I turn my attention to my beloved Leda. She has the drive to be a search dog, but she is atypical in particular ways. She has never needed the immediate gratification of a toy or tennis ball when she locates her target. Leda sits on her haunches watching me intently as Shari is tended to. Once the injured woman is bundled up and sent down the mountain with the EMTs, Leda glides over on her quiet pads and leans against my leg as I rub her ears and kiss her face.

"Clever, clever girl, such a good girl." I pull Leda's collapsible bowl from my pack and fill it from her water bottle. She takes a good satisfying drink and turns back to me showing her beautiful Chessie smile and leans against me harder. She quite literally saved my life in Ohio when I adopted her and now she's saving even more people in Colorado. I sit next to my dog for a few quiet, happy moments listening to the tenacious rain drip softly on the rocks, pleased with our day's work, as Tim, looking like a wraith in the fog, takes his last scout around the area where we found Shari.

Later, much later, I examined that earlier peaceful moment of contentment under the sodden veil of Bear Peak in great detail. But I was absolutely sure of it—even in retrospect. There had been no foreboding ripple or murmuring portent in the air warning me that within days violence was about to blast its way into my life. Again.

CHAPTER 2

Leda, Tim, and I work our careful way down from the near summit of Bear Peak as the weather gets even more tumultuous, with Tim thanking us profusely for the first couple of minutes by yelling into the wind while anchoring his hat to his damp red crew cut. "Veronica, you and Leda did it again. Nobody would have found Shari lying there unconscious in that location without the pair of you. You're awesome!"

"All in a day's work," I respond with a tired grin, while thinking longingly of a scalding hot shower and pepperoni pizza. She was probably thinking of kibble and her bolstered dog bed. (Extra swanky maroon with a gold trim.) She may love it even more than her kibble. Like many abused and neglected rescue dogs, she had issues and it took months to get her to eat up her food properly. Rescue dogs seem to enjoy the little comforts so much more. As we left the spot where Shari was found, we observed behind her a torrent of sparkling water shooting out of the cliff face, possibly a seasonal waterfall that appears only when we get a torrential downpour. Maybe that's what she was looking for when she left the trailhead. We had had a couple of rainy days right before yesterday's good weather. A cool natural occurrence that an acquaintance told her to check out almost cost Shari her life. Mother Nature can be remarkably unrelenting.

Bone-tired by the time I reach my SUV, I load Leda in the back in a hurry. My sanctuary and dog training facility are not far away now. I drive southwest of the city of Boulder and it's not long before I pull up the long, steep driveway toward my home—after using my remote to open the gates at the base of the drive and then close them. We ease into the garage below my house. Leda waits at the back of the tailgate for me to tell her "Yes," and hops down. This is a very important command and one many dog owners never train their dogs on. It can be a lifesaver though; you never want your dog jumping out of your vehicle wildly in a parking lot with moving vehicles. I remove her harness and Working Dog vest, and give her a biscuit. Her favorite, peanut butter. I grab one of the 20 or so designated "dog towels" out of my truck and run it all over her, sopping up the wetness from her fur. Chessies have a remarkable coat which repels a lot of water, so it doesn't take long. As we head up the interior stairs to my abode, I feel a familiar shadow of melancholy seep into me. Of course, I know why. If only Zach were here with me to share the triumph of Leda finding Shari. I lean against the stairwell for a moment to gather myself. The lights are on and that shower is calling me. Leda bounds up the stairs ahead of me where my father, Bob, greets her in the kitchen with that baby talk we dog owners favor and we don't care who hears us. I pull off my sodden hat, letting my mass of long auburn hair loose and peel off my raincoat and rain pants. Somehow my lower layers stayed fairly dry.

"You found her then?" my dad questions me, as I trudge wearily up the stairs to join them in the main living space.

"Leda did; I just follow the superstar."

My dad's light blue eyes sparkle with merriment and pride. "You're too modest, Ronnie. You trained that dog."

"It wasn't too hard," I reply as I wander further into the kitchen. "She's got a wonder nose. Poor Shari is still unconscious though. It looks like she broke her ankle and banged her head when she fell. And smashed her phone. Tim will let me know later about her condition."

"Ouch," my father grimaces in sympathy as he turns to the stove to stir whatever was producing wonderful smells. He tells me he's taken care of the evening dog chores and I tell him he is a most excellent parent.

Leda finishes greeting her second favorite human, drinks copious amounts of water, and then folds up on her deluxe dog bed with a contented sigh. I wonder if Dad would notice if I curled up with her and closed my eyes for just a second. "She's come a long way from that emaciated, hairless dog liberated from a six-foot chain on a porch when the County Dog Warden found her," my dad says.

"That's for sure! And it was the luckiest day of my life when I adopted her from the Dog Warden," I respond. My big, strong, outdoorsman father gets very quiet and solemn.

"It was MY luckiest day. Without Leda, I would have lost you, sweetheart."

I blink and try to lighten the mood. "Best $95 I ever spent."

Dad gives himself a little shake and straightens up. "It sure was. Looks like that new rain gear I got you did the trick," he observes proudly as he changes the subject adeptly and stirs his sauce. My stomach starts to rumble; pasta is clearly in my future. He continues to tease me, "I know it's not glamorous but fashion never means much if you're freezing your ass off."

I laugh in exasperation and head toward the shower with one last wiseacre comeback. "I'm going to get a bumper sticker made up with that saying and stick it on your truck if you say it one more time!" My father's amused laughter follows me down the hall toward my shower, and I hear Leda's kibble pouring into her ceramic, paw-printed bowl. Dad gives her the release word so Leda knows it is fine to start eating. The lovely hot water cascades over my weary head.

CHAPTER 3

The next morning brings with it a feeling of freshness and the trademark clear blue sky outside my window. Back to the stellar Colorado weather. No rain gear today. I pull on my jogging tights and socks, tug on a long-sleeved shirt and maneuver my feet into my jogging shoes as I brush my teeth. My reflection in the mirror shows a good enough face, certainly not beautiful—my emerald green eyes and bright white smile are probably my best features. I pull my long, curly auburn hair into a ponytail and clip it up. I love to eat my dad's pasta, a LOT, so jogging is my penance. It keeps my 5' 6" frame at a healthy 150 pounds, and has the added bonus of helping me commune with any and all of the pups in the morning—while simultaneously exercising the lot of us.

In the kitchen, Leda is already doing her downward facing dog stretch in anticipation of our run. I walk down the hill to my kennel building with Leda and the car keys. Squeals of excitement greet me as Gemma is released from her massive indoor/outdoor kennel run. She's black—a Flat-Coated Retriever and Australian Shepherd mix, who started her life in a drug den, but joined me three months ago after her former owner went to prison. The local Humane Society took her in when the felon's father pitched her out in the street. One of their volunteers, Trixie, had gotten to know me when I put up business cards for my dog training business on their bulletin board. Trixie alerted me when Gemma arrived as a possible candidate for a service dog. She has warm brown eyes and an amazingly sweet disposition considering her start in life. Gemma is in training to be a citrus greening disease detection dog for a family, the Duncans, in Florida that owns hundreds of acres of orange groves. They're so excited for her to get to their property they can hardly stand it, but we have work left to do.

Dogs are simply amazing and can help humans in a million different ways. I had not even heard of this disease when the Duncans contacted me in search of a trainer willing to train a dog to protect their trees. But the research showed me it could be done and I love a challenge. These clients found me online after running across my website and reading the testimonials from several farmers for whom I trained terriers as invasive weed sniffers. Sniffing out those invasive weeds before they can pollinate and disperse across crop lands keeps the corn and soybean fields of my farmer clients in Nebraska significantly more robust and thus more profitable. Citrus greening or Citrus Huanglongbing (HLB) disease is fast spreading, impacting 80% of the citrus trees in Florida, and turns the fruit bitter, eventually killing the tree.

The disease is caused by several species of bacteria and is typically spread from tree to tree by tiny insects called Asian citrus psyllids. The bacteria impact the vascular system of each tree and stop the nutrients from getting through. Recent research has indicated that planting cover crops which inject vital nutrients back into the depleted soil as each crop decomposes may provide a way to make the trees healthier and combat the disease. But right now, it is imperative that Gemma be trained to identify the volatile signature scents released by infected trees AND newly infected, symptomless trees to protect their livelihood. Citrus is an $11 billion industry in Florida and my clients are fourth generation growers.

Pondering my afternoon training plans, I walk with Leda and Gemma up the little lane that runs between my dog training facility and my dad's cabin. My converted house sits highest of all at the top of the slope. The whole place used to be a day spa offering facials, massages, and manicures, but was scheduled for a Public Trustee foreclosure auction after the thoroughly mellow owners (who were apparently no great shakes as business people), racked up years of unpaid loan obligations. My father saw the potential and scooped up the property for a shockingly good price. The whole property is seven acres and fenced all the way around now with an eight-foot-high chain link fence. Security cameras and motion sensor lights cover the grounds, my training facility, and the outside of the two-story day spa which has been remodeled into my home, and the images can be accessed from the monitor on my father's desk. He is a throwback mountain man but extremely security conscious. Months of threats against your child will do that to a parent.

The former day spa has a unique set-up with a garage and storage areas below and a lovely mahogany wood upstairs with oversized windows around the entire perimeter. It includes a central open space, a country kitchen, one bedroom, and one bathroom. A cozy, breezy sun porch extends off the front side. Dad's home is only 800 square feet but he loves it. It's a miniature Alpine cabin with one bed, one bath, a fully appointed kitchen full of gleaming appliances and hanging pans of every shape and size, and a living room with a high vaulted ceiling and river rock fireplace. He has a spectacular view of the Flatirons from his laptop by the window. Dad knew we were in the right place when he looked up from writing the first week here and saw a mama bear and three cubs wandering across the mountain meadow below the Flatirons. He is one of the greatest wildlife spotters you will ever find. Literally any trip with him into the countryside results in a plethora of sightings, from eagles to moose to otters to hawks. Dad writes articles for outdoor magazines and does product reviews of all sorts of outdoor gear. Hence the ultra-glamorous rainwear he foisted on me yesterday. I tap on the door and walk in as his male Golden Retriever, Ripley, greets me doing his usual full body wag. Never just the tail with this dog.

Ripley lived most of his first three years at the end of a 12-foot chain in the back yard of a thoughtless family who never imagined "he would get so big" and take up so much space in their house. That's what puppies do—they grow up. He was supremely neglected but not actively abused. Dad watched and worried every time he spotted that dog from afar as he drove down the road, until one day he couldn't take it any longer. And then Ripley was his. I was a little hesitant to ask him how that all transpired, as you never know with Bob. A midnight commando raid was a strong possibility. But apparently the offer of $100 and a different home was enough to pry the gorgeous Golden from his unworthy family. He is much adored and rarely separated from Dad unless he comes running with the dog pack. He lies under Dad's desk for the writing sessions and leaps up with alacrity when he hears the word "hike." Best of all, he and Leda bonded instantly with each other and are often to be found lying back-to-back in the winter in the vicinity of the fireplace.

"Hey Dad, I'm taking the girls running. Can Ripley come with?"

Dad looks up from his computer deep in thought. "Sure, honey," he replies, "all recovered from yesterday?" I assure him I feel fine and mention that Sergeant Tim texted me earlier in the morning that Shari had regained consciousness and was being scheduled for surgery for her shattered ankle. The dogs and I then load up in my vehicle for the short drive to the trailhead. All three dogs have their sight and voice control tags on their collars to visit the Community Ditch trail and we're off and literally running. A dog with a good off lead heel and responsiveness to their owner—despite distractions—is welcome just about anywhere. My pack of three trots along behind and next to me happily sniffing to their hearts' content, but drops in tight to my left side whenever we pass another person enjoying the trail paralleling the irrigation ditch. A good brisk hour-long run does wonders to refresh the mind. Or let one indulge in more pasta. Take your pick.

CHAPTER 4

I return Ripley to Dad and fill him in on my plans to take Gemma up near Estes Park later this morning for an outdoor training session and bonding. The Duncans want her to travel and camp with them, in addition to her upcoming position as Supreme Orange Grove Protector. I feed the dogs and take a quick shower while my cell phone charges up. I gather my hiking gear together and stuff my accessories in my backpack: sunscreen, Cleveland Cavaliers hat, water, lip balm, gloves, surveyor's tape, tissues, dog treats, bandanna, rain poncho, hand sanitizer, Swiss Army knife, antibiotic salve, thermal Mylar blanket, and bandages. Better to be prepared for anything than to lament something you left behind. My father has trained ME well. I grab an apple and a pear from the fruit bowl on the counter, and last but not least, my little boxed samples mimicking the signature scents of trees infected by citrus greening disease. It's amazing what chemical "scents" they can come up with in laboratories nowadays.

I put Leda on her dog bed and give her a cookie, telling her she has to stay this time. Then I resolutely turn my back on the woeful eyes and head out the door. Leda and I are not separated often and Chessies take their mission very seriously. Their owner is their world and theirs to protect. Dad and Ripley will be heading over shortly to collect Leda for the day, which makes me feel only slightly less guilty. Gemma happily jumps in the back of the SUV, stations herself behind my seat, and presses her nose against the dog screen separating the cargo area from the front seats. "Yes,

I know you're excited to work, but we have a drive to get there first. Make yourself comfortable." We make good time heading north up Route 36 and stop in lovely, quirky Lyons for gas. The town is making a decent recovery from the massive flood that hit it a few years ago; but who can forget the photos of pipes which served as utility conduits jutting fifteen feet up into the air above the water-ravaged roadways?

Gemma is briskly sniffing out the partially open rear window while I sing along to a CD by The Chicks and enjoy the brilliant cobalt blue sky. I never tire of the view as we roll into Estes Park and head toward the famed Stanley Hotel before picking up Devils Gulch Road behind that allegedly (yes sir, it is) haunted hotel made famous by Stephen King and *The Shining*. Based on my personal experience when I stayed there one summer Saturday night for a wedding reception, a couple of ball-playing, phantom children need to cross to the other side—and get out of the fourth-floor hallway. But I digress… We pass through Glen Haven and find the forest access road on the left that heads into the Comanche Peak Wilderness, which runs along the northern and eastern boundaries of Rocky Mountain National Park (RMNP). Gemma and I pile out of the vehicle at a small gravel lot for the Dunraven trailhead and I wiggle into the straps of my backpack. I put on my Cavaliers hat, pulling my tangled ponytail through the back, dress Gemma in her Working Dog vest, and attach her to the lead. She dances enthusiastically all around me with a happy grin, ready for the day's adventures.

But how quickly life can take a turn. As rapidly as bullets can pump out of a semi-automatic handgun, my previous life was decimated. If I had only known what coming events in my current life were to be set in motion that fateful day near Estes Park—the missing scientist, the pilot, the assault rifles, the ex-cons, and the terror—I would have loaded Gemma right back in that vehicle and driven away. At speed.

CHAPTER 5

Comanche Peak Wilderness is a truly magical spot, consisting of almost 67,000 acres in the Roosevelt National Forest, and over 100 miles of hiking trails, but it is not nearly as visited as Rocky Mountain National Park. Gemma and I start moving out down the North Fork Big Thompson River Trail. Walking along the river and checking out the mosses and ferns delicately lining the edges in a lacy fringe is soothing to the soul. The river crossings are fun as Gemma peers down avidly to see if she can spot trout in the water. The bridges have all been rebuilt since the flood a few years ago and the sun dapples lazily across the water today. The light shimmers in hypnotic waves lulling me into an almost trance, until Gemma spots a bejeweled blue dragonfly and pounces. Not to worry; it was way too fast for her.

We only run across a few other hikers and exchange happy hellos. One tanned young man spots my hat and offers his commentary, "You have a crazy good team this year."

I grin back happily with a surge of pride. "I know, right? I could get used to winning." He asks for, and receives, permission to pet Gemma, since she's not actually working yet and heads on down the trail with a farewell wave. The peace threaded through a quiet, sunny day out West is unrivaled anywhere else in my humble opinion. Just the warm fall breeze and only bird song to break the silence. We keep a brisk pace as I am planning a four-mile hike close to the boundary of Rocky Mountain National

Park and a practice session with Gemma today. We pass the private outdoor summer camp, which always reminds me of an old-time movie-making ranch and head through the timber-rimmed meadows with a clutch of historic cabins known as the Deserted Village. These desolate shells are the remnants of a 1908 resort which originally included 11 cabins, a dining hall, a barn, a dairy, and an icehouse. "That's not creepy at all," I venture to Gemma, as we pass by the decaying remnants of buildings pancaking slowly into the earth and sliding toward the river while their sightless window holes stare back at us.

A small clearing next to the trail with young aspen saplings around the edge looks like the perfect spot to train. I walk Gemma back around the bend in the trail and put her in a Down Stay with the lead still hooked to her collar. I hustle back to the clearing out of her sight and pull on my gloves. My sample boxes with the simulated citrus greening disease scent are plucked from their bag, and placed around the bases of the saplings in no particular order. Then I put on a fresh set of gloves and take my dummy boxes which smell like nothing but wood from their bag and place them near different baby trees. Little gold stars on the bottom tell me which boxes are the target boxes.

After collecting Gemma, I stand her at the edge of the clearing and then release her to work with the seek word the Duncans have chosen as her cue. Something short and guttural, I told them—which is why I am now standing in the Colorado wilderness calling out "ROT" emphatically. Gemma gets right to work sniffing around the bases of all the saplings. She's done this quite a few times and seems to be getting exponentially quicker. She moves along the line of little trees and sits down purposefully next to one. I walk over and glance at the bottom. Excellent. She's hit one of the target "disease" boxes. "Good girl, Gemmie," I praise her in a happy, high-pitched tone and she beams back up at me. I pop a liver treat in her mouth and send her out again with the "ROT" command. I'm as proud as can be as she methodically checks the whole line of saplings and sits to alert next to only the target boxes. "All done, Gemma. Great work." I ruffle her fur, pop another treat in her mouth, and gather my boxes back into their separate bags and return them to my pack. In a few weeks, I can take her to Florida to proof our work on the real ROT trees. She gets a big drink, slurping water happily over my hiking boots. Time to hike back the way we came. Dogs are not allowed on the back trails in Rocky Mountain National Park so we cannot continue up the trail toward the beautiful Lost Falls. Oh well. Colorado is filled with gorgeous places where dogs *can* accompany us and rules are rules.

Just as Gemma and I turn back from the boundary of RMNP, a foreign sound churns the sky above us—a whirling, chopping noise. I look up in disbelief. "That can't be, girl. What the heck?" But I'm not crazy. A blue helicopter with a silver nose cone flies in our direction from out of the national park and then right over my head—at a pretty low altitude too. No markings are visible indicating it's a rescue or official chopper of any kind. In fact, I see no identifying tail markings at all, but the sun is in my eyes. One thing many people do not know—commercial overflights of the park are strictly prohibited and have been since 1998, thanks to the efforts of the local League of Women Voters. It is the only national park unit in which blessed silence has thus been permanently preserved. Gemma looks up too in puzzlement, or perhaps in solidarity with my disgust.

I hurriedly pull my cell phone out of my back pocket and cue up the camera, snapping a couple of quick photos before it heads over the horizon. A missed text from Dad stares back at me: "Just checking on you, kiddo. Leda is sleeping with Ripley under my desk. Are you and Gemma headed back out of the woods?" Amazingly, one bar of cell service is evident on my phone even as we head back along the Big Thompson River.

I reply, "Yes, Mr. Safety. Gemma did great work and we should be back to the trailhead around 4:00. I'll call you when we leave Estes. Look what we just saw!!!" I attach a photo of the chopper and hit Send. Then I send a follow-up text. "Thanks for checking on me, Dad. Much appreciated." It never pays to get too snarky with the parent who makes you dinner and lets your dog out to play.

Gemma and I drive south enjoying majestic views of snow-dusted mountains jutting up around tranquil, teal-colored Lake Estes as we cruise back down to Boulder and out toward Eldorado Springs. This week sets up to be a busy one for my dog training enterprise. A Northglenn couple with two Springer Spaniels want to bring Butter and Scotch to board with me for a month or so while their incorrigible pups (their words, not mine) learn basic obedience. This assignment was only accepted on the condition that they then take obedience classes from me with their own dogs so that everyone is consistent with commands and expectations. I don't run the kind of kennel where rich people drop off their dogs to have them turned into mindless automatons. If you do not have time to exercise and interact with a dog, you ought not to have one (or two, for heaven's sake). They enrich our lives so much; we owe them the same consideration. After a little negotiation, Sam and Heather Porter have agreed to my terms, and the quoted fee, and the Springer Duo is scheduled to arrive tomorrow.

Gemma and I arrive back at my training facility, Dogged Pursuit K-9, and we head over to pick up Leda from my father. "All quiet on the Western Front, Ronnie, or the Front Range—as the case may be," my father cracks himself up. I smile back at him as Leda and Ripley surge around us eager for their share of the pats.

"Do you have any interest in helping me get a couple of the kennel runs squared away for new dogs tomorrow?" I inquire of my father. He is stretching his back and it's clear he has been working on his product review articles all afternoon. "What was it today, Dad, handheld GPS or rifle scope review?"

He laughs. "I'll have you know next week is GPS Week; today was a blaze orange vest for hunting dogs. That Velcro across the front of the chest is great and the vest never slips. It even has massive, silver, reflective paw prints on the sides for people who walk their dogs in city neighborhoods after dark. You can't beat it for $16."

"That sounds like a great product. Did you score a couple of samples for my dogs?"

"No worries; they sent me six in various sizes so you should be good to go for a long while. Let's get cracking on the kennels and then I'll whip up some breakfast for dinner." I defy anyone to find a better father than this one.

My kennel facility resembles a glorified pole barn but it's 80 feet x 100 feet, clean and new inside with lots of big windows and three impressive overhead ceiling fans providing cross ventilation to the lucky canines. Three spacious kennel runs line each side wall for a total of six and a large matted training area runs down the center. Each kennel run has a corrugated rubber snap-together floor in the indoor section with an elevated dog cot (chocolate-colored) for canine slumber, and an outdoor area each dog can access via a control unit on its collar. (The dogs and I benefit immensely from the shipping of goods for product reviews to my father. It's one of the perks. The downside is the non-flattering rain gear. I may have mentioned that a time or three.) Their outside exercise areas are covered in pea gravel, which is easier on their paws and simple to clean.

At the very far end of the building is a little efficiency apartment that currently houses 20 bags of dog food and piles of supplies. Stacking up the dog food into a slightly more organized tower, I clear a path to the big box of red indestructible Kong toys that just arrived. This room really needs to be sorted out sometime. Just not today! We make quick work of sanitizing the kennel runs and setting out water buckets, food bowls, and toys for the upcoming arrivals. The three dogs gambol around "assisting" us and testing the Kongs for their soon to be arriving pals. I locate the training collars and leads for the Springer Spaniels and check e-mails on my phone to be sure the Porters have sent me the required copy of the dogs' immunization records. Everything looks up-to-date and we should be good to go for tomorrow. I put in a quick call to the Duncans in Florida while walking back to the old day spa with Dad and the three dogs. They are thrilled her training is proceeding well and we set a tentative date in three weeks for Gemma to make the move South. We will really miss her spirit and vitality but she's going to live like a queen. Oh well, time to feed the dogs and tuck into crispy bacon and eggs. And orange juice.

CHAPTER 6

The nightmare wakes me up in the pitch-dark hours of the night with a start, flooding my mind with graphic detail. I know the feeling well, unfortunately. This horrific dream has tormented me several times a month like clockwork over the past year and a half. In the dream, a heavy weight is pressing down on my chest and massive explosions detonate around my head. My breath comes fast and shallow as I pant with fear. I see Zach's face but cannot touch him. When I reach toward him, his image disintegrates. All my strength is not enough to grab him and hold him with me; I fail again, as I have so many times before. Tommy Arnett's derisive laughter punctuates the scene and a sense of devastation floods me. There's furious, defensive barking and one last loud report of a gun.

And now I am fully awake, sweating and disoriented. Leda is pressed against the side of the bed with her muzzle nudging my hand. Tiny distressed whines issue from her lips. I sit up abruptly and bury my hands in the curly hair running down the ridge of her back for comfort. "I'm okay, girl. Thank you for waking me up. Let's go make some tea and get you a treat." I change my soaked through sleep shirt and wander to the kitchen. I look out into the vast night and see a moving searchlight. This sight is also familiar to me—my father restlessly checking the property every night—*his* residual nightmare of prior events. So, I try my best to shake it off, this echo of my, our, former life—the day when everything changed and contentment was destroyed. I have Leda and my father and Colorado now and that has to be enough.

CHAPTER 7

The following morning, Saturday, dawns bright and sunny again—pretty much par for the course around Boulder. I love the low humidity and sunny days and my omnipresent, iconic Flatirons. The beautiful scenery here, so grand and open, acts as a balm to my soul. Every once in a while, I find myself actually wishing for a rainy weekend so I'll feel compelled to stay inside and clean the house, but that impulse usually passes once I get outside with the dogs. All the glorious weather usually means catching up on the latest Louise Penny mystery only after dark has fallen. A tug of pain jabs from behind my upper arm as I pull on my sports bra and tank top over my head. I massage the big knot of scar tissue at the back of my shoulder with a glob of arnica and knead the area while muttering under my breath. "That's what an old bullet wound feels like after you throw around a bunch of 50-pound bags of dog food, you idiot!" Yoga practice this morning will be essential. I can feel myself getting a bit stressed all of a sudden. The past has a way of rearing its ugly head when you least expect it. A few Sun Salutations and Child's Pose should put me right enough. Or more dog time. Lots and lots of dog time.

Sgt. Tim Donovan calls me from the Boulder County Sheriff's Office with an update on our recovered hiker. "Hi Veronica, just wanted to fill you in on Shari's condition. She's feeling good after her ankle surgery and is all casted up and gaining strength rapidly. She really is grateful to you two and wants to meet Leda when they spring her from the joint."

"That's great news," I exclaim, "Leda the Magnificent will be happy to hear it."

Tim chuckles on the phone line. "Today's my off day but I'm headed up to Larimer County to help out a couple of buddies in their Sheriff's Department," Tim continues. My interest is immediately piqued.

"Oh yeah? I was up there yesterday afternoon training with Gemma. What's going on? Anything you can let me in on?"

"I'm not exactly sure," Tim responds. "A scientist by the name of Dr. Randy Jeffers went missing yesterday. It is believed he may be in Estes Park, or possibly, Rocky Mountain National Park. His wife is not positive what section he was going to hike when he called her, but he sure would not have been equipped to stay overnight. You would think with a national park in excess of a quarter million acres, people would have learned by now to narrow down their intended hiking route just a bit before they head out—so we know where to start looking. And leave their iPhone on. Something strange may be going on, however, because his wife made some odd comments to the Larimer County guys that implied he may have dropped out of sight intentionally," Tim pauses and then continues. "Apparently, he's a star expert witness in the upcoming murder trial of that NBA player, Billy Fulton, from the expansion team in Omaha, Nebraska."

"I know that case," I reply. "Who doesn't? Interesting to see if they can prove his wife's death was actually a murder or whether it was an accidental drowning. That's a pretty strong burden of proof for the prosecution to substantiate. The District Attorney's Office had better have ironclad security because a case doesn't get more high profile than this one. Articles are already appearing online that strongly imply that counsel for the defendant might be trying to intimidate witnesses to the arguments between Billy and Chardonnay Fulton. You wonder what they would be willing to do to make this trial go away…"

I fall quiet for a minute and then Tim says tentatively, "Veronica, I'm sorry. I don't want to dredge up bad memories for you talking about this case, girl. Please don't spend any time today thinking about your old job with the Prosecutor in Ohio. You and Leda are safe here in Colorado and you're doing great."

Leda pushes her nose into my hand and looks up into my eyes. She clearly feels my sorrow. "I'm good, Tim. Thanks for your concern. Just let me know if the Larimer folks need us at any point. I think they already work with a dog handler up their way, but we'll make ourselves available any time. Tell Sylvia I'll see her at yoga in an hour."

"Will do," Tim answers, "I'm off to Estes. If nothing else, I'll get a decent hike out of it." We disconnect and the dogs and I roam around outside before their breakfast while I resolutely try to quiet the dark thoughts in my head, and am only partially successful.

CHAPTER 8

Yoga is flat-out awesome. I only started practicing it when I moved to Colorado. Ironically, I live in a former day spa but take a yoga class in downtown Boulder. I am certainly not the most flexible one in the class, but have definitely gained an inch or two in my stretches since faithfully incorporating several classes a week into my schedule. More importantly, the sense of peacefulness it grants me, if only for those set times of the week, has been vital to my overall well-being. Sylvia meets me at the door and we set our mats down next to each other at the back of the room. She's a striking woman in her mid-40s with long light brown hair, high cheekbones, and the smile of an efficient Madonna. Sylvia remains a tranquil sea in the inevitable storms of motherhood, even when confronted with four daughters' packed schedules, sometimes-conflicting agendas, or occasional flare-ups over borrowed clothing or who ate the last cookies and cream toaster pastry. True story.

Sylvia also uses that calm, empathetic nature as a part-time victim/witness advocate for the City and County of Denver. I cannot imagine anyone better suited to fill that essential role. These advocates serve in the criminal justice system to aid any witness or victim needing: emotional support, assistance with paperwork, or victims' rights information. The valuable service these unsung heroes provide, especially in domestic violence or abuse and neglect cases, is immeasurable. Sylvia looks over at me searchingly as we sit on our mats prior to the arrival of our instructor—who is always ten minutes late. Her time is apparently much more valuable than ours.

"Veronica, how are you doing lately? You can tell me to mind my own business. You know I won't be offended, but Tim seemed rather concerned about you after your call this morning. He is worried that mentioning the NBA murder case and the District Attorney's Office dredged up bad recollections for you. Please don't think we sit around talking about you as a matter of course, but he was worried enough to say something to me." Sylvia's words come tumbling out in a rush, a rare crack in her ever-present poise. "We know something terrible happened when you worked for your county prosecutor in Ohio; everyone saw the stories in the magazines and on the true crime networks, but I don't know exactly how it impacted you. As I recall, the judge didn't allow cameras in the courtroom. It never seemed like something we wanted to make you relive," she continues. "But I've seen the scar tissue on your shoulder from that bullet wound. You're rubbing it now. I'm worried about what scars that event left on your mind. You trust our family and your dad, but you seem so closed off to anything else except your dogs and exercise."

I listen to Sylvia quietly and try to process her kindness, all the while feeling a faint trembling start in my hands as tears come to my eyes. We lean our heads closer together. The story is not an easy one to tell. Every time I do—every time I testified in court—an all-enveloping wave of helplessness threatens to drag me down with it. It was definitely not my fault. I know that intrinsically, but the agony just never seems to recede. So much carnage for absolutely nothing. I will never understand the reasoning behind it. Sylvia sees my internal struggle and grabs my hands tightly with hers.

"Sylvia," I start hesitantly, "It was bad—a bloodbath, and by the time it was over, eight people were dead including my fiancé, two toddlers, and my boss, the Prosecutor. I'm only alive because of Leda." Now Sylvia's eyes fill with tears as if she feels the pain radiating from my heart out through my body. I endeavor to set aside my unsettling retrospection as the other students begin stirring with the arrival of our perpetually late teacher. I squeeze her hands firmly and whisper to Sylvia. "Thank you so much for caring. I owe you the full story. We'll talk more another day." Sylvia gives me a quick hug and we face towards the front, ready to hold the flowing poses and desperate to achieve some hard-won serenity after that emotionally fraught conversation.

Amazingly, I am able to focus just on my yoga practice and my breathing for an hour, so part of the mental training must be sinking in. I am not a completely lost cause when it comes to this yoga stuff. Our instructor may not be prompt but she is good and peaceful. I take my leave from Sylvia with the promise that we will get lunch together soon. Her eyes look worried to me—another reason not to burden others with my tale. It's as if the evil of the man central to this horror seeps out and infects anyone who knows the entire story. Tommy Arnett already inhabits my nightmares. I don't want him sliding into the dreams of anybody else.

CHAPTER 9

I hustle back out to my training facility to get ready for the arrival of the rambunctious Springer duo later in the morning. Table Mesa Drive seems astonishingly packed with traffic this morning, but I practice my patience. When Bob Seger comes on the radio, I blast *Turn the Page* and sing (badly) as I make my way in fits and starts along my homeward route accompanied by that awesome saxophone solo. My love of 70s and 80s rock comes straight from my father. Just don't ask me to sing anything current. Or sing at all actually. I am looking forward to the distraction of working with the Terrible Two. A busy mind should be able to beat back negative thoughts. All three dogs are hanging out with Dad. I try to give an equal distribution of pats and shoulder thumps to them upon my arrival. The carcass of a raccoon dog toy lies near his desk with the stuffing strewn about the room. "It appears that Rocky the Raccoon gave up his life for the cause," I tease my father.

"Leda and Ripley had a tug-of-war," he replies, "And then the disembowelment began. It was so hilarious watching stuffing fly around the room I didn't have the heart to stop them. I know you don't like them to rip up toys but that raccoon had it coming! I made sure they didn't eat any of the innards," he reassures me.

"Did Gemma participate in the destruction?" I ask, curious about her behavior.

"She just watched with a perplexed look on her face and then went back to tossing her Kong around the kitchen." By now, I have picked up all the remnants of Rocky and thrown them in the trash bag, all three dogs looking up at me beatifically, as if they have no idea what could have possibly happened to that varmint.

My cell phone vibrates and I know that Sam and Heather Porter have arrived to drop off the Springers. I look over at the security camera feed and see their Ford Expedition at the bottom of the gated driveway. I buzz them through, close the gate after they drive in, and head outside to meet them at the pole barn. Butter and Scotch are delightful one-year-old littermates. They are happy, bouncy boys with that typical Springer verve. Their people, Sam and Heather, don't seem exasperated with them, more amused at their antics and a little unsure of how to handle this rodeo. That bodes well for the future because, as we talk more and watch the kids play, I feel like they are very open to learning what it takes to have canine good citizens. Then everyone's life will be more structured—but consequently a lot more fun. The Porters inspect the kennel building and seem pleased with its airy and bright vibe. I promise them the dogs will get lots of outdoor time too and will be socialized with the other dogs as well. "They have a lot to learn," Sam observes as he writes me a check for a deposit and turns to keep an eye on the liver and white streaks charging around the yard with abandon, the feathers on their legs flying behind them.

"First they learn, and then you two," I respond, while keeping an eye out for the guided missiles. Heather calls the dogs over and they bound across to her (an excellent sign that they do pay partial attention to their people). We walk them into two kennel runs next to each other and close them up after they get farewell pats. I let the Porters out the gate with promises of text and photo updates and head to the cabin to collect Gemma and Leda from Dad. Peeking over his shoulder at the laptop, I see he's working on an article for *Pennsylvania Game News* called 'Hunt the Benches in Steep Terrain.' "What's this one about, Daddy?"

"Just a little something I've been absorbing over my years of hunting. Finding the spots where the bucks like to lay up during hunting season. There are a few small places that bucks just love, and the less ambitious hunters don't. Like flat spots in steep terrain. That's where you go."

"That sounds like a good one," I answer him back while rounding up the girl dogs. "I'll proof it for you when you finish."

"Excellent," he murmurs, already deep in thought over his writing as I exit the cabin. I have time for a quick shower while the newcomer dogs settle down for a little bit prior to their first lesson. Leda and Gemma buffet me from both sides as I rub their heads and thump their sides lightly as we amble back to my home. The healing power of dogs.

CHAPTER 10

After a refreshing shower, a swipe of blue mascara, and a hurried blow-dry of my uncooperative hair, it's time to return to the training facility. One of these days, I am going to stop making threats to this mass of curls and cut my hair to ear-length. I keep saying it, but can't quite bring myself to do the deed yet. At least it dries more quickly in the low humidity West. I just grab a clip and pile it on top of my head. "Seriously, how did pioneer women handle it? Mine's only shoulder-length and I cannot deal with it," I mutter to myself as I enter the training area.

The Springers are in raptures. I enter Butter's kennel and slip the training collar around his neck, rings up at the base of his head between his ears, and attach the six-foot lead. We move to the center working area of the kennel with the non-slip mats. Scotch watches in amazement at the events unfurling right before his snout. Butter stands at my left side. I kneel with the lead under my knees and place my right hand on his chest. Placing my left hand on his shoulders and giving the Sit command firmly but gently, I slide my left hand down Butter's back, over his tail, and tuck his haunches under with my hand. He complies whilst looking the tiniest bit puzzled. *Why am I sitting on the human's hand?* I tell him 'Good' and release him after fifteen seconds. We practice the Sit command an additional four times. "Good boy, Butter," I repeat enthusiastically while sliding a treat out of the bag at my waist and telling him to Watch me. When Butter looks in my eyes, I hand it to him. "Easy. No sharks allowed. Good boy."

We move on to the Down. Butter sits at my left side, and kneeling on the lead, I put my left arm over his back and place my left hand with an open palm under his left foreleg. My right hand is palm open under his right foreleg. Giving a firm Down, I lift him into the down position—with **no** pressure on his legs from my hands or thumbs. Butter seems amenable to all these new experiences and we practice three more times. Treats are presented and we move on to the Stand command. Butter sits at my left. I kneel and place the rings of the training collar under his throat. My right hand goes palm down into the collar. Saying Stand, I pull my right hand slightly forward and parallel to the floor so that the Springer takes one step into the Stand position. My left hand keeps his rear legs in position. We hold it for a good minute. Scotch's quizzical face appears at the corner of my vision. It is almost his turn.

Butter has been a promising student so the brotherly competition is on. Next, I give the Heel command with him at my left side and start walking as soon as I give the command. I keep Butter's neck even with my left leg. When he gets out of this position, I give a short snap on the lead with my left hand as I say Heel again, and then release the tightness on the lead immediately. We keep practicing until we get 10-12 strides without any tension on the lead. "Good boy!" I praise him with animation. Finally, Butter goes into the Down position and I sit next to him on the matting. By staying close to him, I can reinforce the command with a firm Down whenever he tries to get up. Let's face it, five minutes is a long time for a growing boy to hold a Down, but he got it and any dog can. Just be clear on what you expect. He did good work today. I remove his training collar and lead so he knows he's done working and praise him vociferously. He hops around happily and gets a couple of hot dog treats. Back he goes to his kennel run ready to be the observer.

Scotch does equally well in his first session, although he spends the first few minutes frantically trying to figure out where the hot dog smell is coming from while I get his training collar on him. The key to dog training is to stay consistent, and above all else, be patient. Dogs want to please us; we just need to make sure they know exactly what we want. I run him through the same exercises for almost twenty minutes. That's about the limit of good concentration with dogs in training initially. Scotch gets loads of praise too before he goes into his run next to his brother for a little down time. They're both sprawled out on their dog cots gnawing strongly on their Nylabones as I leave the building. I snap a quick photo of them reclining with the caption "Resting up after a productive first lesson!" and text it to Heather. I quickly double-check my schedule on my phone calendar. A monthly drug sweep at a high school in Denver is scheduled this afternoon. The principal likes me to do the sweep on a Saturday when the mass of teenagers isn't rampaging around the building. It's fine by me. Work is work and Leda is always up for a drive.

CHAPTER 11

I stop inside at the gun safe secreted in the lower level of the former day spa. In addition to my father's Browning .270 and Winchester .30-06 rifles and his various boxes of ammunition, there are other crucial items to be safeguarded. I spin the knob entering in the combination, use my key on the second lock, and remove three clearly marked transport containers. One holds heroin, the second has cocaine, and the third contains crystal meth. These samples have been weighed, dated, marked, and logged out to me by the DEA. They have been obtained for our business as Leda is also a certified drug detection dog, but it's not like the DEA just hands out narcotics and forgets about them. Oh no. They know exactly how much they supplied to me and they can come to the property for a surprise inventory any time they want. So far, I have not had the pleasure of one of those visits, but I keep strict records. Those samples are logged whenever they come out and for what job. When the sweep is finished, they are logged back in religiously. If anything ever goes wrong, it pays to look as professional as possible.

My drug sweep business has grown steadily since I came to Colorado. Many of the clients have come through word of mouth and the rest in response to some cleverly worded ads my father drafted to run in trade journals and business newspapers, as well as an e-mail he forwarded to the entire membership of the Colorado Small Business Owners' Consortium. An ever-increasing number of schools, one amusement park, and a dozen manufacturing plants have hired Leda and me. Businesses simply do not want impaired workers. It is dangerous for everyone if drugs are in play, and apart from the potential for accidents, their insurance rates go up with each incident too. One major client is a trucking firm; the owners treat their employees like family but they want to make sure no one is tempted to add anything extra to the loads heading back to Colorado from the Mexican border. So far, all trucks have come up clean, which makes everyone happy. All in all, my business is expanding at a good clip. Dad is a bit of a marketing genius and he loved the challenge of getting out the word about this unique service Leda and I can provide. He was desperate too.

I was not in a good place when I fled Ohio after the murder trial to seek solace with him and a sense of normalcy in the vast, restorative beauty of the Colorado mountains. Dad hastened along the remodeling of the day spa, and got Leda and me started with a highly respected local dog trainer, Bruce Macklin, who was on the verge of retirement. Dad realized how deeply I needed a goal to focus on—something to make me forget my former life or at least keep the dark thoughts from constantly assaulting me. It was a great plan. Bruce worked us together as a team, and separately, eager to pass along all his cumulative dog knowledge to someone before he rode off into the sunset. Actually, he moved to Moab, but you get the idea.

I had always competed in obedience, rally, and agility for fun with my dogs in Ohio, and assisted two accomplished local trainers with their community dog obedience classes for years. But this was the serious professional stuff. We learned tracking through all kinds of conditions and circumstances. Hot, cold, wet, dry, long distances, steep slopes and rocky side hills, through rivers, down sidewalks, obstacles to clamber over, with distractions like thunder and gun shots. Leda handled everything with aplomb. We started with short scent trails with food rewards when she found the "victim" in an open field. Then Bruce had a person set a two-hour scent trail and lay up in heavy brush. Then Leda did a two-hour night search finding the volunteer in sparse vegetation. Lastly, she tracked two people hiding at once, finding one after the other over a six-hour period.

One volunteer tried to distract her with tempting food and attention. No dice there, buddy.

One grueling and memorable test Bruce set for us occurred way up in the Indian Peaks Wilderness past Nederland, following our "lost woman" from the Fourth of July trailhead onto the Arapaho Pass Trail with its abundance of glacier-fed streams, up to Arapaho Pass at almost 12,000 feet, then down a bunch of switchbacks to Caribou Lake and then another nine miles on to Monarch Lake. Despite it being late July, sections of the trail were still covered in snow through which we had to wade. Nothing daunted Leda over 12 miles of trailing and we rescued our target individual, bundled up in cold weather gear and a sleeping bag, in record time. She got more confident day by day. Bruce was thrilled to have a dog as talented as Leda be his swan song and I was content to put my head down and work to the point of exhaustion with him to quiet the memories in my head. Leda and I showed off our previously acquired skill at agility and Bruce had to admit that Leda was a star at the dog walk, weave poles, and A frame. She also learned to scramble up a ladder, crawl through a culvert, and climb over a fence. She could maneuver up and down just about anything you put in front of her. (Me not so much, but she does have two more feet.) We got better and better. And then we moved on to drug detection.

Bruce started us with finding cocaine. It was bound up in every sort of wrapper he could devise. The thing about odors is they still permeate through the teeny tiny pores that exist in most materials. Leda sniffed out all the cocaine samples, by first learning to associate the smell of the target substance with a favorite dog treat. After a month we moved on to heroin. A month later we included crystal meth in her repertoire of scents. Bruce hid his sample DEA packets in every possible sneaky way you can think of—because that's what drug dealers and smugglers do (try to outwit the good guys). We found packages of drugs buried in coffee grounds, baby powder, laundry detergent, moth balls, gasoline, and chili peppers, in sealed containers of cheese, sunk four feet deep in the mud, covered in axle grease, hidden under three pallets of fruit, inside raisin boxes, burrowed into book bags in lockers, inside modified gas tanks, and in volunteers' pockets. She even made one infamous discovery of a packet soaked in faux deer urine. Disgusting but true. Dogs smell all the way down through each layer—not just the scent on top—and that's when they find the drugs. Good try, Bruce.

Leda continued to excel and I got better at reading her body language and trusting her abilities. If she alerted, she was on to something. Leda is a serious dog; she loves to play with Ripley but she sees no need to chase a tennis ball as a reward for doing her job. She gets some high-pitched praise from me and she's ready to search more. It sounds like Minnie Mouse on helium but she seems to enjoy it! Bruce started to treat me like a professional dog handler and I began to feel like one. We worked six days a week for eight to ten hours a day, portions of it classroom or field lessons with just Bruce and me. Then there were more hypothetical search situations dreamed up by Bruce to test us. That man had to have been a tyrant in a former life. When we worked together, we healed quite a bit (literally and figuratively) and thrived together. Dad built the pole barn for me and my new career was launched. Bruce handed me his list of professional contacts and hit the trail to Utah.

CHAPTER 12

My first school client is another relationship begun in yoga class. Sara Jane Brown attends our yoga class in Boulder and is the tall, elegant, Black principal of a Denver inner city high school. Sara Jane was also a standout basketball player in college. We got to talking after class about six months ago and she was very enthusiastic about my new business. She's tough but fair, a lifelong educator in her mid-50s who came up in the Baltimore city schools initially. Not much scares her. She believes the best of her students until they prove otherwise to her. Her positive disposition and supportive demeanor obviously mean a lot to her staff and her students. They want to make her proud, and by and large, they do. But she is also realistic about how quickly young people can make bad choices and how suddenly drugs can infiltrate a school. And she's having no part of that around her kids if she can help it. I pick up my cell phone and hit her contact info. "Sara Jane, it's Veronica. I have the drug samples and Leda gathered up to head down to your school. We should be at Sunny Slope around 2:00 if that's okay with you."

"Perfectly fine, dear," she replies. "I was just thinking about you. I'm getting a little worried about some of my tenth graders; I think we'll start with their locker section first. And then the teachers' lounge and Room 216. I hate to be suspicious, but one of the math teachers has been coming to school with eyes as red as a sunset over the ocean. For all I know, he's got terrible hay fever, but I need to have you check."

"No worries," I respond. "We'll hit the places of interest at the beginning and then Leda can make a quick, overall sweep up and down the halls. Hopefully, it will be like the last three monthly sweeps and you'll get the all clear."

Sara Jane laughs wryly. "From your lips to God's ears, Veronica. But you know that X-Files poster? Trust No One," she intones.

"Not until Leda says they can be trusted," I reply promptly.

I ring off and concentrate on my driving while merging from 36 South onto 25 South into Denver. Every time I make this drive, it seems like more and more cookie-cutter houses have been crammed onto the former prairie dog plains. Luckily, Dad had the foresight to buy a chunk of land with abundant privacy and no near neighbors. My phone rings again and the Bluetooth connection in my SUV picks up the call. "Ronnie, it's Dad. Just checking on you. All good on the drive to Denver?" I reply in the affirmative. He feels better if I check in at regular intervals. Can't blame him after the events of a few years ago. "Okay, honey, I took the Springers out to play and they've met Gemma. Everything went smoothly with the introductions and all pups behaved. I'm going to take Ripley and Gemma for a hike on the Open Space before dinner. I'll feed everybody around 5:00."

It's great to have him around. "I couldn't do it without you, Dad," I reiterate. "Leave me your *Pennsylvania Game News* article and I'll proof it later tonight."

"That's a deal, daughter. Happy searching."

Leda and I roll up to Sunny Slope High School just shy of 2:00 and I give her the command word, "Yes," allowing her to jump down from the vehicle. I put on her snazzy purple harness and working dog vest. It's good to look official—even on a Saturday. Sara Jane comes gliding out with her usual grace and greets Leda enthusiastically. Leda is essentially a one-person dog (maybe one and a half, if you count my dad) but she is fond of Sara Jane and reacts to her attention with equanimity. I give her a drink from her water bowl to rinse out her mouth and her nose. Pulling the drug transport containers out of my vehicle, I open each container separately to let Leda take a deep sniff from each. Then the sample packets are replaced, locked inside my car, and secured by the car alarm. We follow Sara Jane to the teachers' lounge; I utter the Seek command and Leda starts her preliminary hunt around the room. She noses under the chairs and tables, around the mail slots of each teacher and into the drawers and cupboards around the perimeter of the room. Several bedraggled raincoats are hanging from hooks in a jumble but she turns up nothing there either. We continue out the door and down the hall to Room 216. "Seek, Leda," I urge her on. Leda starts off briskly around the teacher's desk up front and then heads to the storage bins along the back wall. She shows absolutely no interest; perhaps the math teacher has the worst allergies ever or he's been cutting up a lot of onions.

We join up again with Sara Jane in the hall and she directs us to the sophomores' locker section. Leda sweeps up and down each side of the hall and covers all the banks of lockers twice. Nothing. (One or two of them have that particular stench of sweat and moldering gym clothes that makes your eyes water and knocks you back. Even I can smell them! No dog needed. Boys, take your stuff home and wash it.) Sara Jane looks relieved with the negative results and tells me to meet her in the administrative offices when I finish sweeping the rest of the student hallways. Leda and I walk at a moderate pace up and down, back and forth until we've covered the entirety of the high school. The only excitement is a mouse busting out in front of her as we round the corner of the biology lab. "Leave it, girl," I reinforce. Leda looks back at me in offended disgust (a mouse is soooo far beneath her) and then finishes the job. "Good girl." I ruffle the fur on her curly back and give her a treat and a drink. We amble back to the main offices and start toward the principal's office in the back as Sara Jane comes out to greet us.

I start smiling at Sara Jane to give her the all clear when Leda abruptly sits down next to the desk of one of the office assistants and gives three sharp barks. Oh shoot. I might have relaxed too soon. Sara Jane's brow furrows as she asks, "Oh dear. Is that what I think it is?"

"Probably, but let me get my gloves on and we'll see. I pull on my rubber gloves and ask Leda again to Seek. Sara Jane begins to video me on her cell phone. In this litigious world, we want ironclad proof of wrongdoing if something illegal is found. The Chessie nudges at a lower drawer of the desk, sits again and gives three barks. I open the drawer and feel around carefully under envelopes and boxes of staples. At the very bottom—pay dirt. Or more specifically, crystal meth. In a vial. And it's blue. Somewhere bad guys are watching too much TV.

I don't carry field test kits because my tester is Leda. I hold the vial up and Sara Jane gets a good shot of it. She bundles it into a large manila envelope and writes the date and time on it while I continue with the video on her cell phone. She tapes the envelope shut. Sara Jane's lips are pressed tightly together and the disappointment is written across her face. "I'll get this over to the lab our school district uses and have a little sit-down with Jeremy after the results come back. The lab will rush this result to me before he returns to work on Monday. I don't know what he could possibly say, but I'll give him a chance to explain."

"That sounds like a good plan, Sara Jane," I confirm. "Get the report and give him an opportunity. You're a great judge of character. There may be a reasonable explanation. A confiscation he forgot to report or something. No sense leaping to conclusions just yet."

"You're right, Veronica. I think he's a good young man. I will not assume anything yet. Let me write you a check and you and Leda can go enjoy the rest of this glorious day."

CHAPTER 13

We bid farewell to Sara Jane and start winding our way through the streets of downtown Denver on our way back to Interstate 25. The bevy of one-way streets in this city can be somewhat confusing and I probably missed a turn somewhere. I definitely do not know downtown Denver as well as downtown Cleveland. Huffing in frustration, I pull up to a stop sign trying to figure out where this drive went wrong. I look to my left down a long narrow alley running between two blocks trying to orient myself better. I am so busy thinking about being lost that it takes a moment for what is occurring to actually register. Four teenage boys in board shorts and raggedy T-shirts are about halfway down the alley coming in my direction—running and hollering. At first, they look to be playing a game or just running out of high spirits. But no. I should have known better. Kids don't play outside anymore.

They are chasing a brown and white speckled dog down the alley yelling at her, kicking at her, while one even brandishes a broken off broom handle he's swinging at her head. She is desperate and terrified, tongue hanging out as she tries frantically to dodge the crates and pallets stacked in the alley as well as the circling teenagers. One blow connects with her hip and she goes down but regains her feet before they reach her again; her entire side is now covered in grease and she is limping badly. She looks panic stricken and hopeless at the same time. I wonder how long they have been hunting her. By now, I have slammed my SUV into Park and grabbed the baseball bat from behind my front seat. I don't see any weapons in their hands except the broom handle.

I'm actually thinking two things as I start toward the alley. "Oh God, why another alley? Seriously?" and "Mr. Safety is going to be so full of himself when he learns I had to use this damn bat." One of the boys picks up a piece of brick and hurls it at the dog. They laugh uproariously as it strikes her in the side of the head and she stands dazed. They don't see me running at them—too engrossed in their plans, but I'm seeing red. I am never going to be a victim again and I am not going to stand by while they victimize this poor dog. I start screaming every curse word your parents never want to hear you say and wind up with the bat. I go for the one with the broom handle and crash the bat down on his upraised wrist. "You bitch," he wails as he drops to the ground clutching his arm and blubbering like a baby.

"How do you like it, you little snot?" I shoot back at him as he gets an extra jab in the ribs with the Louisville Slugger.

I try to keep my eye on the three remaining miscreants as the beleaguered dog edges behind me panting nervously with blood dripping into her eyes. One of the boys has horrible acne and a vicious grin. He charges me yelling like a demon. I go low and smash the bat into his knee. Two down. Pretty sure that was a busted kneecap. He rolls around on the ground next to his friend and calls me the C word. I hate that word. I kick him in the bad knee before turning to face the two upright ones. The sound of Leda barking out the partially open window of my car is audible from 50 yards away. The remaining teens look a little craftier than the first two idiots; then one of them pulls out a switchblade. They are trying to herd the dog and me back into the alley wall where pallets stacked outside a bodega back door will hem us in. Well, crap. My haste to save this dog might have led me into a bad spot. Time for reinforcements. I reach down to my belt loop with my right hand while swinging the bat at them with my left hand to keep them off us. So far, they look a little puzzled about how to get the knife closer to me while a bat buzzes past them, but I don't like my odds of holding them off forever. Let's flip the odds in my favor.

I press the cargo door release button for my SUV. Very handy and just like the ones K-9 police officers use when they need to free their working dogs from their vehicles quickly. "Leda, Here," I holler at the top of my lungs. Not really necessary as she has already burst through the lifting hatch and is a streak of infuriated brown fur heading right at the one with the knife. They don't know enough to be scared and run, but they should be; she's not wasting any energy barking now. She's like a heat-seeking missile. Bruce trained her on weapon avoidance and takedowns and she's on a mission. Leda latches onto the wrist of the boy holding the knife and crunches down. He drops to his knees and tries punching her in the head. Leda responds by backing up steadily while dragging him by the wrist— and not gently. "Good luck buddy. She's a lot faster than you."

The back door of the bodega slams open violently against the alley wall right next to me. Man, I really hope these brats don't have more friends in the store. A very real shiver of fear runs down my spine. I do not want to get hurt in another stinking alley. Glancing over my shoulder with my bat upraised, I see a tall, muscular Black teenager. He must have heard the uproar and come out to investigate. He takes in the scene: the injured dog huddled behind me and the quartet of lowlifes screaming profanities in the alleyway. Leda has the third one hollering in anguish as she holds on and stares him down with her yellow eyes until he drops the knife. "Watch him, Leda," I instruct her and she never wavers.

The fourth one has now managed to draw a knife from *his* back waistband and brandishes it at us with remarkably stupid bravado. The young man from the bodega steps forward quickly and kicks the dropped knife back behind the pallets. He ducks one wild knife swing from Dumbass No. 4 and punches him right in the face, dropping him to the ground like a sack of potatoes. By now, the first two have attempted to stand and take a sort of halting flight. I menace them again with the bat and they sink to the alley floor. "Everyone stay where you are," I order, as Leda, our new friend, and I stand over the dejected pack of would-be dog murderers. I look back to check on the injured dog. She has crept up behind the Black teenager crying softly and he lifts her up in his arms and wipes the blood off her face. I feel my heart break at the cruelty of some men, and the compassion of others.

CHAPTER 14

The Denver police arrive in short order once I have ascertained from our new friend exactly where the heck this alley is, and put in a call to them. Our rescuer tells me his name is Michael Fletcher and he continues to hold the trembling dog tight in his arms. Once the police check out the four teenagers we have been keeping on the ground, they bundle them into an ambulance and another patrol car and remove them from the scene. The one with the broken wrist is driven away hollering, "That psycho's dog attacked US first. They're the ones you should be arresting." The officers look at them and their knives recovered from the ground in veteran disbelief. It is all the officers can do not to roll their eyes skyward at this ridiculous ploy.

I have identified myself and told them that Sgt. Tim Donovan of Boulder County can vouch for me. Patrolman Andrews responds, "I know Tim from our Rugby League. He's told me what great work Leda does—especially the time she found those two lost young boys who fell off the cliff face and got injured when playing near Eldorado Springs. You sure we can't steal you from Boulder County?"

Laughingly, I tell him, "No, but I am available to help out any time you guys need us." I proceed to write my statement indicating that I stopped these men in the commission of a class six felony in Colorado—aggravated cruelty to a companion animal (sometimes the legal assistant part leaps to the forefront even now). I further explain that they then attacked us with knives; we were in fear for our lives so we took all steps necessary to protect ourselves and the dogs. Michael Fletcher backs me up with his statement. We are in the right, but I worry a teeny bit about us injuring them. However, no Colorado jury would give them a whit of sympathy so I don't waste any more time fretting over it.

Once the police leave, I turn to Michael and ask, "Thanks again for your help. How is she? Do you want me to look her over?"

"Yes ma'am, please check her out," he replies shyly and sets the cowering dog on the ground. She cringes down in obvious fear. I talk quietly to her and Michael while running my hands over her body.

"That's a good girl. You're going to need a nice soapy bath to get all this hair cleaned up, aren't you? You look like a Llewellin Setter. Not very common, especially in a big city. How on earth did you get here?" She winces in response to my exam but does not seem to be in excruciating pain—more scared and traumatized, which is bad enough. Leda wanders over and stands next to her in sympathy and the younger dog leans up against Leda's side. "Michael, she seems basically okay. She needs a couple of stitches above her eye. Is she yours or do you know where she belongs? Do you live around here?"

Michael blinks and looks a little overwhelmed with my barrage of questions. "No, ma'am. She's not mine. I'm pretty sure she is a stray. I live in the back of the store here and sometimes I see her at the other end of the alley. She is usually very timid. I leave extra food for her if I have it and I think she eats it once I go back inside the store. No one has ever come looking for her or posted any signs."

"Well, in that case, I'm making an executive decision and she's coming with me. Also, please don't call me ma'am. I'm not that old! Veronica is fine. And what do you mean you live in the back of the store?" I did it again. Bury the poor kid in questions, why don't you?

Michael looks at me and then down at the ground. "I just graduated from high school a few months ago and aged out of foster care. My mother has been in prison on drug charges since I was 12. The owners of this bodega know me from around the neighborhood and they said I could stay on a cot in the back room in exchange for stocking shelves, cleaning up, things like that." He talks slowly and seriously like a person far older than 18 and pets the frightened dog for comfort.

"Do you like dogs?" I ask him as an idea darts through my head.

"I always have, but I was never allowed to have one in the foster homes," he replies with a sad smile. "Your dog is amazing. What is she, a Chocolate Lab?"

"Close," I say. "She's a Chesapeake Bay Retriever—also not the most common breed. If you want a bigger place to live and you want to learn all about dogs, my father and I have a dog training facility called Dogged Pursuit K-9 near Boulder. We could use the help around the place and you would have your own space and room for this pretty girl too."

Michael looks down at me in amazement with an uncertain smile. "Really?"

"Absolutely," I reply. "Do you need to give notice at the bodega or anything?"

He laughs and suddenly looks more his age. "It's not that formal of a job."

"Great then. Let's go talk to your friends inside and see if it makes sense for you to move on with me. If so, we can stop to see my vet, Stephanie, on the way back to Boulder and get a couple of stitches and vaccinations for this little lady."

"Her name is Cocoa," he tosses over his shoulder as he heads in the back door of the store.

CHAPTER 15

I load up Leda and the freshly named Cocoa in my SUV and move it into a parking spot in front of the bodega and head inside to meet the family which has been providing Michael with a place to stay. Michael is standing at the front counter talking intently to a Hispanic couple. They appear to be in their mid-30s and are listening to Michael with serious expressions as he describes what occurred in the back alley behind their business. The store is a modest size and tidy but packed full of anything a person could name if you crave Latin food. Oh my gosh, those poblano peppers look amazing. Maybe Dad will stuff a batch and bake them if I bring a bag home. How do I keep thinking about food all the time? I approach the couple and Michael introduces me to Lola and José Garcia. As we shake hands, Lola asks me, "What brings you to this part of town today, Miss Veronica?"

"I own a dog training business and was doing a drug sweep at Sunny Slope High School. I got a little turned around heading back to the highway, got lost, and happened to see what was going on in the back alley," I answer. "Luckily for me, Michael heard the commotion and came out to see what all the noise was about. It was a fortuitous time for back-up to arrive."

Lola looks over at Michael with a beautiful smile. "Yes, he's a good boy. We have watched him grow up around the neighborhood for the last six years—since his mother got in bad trouble with the police." Michael stares down at the floor, both melancholy and somehow resigned, when his mother is mentioned.

José picks up the story. "His foster homes were all close to this store and we got to see a lot of him. Most of those places didn't feed him too well, but we always could spare a little extra food for him when he'd come by. He would sweep up, empty boxes, take out the garbage, really anything we would need to pay us back. I really do not understand how the system could just put him out on the street with no help when he hit 18. The guidance counselors did not even try to work with him to find a job. We wanted to help him more, but we have four children with us in the little apartment over our store."

Michael looks at the Garcias and states, "You all did help me; every time I needed it. You never looked away when I needed anything."

Lola hugs him and says, "Well, we fed you and gave you a place to sleep and shower. I was not having you sleeping in the streets. But you make money doing errands and chores for all the shop owners on this street and that hard work is all you, *hijo*."

The Garcias are obviously very fond of Michael and I hope that my idea of training him to help me with my business won't sound completely crazy to them. "Michael's good character is apparent from how he helped me and he has bonded with that poor sweet dog already. I have a growing dog training business and could really use the help. You say he's a hard worker. I would like for him to come live at my father's place in Boulder— and I think Michael would like that too. We can pay him and train him and give him his own little apartment in the dog training building. And he can keep Cocoa." I feel like I'm trying to sell the job to them because these goodhearted people are so clearly fond of Michael. I bring in a business card from my backpack in the car and present it to them as proof that I actually do this dog stuff for a living. The Garcias confer briefly in Spanish and then agree that this seems to be a great opportunity for Michael. He hugs them both, gathers up his couple of bags from the back room while José gives me directions back to the highway, and we are on our way.

Cocoa looks a little calmer now that she has been relaxing with Leda. I give them both water and check Cocoa's eye. The blood has stopped dripping. She needs a bath, but boy, has she got pretty markings. One side of her face is brown and the other is speckled. She resembles a smaller English Setter. She presses forward against the dog screen behind the seats and greets Michael with a little whine. I text my vet to say I'm bringing a new dog for some stitches and she replies, "No problem. I am in my office until at least 6:00." As we start our drive north toward Boulder, I call my father on the hands-free connection in the car to fill him in on my afternoon.

"Hey Dad. It's me. I am headed for home with Leda and two new friends. One human and one canine. How is everything back at home?"

"All good here, Ronnie," he replies. "I took Gemma and Ripley for a hike on the Mesa Trail, finished a product review for *Field and Stream* and took the Springers around the property for their exercise. This is when it's nice to have a fully fenced seven acres. They were really blowing off steam. However, I sense you have a story to tell me about your day..."

I reply slowly, trying to buy some time, "Thanks again for getting them out. They go back to obedience school tomorrow." I hesitate a little because I have to tell him that I went charging into a tight spot with only a baseball bat to save Cocoa—which was probably not the best thought out plan. "Well, let me preface this story by saying that the self-defense lessons you had me take after the trial last year really came in handy. I felt confident and competent today." I hear him give a little groan and say "oh geez." Michael grins sideways at me, waiting to hear how I'm going to get myself out of this mess.

I just bite the bullet and tell him the whole tale beginning with seeing the teens and the terrorized dog, me charging them with the bat (which did not cause the instant dispersal I was hoping for), Leda's timely assistance, and then Michael's intervention with the last delinquent. I downplayed the knives somewhat. Okay, quite a lot. Bob is good at reading between the lines though.

"Those lessons were to help you if you were attacked! Not so you could go charging into an alley on the offensive when you're outnumbered 4-1. And they had *KNIVES!*"

"But Dad—there was a dog that needed my help. I had Leda. And then Michael." He gives a snort of exasperation and I know we will discuss this incident later. I do understand his concern but I would do the same thing again and he knows it. There was a dog that needed my help.

CHAPTER 16

"Well, Michael, thank you for jumping in to assist my daughter," my father continues talking through the car's speaker to Michael.

"You're welcome, sir," he replies. "She had everything basically under control." I look over at him with a wry grimace. I am not sure about the "under control" part, but it will alleviate a little bit of my father's stress.

"Dad, Michael is going to come stay with us at the dog training facility. We can use the help and that little apartment is just sitting there almost ready for use. He wants to learn the business. And Cocoa, the dog we saved, is right here in the car too. We need to stop at Stephanie's so she can put a few stitches above her eye."

"Sounds good," he responds. "I'm ready to take a break from my next article, so I'll head down to the kennel and start moving supplies out of the efficiency and get it cleaned up for Michael. The Springers can supervise. We may have help. Two of Sylvia and Tim's girls called the house looking for you earlier. They wanted to come over to see Butter and Scotch. We can probably draft them into helping with the apartment. The more the merrier. Then we can throw a pile of food on the grill."

"Which set of twins was calling?" I ask. "Jane and Elizabeth? Or Marianne and Elinor?" (You probably guessed this already, but Sylvia is a massive Jane Austen fan. Fortunately, she skipped over Lydia and Kitty as name choices. These girls are smart and definitely not flighty.)

"It was Jane and Lizzie. I'll call and invite them over to make a start on the project with me. If the younger girls are home from their soccer match by now, they can all come over."

"That could work out well," I say enthusiastically. "We would have help and Tim was headed up to Estes Park earlier to work with Larimer County officers. Sylvia was getting one of her families from court moved into new housing. The girls can text their folks to let them know where they'll be."

"I'm on it," my dad replies with his usual efficiency. "I look forward to meeting you soon, young man."

Michael and I arrive at my vet's office around 5:00. Stephanie is the best and takes wonderful care of all our canines. They defy the stereotype and don't seem to mind going to her office at all. This may be because they get bonus treats from Stephanie and all her vet techs from the moment they cross the threshold. She looks Cocoa over thoroughly, proclaims she is about seven to nine months old, and gives her a small shot of Lidocaine near her eye. Her sore hip seems fine, no lasting damage. Stephanie runs a microchip scanner over Cocoa just to be sure no chip exists. As expected, we find nothing. Cocoa gets a few minute stitches above her eye and is brave with Michael holding her. Then she gets her vaccinations. Only one little yelp escapes her during that experience. Stephanie looks Michael in the eye and says, "She's really fine, but since she got hit in the head with a brick, and her hip is tender, I would definitely like to keep her here a little while. Just to make sure." Michael looks downcast and glances over at me for reassurance or explanation.

"It will be over before you know it," I reiterate. "I promise she can come stay at the property afterward."

He nods solemnly. "Okay. I understand." He says goodbye as the vet tech, Helen, comes for the pup.

"First stop is the bathtub, little mama," Helen soothes her on the way out the door. We thank Stephanie and pile back in the car for the short drive to my facility.

Turning toward Michael, I inquire, "What do you think about $500 a week plus free room and board to start off with? My work load varies from week to week, so that may be a more fair way to compensate you, at least at the beginning. Some weeks we'll do less than 40 hours, some weeks more. We can always revisit your wages once we see what training jobs we get."

Michael looks back at me with a pleased expression. "That sounds really good to me. And I'll have my own dog."

That settles that question, it seems. I dig a jumbo pack of peanut M & Ms out of my training bag and Michael and I split them in companionable silence as we drive out toward Eldorado Springs. I show Michael the remote that works the security gate as we drive onto the property and explain that we will get one for him as well. "The gates are always to be locked. Lesson number One. No unannounced visitors that way and no loose dogs escaping. Very important." He nods emphatically and hands me the last red M & M.

Some of the Donovan girls have apparently arrived at Dogged Pursuit K-9, as the blue Jeep their parents got them is parked next to the training building. "Alright Michael. Let's go meet everyone." I glance over to see if he looks apprehensive, but to my relief, he looks interested and eager. Leda wakes up from her nap in the back of the SUV and leaps out when released, ready to go see her dog friends and Dad. We enter the building and spot Jane and Lizzie hard at work with Dad carrying piles of supplies out of the apartment in the back. The dog food bags have already been pulled out. I learned my lesson before and am not hoisting them around again. All the dogs are milling about in the massive space playing with toys and generally having a good time. I am pleased to see that Dad's assessment of the Springers' good nature is spot on and they are happy to play and entertain themselves without any attitude toward the other dogs.

"Michael, let me introduce you to my dad, Bob, and two of our friends, Jane and Elizabeth, or Lizzie." Everyone hurries over to greet him and make him feel at home. He shakes hands all around. The girls, who are delightful 16-year-olds with ready grins and extremely long blond hair, have a real love of sports, dogs, and the kind of pop music I know nothing about, and seem pleased to make a new friend. They are soon chattering away to Michael a mile a minute and he relaxes quickly in the face of their obvious good will. They drag him away to show him his new space. He looks a little awestruck by the building and the neat little efficiency at the far end. My father pulls me aside and says, "You know we have to discuss your guerilla raid down in Denver today. But before I forget, Tim would like you to call him later tonight about this case in Larimer County. I just spoke to him when I called to get permission for the girls to eat dinner here."

"Hmm," I muse. "I wonder if they have had any luck finding that missing scientist. If not, his scent trail is going to be getting pretty darn cold."

By now, Michael is helping Dad stack up the dog food bags in one of the side cupboards. Buying in bulk nets us a great discount, but since we just got a delivery, 20 bags of kibble are waiting for redistribution into storage. The twins have sorted the various bags of dog toys, treats, and training paraphernalia previously piled in the efficiency into separate plastic tubs which I had bought, but not yet had a chance to use. They shift the tubs into another side storage area and the floor of the apartment actually becomes visible. The living room is carpeted in a sturdy gray Berber carpet, which is durable but a bit homier than sitting on engineered hard wood floors like those found in the kitchen and bathroom. The kitchen is functional with a small oven, two burner stove, fridge and sink. The counters are butcher block and there are nice white Shaker style cabinets. The kitchen is open to the living room, which is handy for conversation if you have visitors. In the back of the space is a separate bedroom with a queen bed and en suite bathroom. It has a nice bright shower, with a painted ceramic bowl sink featuring sun symbols placed on a white quartz countertop. Jane follows me to the back with the bedding she has found stored away in the bathroom linen closet. "Veronica, I have the sheets for the bed. Can you help me make it up now?"

"Sure," I reply. "The pillows and comforter should be in the closet as well."

"They are; everything looks ready to go. I just couldn't carry it all at once."

"You need one more set of arms, Jane," I laugh with her as we set to work getting the bed made up.

"I love this comforter with the pictures of Golden Retriever puppies playing on it. They're sooo cute." Jane's happy personality is contagious and reminds me how much fun these girls can be.

I ask where Marianne and Elinor are. "Mari and Elli went to a friend's house for pizza after their soccer match. They won 2-1. They're going to be really mad they missed the excitement over here," she chortles with the natural superiority of a teenager two years older than her sisters.

"Well, don't get too smug," I remind her. "They'll have a chance to meet Michael soon enough and they'll be over here in a flash to meet Cocoa after she is given a clean bill of health by Dr. Stephanie."

Jane grins and shoots back, "You'll have quite the crew of helpers with all the Donovan girls on board. It's fun to see the kennel filling up with dogs."

"It is good," I agree with her. "The dogs rotate in and out a bit depending on what they're being trained for and where they are going to live, but a full kennel means my business is thriving. By the way, do you think you can wrangle a couple of your friends to volunteer to be "lost" sometime soon so Leda can practice finding them?"

"Of course, just tell me when. Dad says all the time how great you are at training dogs and finding lost people with Leda. We want you to teach us so we can get a dog at our house. If we're trained by you, how can the parents possibly object?" She finishes this little speech with a flourish by throwing the pillows on the bed and plumping them up vigorously.

"Hey girl, those pillows are calling for mercy. Ease up. You and your sisters can start taking classes with me. We can set up times next week to work with Butter and Scotch and then you can show your parents how you are coming along. You just have to promise your parents that the four of you will take care of the new dog no matter how bad the weather is or how busy your schedules are. Dogs need attention and that's that."

Jane looks at me earnestly and says, "We know, Veronica. We all talked it over and we can work together to make sure our new dog has the best care."

"Good deal," I smile at her. "Suppose you take a sponge and the multi-purpose cleaner into that bathroom and give the surfaces the once-over?"

Back out in the kitchen, Lizzie is scrubbing the counters and sink with enthusiasm. The fridge is empty, but my father has extra staples in his pantry and freezer that we can bring down to Michael. Be prepared. My dad's lifelong motto. And no, he was never a Boy Scout. The apartment looks so much better already. I run the little vacuum from the hall closet around the Berber and use glass cleaner on the various pictures of dogs at play hanging on the walls in the apartment. Dad and Michael are out in the training area of the kennel and seem deep in conversation as they clean out the kennel runs and fill water bowls now that all 1000 pounds of dog food have been tucked away. Michael seems to be telling him some tale that involves a lot of swift hand gestures. I really hope he's not giving him a blow-by-blow account of the incident in the alley. I'm going to get a hard enough time from Dad as it is. Time for a little distraction.

"Hey, Dad," I call over. "Why don't you and Michael put each of the five dogs in their own kennel run and they can eat dinner and digest for a bit while we get organized for our dinner?"

"Sure thing," he replies. "I'm starting to get hungry and I bet all you youngsters are too." Dad shows Michael my charting system on the dry erase board on the wall which lists each dog's name, breed, age, gender, their food type and amount, any supplements, and whether they have any special requirements. For example, Ripley gets a supplement to keep his arthritis from flaring up. New Zealand green-lipped mussels. Strange but absolutely true and they work like a charm. Starting life on a chain in a dirt yard probably didn't help his body any, but this product sure does.

They move along the feeding station getting each dog's bowl ready one by one. Gemma gets a half-portion of special sweet potato food to help her coat recover from pretty sketchy nutrition when she lived in the drug den. (Stale pizza and week-old red velvet cupcakes scavenged off the kitchen counter when her humans were high and passed out do not qualify as a proper meal.) Dad then shows Michael how to carefully open each kennel door and block the opening with his knee so the dog stays inside. They are not allowed to jump for their food bowl, but must sit and wait until they are released to eat.

This is one of the first things every dog here learns. Wait until you get the release word to eat. In houses with little children, this keeps everyone safe, and the dogs aren't lunging at bowls as they're being set down. The Springers and Gemma can eat upon the release word "Now." Our dogs, Ripley and Leda, each have their own release word, which is unlikely to be guessed by anyone apart from us. When Bruce trained me, he told me never to risk anyone with bad intentions throwing poisoned meat into our compound to harm the dogs. Drug dealers can hold grudges with a vengeance and our work in the schools hurts their profits severely. Michael leans in as Dad quietly tells him the release words and he is clearly concentrating intently through the whole process of feeding the dogs. The guys check off the evening feeding on the current week's chart and we all troop up to the deck outside Dad's cabin to start dinner.

CHAPTER 17

Michael offers to put together a salad with the various accoutrements in the fridge, saying he helped Lola with this job all the time, and the girls light the grill for Dad and get the hamburgers, hotdogs, and asparagus ready to put on the fire. I take a quick minute to place my drug transport containers back inside the gun safe in my abode and sign them back in. That drug sweep seems like ages ago and weariness starts to settle over my shoulders like a familiar shawl all of a sudden. Down at Dad's kitchen, I start carrying the condiments out to the table on the deck. Then the plates and silverware and napkins and soft drinks. It is just getting dusk now, but it's a pleasant temperature for a fall evening. Little brown bats are circling around high in the air catching insects. Jane and Lizzie grab long sleeve hoodies from their Jeep and put them on over the T-shirts they wore for cleaning up the apartment. Dad offers Michael one of his flannel shirts for a little extra warmth and I pull on my Cleveland baseball jersey. My new life in Colorado is as private as possible, but I won't stop supporting my teams. One day, the city of Cleveland will go crazy over a Super Bowl or World Series win. And I'll celebrate just as proudly from a distance.

Once the food is ready and just hitting the table, Dad goes down to the kennel with Michael and lets the dogs come up to the patio to hang out with us. I explain to Michael that this is good socialization for the dogs. "The young ones go into soft-sided crates at the edge of the patio, away from the table and chairs. No begging allowed. The older dogs show the young ones how to stretch out on their side and relax. They have no expectation of getting people food so they pay no attention to us eating. But they can be around their people and be welcomed because they are behaving." Michael nods and it appears to make perfect sense to him.

"You can work with me on this when Cocoa gets here, right?"

"Definitely," I reassure him. "She's going to learn everything these dogs know and if you want to train her for a specialty of any kind, we'll do that too. First, we build up her confidence and get her weight up a smidge. Get her spayed and dewormed. Buy her a collar and license. All that official stuff." I text the vet to check on Cocoa and she says Cocoa is doing well. Just a little stiff. Got a bath and is sleeping in Stephanie's family room right now.

Dad has gotten the Springers placed at the patio edge in the soft-sided crates and they appear drowsy and content to sniff the breezes. Dad has definitely been practicing this with the Springers while I was down in Denver and they do really well on the whole. (Butter has to be spoken to about whining two times, but he finally gets with the program.) I snap a photo and text it to Heather Porter showing the pups learning to be civilized. We all sit around chatting about everything and nothing and put away a lot of grilled food and kettle-cooked potato chips. So much better than regular chips. Michael looks content and engages in a long discussion with the twins about Cocoa being a Llewellin Setter and what breed of dog the Donovans might get in the future. Then the girls look up pictures on their iPhones to see what this strange mystery breed looks like. "Wow, they're really cute," Lizzie gushes. "They look like teeny English Setters. I love all the speckles and spots."

I interject here, "As I recall, a Llewellin Setter is a strain of English Setter, but an English Setter is not necessarily a Llewellin. Confusing, but anyway, they sure are pretty. And they are supposed to be great natural retrievers and very malleable." We all start to wind down from the long day and after everyone polishes off a scoop (or two) of sea salt caramel pretzel ice cream, we're ready to call it a night. Hey, I never said anything about being on a diet, so sometimes ice cream happens.

I drive with the twins down to the gate and let them out. "I really appreciate all the help, girls. It was awesome to have you here. We'll set up times next week for all four of you to come by and train with Michael and the younger dogs. Tell your dad I'll call him in a few minutes about the case near Rocky Mountain if he's made it home. Be careful going down the hill and text me when you get home."

"Yes, Veronica. See you soon, Veronica. Thanks for dinner." And they're away. I just sounded like Ms. Safety, Jr. but I won't apologize for emulating Dad. He's right a lot of the time.

Dad walks Michael down to the pole barn after we say good night. He will get Michael situated in the little apartment and put Butter, Scotch, and Gemma in their kennel runs. I call after them. "Show Michael the gadgets on the dogs' collars that open the sliders in the runs so they can go in or out." Dad waves in acknowledgement and then they disappear in the gathering darkness together. Leda has been following me back and forth from patio to kitchen as I clear everything away and wipe down the surfaces. She's yawning but trying to hang tough. My father has left me a hard copy of his article on finding the spots where bucks like to lay up. Grabbing a red pen, I read through it for him efficiently before marking two minor typos and one suggested paragraph break. I scrawl "Excellent. As Usual." at the bottom and place the copy on his printer.

CHAPTER 18

I get on Dad's computer and Google the Billy Fulton murder trial. As you might imagine, the disputed murder trial of an NBA sensation from the Denver area who plays for an expansion team in nearby Nebraska generates hundreds of hits. Since the body of Billy's wife, Chardonnay, was found in his spectacular 6000 square foot mansion in Superior, Colorado, the case will be tried in Boulder County. Sports fans can't decide what is currently more riveting, the ongoing MLB playoffs or the jockeying for advantage in this sensationalized case by the defense and the District Attorney's Office. Weeding through the results on Google, I reach a few more sane discussions and expert opinions, offered by attorneys who are not involved in this case, about the circumstances of Chardonnay's death. Then I log on to the online Boulder County District Court criminal case docket and plug in this matter, *State of Colorado vs. William J. Fulton.*

I spend some time reading the docket of voluminous motions, discovery requests, and various other pleadings which have been filed week by week as the case moves inexorably closer to the trial everyone is talking about. The real questions at the heart of the matter are simple. Did Chardonnay Fulton drown accidentally in her massive, marble-clad spa tub at the house, or was her drowning a murder staged to look like an accident? And secondly, does Billy Fulton's alibi of being at a private gym workout session at the time of her death hold up to the intense scrutiny it deserves? Billy was known to have been with his wife at a certain point prior to her death and she had a significant bruise on her head when she was found dead in her spa tub.

Scanning down the expert witness lists provided by each side in the case, the name of Randall Jeffers of Water Analytical Solutions, International, pops out at me, as an expert witness scheduled to provide testimony, and presumably a report, for the prosecution. This is the man missing up in Larimer County, according to Tim. Since Dr. Jeffers' specialty appears to be water (if the name of his company means anything), presumably his expert testimony will address issues to do with the characteristics and/or quantity of water found in Chardonnay Fulton's lungs. I vaguely recall information circulating in the tabloid press that Chardonnay was dressed in workout clothes when her body was found floating in the jetted tub. Very odd. Did she slip and hit her head when she was filling the tub in preparation for a leisurely soak? Or did someone bash her over the head and "help" her into the water?

An additional Internet search on the company name, Water Analytical Solutions, International, reveals a surprising array of areas in which this consulting firm deals with water. Of primary interest to me in light of the details of the Fulton case, is their forensic division, which specializes in the investigation, analysis, and reconstruction of water-related issues with regard to products, equipment, manufacturing, accidents, and foul play. This work, according to their website, can include preparing expert reports and affidavits, and testifying in depositions, arbitrations, and trials in State and Federal courts. They highlight their past work on the failure analysis they performed on a dam in the country of Peru, which collapsed catastrophically a few years back with the terrible, resultant loss of hundreds of lives downstream. Water Analytical Solutions was able to prove that the engineering company's design of the dam was not flawed as the Peruvian government claimed, but was weakened by the use of sub-standard materials, which had passed Quality Control through the judicious use of bribes from the construction company awarded the bid— by the self-same government.

In addition, their roster includes a former medical examiner who has testified in several other high-profile cases with suspicious drowning deaths, including one case featured on several different true crime shows. Shockingly, the water found in the lungs of a deceased soccer mom located just off a California beach was bath water, not seawater. The prosecutor in that case brought on Water Analytical Solutions to review the data and back up the county medical examiner whose qualifications were perplexingly being challenged by the defense. The husband was later convicted of drowning her in their tub at home, putting her in a swimsuit and driving her and her belongings to the beach as if she were tragically killed while taking an early morning dip. Then he jogged home, woke up their kids, and made them breakfast. Talk about coldhearted. I'm finding this all very fascinating, but still owe Tim a call. Better to check in before it gets even more late. The twins have texted me that they made it home and their father got home right before they did.

CHAPTER 19

D ad arrives back at his cabin with Ripley. "Well, Michael is getting himself settled in down there," he reports. "We put the other dogs away and gave them each several of those liver treats they can't get enough of. He seems like a super kid. He was fascinated by the gizmos on the dogs' collars that open the doors to the outside kennel runs. We called Gemma back and forth a few times so he could see. Like a kid in a candy store! He's checking out the dog books you have stashed in the apartment and I found the TV remote for him."

"I thought you would really like him too," I reply. "He gives off such a good vibe and the Garcias couldn't say enough complimentary things about him. And he helped out Leda and me big-time; we can't forget that." I realize my mistake a little too late. I am way too tired to have a big discussion about my overconfidence in taking a bat to a knife fight (which in my defense, I did not realize was going to turn into a knife fight.)

"Dad, I need to call Tim about this scientist, Randy Jeffers. Do you want to listen on speaker while I call? It might be interesting."

He laughs, "I know you're trying to distract me, but I'll bite. Let's call Tim right now." Ripley and Leda plop themselves down next to the desk and close their eyes. I dial Tim's number and he answers promptly.

"Hi, Veronica. I was just about to call you. Thank you for feeding the girls tonight. They had a blast and they told me all about Michael and Cocoa."

"Ha," I laugh. "We should really be thanking them. They did a ton of work this evening helping us get the apartment ready for Michael. Dad and I have you on speakerphone. I was wondering how your trip up to Rocky Mountain National Park went today. Any luck finding the missing guy?"

"Hey, Bob," he responds. "Not long until elk season now. I can't wait for us to get out in the woods. Well, it was a long and somewhat strange day. Randy Jeffers is a bit of a superstar at his company. The company itself is not very big—four partners, two support staff and two IT guys. He has a medical degree *and* a PhD in biochemistry. From what we can gather, he really likes doing research and never actually practiced as a doctor. However, his training in both arenas has made him the company's main asset on a number of high-profile criminal cases and business disputes. All related to water in different ways, of course. This is not being treated as your run-of-the-mill missing hiker case for a couple of reasons.

"His wife, Patty, called on the Boulder County District Attorney directly about his disappearance because his testimony is a vital part of the Billy Fulton murder trial. She is afraid that Fulton's fans or entourage may have harmed Randy to prevent him from introducing his expert report and testifying at court. Billy Fulton's wild lifestyle and sycophant hangers-on are the stuff of legend. As you know, he only got worse as he transitioned from his three years of college ball to the pros. Hardly a month goes by without a vulgar tale regarding him or his posse showing up in the tabloids. You may remember the incident where he had the jewelry store in Vegas cleared of other customers and then spent $1.5 million on bling in 30 minutes, or the time he and his crew stole an ice cream truck in Milwaukee and drove it into the swimming pool at their hotel. With four exotic dancers in tow. Feathers were floating all the way across to the swim-up bar. Chocolate crunch bars, ice cream sandwiches, strawberry shortcake bars, and sundae cones all busted loose from their containers and were popping to the surface like tiny, multi-colored sugar missiles for a good hour."

"Well, at least the dancers weren't weighed down by too much clothing once they hit the water," I offer innocently. Tim and Dad both break up laughing for the next few seconds.

"Yeah," Tim replies. "I bet those rescue crews were falling all over themselves helping the ladies out of the pool."

"But the basketball players, not so much," my dad adds. "I thought he seemed to settle down a bit once he married Chardonnay though?" he asks Tim quizzically.

"You're right, Bob," he says. "He did stay below the radar for a while after their wedding in Bali, but it appears the bad behavior had been creeping back in the last year. His minions were hanging around him again and reports surfaced that he and Chardonnay had engaged in several vocal public fights—complete with cursing, shoving, and the throwing of dishes at one particularly upscale restaurant. The chef there is from Glasgow and not known for his placid demeanor. He invited the whole lot of them to vacate the premises or he'd give them 'a right doing.' I think that's Glaswegian for beat down. The moral of the story is simple; never mess with a man waving a cleaver around. Chardonnay had apparently texted her sister on several occasions just prior to her death indicating that Billy was getting very agitated with her for trying to cut off his friends financially. So that's a bit of the context leading up to the events of nine months ago and Chardonnay's untimely demise."

"Given this cast of characters," Dad responds, "I can see why the scientist's wife might be worried about someone in Billy's camp having bad intentions toward an expert who could help imprison their meal ticket or even implicate them personally in a murder. But what makes her think her husband may have dropped out of sight intentionally? Anything specific?"

"This is where it gets somewhat unclear," Tim answers. "Randy Jeffers called Patty from his office mid-morning yesterday. The connection on her cell phone wasn't great since she and her sister were driving from Golden to play slots over in Central City and they were approaching one of the mountain tunnels. He mentioned that he was concerned about a work matter; she assumed it was the upcoming Fulton trial, as he had been prepping for his testimony diligently for the past few weeks, and had alluded to her very recently that certain results were unexpected. Patty was admittedly a bit distracted as she is staying all weekend with her sister and they were in the middle of making further plans.

"Randy said he was going to have a late brunch at that great café, Up with the Sun, in Estes Park, and then take a hike at his favorite place to clear his mind. He absolutely loves Rocky Mountain National Park, according to Patty Jeffers, but she is unsure exactly what trail he was planning on visiting. She's not much of an outdoors person and admits she never paid strict attention when he recounted the trails he explored. And this is where the connection got bad. She idly asked him where he was going hiking, but his response was unintelligible and then the call dropped. But Randy called her again in the early afternoon. She said his voice sounded somewhat muted and he mentioned that he had spotted two strange looking men near the diner in Estes Park and they looked similar to a couple of characters he had glimpsed last week in the parking lot of his company's building."

CHAPTER 20

"Wait, what?" I stop Tim's explanation. "He had been seeing shady characters near his workplace. Why didn't he tell the District Attorney or the police?"

"Good question," Tim replies. "Possibly he didn't really believe it was anything at first, and maybe he was trying not to be an alarmist. He mentioned it in an offhand fashion to his wife; he said the guys didn't look like your usual healthy Boulder outdoors types, and they looked a bit shifty when he caught the eye of one of them. He described them as looking pallid, with some gold chains and slicked back hair. Randy wondered aloud if they might be media sniffing around trying to get juicy bombshell information on the Billy Fulton murder case. Or he may have assumed they were looking for vehicles to break into. Unfortunately, he never seemed to follow up with the authorities after that. I suppose once he thought he saw the same guys in his vicinity far from Boulder he may have started to take it more seriously. You know betting on professional sports is a big money-maker too and I wonder if someone is trying to make sure that Billy Fulton does not go to jail for murder. This is all just speculation, of course. Patty asked him where he was headed and he said something that sounded like Long Lake. That's the last she heard from him."

Tim continues, "When Randy had not shown up by the wee hours of the morning, Patty got Dispatch to call the Boulder County D.A., who then called Larimer County and the park rangers to roll out the troops. District

Attorney Bowen asked my boss if I could go pitch in with the search today just to give the Larimer County guys more coverage. To make a very long story short, that is how I came to be involved in the case of the disappearing scientist."

"That sounds like the title of a Nancy Drew book," I offer absentmindedly while pondering the Long Lake comment. By this time, both Ripley and Leda are flat out on their sides snoring contentedly while the humans chatter on and on.

"Tim, he must have been talking about Lawn Lake. There is no Long Lake in Rocky Mountain National Park, only the one near Nederland, adjacent to Indian Peaks Wilderness. I took a gorgeous late summer hike up to Crystal Lake in RMNP last year, starting at the Lawn Lake trailhead, and stopping off first at Lawn Lake. Lawn Lake is spectacular. It fills a really wide, flat basin at the timberline and is surrounded by Fairchild Mountain, Hagues Peak, and Mummy Mountain. That hike would make sense given that water and calamity of all sorts are his areas of expertise. I'm sure he's studied just what went wrong in that disaster. The lake used to be dammed, and sometime in the early 1980s, the earthen dam failed catastrophically. If I remember the descriptive marker correctly, an estimated thirty million cubic feet of water surged down the Roaring River Valley at an unbelievably high discharge rate. A little posy of wildflowers was left there by the marker. It really touched me."

My father, who has been tapping away on his computer interjects, "They say it was 134,640 gallons per second. The wall of water was about 25-30 feet high. The flood killed three people and did $31 million in damage, just in Estes Park. Wow, that's horrible to imagine. Those folks wouldn't have had a chance."

Tim responds somberly, "You two have the makings of good detectives. The National Park Service (NPS) rangers came to a similar conclusion about the name of the trail and when we spoke to Randy's boss, he confirmed that Randy has mentioned that lake and the mechanics of that dam disaster a number of times in the past. The Larimer County Sheriff's Office attempted to ping Randy's phone but got no hits. The puzzling thing is his vehicle. We searched at the Lawn Lake, the Lumpy Ridge, and the Cow Creek trailheads, which are the three logical and somewhat close access points if you are heading to Lawn Lake. His four-wheel drive was not found at any of the trailhead parking lots. The rangers checked their CCTV footage at the entrance and exit gates to the park, which is basically all that is covered. Randy's vehicle is seen entering the park, but never seen leaving. A search of all the trailheads and visitor center lots by designated team members over the course of today yielded no sign of the green four-wheel drive. However, despite his car not being located at the Lawn Lake trailhead, the Larimer County tracking dog got a hit at that trailhead and started up the trail confidently."

"Oh yeah," I recollect. "They use a Belgian Malinois named Cuda up there, don't they? Bruce introduced me to his handler when I first started training. The Secret Service uses that breed to guard the grounds at the White House. They are phenomenal working dogs and have those gorgeous black markings and black muzzles."

"It was Cuda," Tim confirms. He went up the Lawn Lake trail for three or four miles—that area where the trail parallels the Roaring River Valley. Then surprisingly, the track Cuda was following took a sharp veer to the east slightly north of Bighorn Mountain. The going got pretty rough from that point and Cuda had a hard time getting a scent to follow in the heavy timber and blowdown in that area. Then it started getting dark and that makes it near impossible to track anyone through that jumble of lodgepole, fir, and aspen. Why would Randy Jeffers leave a well-established trail and take off cross-country like that?"

Dad replies, "That's the pertinent question. He was hiking to a spot he loves and where he likes to think things out. He suddenly deviates from that plan and bolts into cover. I wonder if the two suspicious men turned up, he spotted them coming up the trail, and he was trying to lose them. How far into the timber did he get based on Cuda's tracking?"

"That's the odd thing," Tim answers. "That is definitely steep, rugged country. If he was trying to lie low, he sure went pretty far in. He could have just hunkered down and waited until he was confident they had passed him. At one point, I thought he might be cutting across to the Black Canyon Trail so he could head back south and lose the bad guys, but that's a tough cross-country hike. Unless they kept coming after him. And don't forget, Cuda was having a bit of difficulty locking in on a track once we got a couple of miles into that timber. But it seemed pretty definitive that Randy was right there at some point."

"I was wondering if you and Leda might be available tomorrow," Tim questions me. "If I get it approved by the higher-ups, you could either come check the trail again or even go up the Black Canyon Trail and see if Leda hits anywhere his scent cuts across. They are still wondering if he drove or was driven out of the national park; it's not exactly enclosed like Fort Knox. It's hard to allocate all of Larimer's varied resources to this search when they are not exactly sure where Randy Jeffers is—and if anything actually even happened to him. Additionally, their emergency services team is helping Grand County search for four missing hikers in the far southwestern area of the park near Mount Bryant, so their search resources are spread thin right at the moment. In any case, the team is waiting for Randy's cell phone provider to respond to the subpoena that was served earlier today so they can see where his last calls originated. Unfortunately, the pinging has revealed nothing whatsoever. It's a real puzzle and it's only a matter of time until the media ties this lost hiker to the Billy Fulton murder trial. Then the three-ring circus turns into a free-for-all."

"I could certainly make time tomorrow if it would help," I answer. "But they would need to invite me. I work with you in Boulder County and the deputies in Arapahoe County, but they have their own people and I don't want to step on anyone's toes. Of course, the other issue is the scent trail. It's going to start getting fainter and fainter. Leda has trailed a scent that was two days old, but I don't think we can push it past three days. At least, it isn't super hot and dry right at the moment, which helps preserve the scent molecules a tiny bit. My answer is a qualified yes. I'm about half asleep now after a long day and I'm sure you're beat too. Why don't you check with the people in charge after they get the cell phone records to peruse for clues and call me tomorrow if you need assistance? My schedule just includes training sessions first thing in the morning, so I can be ready to leave shortly after you call if they decide they can use us up there. I'll pack all Leda's gear and mine first thing in the morning just in case."

"That would be wonderful," Tim enthuses. "I'll text the command leader up there and let him know you two are available. All we can do is offer. Good night you guys and thanks again for feeding the hooligans."

"Our pleasure, Tim," Dad replies. "Your girls are more than welcome here any time. I have a feeling that they'll be over here like a shot once Cocoa arrives!" We disconnect and say our good nights. Dad strolls outside to do his perimeter check with Ripley at his heels. I stagger across to my house with Leda padding along behind me like a silent lion. I brush my teeth and fall into bed. Out like a light and not a nightmare in sight.

CHAPTER 21

Sunday morning dawns crisp and cool. And sunny, but that figures. I stretch for a few minutes and then pop out of bed. Leda hops up from her dog bed and smiles in my face. There are definitely worse ways to start a day. I scratch her behind her ears and tell her how beautiful she is. We take a quick jaunt outside, followed by kibble for her, and a bowl of cereal, a banana, and a snack-size chocolate bar for me. We walk down to the training building to check on Michael. He greets us with a big smile and it's clear he has already cleaned the runs and filled water bowls. "Good morning, Michael. You got up bright and early this morning. Did you sleep okay?"

"Yes, Veronica," he replies shyly. "I like it here; it's really quiet. Not like the city at all. I hope it's okay that I fed the dogs breakfast this morning. I looked at the feeding chart on the wall."

"That's awesome," I reply happily. "How long ago did they eat?"

"About an hour ago or so. And I had some toast and jam from the stuff Bob brought down for me."

"Good," I think aloud. "Let's pack up my gear and Leda's in case I have to go to Rocky Mountain National Park and then we can do short training sessions with Butter and Scotch and Gemma." He assents readily and we sort through the gear necessary for trailing in the wilderness: Leda's Working Dog vest, her harness, the long line, water bowl, dog booties in case she cuts a pad, water, gloves, bandages, adhesive tape, sunscreen, antiseptic, alcohol wipes, lip balm, bandanna, baseball cap, rain poncho, thermal Mylar blanket, surveyor's tape (pink), knife, whistle, compass, glow sticks for the dark, flashlight, dog treats, water purification tablets, energy bars, and sunglasses. I show him the tiny packet which holds the thermal Mylar blanket. "This is really nifty. A four foot by seven foot blanket is folded up into this packet, if you can picture that. It's an emergency Mylar blanket that reflects up to 90% of a person's body heat to help keep them warm. They are also waterproof and windproof. Very useful in back country rescues, especially if the individual is injured." Michael nods thoughtfully and adds it to the pile of gear. I explain the use for each item to him and he picks them up one by one, looks them over carefully, and puts everything but Leda's garb in the pack for me.

"How do the water purification tablets work?"

"Well, first of all, let us hope never to use them, but Dad wrote reviews on a bunch of them last year and picked out this brand for me. They contain chemicals that purify water by killing a variety of contaminants like bacteria, parasites, and viruses. You do not want to get giardia, believe me! You drop two of these chlorine dioxide tablets in a quart or liter of water, close it slightly and wait five minutes, then you shake and tighten down the lid and wait 35-45 more minutes. And they've killed the biological organisms. Presto! Clean H2O. They are used all over the world by the military, by people in the back country, in emergency situations like natural disasters, and in humanitarian crises." We proceed to stow all the gear in the car. Leda has been observing all of this preparation with laser focus. "Not quite yet, girl," I tell her. "Let's go over here against the side wall of the building and you can practice your Down Stay while Gemma works." Leda looks a trifle dejected, but is obedient as always. It is difficult to explain the concept of time to a dog. They don't know what "later" means. She puts her head down on her paws with a disgusted sigh. Dogs can give some serious attitude!

Pulling out the boxes for Gemma's citrus greening disease detection training, I explain to Michael what the disease is and her importance in safeguarding the livelihood of her soon to be family. By now the dogs have adequately digested, so Gemma gets a quick brushing and Michael sees how to put on her Working Dog vest. This clothing reinforces to her that she is going to work. No goofing off. I take the sample packet of disease scent out and let Gemma get in a good sniff. I ask Michael to take the two batches of boxes outside. As instructed, he wears two different sets of disposable gloves from the big container in the kennel to place the boxes around any pieces of vegetation outside in the dog yard. These separate gloves keep the scent of the "disease" boxes from getting on the dummy boxes.

Gemma waits patiently inside with me, her tail lazily breezing back and forth. "Okay, Veronica," Michael explains. "I put all the boxes in different places out in the side and back yard for Gemma to find. Some of them look tricky to me. I hope she gets them all. I do have one question. How did you train her at the very beginning to know she was looking for the disease scent made by the lab?" I am thrilled with Michael's very smart question. One point for Michael.

"I started by combining the laboratory-manufactured scent with dog food. The dummy boxes had nothing. Once Gemma knew what scent she was searching for, she could pick out the citrus greening disease scent without a food hint. Pretty cool, huh?" Michael stands in the doorway so he can watch the action and I give Gemma the "ROT" command. Michael gives a little snort and then controls his laughter admirably.

Gemma heads off across the yard doing her quartering search pattern. Michael has done a great job of concealing the boxes in devious nooks and crannies, like wedging them half way up the crotch of a small tree and way back under the bench where Dad and Ripley like to hang out in the evenings and watch the hoary bats. (Dad loves their distinct look with white or grayish hair tips making them look like they were dipped in frost. They forage with swift, direct flight like little guided jets and feed on beetles, wasps, and grasshoppers.) Gemma moves confidently around the property like a jet herself, alerting at target box after target box. As an aside, I tell Michael that next session she will get a treat every three or four finds, then eventually she'll get one at the end of her search pattern only. But always lots of praise! The Duncans need to know that when she alerts to a tree or sapling it is definitely diseased and needs to be removed and destroyed. Healthy stock will go unremarked by her.

Gemma moves past the dummy boxes in their spots resolutely, as being of no interest to her work assignment. We finish with no mistakes and she hesitates over just one box, but gives it a second pass and full inhale, and alerts by promptly sitting down. "Good girl, Gemma," I praise her vigorously as she whirls around in a circle, proud of doing a good job. Michael helpfully collects all the boxes again using two different sets of gloves and takes off Gemma's vest.

"That was so cool, Veronica. Gemma did a fantastic job finding the boxes you wanted her to find. How soon will she be ready to do that with real trees in Florida?"

"Probably about three more weeks. Soon we will omit the dummy boxes and spread the disease scent boxes out in a bigger area for her to find. Once she is solid on that, I'll schedule a trip to take her down there and work with her and her new owners and actual orange trees. We are all really going to miss her."

Michael answers with a smile, "She's a neat dog, but she has important work to do down South. I love my orange juice in the morning." Michael takes her back to her kennel run and strokes her fur, telling her what a good dog she is. Point two to Michael. He's not afraid to give praise and the dogs like him very much.

On my hand signal, Leda runs over to the small agility course Dad put together for me in the back yard. When Michael returns, I tell him, "This is the agility equipment all the dogs get to learn on eventually. Yes, Cocoa too." I answer the question evident in his eyes. Leda demonstrates how she goes over the A frame, through a closed end tunnel, and across the dog walk. He seems really impressed by her thudding power as she charges up and down the A frame while still hitting her contact points at the ends. "We will start Cocoa off with baby equipment once she learns her obedience," I tell him and he grins in anticipation. Leda gets lots of praise and a peanut butter treat; she shouldn't work too much in case she has to trail the scientist later.

We go inside the dog training building and Michael pulls a chair up on the side for optimal viewing. I show Michael how to put the training collar high on Butter's throat with the rings just behind his ears on the skull. Time to run through Butter's set of basic commands that he learned the day before. He performs quite well moving through the Sit, Stand, Down, and Heel commands. Butter needs extra practice on the heeling, as he tends to lag slightly. I encourage him to pick it up a little. Lastly, I add in an About Turn while heeling by holding the lead lightly in my left hand to keep Butter in heel position. I turn away from him to my right and walk briskly in the opposite direction, without stopping and waiting for him to start moving. They are always surprised by this at first. *Where the heck did the human just go?* But he seems to pick things up quickly and starts staying with me on the About Turn. Butter goes into a Down Stay next to Michael and I tell him he has to replace Butter in his spot if he breaks that command and give the Down Stay instruction each time he is repositioned. Michael nods and looks serious. Butter fidgets a few times, but Michael is watching closely and gets him back into position promptly before a real break occurs. He has obviously been paying attention and anticipates any time Butter tries to get up.

Scotch runs through the same exercises and he does almost as well. He is rather resistant to the Stand command, so we practice that a few more times and I help guide him into it more smoothly with a liver treat. Interestingly, he forges ahead on the heeling, the opposite of his brother, so pops of the lead slow him down a trifle. He seems to understand the concept; we'll just keep working on his manners. Butter goes back in his kennel and Michael watches Scotch while he practices his Down Stay as his last exercise. Michael asks me a couple of pertinent questions about what he just observed, so I'm feeling pretty positive about my new assistant's potential. I take several cute photos of the Springer Spaniel brothers and text them to Heather with the caption "Second Day of School." She responds quickly. "Such cute boys!" Which, of course, they are. We put the boys in their runs and I text the vet to check on Cocoa. She responds that she looks good and can go home today.

"Really, she can come live with me now?" Michael asks hopefully.

"Yes, she's ready to come home. Dad can take you over to get her at the vet if I have to go to Rocky Mountain."

CHAPTER 22

Just then, my phone rings and Tim's name pops up on the screen. "Hi Tim, what's the news today?"

He answers me in a serious tone. "Randy Jeffers is still missing in action. His car is nowhere to be found. No phone calls are going through to him or his voice mail. And the call history compiled by his cell phone company shows no activity after he spoke to his wife from Estes Park. Two investigators are researching the owners of numbers to and from his phone in the past couple of weeks to see if that generates any leads. If they could match any numbers to those of Fulton's entourage, we may have a lead to interview or a new place to check out. Also, Cuda has come up lame this morning, unfortunately. His handler thinks he twisted it in all the heavy timber and blowdown yesterday evening. So, the command leader would really appreciate it if you and Miss Leda could come up to Lawn Lake trailhead in the national park and double-check that trail of Randy Jeffers to see if we can get any further. The park rangers have kept the trail closed for hiking so that has limited the amount of additional foot traffic at least."

"Absolutely. That's no problem. Let me just get Michael squared away with Dad and I'll load up Leda and drive to the trailhead. Will you be meeting me there?"

"For sure," he replies. "I'm headed up there now, so I will get all the latest information from the searchers, get my gear on, and be ready to hike when you two arrive."

"Great. We're getting sorted out here and I'll hit the road in 15 or 20 minutes." I turn to Michael. "Before we leave the building, please check to make sure the dogs' training collars are off. Those are only for training and can't be left on for safety reasons. Make sure they have water and the kennel run doors are secured." He is already walking down the line and visually inspecting.

"All good, Veronica." We hustle up to Dad's cabin with Leda trotting in front of us. I am pretty sure she understood that phone call because she looks very peppy and alert, and much less annoyed.

We knock and go into Dad's cabin where it smells divine. He's cooking scrambled eggs with peppers and onion and crispy bacon strips and automatically pulls down another plate from the cupboard when he sees Michael with me. "Hey Dad. They do need Leda up in Larimer County, so can Michael hang out with you today? Cocoa can come home from the vet's, so maybe you two can go get her after breakfast."

"No problem," he nods in agreement. "We'll get this food under our belts and then go pick up the new dog. Do you want anything to eat before you leave?"

"I wish, but I need to get going. It smells wonderful," I say wistfully.

"Honey, you may be working all day and evening with Leda. Granola bars are not enough sustenance for that amount of exercise. You need protein. This batch of food is almost done. I have large spinach wraps. How about I load one up with this food and wrap it so you can eat while driving? I can make another batch of food for Michael and me."

"Excellent. Thanks, Dad. I would also appreciate it if you and Michael can get the three dogs in the kennel exercised later today and help him get started on Cocoa's house training if you have time."

"Will do. I am taking a break from writing since it's Sunday. Michael and I will hold down the fort while you are gone." By this time, Dad has packaged my spinach breakfast wrap, and thrown it in a bag with an apple and two soft baked chocolate chip cookies. Good thing I have a lot of hiking to do today. Michael and Dad wish me well and are busy cooking the second pile of food together sociably when I hurry out the door with my Chessie to work.

Leda happily jumps in the back of the SUV but soon settles down in her imitation sled dog pose once she realizes we have a drive ahead of us. Curled up in a ridiculously tight ball with tail over nose. Sound asleep in three minutes. Boy, that capability would be awesome. I could use an Off switch in my brain at bedtime. I do realize rather belatedly that thoughts of Tommy Arnett have not tormented me at all today. Maybe my attempts to achieve some hard-won serenity are paying off—or more likely I have been so busy I forgot to fret over that lowlife. I have finished my spinach wrap while driving northward and am contemplating a chocolate chip cookie for dessert. Yes, it is still the morning. Just then, my cell phone rings and an unknown number comes up on the radio display.

I hit the Bluetooth connection and answer. "Veronica Kildare here. Dogged Pursuit K-9. Can I help you?"

"Good morning. I am sorry to bother you on a Sunday, but this will be my best chance to call for the next few days. My name is Ricardo Cruz. I was hoping you could help me with dog training. I got one of your business cards from the vet tech at Dr. Stephanie's office." He has a very warm and polite tone with a slight Hispanic accent. His name sounds vaguely familiar but obviously we are not acquainted.

"Sure," I respond. "I would be happy to discuss training with you. What sort of thing are you needing help with?"

Ricardo answers, "I travel a good deal for work and my mother lives in an in-law suite at my home situated between Louisville and Erie. I have just gotten a rescue Doberman, Jinx, from a group in Denver. She is red in color and beautiful, but I think she needs help with her confidence. I am not certain what happened to her with her original owners. And I would like her to be trained to obey Mama and also to guard the premises when I am out of town."

"Okay, Ricardo. I can definitely help you with that. I would like to take the dog for a few weeks so she can be trained in obedience and protection. Then I will need to work with your mother at the property. Also, I can solidify the protection training onsite. I am heading up to Larimer County now to assist in a missing person search, but could probably start working with her next week. Does that sound good?"

"Great! Thank you so much. I will feel better knowing Mama has a trained dog with her when I am gone," Ricardo responds. We discuss a healthy fee to which he readily agrees, and say goodbye. I wonder if Ricardo is as attractive as his voice sounded. Anyway, things are looking up for my business. New assignment and a new assistant. I grab the apple, turn up the volume louder on my Gin Wigmore CD, and sing along to *Black Sheep* as I drive up Route 36. Leda sleeps.

CHAPTER 23

I take Route 34 next and stop at the Fall River Entrance Station. The park ranger stationed there was previously apprised that Leda was joining the search and we pass through quickly. Her nametag says Cassandra and she has a pleasant, good-natured vibe as she wishes me luck with the search. Park rangers are some of the real superheroes of this country—underpaid but doing a fantastic job because they treasure their country and all its beauties. They try to hold the line while all around them budgets are cut back to nothing. If you love your national parks, thank the rangers because they love those parks even more. The Lawn Lake trailhead is just a couple of miles west and Tim is waiting in the parking lot there, as promised. Leda stands up and yawns and then starts her elaborate stretches. She might actually be part cat.

"Hi, Veronica," Tim greets me, "and Leda. How can I ever forget you?"

"You probably can't forget her because she's shoving her head into your hip right now."

Tim laughs. "She knows who her biggest fan is." Chesapeake Bay Retrievers are typically one person or one family dogs—very bonded to, and protective of, their owners. But Leda has expanded her circle of people to include Tim, and now his family, as she has spent a significant amount of time with them. She will actually condescend to let them pet her. I get her Working Dog vest, which also protects her from any heavy brush, and her nylon harness out of my SUV and get her ready with several sips of water to cleanse around her nose area. After lathering sunscreen on my face and neck, I take my bandanna out of the pack and fold it across my forehead, tying it in the back to absorb future sweat. The low humidity in Colorado is great for me, but can make trailing a scent a little tougher for Leda. Next, I shrug into my backpack and attach her long line. She leans against my leg while I rub her ears and tell her we have a job to do today.

Tim has a baggie with one of Randy's T-shirts ready for Leda. Patty Jeffers had gotten it from the house yesterday morning and he had taken it up to Rocky Mountain for Cuda to use. She followed his instructions and pulled the T-shirt out of the laundry hamper in Randy's bathroom with tongs and wedged it in a plastic bag. I open this very same baggie wider and tell Leda to Find. The moisture at the end of her nose assists her in locking onto the smell and better remembering it. Her yellow eyes look very serious as she takes a number of good sniffs at the T-shirt. This sniffing intensifies the smell and helps her recognize the odor she has been tasked with finding. Leda turns abruptly toward the start of the Lawn Lake trail with her nose sniffing the air. She has been trained to air scent first and stay with it unless she comes across a recent "hot" track. Then she tracks that scent on the ground.

"And away we go," I say to Tim as we follow Leda steadily up the trail as she continually tests the air. The weather conditions are not horrible, somewhat conducive to trailing an older scent, but it is never automatic. Thankfully, it is not hot and dry. Bruce told me when we were training with him (and every dog trainer needs a trainer too) that a dog can smell a single drop of blood even diluted in five quarts of water or termites inside the wood of a house. Their sense of smell is so far advanced from a human's that it is difficult to comprehend. Scientists in Russia believe that dogs can distinguish over half a million separate odors. Bruce also said current thinking is that dogs can smell between 10,000 and 100,000 times better than humans can—which is why I have no chance of EVER hiding peanut butter treats from Leda.

She seems confident and we go uphill at a reasonable pace. Tim has done enough trailing with us to know that I talk very little in these circumstances. I watch Leda's body language to see if she wavers or hesitates, and do not want her distracted by people talking incessantly behind her—although like most canines, she can tune us out no problem if nothing interesting is happening! I have asked Tim not to tell us where Cuda made his cut to the east off the trail so as not to telegraph anything to Leda through the line connecting us. Scent is carried downwind in a cone shape, which is narrow at the point of origination (Randy Jeffers) and widens with distance. Each raft of skin cells carries bacteria and vapor, which make up the individual scent of the target. Watching Leda's subtle cues, she seems focused on her upward ascent and is having no doubts.

It is a lovely autumn day in early October and the green firs and the aspens with their brilliant yellow leaves are intermingled on both sides of us like a cordon of towering pennants. This would be a wonderful day hike if our job were not so serious. The trail is so very quiet without the presence of any other hikers at all. This locale being closed since yesterday has helped Leda immensely. This is only my second time on the Lawn Lake Trail; it is not as familiar to me as many of the Boulder Mountain Parks and Open Space trails are. We have covered an estimated four or five miles when Leda suddenly halts and turns her muzzle to the right. She stands stock-still and sniffs air in strongly. Moments later, she steps decisively into the jumbled timber to the east of the trail, picking her way over and around the windfall. I clamber after her, dodging pointed branches with their decidedly lethal intent, weaving like an aged boxer with a bad hamstring because she is pulling into her harness pretty severely. I scramble to keep up, because not inhibiting her enthusiasm is key. If Randy is injured anywhere in this area of downed logs and thickets, time is of the essence.

A number of bushes bearing red and purple late autumn berries dot the landscape and thoughts of hungry black bears do cross my mind. This is the time of year when they eat voraciously to put on weight for the hibernation season. Since I proofed Dad's article for a Colorado wildlife magazine last summer, I know that bears get ready for winter hibernation around late November. They just live off the layer of fat they accumulate during the summer and autumn. Their hibernating heart rate is one third of their normal rate (about 8-10 beats per minute), and they typically don't eat, drink, urinate, or defecate during hibernation. The bear's own waste gets recycled into protein. However, Tim is coming along right behind me and he is armed, so he can worry about bears. I'm going to watch my dog.

We are 200-300 yards into this area of close timber when Tim points out to me a piece of pink surveyor's tape fluttering from an aspen. This marks the spot where Cuda had taken the searchers yesterday evening. Leda is confirming his course, so that is all positive. Two highly qualified dogs have now followed Randy's scent this direction. Now we have to make it further into this tangle. It can be difficult to keep all the slack in Leda's long line either gathered up or meted out in tight quarters, but luckily, I have had a lot of practice at it. We press onward and the strain on my legs from this difficult going makes itself felt. I am going to have to step it up on the jogging. I know—or fewer chocolate chip cookies. I have loads of energy typically, but this is a real workout.

Translucent dragonflies flit by and the sun dapples through the leaves in beautiful, swirled patterns. I notice all this abstractly while concentrating on keeping up with Leda. She scrambles and climbs like a mountain goat as we head almost due east. The weave poles and dog walk have been the perfect preparation for her on this slope. The trees astonishingly get even closer together and we have to force ourselves between them at certain choke points. The three of us bushwhack uphill, passing some very tall trees. The only sounds to be heard are two humans breathing heavily and Leda panting. We have gained close to 2500 feet in elevation by this time. Fortunately, I can exert myself at elevation now without my heart thudding out of my chest. The first few months of transitioning from an elevation of 1100 feet in Ohio to living and exercising at 6000+ feet in Colorado were an eye-opener.

I call Leda back to me and give her a drink. She looks a little put out to be halted, but I want to rinse around her nose and keep us all hydrated. Leda's pads and her feet look good after a quick scan—no cuts, scrapes, or broken nails. I pull a couple of twigs out of my curly ponytail and stick an adhesive bandage on one jagged scrape on my elbow. No idea how that happened, but it is not bleeding overly much. Tim gulps down his water while I grab a pair of Berry Blast granola bars from my pack and we engulf them in seconds as we stand at the edge of a massive grove of trees.

We both check our cell phones and confirm that, as we would expect in this locale in the park, neither of us has cell service. You can get decent service at altitude in a number of places here (even the front face of 14,000-foot Longs Peak), just not everywhere and you need a clear line of sight to a tower outside the park. No towers at all are situated in this national park. An oscillating movement ahead pulls my attention up to the left about 20 yards and on a diagonal. Sure enough, it is another piece of surveyor's tape. Tim catches up and looks at it. "Yep, this is where we turned around with Cuda last night because of the terrain and darkness. I cut a super long piece so it would be more visible."

CHAPTER 24

"**G**ood thinking. This is confirmation that Randy definitely headed this way. Both dogs have trailed him on a fairly consistent course. We are lucky to have more daylight on today's search. Let's move along with her and see if we can figure out what is going on with Dr. Jeffers." We start wending our way uphill again through the dense forest with Leda as our guide. I feel a momentary surge of pride over her ability, beauty, and drive. She is a far cry from the half-starved, hairless, and cowering young dog I adopted from the Dog Warden for $95 on the very day she was set for euthanasia. Her belly never left the floor for two weeks—she was that terrorized and subservient; she was so traumatized she barely ate. Now she is confident and phenomenal at her job. This work is a big change from my position as a legal assistant for a County Prosecutor in Ohio working on cases involving child abuse, neglect, and domestic violence. Both careers are important, but in very different ways. The past that got me here was marked by brutal tragedy, but every step Leda and I take toward helping a missing person gives me back a little of my stolen light.

"Tim, according to my compass, Randy was heading nearly straight east which does make me think he was trying to cut over to the Black Canyon trail. These broken branches make it look like he was being pursued or was with someone else—although we have no idea who that would be." Leda continues to lead our ascent at a good clip. The cooler fall weather has helped keep the scent lingering for her and she forges steadily onward through an enormous grove of old-growth spruce. They stand still like sentinels, pungent in their ancient home. Peering through the trees ahead, a slight thinning of the forest reveals itself. The amount of blowdown has definitely diminished and we are walking more or less straight ahead with limited obstacle course action. I hold Leda's long line with my left hand while pointing to Tim to show him that more sunlight is filtering in ahead of us. Streaks of light spread out wider and wider as we leave the silent darkness of the grove behind.

"Now we're making progress," he offers quietly. Turning my head sideways just enough that he can see me grin, I nod in agreement. Another 500 yards of hiking and we follow Leda out into an enormous moraine meadow.

Proofreading Dad's plethora of articles about the great outdoors and hunting in Colorado comes in handy once again. Rocky Mountain National Park has been sculpted and reshaped by cycles of growth, recession, and reforming of glaciers over thousands of years. The slow movement of glacial ice sheets grinds the ground beneath them, thus depositing till on their margins which forms ridges or moraines. At the point where a glacier's downhill progress stops, wide, flat depressions can often be found, circled by the land it has displaced. The level expanse in front of us has grass cropped fairly short, which was most likely caused by the herd of elk currently passing out the far side of the meadow. The herd numbers 18 to 20 animals; they are moving briskly with rotating ears and upraised heads to get away from these intruders in their domain. It is almost shocking to see such an open space after the tangle from which we have just emerged. Looking around the timber-lined edges, it must cover 10 to 15 acres or more.

Leda continues to track dead ahead toward the center of the meadow. She starts to slow and sniffs deeply, first the air and then the ground. This reaction has nothing to do with the herd of elk or any other wildlife; she has zero interest in chasing wild animals—a requirement for a dog that does this sort of work. She really never wants me to be out of her sight anyway, which solidified our trust and our partnership over the years. In almost the dead middle of the meadow, Leda slows to a halt and looks around in a puzzled fashion. This behavior is not typical for her. She seems unsure of her next direction. I release her and let her cast around back and forth in ever-widening circles for a good ten minutes and she returns to the center of the meadow. The grass does seem to be somewhat trampled, but that could be from elk movements. Herds of elk can include dozens of animals at a time. We scout around the trampled area, which displays bright clumps of common cinquefoil with their five-petaled, lemon-colored flowers dotting the damp patches, and a couple of tall stalks of blue vervain, pressed into the ground. Those flowers resemble a candelabrum, and open a few at a time beginning at the base of the spike until a profusion of blooms erupts forth like a flare. Watching Leda's body language even more closely, I see her looking up in the air.

I lead her next to Randy's back trail for a few hundred yards, then turn her around, and tell her again to Find. Still nothing. She looks at me stoically and then follows the trail to the same spot in the center of the meadow. "Leda, Down," I murmur to her while contemplating our next step. She can rest while Tim and I confer. She drinks deeply from her water bowl. Tim and I eat another granola bar apiece, honey oat this time, and swig thirstily from our bottles. "The trail seems to end right here in the center, which is really bizarre. She has checked it twice, Tim. I'm thinking we should take her around the entire perimeter of this meadow and see if she cuts across a hot track anywhere to give us a direction. What do you think?" Leda sidles over and scores a small handful of her liver treats, one at a time.

Tim pauses and considers the options while rubbing the back of his neck. "Yeah, let's do that. I trust her and she says it ends at this spot, but it is worth a try. We did a lot of hard walking to get up here. We'll see what else we can find. It's really strange."

Steller's Jays flit back and forth from the evergreen forest into the sun spreading their bold, noisy, and curious vibe in all directions. Their chirping shook-shook-shook calls cascade all around us in ripples, making the air active and alive. Two swoop to the forest floor edging the meadow as they seek a meal, hopping decisively on long legs. The prominent black crest with brazen punk rock white streaks and the dusky blue lower body on these birds make them real stunners—with an attitude. These jays can mimic birds and mammals in their environment, in addition to copying the sounds of squirrels and even lawn sprinklers. Clever buggers. As usual, Leda takes no notice, but I am transfixed with joy for a moment at their color gradations of blue and vibrant social interactions. But this is no time to revel in birdwatching. Back to our search.

CHAPTER 25

I take my backtrack GPS and push the button marking the location where Leda lost the trail. This is another one of Dad's latest gadgets. I am more of a map and compass type of girl, but Dad has high hopes of making me more technologically savvy in the outdoors. (Oh, the irony, say those of you trying to drag your parents into the computer age.) In any case, it is a nifty GPS-enabled digital compass that lets me mark up to three places. Now we will be able to tell how far away from this location we are and how to get back to it. This is the second place I have marked after also saving the location at the beginning of the Lawn Lake Trailhead (just in case we had to return the way we went out). Tim always marks our trail intermittently with surveyor's tape as a back-up whenever we have to go off trail. I play with my dog for a minute or two and snap her line on again. I kiss her face and tell her what a fabulous job she is doing. She is a valuable working dog, but also my valued pet. Leda and I return to the spot where we entered the meadow on Randy Jeffers' scent trail. I tell her to Find and we start a search circling the perimeter of the vast meadow.

Leda searches diligently for the scent again; her nose is scooping in enormous amounts of information. We just need the right piece of information. About three quarters of the way around the perimeter, she suddenly surges forward and gives three barks. I hasten forward to look and see something, at long last. A thin braided leather bracelet is lying almost fully embedded in the mud at the edge of one tall patch of meadow grass.

From the copious number of tracks in the vicinity, it appears that one or more elk have stepped on it and ground it further into the muck. Leda is very clear that this scent is the same as the one she was told to find. Tim looks at the bracelet carefully and takes several cell phone photos of it and its location before lifting the bracelet up with a pen and putting it in an evidence bag. No scent trail seems to head away from the spot, however. I ask Leda again to Find and she completes the loop around the outside edge of the field without cutting across a trail of Randy Jeffers. I feel confident that she has covered this ground thoroughly and there is nothing left to learn here. Tim and I sit on a downed tree next to Leda and discuss what may have happened to our missing man.

"From the direction he was headed, it does seem likely that he was pushing for the Black Canyon Trail, just maybe trying to throw off pursuers. This is not a hike one takes for the fun of it—cutting cross-country randomly and crashing around between two trails. Leda was very confident getting us to this meadow—as she was when she found that bracelet, which does seem like a man's piece of jewelry. What happened to him from here on out is more puzzling. Any ideas?" Tim asks. I sit and think for two or three minutes while swigging my water.

"I do have a notion, but you may think it's completely crazy," I reply.

"Hey, I'm open to any ideas right now," Tim laughs. "This whole situation is crazy. It's like aliens abducted him from the middle of this big-ass field." He rummages in his backpack and pulls out a plastic container filled with unsalted cashews. We munch on a handful each while I decide how to broach the next subject. A diet root beer would be so good right about now.

"Actually..." I start to voice my thought.

"Please tell me this does not involve any flying saucers," Tim interrupts jokingly.

"Nope, no flying saucers, but flying, yes. I'm connecting possible dots in my head. Based on how long it took us to hike up here today and if we estimate about what time Randy started up the Lawn Lake Trail Friday after lunch, we can assume he made it up to this location in the late afternoon. Now, bear with me. I was over in the Comanche Peak Wilderness working with Gemma right around that same time Friday and saw a helicopter coming from the west out of the national park and toward me in the wilderness area. No overflights are allowed in the national park as you know, but that is definitely where it came from. No markings were visible on its body, but it seemed larger than your average rescue chopper—like a heavier body. We should check with the National Park Service when we get back to see if any rescues or allowed flights were logged for that afternoon."

"If not," I continue, "Perhaps Randy was caught and subdued by his pursuers and taken away in that helicopter. It would certainly explain the trail ending and Leda looking skyward in confusion. The center of the meadow did show that big flattened area—although it's hard to tell if that was a chopper setting down or a massive elk bed."

Tim looks thoughtful as he checks his (non-existent) cell coverage and says, "But how did the helicopter know where to come and get Randy and the supposed bad guys? No cell coverage up here with this meadow being hemmed in by tall trees, so it would have to be a satellite phone, right?"

I agree with him. "That is what I was thinking. Maybe they followed Randy and when they saw him start to cross this big, open area, perfect for setting down a chopper, they caught up to him, subdued him, and called in their pilot using a satellite phone. Coverage is known to be very spotty in this quarter million-acre national park, so someone planned ahead. Why they have a helicopter on standby is a question that needs investigation. Anyway, their taking him away into the air would explain why the trail ends in the middle of the meadow."

"And the bracelet?" Tim queries.

I respond thoughtfully, "Randy either lost it in a struggle or dropped it from the helicopter as he was being taken away. Leda found no scent trail of him walking out of that meadow. The good news is this: I snapped several pictures of that helicopter as it flew overhead and texted them to my father. He is a great researcher. If the NPS has no record of an approved flight for that day and time, he can blow up my shots on the computer and start digging around for a lead."

Tim shakes his head and says, "It makes as much sense as anything else I can dream up. Let's hike back out of here and check on the status of the investigation."

CHAPTER 26

The three of us get ourselves together and hightail it back the way we came in. Leda is released from her long line so she can move around a tad more freely. She never gets far from me even when she is not working. I use the GPS backtrack device to guide us smoothly down the mountain and toward the main trail. We go around a rocky outcropping and see some yellow-bellied marmots basking in the late afternoon sunlight. They are very close to hibernation time, but seem keen on one last play party. The bold ones stand up on their stocky legs presenting their yellow chest and the white patch between their eyes, which makes them look eternally puzzled. They hurl abuse at Leda, but she barely deigns to look in their direction. Their chatter is of no consequence to her, and she looks over her shoulder and smiles back at me. "Aren't those rodents the silliest things, girl?" She wags her tail in agreement and keeps heading out of the mountains.

Tim and I chat about the girls' sports activities and their desire for a dog. Tim is rightfully concerned about the time commitment since they are so active on a variety of teams. I offer my help and remind him that it would be a good thing for the girls to have a running companion and protector when they are off training for their various sports. I mention an article I just read about diabetes alert dogs being trained to smell the difference in Volatile Organic Compounds (VOCs) in a diabetic's saliva if their blood glucose level gets too high or too low. This first alert from the dog gives the person a chance to check their glucose level before an issue has become evident to them, and remedy the problem. The uses for which dogs can be trained have been growing in leaps and bounds.

We wade back through the dense forest area lying between the Lawn Lake and Black Canyon Trails; it is easier for me going downhill and not being attached to a harnessed dog on a long line, but I still won't win any awards for grace. Up and over and around trees until we pop back out on the Lawn Lake Trail and head toward the parking lot. We arrive back at our vehicles and find one of the Larimer County deputy sheriffs leaning non-chalantly against his vehicle at the trailhead. I take off Leda's official gear, get her a drink of water and a biscuit, and load her and my equipment into the back of the SUV, rolling down all the windows partway to keep Leda comfortable. Meanwhile Tim goes to compare notes with the other officer. Leda hops in, promptly collapses in an elegant heap, and then rolls over flat on her side. She worked hard today and I can sense a power nap coming on. Yep, those enigmatic eyes are closed already.

Tim is still deep in conversation with the Larimer deputy on the other side of the empty lot, so I climb into the front seat and take the opportunity to pull off my sweaty shirt and sports bra. I choose a clean dry sports bra and long-sleeved hoodie from my bag of extra clothing behind the front seat and pull them on. Much better. I take off my bandanna and release my hair from its ponytail. Ugh, more sweat. I twist my hair up in a coil and clip it to the top of my head. Not sure why I bothered with the blue mascara and eyeliner this morning; most of it appears to be smeared around my cheek. I start laughing and wipe it off with my damp bandanna. I peel off my adhesive bandage and check out the ugly scrape on my elbow. It's done bleeding. I take my little jar of arnica salve from the glove box and rub it on the scar tissue on the back of my shoulder. Leda is snoring like a warthog and somehow still manages to look twice as glamorous as I do right now.

I grab a bottle of cold spring water from the cooler on my passenger seat and pour a packet of strawberry-flavored electrolytes into the bottle, shake it up, and gulp it down in four swallows. It is tough to remind myself to stay hydrated in the more arid Mountain West. Then I pull two more cold bottles of water from the cooler and amble over to the officers to hand out the waters. Sitting down was a mistake. I'm feeling kind of stiff. Sylvia and I really need to intensify our yoga workouts just a smidge. Can't wait to break it to her.

"Veronica, this is Bryan Campbell. He came from Denver P.D. originally and he's been a deputy here for a year or so." Officer Campbell is tall, red-haired, and keen looking. If he were a dog, he would definitely be an Irish Setter. We shake hands and all stand in the fading sunlight relaxing for a moment, hydrating, and listening to trilling birds. Lazy, puffy, shape-shifting clouds scud across the sky. I am reminded again of how much I love Colorado. The Chicks got it right. Wide Open Spaces.

CHAPTER 27

Tim and I part company as he heads off with Deputy Campbell to visit the command center and get the latest updates on today's search in other areas. Leda has gotten up to keep an eye on me as I talk with the officers and she waits steadfastly for me to get back to the car. Deputy Campbell confirms that no contact was made by any of the team with Randy Jeffers. Tim can pass on our experiences to the command leader and get confirmation from Patty Jeffers about whether the woven leather bracelet is, in fact, Randy's. He has worked with Leda and me often enough to know what is the pertinent information to convey about the search. It will be interesting to talk to him later and see what response he gets to the helicopter theory. The liquid breeze has picked up as evening encroaches and a shiver of coolness passes across my body. Leda and I are going to head south toward Boulder and home and dinner.

I wind my way out of Rocky Mountain National Park and cut through Estes Park as the day's light starts getting softer and dimmer. The horizon has an otherworldly glow about it, like time has slowed down. The dying sun flickers up the cliff faces like flames. A massive train of elk wanders in front of me and crosses the road in a leisurely fashion. Two yearling calves are the sluggish caboose. Their sense of self-preservation is clearly absent. Leda is asleep again, yipping and twitching her paws in her sleep. Maybe there, she allows herself to indulge in an undignified but pleasing dash after a marmot. I will never know. I laugh in the rearview mirror, and right now, today, I feel content and almost free of my haunting memories.

CHAPTER 28

Time to check with Dad and Michael and see how their day went. I call from my car using the Bluetooth connection while sailing like a galleon through Lyons toward home. A new housing development scars a previously pristine piece of land and a pang of dismay jolts me. The developer's self-congratulatory sign posted by the road advertises lots for sale in the Sanctuary at the Preserve. One can buy a lot on Mule Deer Lane or Gray Fox Circle. Oh, for Heaven's sake. Why are these new projects always named after the animals that are being displaced? Is the irony really lost on the property developers? Leda sneezes three times in the back of the vehicle and looks so sheepish that I start laughing. Nothing like a dog to make you feel less disgruntled.

"Hi Dad, Leda and I are headed back from Estes. How was your day?"

"Real good, Ronnie. Did you and Leda have a successful manhunt?"

"Ha ha, Dad," I laugh. "I've told you a million times we don't call it that anymore. That makes it sound like we're in some 1940s B movie chasing an escaped convict through a Mississippi swamp. Unfortunately, we did not locate Randy Jeffers. His trail just ended in the middle of a mountain meadow, but more about that in a minute. What did you guys do today?"

"Well, honey, Michael and I drove over to Stephanie's house first and collected Cocoa. She is a very kind dog and so beautiful with all her brown spots and freckles. She started off being timid, but she clearly remembered

Michael and was soon crawling all around him. Cocoa seems to have suffered no physical ill-effects from her narrow escape, but she will need confidence boosting for sure. The other dogs will help with that. None of them has a shy bone in their body. We took her home and let her wander around the property loose for an hour or so. Michael and I went around the fence and checked to make sure everything looked tight and together and she just followed us, tail coming up bit by bit. I don't think she's ever been out of the city before.

"Then we got Ripley out and let them meet each other. He's so mellow that he definitely provided a calming effect on her. She latched on to him and followed him around like his spotted shadow. I even saw a play bow out of her at one point. Then we added Gemma to the mix and all went well. Everybody just rambled around outside and enjoyed the sunshine playing with toys and chasing leaves. Last but not least, the Springers joined the action. Boy, did they like her. We got them calmed down after a bit and she stopped hiding behind Michael's leg. I knew we had the pack all socialized and sorted out when Cocoa and Butter laid next to each other chewing on Kongs, Scotch and Gemma played stick tug-of-war and Ripley dozed in the sun next to the bench lazily watching the pride like the senior lion in charge.

"Nobody showed any signs of aggression, they took turns drinking out of the water tub, and waited politely for their treats. We figured we might as well get in a bit of practice to help you out since you had such a strenuous day. We did run-throughs on Long Sits and Long Downs after I showed Michael how to work with Cocoa. He kept her on a lead and stayed right next to her for the exercises. It looked like a little obedience trial in the dog yard. Cocoa seemed braver with all the dogs there and, all in all, it was a satisfying day. Michael is getting Cocoa acclimatized to the apartment. I went over the house-training basics with him—you know, take her out a lot, praise her profusely when she potties etc… She seems like a smart girl so I don't think it's going to be a tough task."

"Thanks, Dad. I really appreciate it. I left you with a lot of work to do today and dogs to keep track of. Our girl Leda did well on the trail. She followed Randy Jeffers' scent confidently right up the Lawn Lake Trail for four or five miles. Then she took nearly the exact same cut to the east that Cuda had followed the night before. That area looked like a bomb went off in there. Tangled woods and blowdown. It reminds me of that area in PA where you used to hunt grouse. You know, on that ridge up behind the camp. No one takes a pleasure walk in a spot like that. The three of us bushwhacked through that mess and finally came popping out into a moraine meadow. We saw a bunch of elk by the way. One big bull with a massive rack. Then it got weird. Leda trailed into the center of the meadow and lost the scent—like nowhere to be found. She did find a braided leather bracelet that has got to be Randy's from her behavior, but no scent trail took Leda out from that spot. She worked that ground over good; we even did a perimeter loop and she never cut across his trail elsewhere. The scent was just gone."

"Wow," my father responds. "Leda is the best. I can't imagine that she just lost the trail. The weather was reasonable for a two-day-old trail and you said she found it distinctly up to that point. What are you thinking happened?"

"Well... I think he was taken away by helicopter. The open meadow is a perfect spot to set down a chopper and he would have been in that location late afternoon Friday. That's the same timeframe when that helicopter flew out of Rocky Mountain National Park and toward Comanche Peak Wilderness when I was up there working with Gemma. What are the odds? They are not permitted in the national park, but there it was. It looked different from a rescue chopper and nothing was on the news about anyone being injured. Tim is checking with the park rangers to see if any permitted flights were logged that day. If not, it really needs to be checked out. Remember I snapped a couple of photos with my phone and texted them to you? Maybe you can take a look at them, blow them up, and see if you can glean any information from the helicopter. Or better yet—check social media and see if anyone else commented on the helicopter being over the park. It's odd enough that it should have drawn some interest or outrage even. There might be better pictures than the hurried ones I snapped. You're the fanatic researcher of this family. Have at it."

Dad chuckles, "I just have tons of practice looking things up to bolster the facts of my articles. But this is my kind of research project. It involves the outdoors *and* a mystery. I assume you are thinking the helicopter was called in by satellite phone or was pre-arranged—because cell service has got to be quite sporadic up there."

"That's what Tim and I were thinking," I confirm. "Either someone chased him there and then called for the pick-up or he had already planned a pick-up spot himself for an unknown reason. Tim should call us later tonight with more information from Randy's phone logs. The police were going through those numbers all day, according to him."

"Alright, honey," Dad continues. "I can start looking into the helicopter thing. Are you almost home? I made some pasta with vegetables and can throw a batch of garlic bread in the oven. Michael and I are waiting to eat with you."

"You two must be starving; you didn't have to wait!" I exclaim.

"No worries, Ronnie. We had plenty to do around here getting the dogs fed and squared away and we'll just get the table set so you can eat as soon as you get here."

"Okay, Dad. We'll see you soon. Love you." Leda stands up in the back and presses against the screen behind my seat snuffling my hair. Her silent loyalty is so endearing. She's ready for her kibble. Hmm. Pasta. Things are looking up. I burned a ton of calories today. Cheesy garlic bread awaits.

CHAPTER 29

The velvety darkness deepens around me and bats flit like torn pieces of shadow overhead as we move through the gates at Dogged Pursuit K-9, trigger them closed, and head up the steep drive to the training building. I leave all the gear in my truck and clamber out looking less than agile. Leda hops out and trots alongside me happily testing the night breezes to see what happened here while she was gone. I go upstairs in the former day spa building and scoop out Leda's kibble into her bowl. Her release word barely leaves my lips and she's engulfed half the kibble. I turn on a lamp in my bedroom and the other half of her kibble is gone. Looking out, I see soft rectangles of light slanting out of the windows of Dad's cabin, casting magic lantern patterns on the ground beneath. We head down to join the party. Michael is seated on a kitchen bar stool talking quietly to my father, who is once again stirring pasta sauce. It smells heavenly. The partnership of basil and oregano is sweet and minty. Michael seems to be bonding well with Bob. It's hard not to because he's a compassionate and fascinating guy. Admittedly I'm biased, but he's a rock when you need one.

Cocoa is lying next to Ripley on the living room rag rug, but joins him when he comes to greet us. She clearly remembers Leda, her pal from the dreadful alley. The dogs mill around sniffing in their convoluted dog circle until they are satisfied and then plop themselves down near the kitchen table. Cocoa looks a little nervous every time someone gets to their feet, but subsides when she realizes they are not "after her." She will see from the two older dogs that begging is not allowed and learn through osmosis. I kneel down quietly next to the new addition to the pack and let her sniff my hand softly. She has the gentlest face and tears come to my eyes when I think what those juvenile delinquents would have done to her. Dad waves me to a chair looking concerned; I must look very tired all at once. My shoulder aches, specifically when my head turns to the right and the scar tissue pulls deep inside. Leda rolls over onto her back and flops her head to the side at an awkward angle. It doesn't seem to bother her. She looks content. I look around at our little gathering and feel sudden contentment too. It's wonderful to have people you can count on. That's the only thing that gets you through the dark times.

We fill our plates and start eating like ravenous wolves while discussing all the details of the day. "Are you happy to have Cocoa here now, Michael?

"Yes, I am," he replies enthusiastically. "Thank you so much for giving us both a home. I love it here. Lots of outdoor space for a big guy like me and my own place too. Cocoa has been real good inside. I watched her and she hasn't chewed or peed on anything."

I laugh back with him. "You'll be a dog trainer before you know it. Just stick with Dad and me. And I can use the help. We have a new client in the pipeline." I fill them in on the call from Ricardo Cruz about his red female Doberman. "You can help me teach Jinx to be an obedient watchdog for Ricardo's mother."

"Ricardo Cruz," Michael almost yells in surprise. "He's the third baseman for our baseball team. He's got a great glove and he batted like .315 during the regular season this year. He is from Venezuela originally." Well, that explains why his name sounded familiar to me. I love sports too, so this is embarrassing. Now if he were the third baseman for Cleveland, *that* I would have known.

CHAPTER 30

We sit around in contented silence after the meal, enjoying the peace and quiet and watching the flames from the fireplace nibble greedily at the logs, showering sparks like pinwheels up the chimney. The dogs do what they do best. Rest and relaxation. Occasionally a stray yip or paw twitch punctures the air as one or another pursues a mythical creature at top speed in fantasyland. We all smile when that happens, to see these three formerly neglected and abused dogs so relaxed and trusting in their small pack. Dad transfers the photos of the helicopter I texted him two days ago to his computer, and sinks deep into thought as he scrolls through websites doing his master research thing.

Meanwhile, Michael and I wash the dishes and he tells me about his day helping Dad work with the dogs. He blows several flimsy soap bubbles at me and it's very easy to see why he charmed the Garcias. He has a kid's kind nature hidden inside the disguise of a college linebacker's body. His sparkling brown eyes and youthful enthusiasm are infectious and I get a second wind as we discuss our schedule of training for the next week. He makes me promise to let him help with Ricardo Cruz's rescue Dobie. I never had a younger brother but I can see why people recommend it. Keeping busy distracts my mind from dwelling on the past. Just as I contemplate this truth, my cell phone rings and Tim is on the line.

"Hi Tim, did you make it back from Estes Park okay?" I inquire.

"I sure did. No commuter traffic since it's Sunday and Sylvia and the girls saved me some chicken Parmesan and garlic mashed potatoes with string beans. A little fancier than our granola bars and cashews!" We are both amused by that comparison. Then I ask permission to put him on speaker so Dad and Michael can listen to any new details Tim has acquired about the investigation.

Tim continues, "No problem; we can all hash it out together since Dogged Pursuit K-9 and its employees are part of the case now. I filled in the command leader and his team about our trail up toward Lawn Lake and the eastern veer into 'the Black Forest,' which supported Cuda's work from the day prior. I also explained in explicit detail what occurred when we reached the meadow and how Leda found no trail leading out of that open field, but she did find the bracelet. They really didn't know what to make of our guy presumably disappearing into thin air like that. Of course, they don't know Leda the Wonder Dog like I do, but I emphasized strongly that Leda was on a solid trail up until that point. Then I hit them with the helicopter theory."

My dad looks up over the top of his reading glasses with sudden, sharp interest and interjects here, "How did that notion go over, Tim?"

Tim gives a wry chuckle and responds with his typical dry understatement, "Well, nobody mentioned flying saucers or E.T., so that was a positive. I texted the photo of the bracelet to Patty Jeffers and she identified the intricate woven pattern and the tiny seashell tied in the center of the leather design as belonging to her husband. So, that bolstered Leda's find as pinpointing a location where Randy was situated very recently. Patty was positive she recognized the piece of jewelry because she has seen it every day on his wrist for the last 12 months. Randy bought it in Mexico when he was working on a water desalination plant prototype with several investors near the Tampico coastline last year. I also texted a copy of the bracelet photo to his boss, Glen Gerard. He confirmed the bracelet as being

Randy's as well. And he had a lot of useful information about Randy to add. Ummm, let me look at my notes here…

"Glen stated that Randy was transitioning in his professional career away from the criminal and civil court type proceedings which need an expert witness on water issues of all kinds (i.e., contested irrigation rights, staged drowning deaths, and dam failure) toward bolstering experimental desalination projects—the separation of salt from water, in oceans, inland seas, or the ground. A number of nations rely on desalination as the main method of providing their citizens' water supply. Randy has been traveling a good bit to South and Central America in the last year or two working on coastal desalination projects from small to enormous. Glen said the next arena Randy envisioned entering was the continent of Africa. Hundreds of cities across the globe desalt water in one way or another, whether it's by flash distillation, electrodialysis, or reverse osmosis. In fact, Israel and the Saudis get the majority of their drinking water from desalination. Here in the U.S., Tampa Bay's Seawater Desalination Facility, for example, can provide up to 25 million gallons per day of drinking water to the region.

"Amongst many other things, Randy is an expert in a newer technology that creates a membrane for filtering seawater that replicates the membrane of a living cell. This new membrane does not require the water to be forced through it, which is what generally takes significant amounts of energy and increases costs. So, having said all that, I gained some insight into what Randy works on when he isn't preparing to be an expert witness in an NBA player's high-profile murder trial. We have double confirmation that the bracelet is Randy's, and Leda took us to the spot where he vanished. Deputy Campbell is working with the park rangers right now checking computer records and logs to see if any emergency overflights were necessary on Friday or if other overflights were preapproved by the NPS or the Federal Aviation Administration. He'll let us know what they discover."

"Wow," Michael offers in amazement. "Randy really is a smart guy. I bet he knows everything about water. My science teacher last year told us droughts were getting worse around the world, increasing by almost 30% in the last 20 years and fresh water was Earth's most valuable resource. She said over two billion people live in water-stressed countries. How great to be able to create drinkable water from salt water."

Dad responds with a proud smile in his direction, "You're right on, Michael. That's quite an eclectic list of projects. Randy seems like a person who contributes to the world in a positive way and he's got the smarts to do it. We need to redouble our efforts to figure out where he is and bring him home. Give me a couple more minutes comparing these photos Ronnie took with other ones on this website and we can talk about that helicopter." Just then, Ripley flails his legs in a desperate attempt to run down that uppity rabbit in his dreams. He bumps into Cocoa's rib cage and she leaps up looking startled as she careens off the sleeping Leda's shoulder. Leda opens her peculiar amber eyes and regards her fellow canines without blinking—like the Sphinx in contemplation of life's mysteries. With a sigh, she lowers her head and nods off. The other two rearrange themselves looking embarrassed while the humans crack up. You literally cannot be in a bad mood around a dog. Or three.

CHAPTER 31

D ad is still correlating information, so Tim goes on with the extra information which has been gleaned by the various team members today while Leda was on her afternoon constitutional. "Henry Akers, the command leader, delegated the cell phone records review to two Estes Park officers, who have been brought onboard for their forensic expertise in just this area. They downloaded all Randy Jeffers' call logs and texts for the past six months, which were stored and consequently supplied by his service provider, and started winnowing down contacts once they could definitively say which numbers belonged to which people. He made a ton of work calls on that phone so the officers are charting which phone numbers are affiliated with each of the ten projects he currently has ongoing. Interestingly, so far, none of the numbers can be traced to any phones registered to members of Billy Fulton's entourage or to Billy himself. Of course, that is just known numbers. Two numbers seem to be from prepaid disposable phones and that research takes time to wade through. Those burner phones can be purchased at a multitude of different drug stores, big box stores or grocery stores, so the Estes Park guys are getting the numbers checked against a database, which should tell us point of sale and potentially lead to security camera footage of the purchasers. That may be a lot of work for nothing, but it's a loose end to follow."

Tim goes on, "Looking at the texts and numbers, just about every communication apart from those to his wife seems to be work-related, you know, to the boss, co-workers, different companies related to the clean water industry, prosecutors, and other experts in his field. He is not showing any real signs of alarm and they do not see any indication of an affair or efforts to deliberately go off the grid. No flirtatious messages or the ubiquitous sexting to another woman, for a blessed change. His last calls were the two from Estes Park to his wife on Friday and then the cell phone reveals nothing else. Pinging it did not reveal a current location. It must be totally turned off or destroyed. Unfortunately, he apparently disabled the Find My iPhone feature on his cell phone anyway. However, he did subscribe to the carrier-based GPS tracking offered by his major cellular carrier. The phone's location is updated frequently and can be relayed to the mobile account holder on an interactive map. You can see where a phone is currently located or where it was last powered on and connected to a network. Patty did have access to those login credentials and the officers determined that Randy's cell phone was at work Friday morning and then moved north, being last powered on near Estes Park and heading into the east central part of Rocky Mountain National Park. After that, radio silence," Tim concludes his briefing on the cell phone issue.

"Another Larimer County investigator was assigned the bank subpoena review and got the records from the Jeffers' bank late this afternoon. Thus far, he has not flagged any unusual deposits or withdrawals at any time during this year. The scope of the subpoena was limited to the current year only, but at least we have nine months' plus of data to scan through. Everything looks aboveboard, no bribes incoming or blackmail payouts outgoing that we can identify initially. Patty recognized one large withdrawal as a big chunk of money they took out in early August to make payment for her niece to attend Penn State. The university confirmed that payment. Randy holds certain patents related to field test kits for various water quality parameters and gets a steady income, apart from his job, relative to the worldwide use of his research and derived products. They are clearly willing to share the wealth with family members as they also previously paid for Patty's nephew to attend Rutgers. Phone interviews were conducted with their closest relatives, which is not very many folks. Randy is an only child and Patty has one sister with two kids. Neither of the Jeffers has any living parents, so the close circle of relatives is extremely small. Nothing negative or alarming was reported to the police officers who called inquiring about Randy and his relationships within the family. By all accounts, he is a stand-up guy."

CHAPTER 32

I get up and wander into the kitchen for a glass of lemonade, still feeling parched after the day's hike up the mountain and down. Okay, I admit to grabbing a couple of peanut butter cookies while in the vicinity too, but I did pass one to Michael on my way back to my chair. Michael looks engaged and he has been following Tim's recap with good attention. That's terrific news for me. My new trainee needs to have that desire for learning and wanting to figure out puzzles—so much of training a dog out of a certain behavior is deciphering what is causing the issue in the first place. And Michael takes the initiative to take all three dogs out for a bathroom break after Tim finishes relaying his information. I could definitely get used to having an assistant. The recliner is pulling me down into its depths after all that climbing today. The dogs come bouncing back inside and mill around getting petted for a few moments. Michael sits on the floor by the fireplace and Cocoa crawls over and leans against his leg while he rubs her speckled tummy. The bonding process has begun. Dogs most definitely choose us, not the other way around.

Dad looks up from his computer screen and scans the notes he has been taking on his legal pad. "I think we might be onto something with the helicopter theory," he announces in his usual low-key manner.

I hear excitement in Tim's tone as he says, "Really, Bob? Because I just got a text from Deputy Campbell that says they can find no approved helicopter overflight for that day and time at RMNP. And the ban has been in place for over twenty years; it's not like people don't know about it."

Dad confirms, "I blew up the pictures Veronica sent me so I could get a good visual of what exactly this chopper looked like. I also searched social media online including hiking websites for that day to see if others took pictures that corroborated the time and location of the helicopter or made additional comments about its appearance. One thing I factored in is that this helicopter has to be able to fly at an altitude of at least 12,000 or 13,000 feet to clear the peaks—given the location to which Leda trailed Randy and then the approximate course it took to fly near Ronnie's previous location in Comanche Peak on Friday. A significant percentage of helicopters cannot fly that high and carry any kind of a load. The lift generated by helicopter rotors depends on a number of factors and density of air is one of them. Lift produced is proportional to the density of air, so as you go higher above sea level, air density begins to decrease, thus producing less lift. Helicopters which can go higher typically have incredibly powerful engines and large rotors, while still being extremely light due to their fuselages and internal furnishings being produced from super light composites.

"Looking at the hikers' pictures on social media, and boy did they post about it, and Ronnie's photos, I have identified three key points. First, it appears a heavier duty helicopter was initially spotted by hikers flying out of the Neota Wilderness at Long Draw Road slightly southeast in the direction of Fairchild Mountain about 45-60 minutes before Ronnie spotted it. The next postings show it was then seen flying from inside RMNP toward the northeast at verifiable times in the late afternoon Friday by Ronnie and several other hikers scattered across the wilderness. Lastly, the helicopter seems to be a Cumbre Negra—which translates to Black Summit by the way—a utility helicopter created and produced by a newer aeronautics company out of Argentina. It was designed to meet the requirements of both civil and military applications, including transport, offshore operations, search and rescue, and medical evacuation uses. The carbon fiber composite reduces the weight of the bird by up to 50%, which is key at altitude.

"It comes with an HF/UHF radio and Doppler navigation. People on the ground could have called it in with an HF radio of their own since those frequencies are suitable for mountainous terrains which prevent line of sight communication. The high frequency band is used in aviation air-to-ground communication. Incidentally, the Cumbre Negra is extremely capable of flying at very high altitudes as it was initially envisioned to operate in the glacial fields and higher elevations of the Andes Mountains. Those geographical locations can range from 13,000 to 22,000 feet at their maximum. Plotting the course from the moraine meadow toward the North Fork Big Thompson River Trail that Ronnie and Gemma were on, the helicopter could have easily stayed below that top altitude and carried cargo. This utility helicopter also attracted international buyers like Peru, Pakistan, and Nepal. The Ecuadorian military ordered four of the helicopters and utilized them in search and rescue and Medivac missions in the north of the country.

"It holds up to 10 passengers, flies between 150-175 mph, and has a range of almost 400 miles. Interestingly, by 2019, the government of Ecuador withdrew the remaining Cumbre Negra choppers from service, due to recurrent maintenance issues and difficulty obtaining essential parts. As of 2019, those helicopters were stored at an Ecuadorian Air Force base and were being offered for sale to any potential buyers—military or civilian. I have compared the photos associated with that offer for sale and they look identical to the pictures taken in Colorado on Friday. Incidentally, I do see anecdotal evidence that one of the Cumbre Negras was purchased by a wealthy young South American businessman who may have criminal ties. The record is not as clear on the purchasers of the other birds. They could be anywhere in the world. Of course, we can have an expert do a visual comparison for us, Tim," my father concludes modestly after completing his showcase of research ingenuity.

CHAPTER 33

"That's great research," Tim enthuses. "One of the pilots for the State Police can review the photos you compiled and the specifications of the Cumbre Negra to verify that conclusion. We might be making progress. That kind of aircraft is going to attract notice from the right person with aviation experience. Text me a photo please of your notes and I'll get this information over to the command leader. He can assign an officer or two to check local airfields, airplane storage facilities, and mechanics inquiring about this rather unique helicopter. I want to touch base with Henry Akers anyway to see if their interviews and alibi checks of Billy Fulton and his entourage around the time of Randy Jeffers' disappearance or afterward turned up any red flags or discrepancies. Of course, that would not account for a random sports fanatic who wants to help his favorite player beat the rap by taking out an expert witness. It's kind of a reach, but an article in the *Denver Press* last month detailing Randy's fascinating career and upcoming testimony in the Fulton case may have made him the target of some crazy basketball lover. Well, I think we should call it a night. We have a bunch of irons in the fire; let's see what tomorrow turns up."

We all say good night and hang up from our lengthy phone call with Tim. My eyelids are so heavy now. Dad and Michael stroll down to the dog training building to check on the Springer brothers and Gemma before Michael and Cocoa head into their own little apartment. The moon glimmers at three quarters full in the night sky, a ghostly cloud hanging near its bottom like a lacy ruff. I sleepwalk over to my house with Leda and give her a peanut butter biscuit before bed. Dad will be performing his restless, inevitable tour around the property checking for any anomalies or intrusions before he and Ripley settle down for the evening. I almost fall asleep leaning against the counter brushing my teeth. Not a good look. Time for lights out.

I jolt awake abruptly in the very witching time of night and Hell itself has definitely breathed out its contagion to my world. I fight my way out of a strange dream where I am standing in the middle of the moraine meadow with Leda. Zach is right there, just in front of us. We hurry forward to greet him, happy at his presence, but as we get closer, he keeps drifting backward and upward, his shape diaphanous and edges blurred—until he is gone, dissolved in the mountain air. I bolt upright in the bed and touch my cheeks to find them wet with tears. I have been crying in my sleep. Leda has gotten up from her dog bed and climbed onto the bottom of my bed. She stares at me in her unflinching fashion; her eyes look mournful too and I wonder if she knows that Zach was here with us for a moment, but we have lost him again. I bend over and hug her, saturating her fur with my tears. My salvation.

CHAPTER 34

Monday morning finds me up early and thankfully feeling full of energy. I push away last night's unsettling dream and focus on the strange vanishing of Randy Jeffers and what steps can be taken next to unravel the mystery of where he is now. His wife must be so worried. I check my cell phone on its charger to see if Tim has texted me any good news over the night. Nothing yet. After Leda has been outside for five minutes and been fed, I do a series of yoga stretches to loosen up everything after yesterday's extensive search. Leda gets bored and grabs her Nylabone ready for a pleasing gnaw around the ends. I eat a container of blueberry yogurt with pumpkin granola sprinkled on top feeling extremely virtuous. This feeling will last until my first cookie of the day has been inhaled. Probably sooner rather than later.

I take a hot shower, get dressed, brush my hair for the ten seconds it takes for the brush to get caught in the curls, sigh in disgust, twist it up, and clip it on top of my head—for something new and different. We venture outside into the brisk early October air. Leda plays in carefree fashion, running around with a stick for a moment; it's wonderful to see her usual reserved nature loosen up. The sky is a brilliant blue, so bold it looks unreal, like a Western painting unfurling down to the horizon. The best weather ever for being outside. The famous Flatirons look back at me from across the road with their placid, stoic faces. How many endless years have they stood guard just like this, mutely returning the gazes of generations of people over time? Birds of prey wheel overhead drifting on thermal currents with silent wings. My spirits lift. Time to get some work done.

Michael is up and working away in the training building when we arrive. "Good morning, V. It's a beautiful day today. Ready for dog training this morning?" Cocoa follows close at his heels. She looks more relaxed after just a few days away from the big city. But who wouldn't be? (Michael seems to be settling in as well—he feels comfortable enough to give me a nickname. I like it.)

"Absolutely, Michael. Thank you for taking care of all the kids this morning."

"No problem. I like it in this building. The dogs and I wake up together. I wanted to ask you—what were Chesapeake Bay Retrievers originally used for? Leda is such a neat-looking dog." Hmmm. A chance to talk about my dog. Can't pass that up!

"Well, they were developed in the Chesapeake Bay area, no shock there, in the 1800s to retrieve waterfowl, haul nets, and rescue fishermen. The foundation stock came from two puppies that were saved from a sinking ship in Maryland in 1807, which were bred with local dogs for certain traits. They have a double coat to protect them from cold water and ice. The oil in the outer coat and the sort of wooly coat underneath repel water and keep them warm and dry. They come in three colors, brown like Leda, sedge, which is a reddish yellow or red, and deadgrass which is sort of a dull straw color or tan. The American Kennel Club recognized the first Chessie around the time of World War I; they were one of the nine original recognized breeds. They are known for their tireless energy, protective streak, and very strong will—which is why they are definitively not a good dog for first-time dog owners. And last, but not least, Teddy Roosevelt owned several."

"Cool," Michael replies. "I can't wait to see her swim sometime."

"Yeah, it is neat; she loves it. She'll swim out in a giant circle just powering through the water with a retrieving dummy in her mouth. Okay, let's get started on our work on dry land today." We both grin and head over to Gemma's kennel run.

Gemma, Butter, and Scotch have been fed over 90 minutes ago according to the wall chart and they have clean runs with full water bowls. I put Leda in a Down Stay and have a gloved Michael place Gemma's little training boxes that mimic the scent of citrus greening disease's VOCs out in the side yard. We no longer need the dummy boxes. Michael then puts Cocoa into a Down Stay next to Leda and watches her while Gemma works around the yard. Cocoa is holding her Down Stay very well. Dad and Michael have clearly been working with her in my absence. She watches bright-eyed as Gemma does her thing. Gemma is fabulous and relishes the praise showered upon her. I feel confident that the Duncans' orange groves are going to be ably protected by Gemma very soon.

Michael puts Cocoa in a kennel run and we dress the Springers in their training collars and get leads off the wall hooks. We work them outside together. I work one dog and then watch while he works the other. "You're picking this up very fast, Michael. Good job. Remember on the About Turn to give a little pop if Scotch lags. Nothing too hard, just a little reminder. Then praise. That's it," I encourage him. We add Left and Right Turns to the heeling. "Normally we will train with the dogs two or three times a day. It is better to have their undivided attention for a 15-minute period a few times a day, than to try one long session. We'll be picking up the pace after this missing person is found."

The Springers seem to adore heeling and both of them trot along looking up at us and happy to be working. Sam and Heather are going to really enjoy taking these boys everywhere with them. I take a short video of each dog working with Michael and send them to Heather. She responds with a text showing two spotted dog faces, a rose-colored heart and the massive thumbs up emojis. I show Michael and we exchange a pleased look. We take off the training collars from Butter and Scotch and use mini hamburger-looking training treats to practice the Leave It command. Very important if you want your dog NOT to pick up and eat a potentially dangerous item. We place the treats in front of each dog while they are in a Down, and tell them to Leave It. At first, they don't really comprehend and snag a couple of contraband treats, but the stern command starts to sink in eventually and they each watch their treat avidly until given the okay to eat it. They get effusive praise and go back into their runs.

Leda is released from her Long Down by hand signal and she trots over to me ready for action. I run her through a closed tunnel and massive concrete pipe several times in the agility section of the training yard. She finishes with the dog walk, which always makes me crack up, as she creeps along the top like she's trying to surreptitiously burgle a house, before running down the last ramp and leaping up in the air next to me. Her high spirits are infectious. I thump her shoulder and haunches while she hops around like a pup. Back she goes into a Long Down and Cocoa comes out for work next. Michael starts to run through her basic commands: Sit, Down, Stand, and Heel as I watch and offer little corrections. It is certainly impressive to see how quickly he is absorbing the lessons and his quiet patience with the dogs.

"You and Cocoa are doing great. Your demeanor with her is just right. Be calm and encouraging. Training can be frustrating—if you let it be. Dogs want to learn and please us; we just have to show them what we want calmly and consistently. If you really aren't getting a specific command through to a dog, take a break, do a different command the dog knows well and praise her like crazy. End on that positive note and come back to the tougher one later. We'll start you out with obedience training at first, but eventually I would like you to help me with doing the drugs sweeps at schools and companies. Once you are trained, I plan to expand that part of my business quite a lot. Sound good? Okay, get that collar off Cocoa, and then we can take everyone for a ramble around the property. I'll run up and get Ripley from Dad while you do that."

Dad looks up with a grin as I run in and scoop up Ripley for playtime. He is considering a set of fancy binoculars on his writing desk, so is apparently working on a product review for one publication or another. Heaven knows what these binoculars can do—maybe shoot laser beams out the bottom. The gear keeps getting more and more advanced. I cling to my paper maps and threaten him with bodily harm when he tries to replace them. Ripley is happy to join the pack and Michael and I crisscross the seven acres with all six dogs while they examine the property for evidence of animal visitations. We have a moment of group panic and flee calling the dogs Here Here Here as we spot a smallish skunk (with a lot of black and hardly any white) not far away, until we realize it's outside the fence. How to Make Grown People Scatter in Terror 101. "Dang, that was embarrassing," Michael says doubled over with his hands on his knees.

"Hey, discretion is the better part of valor," I reply while massaging the stitch in my side. The dogs think the running headlong game was pretty fun—minus the skunk.

CHAPTER 35

Socialization with Butter and Scotch is going swimmingly and I look forward to working with their parents in two or three weeks and getting them integrated into a happy family unit. We walk up to the training building and I show Michael how to clip Cocoa's nails and wipe her ears with the ear cleansing pads. She isn't too squirmy for a dog that was living in the streets and probably was not ever handled much. He is very gentle with her, so his future working with dogs looks promising. Michael is apprehensive at first about cutting too much nail and hitting the quick, but once he sees how well the guard on the clippers works to help prevent such a thing, he relaxes. We go through the same routine with Gemma, Butter, and Scotch, and run a brush over each dog. They are all looking spiffy and ready for a nap when we finish up. I check e-mails on my cell phone and see that another high school in Arvada would like to hire me to conduct a drug sweep later this month. I call them with my available days and we are able to confirm a date and time. The number of schools contracting with me for this business has been increasing steadily as Leda's reputation spreads through word of mouth among school administrators. It probably helps that she located cocaine in second-degree felony weight at the third school that hired us! One drug dealer taken out of that school at least.

My cell phone rings and I answer Tim's call. "Good morning, Veronica. How's everything over at the ranch?"

I adore his favorite name for the property. "We're all good. Thanks for asking. Michael and I are just roaming around with the dogs and Dad is writing up a review of super-secret spy binoculars." Tim busts up laughing.

"Well, the girls are off school today for one of those undefined holidays they get every so often for no reason, and Sylvia has a day off too. They would really like to come see Michael and Cocoa. I'm going to Estes Park later today but I thought you all might like to eat breakfast with us. I can tell you what additional information I gleaned from a very lengthy conversation with Randy Jeffers' boss, Glen Gerard, this morning."

"Okay, now you're just bribing us—first food and then potential clues to our mystery. How can we resist?" I say with a smile. "I'll go let Bob know and you guys can head over as soon as you're ready."

"Good deal," Tim replies. "We'll pick up provisions on the way. See you soon."

CHAPTER 36

The Donovan clan comes rolling up to our gate 40 minutes later in two vehicles and Michael buzzes them through. Dad is more than happy to hear visitors are on the way and starts pulling eggs, rashers of bacon, and vegetables out of the fridge in my house. It is a good deal bigger than Dad's cabin and is a perfect spot to host people with its striking upstairs view of the Flatirons. My mouth starts watering because it looks like omelets are on the menu. He starts slicing and dicing his veggies and I run a dust cloth around the end tables and push the vacuum around the living room. Having visitors is always a powerful incentive to clean up the joint a little.

Michael and Cocoa can be heard through the open window greeting Lizzie and Jane, whom he knows, and being introduced to Sylvia, and the other set of twins, Marianne and Elinor. The girls are all fawning over Cocoa, who accepts their adoration with aplomb and visits them all in turn like a queen bestowing favors on her subjects. Understandably, she seems more trusting of females, which makes her instant trust in Michael all the more telling. Marianne exclaims with delight, "She even has spots on her tummy and the roof of her mouth." She's not going to be too spoiled, I think to myself facetiously. But if ever a dog deserved a heaping dose of spoiling, it's the spotted dog. Sylvia and Tim leave all the kids outside with Cocoa and come up the stairs carrying boxes of pastries and bagels. I call out the upstairs window to Michael that they can get the Springer Spaniels and Gemma out of the kennels if they want to join in the fun.

He waves his acknowledgement and the pack of teenagers sets off for the training building.

Sylvia and I exchange a quick hug and start putting out the bagels and pastries on big platters. We pull containers of regular and chive cream cheese out of the carrier bag and add pitchers of orange juice and ice-cold water to the big farmhouse table. Dad is working the skillets getting ready to pour in omelet fixings and he's drafted Tim to finish making a big pile of bacon using the griddle. Ripley and Leda arrange themselves on the edge of the kitchen for optimal viewing of all this sudden activity. It's a solid plan as they collect lots of pats as we all move around getting food ready for the table. I also carry a pile of silverware to the table out on the covered sun porch that leads off my living room. The teens can eat at the farmhouse table and Dad and I can eat with Tim and Sylvia outside to discuss developments in the disappearance of Randy Jeffers. We have everything ready in short order and a herd of kids and dogs flows up the stairs from outside in true tidal wave fashion. Everybody grabs a plate and fills it from the kitchen counter buffet while the dogs throw themselves down to cool off after playtime. We leave the younger ones to eat and keep talking about the baseball playoffs and the adults head out to the sun porch.

An incoming call comes through just then. "Dogged Pursuit K-9. Veronica speaking." It turns out to be Steve Sherman, my contact at Sherman Brothers Trucking. He wants to set up drug sweeps at two locations they own starting next week and running for three consecutive weeks. Steve and his brother, Scott, are not wasting any time. Apparently, one new employee is giving them serious cause for concern and they want to be sure no drugs are entering their workplaces or being run through their terminals. They are usually very careful about new hires, so this worker must be quite devious if he slipped through the cracks in the system meant to keep him out of this family-owned and run company. After assuring Steve that I will be able to get him on my schedule immediately, we arrange dates and times. My spirits lift; all this upcoming work should help boost my business bank account balance. And I can start paying Michael wages right away in addition to his free room and board. Now, back to finding the missing scientist.

CHAPTER 37

"Okay, Tim," I begin, as we all tuck into the mounds of food on our plates. Wow, that omelet with red peppers is awesome! "What new information have you collected already today? No sign of Randy, I assume?"

"Not a trace. His credit cards and ATM card show no activity. His car has not turned up and his phone is apparently still turned off. He has not contacted his wife or boss. Larimer County deputies are running down local aviation insiders to check on this helicopter information Bob pulled together for us. Other officers are also checking on associates of Billy Fulton and it appears that the majority of them were on the road with Billy at games on the East Coast at the time Randy vanished. As you know, he's out on that million-dollar bail so he can keep playing basketball. Crazy! I suppose the league is waiting to see how the judicial process plays out. He was definitely at a game in Boston on Friday. Plenty of video footage exists of him slam dunking.

"However, the whereabouts of two of his posse that night still have to be confirmed. That's in the works. Billy was acting a bit evasive when questioned by phone and making cryptic statements to the investigators about Randy's fate, so his involvement in the situation is unclear at the moment. It seems extreme, however, when measured against his previous form. But it is a murder trial. You would think he would know that one expert witness could be replaced with another eventually; all it does is delay the inevitable trial. But I am not sure how bright he and his buddies actually are."

"Not very," Sylvia offers, "if the ice cream truck in the pool incident is anything to judge by. Wasting perfectly good chocolate crunch bars like that." We high five each other and look smugly at Dad and Tim as they laugh and shake their heads at us. Leda and Ripley roll onto their backs and go to sleep. Way too much talking, not enough action...

"This morning I had a follow-up interview with Glen Gerard, Senior Partner at the Water Analytical Solutions office," Tim carries on. "He walked me through a broad description of the roughly ten projects Randy has in his queue at work at present. He did preface the entire conversation by saying he is not privy to all of the exact details of any reports or conclusions Randy had come to on any of his cases. Each of the four partners has their own directory on the server and therefore information is not stored in one central place with everyone in the firm having access to it. Each partner is solely responsible for his or her own clients and expert reports; therefore, only a brief summary is available of each partner's projects. In this structure, matters are separate if two of the company's partners need to testify or report on two distinct issues within the same case. It is a sort of firewall or information barrier to prevent exchanges or communication that could cause conflicts of interest.

"Besides the four partners with their own areas of specialization, Water Analytical Solutions, International has two long-time administrative assistants and two IT people—one of whom has been with them since inception and one is a more recent hire who speaks fluent Spanish. The firm's expansion into Central and South American markets, based on the work projects of two of the four partners, has been enormously successful. Obviously, the most high-profile case of Randy's, and potentially the most explosive, is the Billy Fulton murder case. The office had been getting the odd obliquely threatening letter or crank phone call in the wake of the *Denver Press* article last month, but no real specific threats of harm were made. The article focused on Randy Jeffers' eclectic career in the field of water and mentioned his engagement as an expert trial witness for the prosecutorial side in the Fulton case. Glen stated that Randy did not seem unduly bothered by any negative feedback he got on this case or any others.

"Apart from the Fulton murder trial, Dr. Jeffers just appeared as an expert witness on another homicidal drowning case in Virginia. A father was tried in a matter where the drowning of his teenage son at a nearby lake was initially ruled an accident. The father was the non-custodial parent whose son had arrived for his two weeks' visitation in the summer and they had gone canoeing on the lake together. The father claimed that his son had gone in the water from the canoe to swim, had gotten a cramp, and drowned before the father could get the canoe back over to him for assistance. However, the mother informed investigators that the father was furious about having to pay child support and she suspected him of murder.

"Further examination several days after the initial autopsy showed bruises, which were revealed later on the boy's shoulders when the tissue was peeled back for more detailed examination. They were consistent with a canoe paddle being used to hold the boy under the water until he drowned. Randy testified to all those details, as did three other experts. That defendant is behind bars and does not have access to significant amounts of money; he would seem unlikely to be coming after Randy. But we are having an officer follow up with the prison to see if any of this defendant's recorded calls or letters mention going after Randy." Dad glances over at me while Tim talks about this case hinging on child support and the murder of a child. He knows I am thinking about the last abuse case I worked on before everything in my life went so drastically wrong. I manage a tiny smile meant to reassure him and force myself to concentrate on Tim's report.

"Randy also teaches two courses annually at the Forensics for Truth Center, in which he instructs on the most recent and effective forensics techniques to help law enforcement personnel ascertain if a drowning is accidental or foul play. He has personally trained dozens of investigators on the proper identification of water homicides, how to secure a water crime scene just as they would a land crime scene, to carefully observe and document the scene of the death as soon as the body is found due to the impact of water on the permanence of the evidence, and the proper collection of evidence from deep water by divers. All other causes of death, like heart attacks, accidental overdoses, strokes, or seizures have to first be eliminated before a medical examiner can move on to consider drowning as the cause of death. However, some experts think that up to one in five drowning deaths may actually be homicides.

"You are all aware of cases on the true crime networks in which an individual drowns and the autopsy later reveals that the deceased was given an overdose of their meds and then 'helped' under the bathwater by a killer. He trains investigators in how to make sure the medical examiners have all the necessary facts to issue a ruling. His MD degree in conjunction with his biochemistry PhD make Randy particularly well-suited for these types of examinations."

"I'm beginning to see that Dr. Jeffers is an extremely brilliant individual. He is quite accomplished in a number of different arenas—which may make it a little trickier to pinpoint exactly who is after him," Dad offers while polishing off the last chunk of his blueberry bagel.

CHAPTER 38

Tim continues after glancing at his notepad, "Well, if you find that interesting, Randy's next couple of projects should be right up your alley, Bob. Randy Jeffers also consults across the country on the hot topic of dam removal, which grew as an adjunct out of his studies on dam structural failure. Dams were initially considered instrumental in the growth of the United States, providing water storage and drinking water security, protection from floods, and the generation of electricity. At last count, 90,000 dams had been put in place nationwide for these purposes. But, as you probably know from the recent spate of articles, over 1500 dams have been taken down in the last few decades. Randy contributes the scientific studies that are a part of the whole picture in making decisions on these dams. He reviews the impact of each dam in its particular ecosystem, including fragmentation of habitat, effect on fisheries, public safety, and what actual percentage of the region's power or fresh water is presently derived from the dam."

Dad joins in, "Ronnie and I have a little firsthand knowledge of this very subject as a matter of fact. We submitted lengthy public comments when the Brecksville Dam in the Cuyahoga Valley National Park was being considered for removal a few years ago. It previously provided water to a steel company and was built 8 feet tall and about 160 feet across the Cuyahoga River on top of a wooden dam originally put into place in the early 1800s. Opening up that river flow through dam removal has already started to improve the water quality and habitat for wildlife, and the kayakers are ecstatic."

"That's so cool that you two contributed comments on that project," Tim responds. "Most everyone has heard of the negative impact certain dams in the Northwest have had on the salmon fisheries. This directly impacts the local tribes, sportsmen, and Orca whale and bear populations. In 2018, for the third consecutive year, every calf born into one of the killer whale pods in Puget Sound failed to survive. Their numbers were at a 30-year low. A diminishing supply of Chinook salmon, their main food source, is one of the primary reasons contributing to this situation. In any case, a number of factors are considered before dams are removed, and Randy plays a big part in those decisions.

"People get very passionate about these issues and Randy has had several encounters with irate folks, but he simply follows the science in his reports and, in general, invested individuals realize he is not the decision maker. None of his dam projects in the past year have featured any threatening incidents that he reported to Glen, although controversy has been ramping up recently over one in Nevada and whether a certain freshwater mussel should be federally listed as endangered. One local conservationist has ranted and raved about Randy's environmental study to the point where he has been removed from public meetings on at least two occasions. He does live part of the year in Colorado so that connection is being looked at by one of the Larimer County officers also.

"As a related point of interest, Glen told me that the big surprise out of the dam removals of this century has been how fast the reclaimed rivers repair themselves. Glen indicated that one reason why Randy returns over and over to the Lawn Lake Trail as a favorite hiking spot is his keen interest in observing how the banks of the Roaring River have been altered by the high impact flow of the burst dam, and how nature is reclaiming the southern shoreline of the lake. The power of Mother Nature is astonishing."

The other thing that's astonishing is how much food five teenagers can put away in 45 minutes. They're like the proverbial locusts. They have polished off every bit of the food on their table and are now in the kitchen washing the dishes. Mari and Elli are telling Michael about their campaign to add a dog to their family and the whole lot of them are discussing possible breeds. I think Tim and Sylvia are going to have a hard time standing their ground on this issue. The girls sound like they are preparing to give the Pro argument for the school debate team on the issue of whether a dog should be acquired by the Donovan household.

CHAPTER 39

I ask Michael to take the dogs out and the girls volunteer to help; they all go hurtling down the stairs followed by a pack of happy dogs. Tim continues with his recounting of the morning's conversation while flipping through his notes. "Another issue Randy is working on currently, according to his boss, relates to a new company seeking to enter the playing field through the mass manufacturing and sale of a mid-pressure reverse osmosis commercial unit which could provide hundreds of gallons of at least 95% pure water to towns and villages throughout the Americas and Africa at an incredibly economical cost. A reverse osmosis system features a semi-permeable membrane, which passes water through due to its molecular size but screens out contaminants by trapping them.

"This client, Agua Pura Ahora S.A., based out of Loveland, has a proprietary synthetic material which creates membranes incredibly effective at rejecting contaminants (like chlorides, sulfates, arsenic, pesticides, lead, and mercury), but durable enough to stand up to the greater pressures needed for efficient operation. Additionally, they have developed a sediment pre-filter with unique characteristics to ensure that fine suspended particles in the source water do not clog the membrane. Per Glen, this project is near and dear to Randy's heart as he has worked on numerous projects in Central and South America and is well aware how life-changing these reasonably sized and priced units could be for far-flung towns and villages without easy access to potable water. Lives could be bettered almost instantaneously if these systems are put in place. Particularly in Africa, women and children have to travel miles each day to collect water for their families, carrying heavy containers and being exposed to treacherous terrain and often hostile people. They have no time for education when clean water is scarce.

"The principals of this local company have hired Randy to do the technical report addressing the effectiveness of the membrane and the sediment pre-filter. They have secured the support of a number of well-known politicians, celebrities, and a cadre of internationally known soccer players as initial investors based on their preliminary results and the placement of successful prototypes in villages throughout Guatemala. The company is planning an IPO, or initial public offering, very soon in which shares of the company will be sold to institutional and individual investors.

"Apparently, this is how a privately owned company becomes publicly held. The IPO will raise new money for the company, increase public exposure, and can make a profit for the original private stockholders. The shares will be listed on one or more stock exchanges and can be traded in the open market after the IPO. According to Glen Gerard, an IPO is highly regulated and includes the ongoing requirement to reveal any pertinent information as it becomes available.

"The owners hired Randy specifically because of his reputation in the water purification field and his ability to translate the technical data collected into the research report needed to get final SEC approval. At present, just the preliminary prospectus (or red herring prospectus) has been issued. Incidentally, it is called a red herring prospectus due to the large warning statement printed in red on the cover which says that the offering information is not complete and may be changed. Brokers are permitted to collect indications of interest from their clients during this quiet period though—and interest has been extremely high. Once the stock launch officially begins, those indications of interest are converted into orders to buy. Randy recently told Glen that he should have his review of the data completed and the report ready by mid-October. Randy was excited about this venture due to the access to clean water it could bring to millions of people.

"Randy also does pro bono work on water quality issues for entities which need an expert to figure out why their water samples are showing bacterial contamination, but do not have a ton of money necessarily. He has done this type of investigation for senior centers, day cares, and churches. He's such a good guy; he never charges them a dime. At one local Baptist church, everyone was stumped by repeated bad water samples, despite the custodians disinfecting the system with chlorine. Once Randy determined that the well was not contaminated, he knew the problem originated somewhere in the distribution system. While inspecting the system, he spotted the immersive baptismal font and had a hunch. The waterline serving the font was connected to the whole system, but sat stagnant in between baptisms, which likely caused the contamination. Although the system was disinfected, the water in this dead-end line was never replaced. This contaminated water was then periodically pulled out into the rest of the system causing bacteria counts to register on the tests. Once the custodians knew to flush out the water to the font routinely, thus keeping the water in the line fresh, the drinking water supply was chlorinated and then tested out fine. Glen said that Randy especially enjoys these sorts of professional puzzles.

"And Randy is consulting as well with a handful of East Coast cities on ways to absorb rainwater and prevent it from running off into local rivers. Untreated storm water runoff carries trash, oil, bacteria, and nitrogen into bodies of fresh water. Two effective options he has suggested are green roofs on all new buildings, which use gardens up top to hold and store, or evaporate, rainwater before it hits the ground, and bio-retention planters that run parallel to sidewalks and capture water to disperse through their soil. Of course, both of these solutions also provide appealing miniature landscapes for passersby to enjoy. Unless someone is really averse to seeing grass on a roof, I can't imagine how this could be the source of the mystery," Tim chuckles.

"The last interesting thing I learned from Glen Gerard is that both his IT people checked Randy's directory of projects on Saturday at Glen's request. A function exists that allows them to see that Randy accessed the computer system Friday morning and copied his entire directory to a thumb drive. This lends credence to his conversation with Patty that day in which he told her he had something to figure out related to work and was going to take a hike to think it through. Perhaps he intended to review the pertinent file on his laptop while he ate brunch in Estes Park and then mull it over while hiking. Unfortunately, since he copied his entire directory of ten projects, we are no closer to knowing which item was worrying him. And to top it off, they found that Randy recently added another password layer to protect his directory at work, so Glen's people have no access to Randy's documents at the moment. Julio, the younger IT guy, said Randy expressed worry recently about the tabloids hacking into his computer for the inside scoop on the Fulton trial."

"Well, that was certainly a thorough and all-encompassing overview of the business life of Randy Jeffers," I say with a smile directed at Tim. Sylvia and Dad nod their heads vigorously in agreement.

Dad offers his insight, "But the takeaway is really that Glen seems unaware of any current, specific threat or unsettling activities that Randy mentioned to him. And the combined Larimer County, Boulder County, and National Park Service team is working hard to narrow down the possible threats to Randy—so that may get us closer to an answer."

"That's right," Tim concurs. "I think something happened on Friday after his lunch in Estes Park that resulted in him running and/or being taken. We just have to figure out what."

CHAPTER 40

The four of us stand up and start clearing the table on the sun porch. We did a decent job of wiping out our pile of food too. Detecting must make us hungry. That's what I'm going with anyway. As we head outside to check on the kids and dogs, Tim gets an incoming call and we listen to his side of the conversation. "Good morning, Mrs. Jeffers. What can I do for you? Yes, that's correct, Veronica is the one who trailed your husband with her dog Leda. Yes, they are very good at what they do. The only caveat is that the scent trail is three days old at this point. Well, I can certainly ask her for you. Let me check; I happen to be at her house right now." Tim puts his phone on mute and turns to me.

"Patty Jeffers is aware that you and Leda trailed Randy to that high mountain meadow. She really would appreciate it if you would consider taking another trip to Rocky Mountain National Park with Leda to scan other parking lots, trailheads, and visitor centers again, starting on the eastern side of the park, to see if Leda can find any other trace of her husband. She thinks it is so odd that his car has not been found and just wants everything double-checked. Patty did mention that Randy loves to wander around viewing the displays at the various visitor centers when he's thinking about a work project. She may be clutching at straws, but she puts a lot of faith in Leda and you, and it would ease her mind at the very least."

I ponder my answer for a moment, "I'm certainly willing to go, but what about Cuda? It's really his territory and he followed Randy's trail to nearly the same distance out that Leda did."

"I forgot to tell you with everything else going on, but Cuda is still lame. His handler let me know this morning. That leaves you guys, I guess."

"Sure then," I reply. "Most of my gear is still in my car. I can load up and hit the road in a quarter of an hour." Tim returns to his call and informs Patty Jeffers of my decision. She can be heard thanking us profusely through Tim's phone; I sincerely hope she is not setting herself up for disappointment.

Tim turns to thank me also and says, "There is one small issue though. I have to get over to Superior to Billy Fulton's mansion. Two of his associates have been located there, supposedly house sitting, and claim to have been there during Billy's entire basketball road trip. That means they were in town when Randy Jeffers disappeared. The District Attorney wants me to question them about whether they are involved in this matter, trying to help out their good pal Billy. I won't be able to follow you on the search like normal."

"I can accompany her, Tim," my dad offers. "I still have solid trail-blazing skills left in me, and Michael is here to watch the place and the other dogs."

"Thanks for the offer Dad, but I have another assignment for you," I respond thoughtfully.

Sylvia speaks up, "I can go with Veronica. I'm off today. The girls can hang out here or take themselves off for a hike. I can handle a tough climb, if necessary, thanks to our yoga class." We share a smile as we think about the more advanced poses we have been trying to learn for the last few weeks. I'm probably never going to get the Firefly Pose and neither one of us is ever going to master the King Pigeon Pose! Nobody's back should be able to do that.

Everyone agrees to the plan and Dad is designated to keep an eye on the teenagers and dogs while Sylvia and I get Leda's gear together and grab cold water to add to my backpack. I lift an extra backpack from the storage hooks and fill it with additional supplies for Sylvia. "Dad, I would appreciate it if you would check social media for any photos of Randy from Friday anywhere in RMNP. Look on Trip Social Colorado, the hiking websites, and any other sites you can find where people post their personal photos and see if you can spot Randy or his car. We had good luck using hikers' posts to confirm the presence of the helicopter, so it's worth a shot."

"That's a great idea, Ronnie. A photo of Randy Jeffers accompanied that *Denver Press* article, so I can use that for comparison. You know I love a good research project. Ripley can supervise. Ronnie, be careful!" Dad adds as he heads back to his cabin with the yellow dog at his heels.

Tim drives off toward Superior to talk to the ice cream truck bandits to see if they have graduated to something a lot less amusing as they have gotten older. Sylvia instructs her girls to make themselves useful around the place or go take a hike on the Mesa Trail while they're on this side of town. The Springers and Gemma and Cocoa are most likely going to be worn out later today with so much teenage attention. I suggest that they practice Long Downs with all the dogs as a group today where there are minor distractions. You can never work on attention exercises enough.

Michael and I chat for a moment about feeding and what the dogs need during the afternoon and he assures me that he and Dad will handle everything. I ask him to check the board for heartworm preventative dates as Gemma is coming due for her tablet. He confirms he knows where the meds are kept. I make a mental note to check the board for flea and tick preventative due dates for all the dogs as well. Yes indeed, having an assistant is awesome. Leda stays pressed close to my side; she has seen the backpacks go into the SUV. I ruffle her ears and tell her we're going to work again. She smiles back at me and jumps up in the truck with a showy high arc. Not too bad for a dog that could barely stand up when I first adopted her.

CHAPTER 41

Sylvia and I drive northward on Route 36 and I thank her for volunteering to accompany me. "No problem," she replies. "I always wanted to see Leda in action. How did she get her name? It's very unusual."

"It's right out of a college class I loved. She is named after the poem *Leda and the Swan* by William Butler Yeats. That poem and another one he wrote called *The Second Coming* are just phenomenal—easily my two favorite pieces. You probably know the famous lines from it: 'And what rough beast, its hour come round at last,/Slouches towards Bethlehem to be born?'" She hesitates for a minute as I pull out my sunglasses at a stoplight and push them on my face. The sun here is ever-present and shockingly bright in the clear air. When snow is on the ground in the winter and it's sunny, my eyes will barely open due to the glare. Sunglasses stashed everywhere is the solution to this issue.

"Veronica, I couldn't help noticing your reaction when Tim was talking about the boy who was drowned by his father who didn't want to pay child support. Did that bring up unpleasant memories from your former job with the prosecutor in Ohio?" I need to unburden myself and tell Sylvia what happened nearly three years ago, but I hate to taint her life with the story. On the other hand, she is a good listener and accustomed to hearing tough stories in her career as a victim/witness advocate. The longer I go without telling the whole tale to a friend, the more the contamination associated with it lingers in my body. It seems like it might be easier to talk while driving. Looking straight ahead, I can try to get it out without having to see the sympathy in Sylvia's eyes.

I take a deep breath and start telling the terrible, awful, unbelievable true story. "I was working as a legal assistant in the county in Ohio where I grew up. Prior to that time, I had trained with a major international law firm as a younger legal assistant, but wanted to stop traveling all the time for cases and get another dog. My father was still living in Ohio, too, writing his articles and doing product reviews, but he wanted to move out West and was looking around online for properties to buy. The Prosecutor, Charles Jackson, was intrigued by my work experience and brought me in to interview with two of his assistant prosecutors who handled child abuse and neglect cases, domestic violence cases, and child support and paternity cases. It was a pretty well-educated and prosperous county, but you would be amazed at the things that went on behind closed doors. You probably have a good idea based on what you've seen down in Denver."

Sylvia nods her head firmly and presses her lips together tightly. She's undoubtedly thinking about a case that broke her heart; it's an unfortunate side effect of doing these types of jobs. I really don't want to add to the bad visions in her head, but she murmurs, "So you got the job then?" and encourages me to carry on.

"I did get the job and hit it off with my two assistant prosecutors right away. One did primarily abuse, neglect, and domestic violence cases, and the other usually covered paternity and child support, but there was some overlap. In the child support cases, we tracked obligors once the child support orders were set up through a divorce to ensure payments were being made by the obligor. If they didn't pay, they got brought into court to face our two tough-as-nails judges. In paternity cases, we used DNA testing to ascertain the biological father of each child and set up a support order on the non-custodial parent which factored in both parents' income. Those cases were sad to me because oftentimes the 'father' never wanted visitation with the child and he resented having to pay support. But it was his obligation to support the child he helped create, not the taxpayers of our county. The abuse, neglect, and domestic violence cases were horrific and it is still hard for me to accept the way people act toward those they have power over. We worked closely with the Sheriff's Department on a number of these cases, especially when we needed subpoenas served. I started dating one of the deputies, Zach, and we became engaged. He possessed great compassion for people and a real zest for life. He and my father hit it off right from the get-go and I was really happy and outgoing—a lot different from the way I am now...

"Anyway, after two years or so of doing the job, it was time to get my own dog. Dad and I had a Golden Retriever before named Alex that we shared. He would take care of Alex at his place when I traveled the country for work. He was an awesome dog who loved everyone and worked as a therapy dog in nursing homes whenever I was in town. He was so quiet and loving with the elderly. Alex was about 13 when we lost him to a tumor, the bane of Golden Retrievers everywhere. Soon after, one of my friends saw an ad that the Dog Warden was running in the local newspaper, which listed available dogs for adoption. It was short. It said something like: *Young female Chesapeake Bay Retriever. Time running out. Can you help?* I had never dealt with a Chessie before, but when I showed up at the Dog Warden's office and took one look at her eyes, it was all over. And that's how I got Leda.

"They told me her story. She was only a little over a year old and terrified. She was emaciated and had no hair. She was slowly starving to death on a six-foot chain on some monster's porch when the Dog Warden showed up based on a neighbor's tip and liberated her. He basically informed the owner that she was going with him then and walked off with her. The owner didn't fight it. But no one adopted her week after week; she looked too scared and wouldn't eat. Eventually, she was scheduled for euthanasia." I look over at Sylvia for just a moment and her eyes are filled with tears.

It's only going to get worse from here—the telling. The things people do to animals and humans. It will break you down.

"They were so hopeful that someone would save her at the last minute when I showed up. Little did they know, I did not even need to hear her back story. The desolation in her eyes was devastating and she was absolutely going with me. She was a project for me to work on—get her healthy and bring her back to life. A new dog to love and focus on would help me deal with stress from the tough cases at work. Zach and I took wonderful road trips with her on our off times. She cost me $95 and she saved my life less than three months later. Literally.

"I had trained in obedience with Alex and he loved agility too. I had always tried to absorb everything from the trainers with whom I worked and had hopes of teaching Leda obedience and rally. She gradually started to trust me, and Dad and Zach, and her belly started coming off the floor. It was a struggle, but I started getting her to eat. We got rid of her mange. She got fish oil supplements and sweet potato-based food to get her hair to grow back. When I first got her, the only part of her body that had hair was her head. I loved watching the coat start to come in on her body. We were making progress and she was bonding with me. We started doing basic obedience lessons and took long hikes together to build up her unused muscles. She started to enjoy life for the first time ever."

CHAPTER 42

"Right around this time, we got a case at work that involved a paternity issue and a domestic violence issue. This local man, Tommy Arnett, had two little children with his girlfriend, Joan. Initially, they lived together and got no public assistance, so no paternity order was needed. Then he started bashing Joan around. It was awful. You've seen it in your job. She contacted a helpline in our county and our victim/witness advocate made arrangements for her and the children to move into the safe house which had been established for victims of domestic violence. Tommy was arrested and a court date set, but he was out on bond, albeit with a restraining order in place. Then he received the additional paperwork informing him that he was going to owe child support for his two kids going forward—since he was no longer supporting them by residing in the same residence. Of course, this infuriated him because he blamed the Prosecutor's Office for 'breaking up his family' when Joan and the little kids were moved to a safe place. Joan and the children were doing well and she got a job, and then an unbelievable disaster struck in the early spring about three years ago.

"Tommy Arnett spotted Joan and the kids at a park playground that is not one of the most highly visited ones in the county. Debbie was three and a little firecracker. Pete was four and all boy. He never met a mud puddle he didn't want to jump in. It was a blustery day, kind of raw, but Joan probably wanted to get them a little fresh air, burn off some energy so they would sleep better, that sort of thing. We can only speculate. Due to the weather, no other people were at the park, except for a lady way at the back of a long soccer field walking her dog near the tree line. She lived adjacent to the park so was not parked in the parking lot there. Tommy got out of his pickup, marched over to Joan, started yelling, pulled out an unlicensed handgun, and just shot her in the head. Then he shot the kids." Sylvia draws in a sharp breath as she pictures the scene. I wish I could stop picturing it.

"The lady walking her dog heard a bit of the yelling, but definitely heard the gunshots. She had to run back to her house to call it in, as she had left her cell phone on her kitchen table inadvertently. By the time Dispatch got the call and the deputies made it to the park, Tommy Arnett was gone and she was not close enough to describe him or any vehicle except a blue or black pick-up. Joan and the two babies were already dead when the paramedics arrived. Police fanned out and started searching the area, but he was long gone—because he was on his way to the County offices."

"Oh no," Sylvia says. I drive as if on auto-pilot while preparing to tell what happened next. Leda leans against the dog screen in the back whining softly under her breath.

"I had had Leda for about three months. She had a stubborn kidney infection that we were having a hard time knocking out right at the time this all occurred. My boss, Charles, was a big dog lover and said Leda could come to work that week. Dad was out of town looking at properties in Colorado and Leda needed medicine and a couple of potty breaks during the day. Everyone in the office was invested in the project to restore Leda to health; they had all seen pictures of her as she gradually improved. Nobody was allergic and my boss said it was fine for her to come sleep on her dog bed in my office.

"It was late morning and I was just getting ready to take her out for a quick break when Zach showed up at our office on the third floor. He came in for a quick hello, gave me a kiss and Leda a pat, and then headed over to talk to my boss about an upcoming trial. I wanted to chat with Zach for a few minutes, but I felt oddly restless that day and decided to take Leda out first. I put on my winter coat because it was really cold for early spring and Leda and I headed down the back stairs of our county building. I walked her over to a small patch of grass that bordered the alley between buildings and let her pee. She was sniffing the breeze with contentment and I was enjoying looking up at the clouds. I still remember thinking how cold and sharp, but also invigorating the air felt. Little bits of frozen rain floated through the air as I turned to go back and reached for my key to the alley door. Then my whole life exploded.

"I heard a multitude of rounds fired from a semi-automatic handgun upstairs in the building. I don't shoot, but I have been around guns with Dad and then Zach my whole life. Responsible gun owners. I thought to myself how strange it was to hear that through the closed windows. There was pounding on the metal stairs and this maniacal laughter and Tommy Arnett burst out through the alley door. He looked demented and thrilled at the same time. He still had a gun in his hand. I took all this in at the same time I was trying to draw Leda back behind a dumpster in the alley for cover. We almost made it, but did not move quite fast enough. Tommy looked right in my face and smiled. He raised the gun and shot me.

"I was turning away so it entered the back of my shoulder. My winter coat helped absorb a good deal of the force, I think. A starburst of hot pain exploded in that area, but I kept trying to wedge Leda and myself back behind the dumpster. He said 'trapped like rats.' And I was pretty much thinking we were done for at that point. He started around the corner of the dumpster and raised the gun again. I found out later, that the workers in the County Auditor's Office had called 911 when the shots were fired one floor above them and reported that the assailant was heading down the back stairs. By this time, the two deputies assigned to work the entrance to the courthouse across the street ran down the alley. I was resigned to the fact that they weren't going to get to us in time. It was so bizarre, the almost slow-motion way that gun was being aimed at us. Suddenly, Leda surged forward from around the edge of the dumpster barking like a demon dog and it startled him for just a second. The muzzle of his gun went up in the air briefly and the leading deputy shot him. He dropped like a ton of bricks 15 feet away from me.

"The deputies cuffed him and started over to check on me. I staggered to my feet and dodged them because I had to know. Leda and I ran up the back stairs of the building and came out in our office. Blood was dripping down my arm and leaving a trail falling off my hand like bloody rose petals across the carpet. There was no security then or locked section away from the public—so naïve as it turns out. Everyone in the office when Tommy Arnett charged in was dead. Our receptionist, Carol, my boss, and Zach, and the two administrative assistants were all standing near the front of the office when he ran in. So incredibly unlucky. He shot Zach, who had had his back to him, in the head first, and then everyone else. It was a slaughter. All the assistant prosecutors were at court, so they were spared, thankfully. If Leda and I had waited to go out for five more minutes, we would have died there too. I sank down to the floor just outside the main office. That's where the other deputies found me as they ran in—sitting on the floor bleeding and crying with my dog on my lap."

Sylvia reaches over and puts one hand on my right hand on the steering wheel for a quick squeeze. "Oh my God, that's so awful. I'm really sorry you had to go through that. I can't imagine."

"Yeah, it was bad, but I was alive unlike so many others." I reply slowly. "The aftermath almost did kill me. The whole building was locked down and there were police and paramedics all over the office making sure the area was clear of other gunmen, checking all my co-workers and fiancé for vitals, and then investigating the scene. The paramedics got my coat off and were trying to get the bleeding stopped while Zach's fellow deputies were trying to find out from me what had happened. Most of them had tears running down their faces when they saw Zach and the scene. Our prosecutor had been in office for decades and the Sheriff and Charles were very close friends.

"Leda was standing next to me almost snarling under her breath and trying to protect me from everyone. She was so upset. I had to call my friend to come get her out of that stressful situation. She looked back at me like she was going to the executioner when the K-9 deputy walked her out to go with Susan. I called my Dad right away and gave him a very brief account of what had happened. He promised me he would fly back from Colorado immediately. All I could think was: he has to hurry because Leda needs him. My father tried all my life to make me safety-conscious and aware. That's why I call him Mr. Safety. This was one eventuality we had never considered. I knew he would be blaming himself for my getting hurt—which is nonsense. It was all that demon Tommy Arnett." Sylvia gives a little snort because she has seen Mr. Safety in action. I'm 30 and he still tells me to watch my flanks when I cross the street. I give a tiny grin back to her and the tight band across my chest feels an iota looser.

"Meanwhile my shoulder would not stop bleeding and the paramedics were getting worried. They insisted on heading to the Emergency Room and the deputies could follow me there to ask more questions. That whole part is sort of a blur. A nurse said the gunman did not die when he was shot and I vaguely recall being worried that he was going to come after me in the hospital. I may have been faint from blood loss, because even though I was aware of huge bursts of activity swirling around me and anguished voices, a lot of what happened at the hospital was hazy. But the ER docs got me patched up and the bleeding stopped eventually. I was able to tell the deputies in more detail what I had seen and heard. By then, the authorities knew that Tommy Arnett was also responsible for the slaughter at the park.

"They had identified Joan and the children and knew of his aggressive behavior toward her that had resulted in that restraining order being issued earlier. But this time, unlike the other times, Joan ended up in the morgue instead of in intensive care. The other people working in the County building that day could report what they had heard regarding the gunshots and a man running down the back staircase afterward. But I was the only one he shot who survived and the only one who saw him with a gun in his hand coming out of the building. So, I was going to be the star witness against him, followed by the two courthouse deputies who arrived just as he was about to shoot me again.

"The next few months were truly awful. The media coverage was intense; I was trying to heal up while also mourning my fiancé and my co-workers. I was also devastated that the lives of Joan and her children had been cut so tragically short just when things had been looking up for them. My life felt unmoored without Zach and without my job. I was doing worthwhile work for my county and that was ripped away too. A neighboring county's prosecutor actually had to try the case due to the murder of our prosecutor. My father was a rock and tried to make me feel secure. I was so jumpy about everything, especially after inmates at the County jail reported that Tommy Arnett had been making threats against me. Dad instituted his security and surveillance measures which he continues to this day, even here in Colorado. I knew intellectually Tommy was locked up, but a tiny internal part of me still worried he was coming after me. Leda was the other thing that gave me solace. I could talk to her and cry in front of her and she always gave me sympathy. She knew my heart was breaking and she never wanted to ask me questions or make me go over the details again and again like I had to do when preparing for court. Dad spoiled her rotten because he knew her lunge at Tommy bought us enough time for the deputies to take the monster down. We took long walks in the woods together and as she kept getting better and stronger, so too did my shoulder, which started to heal. My soul not so much."

CHAPTER 43

"I became more withdrawn and anxious around other people. I really just wanted to stay with Dad and Leda, but had to get ready to testify at the murder trial. Unbelievably, Tommy had pleaded not guilty to all the murders and the attempt to murder me, so the whole county had to suffer through a trial. It was ascertained during the investigation that he had seen Joan's car outside her new job and placed a GPS tracker on it. Then he waited until she was with the children in a remote location and carried out his dreadful plan. The judge did not allow cameras in the courtroom, which in some aspects was unfortunate, because then it would have been televised that Tommy Arnett spent the entire time I was testifying against him threatening me with violence. At first, he just glared, then he started muttering under his breath, and finally he started screaming 'I'm gonna get you' and 'you're a lying bitch.'

"That was after the prosecutor asked me to point out the man who ran out of the County building with a gun, and who shot me. The judge warned him repeatedly that he could lose his right to be present at his trial and would be removed if he continued his disruptive behavior. Citing him for contempt of court was clearly not going to shut him up. Tommy would settle down temporarily and then something would set him off again—usually directed at me. He seemed to transfer all his rage against Joan onto me since she was no longer around to be his target. It shocks you to your core to feel another person's hatred emanating off them in waves and almost being crystallized inside you.

"The courtroom was in constant turmoil with the prosecutor imploring the judge to gag the defendant, the courtroom deputies looking outraged because they had to listen to Zach's killer lie through his teeth and abuse me, and the defense attorney yelling back that gagging was a violation of the Sixth Amendment. However, the judge, in no uncertain terms, referred the defense attorney to the Supreme Court's ruling of 1970, which did give him the right to gag the defendant as a last resort, and then cited **him** for contempt of court when he wouldn't stop arguing. My energy was focused on just surviving this onslaught of hostility and getting justice for Zach and my boss and my friends and our client, Joan. Every day, my father sat through my testimony about Joan's domestic violence matter, the paternity support issue, the restraining order, and Tommy's attempt to murder me. He had to listen to that unhinged man make threats toward me and watch him glare at me in an effort to intimidate me. Sylvia, my father never sat back in his seat a single time; he sat poised on the front edge the entire time. Because if that killer made one move toward me or even looked like he was getting out of his chair, Dad wasn't waiting for courtroom security. He was taking him out. Leda wasn't there to protect me, but I had Dad.

"Eventually we got through the trial, but it took almost a year from the time of the crime to the sentencing. He was found guilty on all counts, and was dragged out of the courtroom hurling imprecations at the judge and me. Thankfully, he was sentenced to life in prison without the possibility of parole. Dad found the decrepit day spa property scheduled for a Public Trustee foreclosure auction in Boulder County, bought it, and started getting it remodeled and the property fenced. We both wanted to take Leda and go to a place that didn't have horrific memories. Dad got the idea to have me train with Master Trainer Bruce Macklin to become a dog trainer with a business. He's a smart man. He knew the constant outside activity, exercise, and mental challenge of learning new skills would help me heal and recover. And I could do it with Leda. He also signed me up for self-defense lessons with a wonderful local police officer. Penny is a 5 foot 4 human dynamo with strawberry blond hair. She teaches martial arts to women in Arapahoe County and I'm certain once they complete her classes, the vast majority of them are confident in their survival skills if attacked. She wants women to stop feeling like victims, and to stop being victimized. And that's how we got to where we are now," I finish, thankful that I can stop talking and that I made it to the end of the telling.

Sylvia says to me very quietly, "These are the types of things that will make you or completely destroy you. I am really proud of you for what you have done since you came out to Colorado. You have found another way to help your community. You keep drugs out of schools, help find lost hikers, teach people how to have obedient, well-mannered dogs, even pitch in on this case to help out a neighboring county when their search dog is injured. You may not talk as much and laugh as much as you did before, but you do a lot of good and I think you are healing more and more the longer you live here. You are a strong role model for my girls and you know the Donovan family loves you very much." I made it through the whole story without tears, but now they start to flow. But they're a different kind of tears. The welcome kind.

CHAPTER 44

Sylvia and I stop by unspoken agreement on the edge of Lake Estes. We let Leda out to stretch her legs while we try to loosen up ourselves—physically and emotionally. Leda does Downward Facing Dog and then Cat-Cow. That reminds me. "We definitely need to go to yoga soon," I groan.

"You're not kidding," Sylvia agrees. "I feel like a pretzel. Just imagine if we had to drive for more than 90 minutes." We both crack up and the dark clouds that hover over me with any recollection of Tommy Arnett lift upward. I visualize them floating up and up into the sun until the intense heat burns them up, and feel much better all of a sudden.

We grab a panini sandwich and fries from a restaurant on the corner and sit along the shoreline of the lake to eat. I pour Leda a drink of water and she watches me with rapt attention until she gets her two peanut butter biscuits. It is oddly relaxing watching people kayak and paddleboard around Lake Estes' surface area of 185 acres. The marina offers a plethora of activities for people, including bike and pontoon boat rentals and, as the end of the season nears, people are taking full advantage of the fabulous weather. The water ringed by snow-capped mountains is my favorite Colorado look; this water is so crystal clear that the mountains are reflected back at you. One kayaker flips over in his kayak and I start to rise to my feet in instant concern. But he pops right back up to the surface and does it again a few moments later. He is just practicing his maneuvers to right the kayak. He's very good at it. Dad would definitely approve of this safety pre-planning!

I turn to Sylvia and ask, "So, what do you think of this push from the girls to get a dog this year? Do you and Tim have an inclination which way you are leaning?"

"Well," Sylvia hesitates for just a beat. "I think we are going to let them get one—with your input on breeds and size, of course. They have presented strong arguments to us over the past year and have shown they can take on responsibility by helping with your dogs. They have promised to do all the care themselves and to consult you with any questions. They are all good-hearted girls and even though we hesitated because they are super busy, we feel confident they will follow through with their promises. I'm just worried they may have swiped Cocoa from Michael by the time we get back. She's a little darling."

"That she is," I reply with less than full attention. "Once you decide for sure, I'll go over breed characteristics with the four of them and see what they are looking for in a companion." My brain is already scanning through possible dog breeds for the girls. I know Mari and Elli favor a Golden Retriever and Jane and Lizzie want a German Shorthaired Pointer. Hmmm. Perhaps a Vizsla. Reluctantly, I drag my attention away from dog breeds and back to the case. I had better check in with Dad to see if he has any leads for us to follow.

But first, Tim calls us. "Hey there. Just wanted to let you two know that we finished interviewing the two so-called friends of Billy Fulton. I use the term loosely because I think these are just secondary hangers-on, who enjoy the high life on Billy's dime. These are not guys from his original college crew, but ones he's picked up since he's been in the NBA. Having said that, they both made certain odd and frankly, not very bright, comments to me and the other officer about 'no scientist is going to take Billy down' and 'like Chardonnay found out, it's not good to mess with Billy.' It is astounding how many people are leeching off this one superstar player.

He's going to finish his playing career and be totally bankrupt. You can see it coming like a train roaring down the tracks. No wonder Chardonnay was frustrated. What is truly amazing is how long she stuck it out with Billy. Anyway, I'm going off on a tangent…

"They actually admitted they were in Lyons on Friday. Now, if you're in Lyons, you're not far away from Estes at all. These don't strike me as the kind of guys to enjoy Lyons' quiet, outdoorsy vibe. They surely aren't the type to be visiting the Whitewater Park or going antiquing. I could maybe envision them floating on tubes in St. Vrain Creek with a beer in hand. Just maybe, if it were summer. They claim they were there for the opening of a new brewery, but I checked with Lt. Dolan in my office, who is into all the craft brewery stuff, and takes his days off visiting breweries with his husband and he was not aware of any advertised event. According to them, they drank so much they can't remember the name of the place. Lt. Dolan is checking online and with the Chamber of Commerce to see if any such event was scheduled for Friday.

"Their comments seemed like a whole lot of bluster, but we're just not sure. I'm sending their pictures over to the park rangers; they can go through CCTV footage of people entering the national park on Friday to see if they can spot these geniuses. Oh, and by the way, Syl, the girls checked in and they went with Michael and all the dogs to hike on the Homestead Trail. Michael said to tell Veronica that they are keeping the Springers and Cocoa on lead. Gemma and Ripley will do their usual thing and amble alongside loose. And he remembers to keep Cocoa away from other dogs since she's not getting spayed until she goes back to Dr. Stephanie next week. So not to worry. At least, they have enough hands for all the leads."

"I'm starting to like this new assistant more and more," I declare with a laugh as we get ready to say goodbye to Tim on the phone. "Oh, one thought, Tim. Why don't you send the photos of Billy's good buddies over to Dad by text? He can scan through social media for them too while he's looking for Randy Jeffers in posted photos from Friday. Who knows, if they did do something to Randy, visual evidence may exist of them being in his vicinity at RMNP."

"Excellent idea. I will shoot those over to Bob and he can do his research thing," Tim responds. "In the meantime, I'm going to figure out just what game these two pals of Billy Fulton's are playing." Sylvia and I get up and start to gather up the remnants of our lunch. Leda hops up, no doubt wondering when her part of the job is going to start. She thrived in her training with Bruce and loves any chance to get out and work with me. We pile back into my SUV, cut over to Route 34, and arrive at the Fall River Visitor Center to start our checks of parking lots, visitor centers, and trailheads as requested by Mrs. Jeffers.

CHAPTER 45

Dad texts me that he is still scanning through Friday's social media and hiking website posts in an effort to locate Randy somewhere, anywhere in the park. I text back that he should let us know if he finds a clue; we are going to start at the closest visitor center and work our way west around the park. The day is lovely and worse ways exist to spend our time. I am just sorry for the worry Patty Jeffers is undoubtedly experiencing.

The Fall River Visitor Center—which borders the entrance to the park—is a typical Western-looking visitor center with a heavy beamed timber arch above the front entrance. The rustic look of the wood and stone construction blends together perfectly with the awesome tree spattered mountain peak rising up behind it in graduated layers. It's a sprawling building with copious amounts of parking on two different levels. The Visitor Center and Gateway buildings are covered by a cool timbered walkway featuring McGregor and Deer Mountains on either side. The visitor center also includes a restaurant and a gift shop with plenty of gear to entice all family members.

I stop the vehicle and let Leda out of the back with her release word. Most likely, we are going to get a lot of practice popping in and out of the SUV for short stints today. Leda's Working Dog vest goes on, so it is clear that she is here to do a job. Then I attach Leda's long line, give her a few sips of water, and let her sniff inside the baggie with Randy's T-shirt. I tell her to Find and walk her briskly around the parking lot as she samples the breeze.

Sylvia walks behind us, scanning the lot for the scientist's missing vehicle on the off chance the earlier searches overlooked it. The parking lot is busy but not terribly crowded, it being a weekday. Leda traverses back and forth across the upper and lower parking lots. Nothing appears to catch her nose. We slowly check the timbered walkway as a herd of mule deer in the meadow munch along lazily without a care in the world. Wait until winter, deer. We do a thorough tour around the outside of the immense center. Most of the visitors recognize that Leda is working so give us space. I vaguely hear several "Ooh, look at the pretty Chocolate Lab" comments. Well, thank you. She is pretty, but not a Lab. No offense to the many wonderful Labs who live with their families across the country. I tell Leda to Find again and we walk into the center. Sylvia finds the ranger up front and fills her in on our mission. "No problem," wafts over to us as the athletic-looking ranger observes Leda at work with sharp interest. Leda works around the perimeter of the main room and then we start moving among the full-sized wildlife displays, interactive topographic map displays, and the racks full of maps, videos, and books. She has ground to cover, as Bruce used to tell me in training, and she works efficiently.

She stops for a quick moment and I feel a surge of hope, but quickly realize she is just giving the enormous, life-size elk sculpture the side eye. It does look like he's plunging down that rock right at us if you glance at him fast. She looks back at me over her shoulder in near embarrassment, but I pretend not to notice anything. No need to make her feel silly. "Good girl, Leda. Find," I encourage her. I run her past the racks of garb with Rocky Mountain National Park emblazoned on them and she moves along rapidly. Leda passes the wall with the giant carved bear and wolf heads for sale without a flinch. Not going to catch her twice that way. Her tail is up as she trots nonchalantly past. She stands at the entrance to the restaurant and takes a hearty sniff. No need to run her through the eating area. She has covered both floors of the complex and the outside viewing balcony. No indication of Randy Jeffers has been found within this visitor center. The three of us head outside and Sylvia marks off this location on a little pocket map the ranger had provided to her. Good thinking. This is why the Donovans make excellent back-up.

CHAPTER 46

We pass through the Fall River Entrance Station, have a brief discussion with that ranger about Leda, and take a look at our pocket guide. "Navigator, where to next?" I ask Sylvia as we climb back into the car after offering Leda a drink.

"Let's stop for a second at the vantage point overlooking Sheep Lakes. She can check the parking edges and we can see what wildlife is out today."

"Sounds like a solid plan," I reply as we drive westward. We pull to the side and look out across the interconnected meadows and the shallow Sheep Lakes, carved by the glaciers in their undulating journey eons ago. The edges of the closest lake are churned up with damp earth in a ring backing away from the lake for 15 feet or so—testament to the popularity of this spot as a multi-species watering hole. The pines and aspens alternate stripes going up from the valley floor and onto the mountain in the background like an unraveling sweater. Sylvia jumps up and down when she spots four bighorn sheep ewes with their straight spike horns. Two landscape painters have set up facing one of the lakes, easels pointing at the slope of the mountain, brushes moving languidly as they decide on their colors. One gauzy cloud dangles over the tallest peak like a parachute coming in for a steep landing. Leda works up and down the sides of the road with caution for two hundred yards and not unexpectedly, she finds nothing here. Time to leave this peaceful spot behind.

We then clear the Alluvial Fan parking area as Leda gets no hits. When rushing water from the Lawn Lake flood in 1982 entered this valley and lost speed, a fan of rocks, boulders, debris, and sand—covering 40 acres—spread out in this area in an impressive display. The information marker states that some boulders, which were moved over six miles by the flood, weighed in excess of two tons. That is quite the display of power. The afternoon soon becomes a repetitive blur of getting in and out of the vehicle with Leda and our gear and crossing off the Endovalley Picnic Area and Horseshoe Park from our map. No need to stop at the Lawn Lake Trailhead again as Leda had previously worked that area. A ping on my phone alerts me to a text from Dad. He tells me that he believes he has spotted just one of Billy Fulton's house sitting pals in photos in Lyons on Friday night, but he is double checking. I reply with a comment wondering if only one is there to establish an alibi, while the other one is up to no good. Dad sends me back the smiley face emoji holding his finger up to his lips. He enjoys emojis just a little too much for a man his age. We climb back into our seats a good deal more slowly and head for Deer Mountain Trailhead. Leda dozes peacefully in the back. The afternoon sun makes me a little drowsy so Sylvia and I sing along to the Pistol Annies as we drive. Nothing like a little *Hell on Heels* to wake you right up.

We park in the roadside spots at Deer Ridge Junction. We are lucky to find a space on such a gorgeous day to be outdoors, and considering the popularity of the hike to Deer Mountain. I am in awe once again of this dazzling national park. I feel calmer here and sense that some of the poison dripped into my soul by Tommy Arnett's hatred is melting away. Zach would have loved this territory. Breathing in several big gulps of invigorating air, I get Leda ready to work again. She is as eager as ever. Sylvia tells me, "Believe it or not, there used to be a chalet here. From 1917 to 1960, this spot had a lodge, cabins, gas station, restaurant, a ski run, and even a 50-foot-high viewing tower. When RMNP acquired the property in 1960, the structures were all torn down over the next year."

"Wow," I answer. "I bet the view from the top of that tower was awesome."

"It was incredible the distance you could see," she answers. "In fact, once the park bought certain pieces of land from private owners, they tore down similar structures at Sprague's Lodge, the Brinwood Ranch-Hotel and Fall River Lodge. The biggest one though was Stead's Ranch. It spread over 600 acres and had a lodge, barns, cabins, and even a golf course. They could host almost 200 people. It seems a little sad in some ways, even though I know their intent was good, but people had vacationed for decades in those rustic, Western lodges. It was the end of an era. Not everyone loves being in a modern campground."

"I learn something new about Colorado every time we go on a road trip together," I applaud Sylvia.

"Good thing you're paying attention. There's going to be a quiz on this information later," Sylvia jokes with me before we stand together in silent contemplation of the landscape. It almost feels like the spirits of happy vacationers are still drifting through the pines remembering a time when life was simpler and more innocently "commercialized."

We check the parking edges for Randy's scent and then head into the stand of towering ponderosa pines at the beginning of the trail. After 1/10 of a mile, a trail forks off to the left. We travel a half mile up the trail toward Little Horseshoe and then backtrack to go a half mile up the main trail toward Deer Mountain. Sylvia is walking along behind me humming very softly under her breath. It seems the peaceful aura has enveloped her too. A mother of four teenage girls has got to enjoy what little time she gets to herself—even if it does mean tagging along behind a Chessie and a Midwesterner. Leda hits on nothing again and we head back to the road. We sit in the back of the SUV and eat trail mix with carob chips, peanuts, and raisins. Leda chomps down two egg and cheese flavored biscuits after taking them out of my hand very daintily. A wave of love for her passes over me. She is such a cool dog. We lean against the side of the cargo hold and smile at her and each other. A tiring day, but somehow a restorative one too.

CHAPTER 47

My cell phone ring tone (*Bad to the Bone*—it needs no explanation) startles us out of our reverie. I only have one bar of service, but Dad sounds like a thunderclap when he exclaims, "I found him, Ronnie. I found Randy on Friday at Rocky Mountain National Park." Sylvia sits bolt upright and leans in toward me and the speaker.

"Really, Dad? Where?"

"I can see him in the background of tourists' pictures posted on Trip Social Colorado. He was in the parking lot of the Moraine Park Discovery Center and headed toward the building, it looks like. From the comments posted with the photos and the height of the sun in the sky outside, he was there in the early to middle afternoon."

"Great work, Dad, we're actually very near to there. We'll head directly there now. I'll skip stopping at Beaver Meadows Visitor Center. Moraine Park is a seasonal visitor center, and coincidentally, I think it closes around October 9th. That's only a week away. Text me if you find anything else. Thanks, Dad."

Sylvia calls Tim to update him on our plans with this new information garnered from social media. He promises to relay that confirmation to the command leader, Henry Akers, and let him know we are headed over to Moraine Park Discovery Center with Leda. Tim laughs and says, "We can rule out the great Owyhee River Mussel conservationist, who confronted

Randy at the public meeting on the environmental study related to the possible dam removal in Nevada. He actually is in Colorado, but he broke his leg last Wednesday rock climbing. He's totally laid up and running his poor wife ragged with his demands for the TV remote, food, books, aspirin, and just about everything else under the sun. This came directly from her unhappy lips.

"No way either one of them harmed Randy, but she may harm the freshwater mussel savior soon. You two let me know if you find anything with Leda and I'm going to keep working on figuring out where Billy Fulton's other house sitter friend was on Friday. So far, we can only confirm that one was in Lyons. On an interesting note, the friend whom we have not yet placed in Lyons turns out to have a police record, for disturbing the peace and assault and battery. So we know there is a certain propensity toward mayhem there. Talk soon." Sylvia looks over at me with a huge grin as we head south down Route 36, just short of the Beaver Meadows Entrance Station, and then keep traveling south on Bear Lake Road for another mile. The visitor center closes at 4:30 so we need to hustle down there.

Sylvia laughs, "The mussel conservationist better be careful or she's going to brain him with that TV remote!"

"Poor woman," I reply. "It makes you wonder how he came to fall off that rock face in the first place! I wonder if they were climbing together."

Moraine Park Discovery Center and Museum is a gem. And as an added bonus, the amphitheater built into the rock hillside at the base of Eagle Cliff Mountain can serve as a stunning wedding venue for up to 100 guests. Not bad for a few hundred-dollar fee. Towering pine trees above it offer serene shade around the stage area, and views of Moraine Park and the Big Thompson River add to the ambiance. The amphitheater features huge stone steps and long wooden plank seats, and was constructed by the Civilian Conservation Corps (CCC) starting in 1936. Its design incorporates naturalistic principles, uses native plants and materials, and the amphitheater is molded into the bowl shape of the existing topography organically. But the CCC also did other Rustic design work at this location for the National Park Service in the 1930s, one perfect example being their conversion of the Moraine Lodge's Assembly Hall (the prior incarnation of this property) to a museum. The building blends stone and timber seamlessly into the surrounding terrain and features hand-tooled construction work. The look of the hefty stone fireplace chimney and stone bottom segment of the historic building is quite impressive.

In the ten years the CCC was active in this country as a response to the unemployment spun out of the Great Depression, over 3.2 million young men from cities labored around this country's parks and forests on conservation and construction projects that survive and enhance to this day. Approximately three-and-a-half billion trees were planted and tens of thousands of illiterate workers learned to read and write in the CCC camps. They made about $30 a month, sending all but $5 a month home to support their relatives. More importantly, they were provided clothing and shelter and plentiful food. You have to admire so many young men willing to work so hard to earn an honest wage. Being a History major at university regularly stands me in good stead and the history of America is fascinating.

I focus my attention on the current visitor center and its stunning surroundings. The views of Moraine Park and Longs Peak are breathtaking. I know from prior visits that it has a half-mile nature trail for the kids, with an activities booklet they can complete along the way, a tiny but packed bookstore and gift shop, and fascinating interactive natural history exhibits on weather, climates, ecosystems, the glacial periods, wildlife, and geology—all topics near and dear to Randy Jeffers. Given the lateness of the afternoon, Leda just checks the parking lot quickly on the way inside the museum. I feel eager and hopeful that we can pick up a tangible sign of our missing man, and the tiredness of the long day melts away.

CHAPTER 48

Leda takes a deep sniff of the baggie hovering in front of her, mostly to humor me because she has that scent locked into her brain. She walks purposefully toward the back corner of the parking lot and then heads up the walk toward the museum. She weaves in and out of several people strolling about and heads to a timbered bench outside. Leda circles the bench and pulls me off toward the building.

Sylvia murmurs, "Now we're getting somewhere. Things just got interesting."

Leda looks very engaged now and we enter the building. The closest ranger sees her Working Dog vest and says nothing, but Sylvia slides over and explains to him anyway that we are working with the National Park Service and Larimer County on a disappearance. He's about 40 with long brown hair pulled into a ponytail and a face alive with personality. His nametag says Rory. Of course, it does. An original name for an original character. He nods his understanding and asks if he can follow at a distance. Sylvia gives him the "sure, come with us wave" and off we go.

Leda dodges two small children playing tag near the immobile but still fascinating pine marten display and carries on searching for Randy's scent under the vaulted timber ceilings, hanging educational banners, and lighted instructive displays. The room is fairly dim, with a soothing, timeless feel, and I try not to run into any display case corners. A random tourist pondering the exhibit which asks "If a Glacier is Frozen, How Can it Flow?" looks so deeply engrossed in that question that Leda's sudden appearance startles him and he jumps a foot in the air. Leda criss-crosses the floor testing air currents and starts to zero in high on the wall featuring the famous taxidermy mountain lion. A straight-backed chair stands off to the side of the lower exhibits and Leda shows serious interest in that chair. She sniffs the ground from there and picks up a river of scent. She seems a little puzzled and begins looking up at the mountain lion quizzically. Unbeknownst to me, the tourist has followed us into the display area and emits a raucous laugh. "Looks like your dog tracked a cat!" Oh geez. Seriously? Sylvia and Rory the Ranger confer, with Sylvia pointing at Leda and then the cat. Rory then ambles around the room personably herding the two remaining tourists out of the building as it's closing time by now, and then locks the door so we have privacy for the search. Sylvia is doing fantastically well in her first mission with us—running interference for Leda, explaining quietly how she works to onlookers, and showing huge faith in Leda's nose.

The ranger returns eagerly and carries the nearby chair over to just under the mountain lion on his lofty rock pedestal attached snug against the inside timbered wall. He gestures to me with a magnificent flourish like a magician pulling a rabbit <u>and</u> a dove out of a hat and smiles at me in encouragement. I hand Leda to Sylvia and step on the chair carefully. I reach up and feel around the rock base on which the cat is mounted. This is probably gonna result in a big collection of dust bunnies and dead bugs, I think with a grimace. Then I happen to look down at Leda and she is still targeting on the cat. Now many Chessies are known cat chasers. Sorry! (Heads up to cats everywhere.) But she is wearing such an intent look. I know what that means. After three days of scent dissipating and scores of people traipsing through this jewel of a building, Leda KNOWS that Randy Jeffers was here.

I contort my hand carefully behind the mountain lion's right hind leg. Nothing but dust. Next, I reach carefully behind the lone pine cone standing upright in gluey puzzlement underneath the cat's belly. All clear.

The final area to inspect is behind the mountain lion's right front leg. And there, in the tiny sliver of space between the lion leg and the wall, my fingernails graze an object. I jiggle it loose from its hiding place in a normally very public room. Rory the Ranger exclaims in delight as I pull out a computer thumb drive in a tiny plastic wrapper.

He looks at Sylvia and says, "This is the most interesting thing I've seen at work all year."

Sylvia turns to him and with perfect deadpan delivery replies, "I bet. It's not every day you pull a clue out of a stuffed cat."

I clamber down while laughing and almost fall off the chair. It's no secret; I have terrible balance. Yoga is not helping. Leda saunters over and sniffs the plastic wrapper, looking very smug. I hold it by the corner and drop it carefully in a paper bag Sylvia has brought me. "Good, good girl, Leda. Such a good girl." She yawns and leans on my leg while I pull her left ear gently. She's ready for a nap after a hard day's work. Biscuits first though.

CHAPTER 49

We thank Rory for his assistance and head back out to the vehicle. He looks a little disappointed to see us go, but at least he had an exciting interlude today. We caution him that the discovery of the thumb drive is to be kept confidential due to the open investigation and he nods his understanding. Leda jumps in the cargo area and lolls back against the sidewall, the picture of contentment. I pull out my cell phone and call Dad while Sylvia calls Tim. With everyone on speaker, we can have a decent four-person conversation. I start off the proceedings, "Well, I'm guessing that Leda finding a computer thumb drive that Randy Jeffers hid in the Moraine Park Discovery Center definitely confirms that something alarming was going on in his life on Friday." We wait for the excited responses. And here they come.

"I knew she could do it," my dad praises Leda.

Tim joins in, "She's the best! Where was it hidden?"

Sylvia adds to the mix. "You would never believe it in a million years, but he stashed it away behind the leg of the stuffed mountain lion up on the wall. Everyone thought Leda was just pointing at a big cat, but she knew better."

"That's our girl," Tim says. "I'll let Henry Akers know and we can get the thumb drive over to his computer specialist to look at the contents and see if it helps us find him. It goes without saying that **nobody** discloses we found this thumb drive. Randy hid it for a reason. There has got to be information on it to help narrow down what is going on with Randy. We have a possible sighting of a guy who may be one of Billy Fulton's entourage entering RMNP on Friday, but this particular footage is very grainy and the guy has a hood up and turtleneck on. I can't swear that it's him."

Dad comments pensively, "I wonder if the command leader would make a copy of the thumb drive and allow me to peruse it. I have time and the ability to research and I can do an extra review for information—just to assist his guys, of course. The more eyes the better at this point, I would guess."

"I am pretty sure Henry would go for that," Tim answers with alacrity. "I imagine right now he just wants Randy found; it's not like you work for a competitor of Water Analytical Solutions. And you located the photos of Randy on social media to begin with outside Moraine Park Discovery Center. If he agrees, the ladies can take the thumb drive to Henry and get a copy made before they head back to Boulder. We have to figure out where he's disappeared to."

We all hang up and Sylvia and I sit in the front of the SUV and watch the gathering dusk settle in behind the rustic visitor center like the curtain dropping gradually on a magnificent stage. We are both tired from exercising out in the fresh air for hours—but it's so much better than being hunched over your computer and chained to your desk at work all day. This is a definite advantage to no longer working as a legal assistant. We sip our water and chat until Tim calls back to confirm that we are to take the thumb drive to Henry Akers at the command center. He has gotten permission from him to make a copy for Dad to examine while the police work on the original copy. We all hope the answer to Randy Jeffers' disappearance is contained on that thumb drive. Something serious caused Randy to conceal it behind the lion. We desperately need more information to point us in our next direction.

CHAPTER 50

We drive over to the site of the Larimer County Sheriff's Office sub-station in Estes Park to meet the computer technician who has been assigned to wait for us in the parking lot. As we pull up under a towering streetlight, we are approached by a tall, lanky kid, who introduces himself as Jonah. He looks about 15, but I assume he's got to be at least 21. Jonah takes the paper bag we hand him with the computer thumb drive and tells us it shouldn't take too long to copy if we want to wait. Leda stands up upon his approach watching silently for any nefarious intent by this unknown individual. "It's okay, girl. He's a friend." She pays absolutely no attention to this reassurance and continues to watch Jonah steadily through the glass. He gulps nervously, turns on his heel, and trots back into the building eager to get to work.

Sylvia says, "Well, he seemed a little freaked out by Leda."

"It's the yellow eyes," I reply. "It gets them every time." Leda flops down in a heap with a grunt, resting up until she feels she's needed again.

Jonah returns in short order and cautiously hands me an envelope through the window while Leda levers herself up and watches him impassively for any sudden movements. "Thanks, Jonah. We'll get going back to Boulder with this. We appreciate your help."

"You're welcome, ladies. Good luck with it." Leda sinks into a sit. Apparently, she's decided that Jonah poses no immediate threat. We start the drive back toward Boulder with the little cache of information it took all day and one close encounter with a stuffed apex predator to unearth.

The drive back goes smoothly enough. Leda is flat out on her side giving tiny yips under her breath. I really hope it's a rabbit she's chasing in her sleep and not poor Jonah. She'll never tell. We're past the worst of the time when commuters are attempting to make their way home from work. I also don't miss the commute that comes with having an office job. Sylvia spots the new housing development on the way home and she groans in disgust. "Really? Sanctuary at the Preserve. That's the exact opposite of what it is to the animals any more. Too bad the Open Space department couldn't acquire this land."

"I know," I commiserate. "But they have protected tens of thousands of acres in our county. They can't save it all. Unfortunately." By mutual agreement, we change the subject to a topic more pleasant than the despoiling of nature and plan out our schedule of yoga classes for the next few weeks, working around my upcoming drug sweeps for clients and Sylvia's work schedule for the City and County of Denver. Before we know it, we are passing through the gate onto the Dogged Pursuit K-9 property and driving up to my home. Both Donovan vehicles are sitting near the building. Good news. That means we can all have a strategy meeting.

CHAPTER 51

The upstairs is full of teenagers and dogs. A sudden uptick of my mood reveals I must be healing a little bit inside. All this activity in my personal space would have been overwhelming to me when I first came to Colorado, but now it just feels welcoming. The older twins are setting the table and the younger twins are tossing a salad with a proliferation of vegetables. It looks gorgeous with the rainbow of colors decorating the romaine and spinach leaves. Way too healthy, but nevertheless gorgeous. One of them has put the Best of the Eagles in the CD player and the beginning of *Take it Easy* soars through the room. Sylvia and I throw our stuff on the floor and belt out the lyrics about that famous spot in Winslow, Arizona, while the assembled members of our human pack dissolve into laughter and the dog pack leaps around in excitement. No better song than that one exists. You know I'm right.

Tim is sitting at my desk with his laptop looking up information on the Internet and gives us a distracted wave. Sylvia wanders over and kisses the top of his head while he pats her hand absentmindedly. Dad and Michael are in the kitchen making one of Dad's famous concoctions involving chicken, potatoes, and broccoli. Michael puts two cookie sheets packed tight with the garlic bread my father is famous for in the oven. Things are definitely looking up in the culinary department. The dogs have all greeted Leda and are sprawled out in clumps around the living room, tongues lolling out happily. I feel positive about Gemma integrating smoothly into the

Duncan household in Florida. They also have a poodle and this socialization bodes well for a successful future meeting between them. Cocoa lays with her back against the bottom of the couch, probably to make her feel more secure, and keeps a steady eye on Michael. I look her over closely and am pleased to observe that she looks fairly relaxed for a dog that's only been off the streets for a few days. All of the dogs seem content to lounge about; the kids must have kept them all very busy today. It's the perfect way to have a well-behaved dog. Lots and lots of exercise and tons of attention. I roll a little video and text it to the Porters so they can see how polite their boys are being. I take Leda downstairs briefly to feed her, and 21.9 seconds later, she looks up at me and grins. All done.

When Leda and I go back upstairs, Dad and Michael are carrying food to the table and the girls are pouring out glasses of lemonade for everyone. Elli remembers napkins and scurries out to the kitchen as we all fit ourselves in around the big farmhouse table. Just enough room for nine. I look at Dad and laugh, "I guess you were right to insist on getting the gigantic table when we furnished this place, Dad. I never ever thought we would fill it up when we first moved here."

"It's nice to have this many good friends to feed now," he replies with his patented cheerfulness. "What I should have also insisted on was a bigger pantry!" Everyone laughs as we pass platters of steaming hot food around the table, serve out the salad, and take pieces of cheesy, garlicky bread out of the big serving bowl emblazoned with the helmet of our favorite football team on the side. No, not the Broncos. The Springers have a moment of lunacy when a piece of potato hits the floor. Michael gets up quietly and calls them over to reposition them in a Down next to Gemma. Order is soon restored. Gemma looks at them condescendingly. Silly pups.

CHAPTER 52

"**M**ichael and I were having a talk while we prepped the food for dinner and he has something he would like to share with you, Ronnie," Dad says, as we all dig into our food. Michael looks over at me and puts down his fork. He is hesitating and looks slightly nervous. Don't tell me I'm losing my assistant already.

He gathers his courage and begins, "I was thinking I would like to take Criminal Justice classes at Flatirons Community College when they start a new semester. Jane looked online and the first course I would need is Intro to Criminal Justice. Then I would take Policing Systems. Lizzie even found three small scholarships I can apply for which could help pay for the courses. It just came to me after watching Sgt. Donovan and you do your jobs. I would really like to become a K-9 officer. You can teach me to train dogs and I'll be further ahead when I finish school in a few years." He finishes in a rush and then holds his breath waiting for my response.

"I think that is an excellent, well-conceived plan." Michael exhales. "We can all definitely help you make that happen. If the scholarships don't work out, or take a while to come through, you can use the money you earn for being my assistant. I really plan on expanding my drug sweep program and building up my client base of schools and other businesses. You can start learning how to help me with that. And of course, I'm sure Dad will let you keep living here with free room and board."

Dad looks over at Michael and smiles, "Definitely. You're part of the team now. I like having a sous-chef too." It's quite evident that Dad is genuinely fond of Michael already. He misses Zach, his hunting and fishing buddy, terribly—so Michael's arrival in our lives at this time feels like divine intervention.

Tim chimes in, "I'll do whatever I can to help you as well, Michael. You can go on ride-alongs with me and I'll introduce you to the K-9 patrol officers from the surrounding jurisdictions. Of course, by training with Veronica, you'll learn all the dog stuff the right way."

Mari and Elli pipe up. "Please can we take lessons too, Veronica? We want to learn."

Tim and Sylvia look at each other and nod in agreement. Then Sylvia says, "Your dad and I have decided that you girls *can* get a dog, as long as you promise to be completely responsible for its care. The four of you have to arrange amongst yourselves all the details necessary to feed and exercise and train—all that good stuff. Oh, and Veronica will help you pick the breed. No squabbling over that decision. Fair enough?" The girls start shrieking in excitement and talking all at once.

Michael is beaming and I can see he's happy that he'll have training partners. Or maybe he's thinking he won't have to keep such a close eye on the girls to make sure they don't swipe Cocoa from him. She is dozing against the couch now, but every so often she opens her left eye to get a visual check on Michael. Approximately ten potential dog breeds have been thrown out by the two sets of twins in the last 60 seconds. This may be harder than I thought. I'll have to sit down with them when they're not so wound up and get suggestions and see what characteristics are most important to them. That should help me pare it down to a breed with which they can all be happy. It looks like I'm going to be running a whole lot of obedience training classes in the not-too-distant future.

CHAPTER 53

We all enjoy the hearty meal (made even more tasty because I did not have to participate in any way in its preparation) that Dad and Michael have provided for us. They even rustle up two pecan pies from the storage freezer and we enjoy dessert with vanilla ice cream. Sylvia looks at me and says playfully, "Good thing we hiked all over creation. I don't feel guilty at all."

"Me neither," I reply. "I feel so not guilty, I'm having another scoop of ice cream."

The teenagers clear the table and head to the kitchen to deal with the dishes. We send them all out to the sun porch afterward with the coffee table book on dog breeds and tell them to start their research. I'm curious to see what their list of possibilities will include. The rest of us sit, satisfyingly full, at the farmhouse table and privately discuss the status of the investigation into the vanishing of Randy Jeffers.

Tim confirms that as of tonight, Randy's vehicle has still not been located, his cell phone still seems to be turned off so pinging is of no use, and no activity has occurred on his bank account or with his ATM card. According to his wife and co-workers, he has made no effort to contact them since he last spoke to his wife Friday afternoon. The Larimer County Sheriff's Office was able to copy the thumb drive for Dad to peruse; however, they want us to know that half the files on it are password protected.

"They are working on getting around that security measure now, but no luck yet," Tim informs us.

"If Jonah's working on it, maybe he needs Leda standing over him for additional motivation," Sylvia jokes. Dad and Tim look puzzled so we fill them in on Leda's interactions with Jonah. They are both amused, as they picture Leda piercing Jonah with her gimlet eye.

Then Dad says, "I can take a look at the files which aren't password protected first to see if I spot anything. In the meantime, maybe the Sheriff's Office will figure out a way to open the other files. I'm guessing what we need to know is on those protected files, though. It only makes sense."

Tim agrees, "That would be great, Bob. They will let me know when they've cracked it. Glen Gerard's two IT guys are still working away on the extra password layer on Randy's work computer directory as well. However, at the moment, besides us, only Larimer County knows about Leda finding the thumb drive. I have also learned that the investigative team going through footage on security cameras near Randy's work has spotted two individuals lurking near his car around the time he mentioned to his wife. The footage is not really clear enough to see what they were up to, or to spot very many distinguishing features, but the sizes and body types are not inconsistent with the two house sitting pals of Billy Fulton. They are working on getting that footage cleaned up.

"Another team member is trying to get Billy Fulton to agree to an interview just to gauge his body language and so forth when this disappearance is discussed with him. At present, his attorney is advising him not to cooperate and we are not having much luck convincing them otherwise. I mean he was clearly gone playing basketball when this happened, but it would be nice to ask him if he thinks any of his friends might have taken it upon themselves to help him with his legal troubles. We learned from one of Chardonnay's friends who was interviewed for the murder case that several of Billy's pals apparently have access to one of his bank accounts 'in case they need anything while he's playing ball out of town.'

Understandably, this was a huge bone of contention in their marriage. Now you have to wonder if they used Billy's money to get up to no good."

"Moving on to the helicopter," Tim continues. "One of the officers had luck when he telephoned a privately owned airfield on the outskirts of Walden. The manager there confirmed that he had a new customer fly in a Cumbre Negra last week, so you were dead on there, Bob. The airfield's mechanic was needed to clear a fuel line that was clogging according to the pilot. The infrared was also non-operational, but that fix requires a replacement part from the manufacturer in Argentina so the mechanic advised the pilot that was not something he could immediately address. Two men picked up the pilot at the airfield after he made arrangements for the repair. Those two never got close enough for anyone to get a good look at them. Two white guys in their early 30s, maybe, with dark hair and wiry builds is all we got. That narrows it down to 30% of the population, including, again, the two friends of Billy Fulton's we've been trying to track. The pilot asked to hangar the helicopter at the airfield for a short time and said he would be back for it soon. Also, he talked the manager into giving him a discount if he paid cash so we have no credit card receipts to check. This is just a Mom-and-Pop operation, where the owners live onsite, so they never sprang for security cameras.

"Once the fuel line problem was corrected and the bird was refueled, the pilot turned up for it two days later in a blazing hurry. Since it's not the typical helicopter one sees around here, the mechanic and the manager both tried asking the pilot about it—you know, how he got it, where he was going, that sort of thing. The manager indicated that the pilot looked like an ex-military type, pretty intimidating and non-communicative. He saw a veteran's patch on the guy's jacket—a fairly distinctive one too. It was a brown roped circle with four helicopters flying against a gray background at the top with the word IRAQ, a banner of OPERATION DESERT STORM in the middle and a tank at the bottom with a dark brown background. The manager is sure of the details as he collects American military memorabilia. The pilot pretty much shut down their inquiries with brusque comments about his owner being an intensely private, rich guy who collects unusual aircraft. The pilot tried to play it off like he was just flying this freshly acquired helicopter to its new owner. Since he indicated he was flying for pleasure in visual conditions and staying below 18,000 feet he declined to file a flight plan. It's not a great idea, but it's not illegal. But they did see it head off very swiftly to the southeast, which is toward Rocky Mountain National Park and Comanche Peak.

"The dates and times track with the sightings of the helicopter over and around the national park and when we think they scooped up Randy from the meadow. But we did catch a break. The mechanic noted the faded registration number on the tail and it started with HC-AA. He later spilled pop on his notebook, but we did get that partial number. The registration numbers in that series are allocated to Ecuador. We have a contact at the State Department checking with Ecuadorian leaders on those Cumbre Negras that they offered for sale."

Heading to the kitchen, I pull another pitcher of lemonade out of the fridge and return to the table to refill all our glasses. Talking over all the details is thirsty work. The kids are still on the sun porch with most of the dogs and are now discussing the Criminal Justice curriculum at Flatirons Community College and how many total courses Michael will have to take. Jane tells him she will print out the applications for scholarships tomorrow and they can start filling them in for submission. It sounds like the plan is coming together well. Dad starts a fire in the fireplace and it makes me warm inside to look at the amber and red flames curling around the edges of the logs with tiny, tentative fingers, and to hear the snapping and crackling begin. After the murder trial, I was sure I never wanted to be around crowds of people again. But now, more at peace than I have been in months, it occurs to me that it's quite nice to have this kind of company in my house.

CHAPTER 54

The girls head outside with Michael to get the dogs to potty and then get the boarding dogs into their kennel runs. They stand outside and look up at the stars twinkling above us while Tim and Sylvia gather up their belongings and say goodbye to Dad and me, promising to touch base in the morning.

Mari calls out, "Look at that shooting star. Ooohh. There's another one—and another one."

Looking up, the sky seems full of blazing stars headed downward in flamboyant arcs. The night sky is beautiful without the light pollution so pervasive around urban areas. Michael heads inside to his place with Cocoa after we discuss plans for the morning. I ask him not to feed the dogs early as Gemma will come for a morning jog. Dad and I walk back to his cabin. He and Ripley are planning a late-night session of reviewing the thumb drive for any obvious, or not so obvious, clues.

I ask, "Is all this investigating leaving you time to work on your articles, Dad?"

"Not to worry, honey, I have a deadline in two weeks, but that article on primitive weapons is almost fleshed out. Helping find Randy Jeffers is more important. That man is brilliant; the world needs him a lot more than it needs another article from me on muzzleloader season. I just really hope we find him alive."

"I know Dad. I'm worried about that too, but at least Leda didn't find any indication he was killed in the moraine meadow." Leda hears her name and circles back to get her head rubbed. She closes her eyes blissfully. *Ahhh, that's the spot, Mom.*

I wake up very early Tuesday morning and take a peek outside. News alert. It's going to be sunny and clear. The sunshine and low humidity here never get old. I pull on my jogging tights and long sleeve T-shirt. I fight the brush through my curly hair and do two quick braids before pulling on my baseball cap. It occurs to me belatedly that my shoulder feels more flexible, with less pulling of the scar tissue. The arnica seems to be helping. Twelve jars later. I grab my running shoes and thump Leda on the sides. "My goodness, Leda. You goofball. That tail should be registered as a lethal weapon," I say as she slams it against my legs. She bounds around crazily like a jackrabbit on hot coals for five minutes and then runs down the stairs to wait for the slow-moving human. I grab a banana and eat my healthy breakfast as we walk over to Dad's cabin. It needs something else. Like a coating of chocolate.

Dad is already up and typing away vigorously on his computer keyboard, with a cup of steaming coffee by his side, and wearing the blue plaid flannel shirt I bought him last Christmas. He's pretty easy to buy gifts for— anything outdoor-related will pass muster. He was almost certainly up and roaming around the property in the middle of the night with Ripley. I don't think he has slept very well since the murderous events in Ohio and the subsequent trial. Tommy Arnett's black soul has that effect on people. But Dad gets up early every day regardless to enjoy the sunrise on the Flatirons while sitting at his strategically positioned desk. Leda and Ripley greet each other happily and carry stuffed toys around together. Ripley has chosen the moose and Leda the T-Rex, of course.

"Good morning, Dad. Any luck with the thumb drive yet?"

"Morning, Ronnie. Well, I think we can eliminate the storm water retention projects as the source of any harm befalling Randy. I analyzed that entire file and the municipalities who brought him onboard are actually thrilled. They are having significantly less flooding and polluted water entering their local bodies of water. The rooftop gardens and sidewalk planters have added splashes of color to the neighborhoods and a booming increase in butterflies. They have also installed permeable interlocking bricks in spots to allow water to filter down through to the ground more gradually. Teachers are taking their kids on field trips to view the projects and have started to add school gardens to their science modules. In Pittsburgh, they have grown so many vegetables that the kids are taking home healthy food every week for their lower income families. It's basically a win-win situation. I read through all of the local articles clipped into the file and the minutes of the council meetings debating these projects and the resistance was very minimal. No one was even dragged out in protest—unlike the mussel crusader."

"It's good to know that we can eliminate one of the files anyway—so butterfly haters have probably not invaded Colorado." Dad laughs at my pitiful joke like the good father he is and takes a big gulp of coffee.

"Send Michael up here to join me for breakfast if he wants," Dad offers. I nod in acknowledgement, tell him I'm taking the dogs running, and leave with Leda and Ripley to get Gemma. Michael comes out of the apartment in the training building to greet me. He has his usual beaming smile. He really is the nicest kid. Cocoa thinks so too and follows right at his heels. I reach down and pet her gently. Her tail is at about half-mast now. We're making progress. The tiny line of stitches above her eye looks clean and sealed. She'll get those out in a week or so.

"Hi, Michael. I'm taking these three running. Please feed the Springers and Cocoa and then you're welcome to join Dad for breakfast at the cabin. If you're lucky, he'll make some of his famous French toast with Geauga County maple syrup. We get it shipped to us from a family-owned farm near where we used to live in Ohio. We'll do some training when I get back from my run. We can go shopping afterward. Do you need anything you can think of?"

He looks down at the ground and then back up at me shyly. "Can I get a track suit or sweatpants? The girls and I are planning to do a lot of hiking and jogging once they get their dog, and Sgt. Donovan said I could practice on the obstacle course they use for officers in training. I have to get in shape. He told me how hard you work when Leda is trailing a missing person through the mountains. I don't think I could keep up now. The only running I did in the city was to stay out of the way of the gangs," he finishes with a rueful grin.

"That was a good thing to avoid! We can get you a pile of workout clothes for sure. I know just the place."

My three canine companions and I set a modest pace up the Doudy Draw/Community Ditch trail. They sniff the base of every other bush and then sprint to catch up to me. They never seem to tire of it. The morning air is cool and fresh and we have the trail mostly to ourselves. A pack of coyotes is howling higher up in the hills. It almost sounds like children laughing, yipping and high-pitched. Then a siren sounds far far away and I realize they are responding to its wail. I call the dogs over to sit on the edge of the trail to allow one mountain biker to pass. He smiles appreciatively; he's moving much faster—why slow him down? It feels good to stretch out my legs and look at the scenery in a leisurely fashion. When Leda and I are trailing, there's not time to look around much. We're managing nine-minute miles on this run, so no records are being set. I remind Gemma firmly that she is not going in the deep irrigation ditch alongside the trail ever again. The cattle like to stand in it and I don't need any more bouts of giardia out of her. The effects are frankly disgusting. We hit our turnaround landmark and head back making sure to close the gate at the halfway point behind us. It controls some function of them moving cattle around during the year. I just leave it like I find it. The four miles went by quickly and I feel rejuvenated.

CHAPTER 55

After the dogs are fed, I take a long hot shower and dry my hair quickly. I pull on a pair of jeans and an ancient Cleveland Force soccer jersey purchased from a yard sale in my hometown. It's seen better days and might have a few teeny holes, but that logo is awesome. The mystery guy is enveloped by a blue and yellow tornado of power while kicking a disproportionately large orange soccer ball. I put on my hiking boots and collect Michael from Dad's place. They are happy to report that they decimated a platter of French toast between the two of them. That banana seems like it was ages ago. Luckily, Dad saved me two pieces and heats them up in the microwave before dusting them with powdered sugar. Heaven. We leave Dad and Ripley, as honorary manager, to work on the thumb drive; he says he has an idea. He'll tell me later if it comes to fruition. Michael and I wander down to the training building.

We get Butter and Scotch into their training collars and run through their preliminary exercises. Steady repetition is what builds an obedient dog. They are a tad unfocused this morning, but settle down as we move through the Sit, Down, Stand, and Heel commands. We then do a heeling module in which we vary straight line heeling with About Turns, Left Turns, Right Turns, and then Circle Left and Circle Right. For a teenager with the build of a Division-1 college linebacker, Michael has exceptional gentleness with the dogs and shows a high level of maturity and patience. All indications point toward him becoming a terrific K-9 handler.

Lastly, we practice the Sit Stay. Butter starts sitting on my left side, with the rings of the collar between his ears on the top of the head. The lead is folded up in my left hand until it is taut above his ears. I give the Stay signal with my right hand and step directly in front of Butter and count to ten. Then I swivel back into heel position. I release the pressure on his collar and praise him happily. I do this exercise several times and tell Michael each day we will gradually back farther away from the dogs when standing in front of them. Michael nods and then works through the exercise three times with Scotch. He gets more distracted than Butter, but Michael does a good job reinforcing the command. We get a handful of treats from the storage bin on the side wall and practice the Leave It command with the Springers. They do a stellar job resisting temptation until told they can have the treats as we put them down one by one. I tell Michael it usually takes about three weeks of steady work before the dog actually gets what we are asking him to do with all this training.

Cocoa comes out of a kennel run when the Springers go back in and Michael runs through the beginning obedience exercises with her after putting on her training collar. She is slightly timid, but not overtly submissive, which bodes well for her future confidence level. She gets weary after 15 minutes and I remind Michael that she still needs to build up her stamina. We'll get Dad and take all the dogs hiking in the next few days with any luck. We finish on a positive note and reward her. She looks up at Michael with her sweet eyes and half-speckled face and I can see the trust she already has in him. Amazing the resilience dogs can have. Finally, Michael pulls on gloves and takes the citrus greening disease training boxes out on the property.

"Should I hide them close or far?"

"Take them all the way out and around, if you would. And make sure they are not visible—really hide them. We don't want her to see the boxes, just find the smell. Gemma can work a big territory to find them today. The groves she'll be checking for the diseased plants cover hundreds of acres,"

I reply. Michael returns after 25 minutes and gives me a thumbs-up. In the interim, I run a brush over Leda's wavy coat, wipe out her ears with the cleansing pads, and trim her nails. Once released, she wriggles around on her back throwing her hind end from side to side violently and rubbing her head on the matting. "You realize you look ridiculous, right?" She hops up grinning at me and leans against my knee. I kiss the top of her head and think about how lucky I was to adopt her just before she ran out of time at the pound. Another dog nobody wanted with oceans of love to give.

CHAPTER 56

Gemma is eager to work and searches the entire property when given the ROT command. She trots along with her black plume of a tail waving back and forth gently as she alerts to the scent from box after box. She covers the entire seven acres briskly and has no bobbles. I text the Duncans in Florida and tell them Gemma is ready to work in their actual orange groves. Arrangements are made to drive her there in about two weeks and polish off her training in the field, while also training the Duncans' son, who will be her primary handler. The son responds almost instantaneously with enthusiasm and a photo of the dog bed they have bought for Gemma. It looks very cushy. It's a clever camouflage design using the paw prints of bears and deer as the markings. I text the photo to Dad with a caption "You should review this product next. Ripley volunteers to be the tester!" He texts me back a request to come up to his cabin. Then he sends me the smiley face emoji with the jazz hands. Seriously, Dad?

Michael begins cleaning out the kennels and wiping down the mat flooring with disinfectant. He can take a shower and we will leave in about an hour to go shopping. Leda and I head up to see Dad. As we walk, I look up and see jet trails feathering out diagonally overhead, white against the brilliant blue sky. A Cooper's hawk does his trademark flap-flap glide overhead and shows off his steely blue-gray on top and vibrant reddish bars underneath. His coloring is truly gorgeous and I watch him silently until he flies out of sight, before turning away reluctantly.

Dad is hunched over his computer intently and motions me over to join him. He has Foreigner pumping out of the stereo behind him. Oh boy, Dad must be on a real roll now. The classic *Double Vision* is blasting out into the cabin. Couldn't be a more appropriate song! In addition, four coffee cups sit there on the desk circling him like sharks. He must be so engrossed in his work that he has been grabbing a new cup every time he wanders into the kitchen. Where in the world did the one come from that says 'World's Greatest Mechanic'? And what the heck is the sludge at the bottom of that cup?

Dad impatiently twists the volume knob lower on the stereo. "Ronnie, listen to this. The Larimer County computer experts are diligently working on the files that are password protected on the thumb drive, with no luck yet, but I had an idea. I ran it by Tim and he said it was fine to pursue. I called Patty Jeffers and asked her for vital details about Randy, like birth date, hometown—Fort Lee, New Jersey, by the way—favorite sports team, the Yankees, of course, but we won't hold that against him, names of his pets etc… I'm trying to solve the password using this program I uploaded from a website for people who like to crack codes. You enter the variables and it processes them in ultra quick time in differing combinations. You know like Yankees03171962$$ or PandaFort Lee%%. It has been searching the possibilities for about an hour or so now.

"The only sticking point is whether I entered in all the right variables. He is a scientist so he may use one of those crazy combination strings that has absolutely no meaning and is so convoluted you have to write it down and hide it in your desk—thus negating the totally secret aspect. Anyway, we shall see. In the meantime, I am going to examine the next file on the directory, which is *not* protected. That's the dreadful Virginia case of the man who drowned his son to avoid paying child support. Interesting that this one is a file that has not been made more difficult to view," he trails off thoughtfully.

I respond while heading into the kitchen to grab a huge glass of water for Dad to dilute some of the way too strong coffee in his system, and snag an apple for myself. "Maybe since the case was already adjudicated, and the father sentenced and shipped off to prison, Randy did not feel the need to encrypt it. Everything is a matter of public record at this point and all four of the expert witnesses testified to essentially the same facts regarding the autopsy. It seems less likely the defendant would single out Randy, but you probably need to read the transcripts."

"I'm thinking the same thing, Ronnie. Tim placed a call to the warden of the prison in Virginia where the father is being held to see whether they have intercepted any threatening calls or letters from him to that prosecutor, Randy, or the other experts. His own family members condemned him publicly and vocally at the time, according to the media coverage, so it appears unlikely a relative is taking retaliatory action on his behalf. But stranger things have happened. You know that from personal experience with that one felon you guys put away in Ohio sending a graphic and disturbing birthday card to your boss every year."

Dad glances up at me belatedly with concern to see my response to a discussion of my prior job and my murdered boss, but I feel oddly calm. Almost. I may finally be regaining my footing in the world. "Right? Who would think that someone else would actually succeed in killing Charles? One new lunatic that was not on anyone's radar. Charles saw it as an occupational hazard of having that job, but I always worried a little about Gus Staines getting out of jail and coming after Charles. It's not a huge county and Charles went jogging every morning near his home. He wasn't really hard to find. None of us turned out to be, I guess." I stop talking abruptly. This is a black hole of thinking I do not want to go down, and I mentally give myself a shake. We have a missing man to find and I am going to try my level best to focus solely on my present and not my past.

Dad changes the subject adeptly. "Oh, by the way, honey, you got an e-mail from a company near Golden that is a distributor for several outdoor gear companies. Apparently, their warehouse is enormous and involves a number of pieces of heavy equipment, forklifts and so on. The director of operations is concerned about possible drug use on property and they would like to engage you to do a drug sweep in two weeks or less, depending on your availability. I told him you would get back to them today to arrange a good time."

"You're the best, Dad. I'm going to have to start paying you an administrative assistant salary too."

"Not at all, you help me out all the time by taking Ripley running when I'm working on an article on deadline." I quickly e-mail the company in Golden and offer up five or six days when my schedule is entirely open. Leda is getting to be an extremely well-traveled drug detection dog. We have accumulated clients in a number of the surrounding communities and I feel positive about getting even more business with Michael as an assistant and possibly another trained dog.

CHAPTER 57

Leaving Leda with Dad, Michael and I drive to the nearby military surplus store, always a favorite for outdoor apparel, camping and hiking gear, and boots. Michael wanders around looking at the stocked shelves in wonder. The shelves and racks carry vast quantities of gloves, jeans, overalls, hats, military and tactical paraphernalia, and camping and hiking gear. It's the proverbial kid in the candy store scenario for any outdoor enthusiast. We discuss what he needs for hiking, dog training, and just lounging around and start to make a stack of stuff on the counter. It isn't exactly like the scene in *Pretty Woman,* where Julia Roberts shops like a fiend, but it is just as satisfying.

"Veronica, this is so much. It will take me a long time to pay you back. I really don't need all of this right now."

"Of course, you do," I reply. "This is Colorado; you're going to be spending significant amounts of time in the great outdoors and need to be warm and comfortable while you are helping me grow the business. And you know my dad, right? Mr. Safety. You need the proper gear. Plus, we just like you. No worries. You are already earning your keep around the place and helping Dad when I'm not there. This is payment for services already rendered for Dogged Pursuit K-9. Once we find Randy Jeffers, we will sit down and figure out your hours to fit around your classes in Criminal Justice. We can go to the bank of your choice in the next few days and get you set up with your own account." I punctuate this speech by adding a pair of gloves to the tower of apparel threatening to topple off the counter at any moment. The sales clerk hustles over to save the day, and wisely starts tower number two for us.

Forty-five minutes later, Michael and I head back to the SUV swinging six bags of gear and he has new boots on his feet. They give off that new leather smell and squeak ever so slightly. "Dad has dozens of different conditioning treatments for the boots, not just mink oil. You will have to consult him on the best ones. He gets a multitude every year to try out and review. We will literally never have to purchase any waterproofing treatment for the rest of our lives. And you will have to break those in bit by bit. You don't need to get blisters right off the bat."

He laughs in delight and responds, "I can alternate with the high tops we bought. I love the black sneakers." Now he finally sounds like an 18-year-old kid who never had much growing up. Out of everything, he seems the most pleased with the collar covered in a pattern of tiny paw prints that he chose for Cocoa. That reminds me. I text Stephanie's office and confirm Cocoa is scheduled for her spay next week. The last thing the world needs is more unplanned puppies when 1,500,000 good dogs get euthanized in shelters every year in the United States.

CHAPTER 58

Tim calls me as we drive back to Boulder and the call connects through my Bluetooth. "Good day, Veronica. How are you?"

"Great, Tim. Thanks for asking. Michael and I are driving back from the military surplus store with a bunch of goodies. Do you have any updates for us on the status of the search?"

"Man, I love that store," he answers promptly. "Last time we took the girls, it took two hours and an $800 hit to the credit card before Sylvia could drag us out of there. Highly dangerous! Anyway, I do have a puzzling update of sorts. A former work colleague of Randy Jeffers' was in Granby last evening and swears he saw Randy there. I really am not certain what to make of his claim. He says he is sure of his identification, but that's on the complete opposite end of the national park where Randy was last seen and his phone is still not turned on. Also, it was getting close to dusk at the time this former work colleague allegedly saw Randy crossing the street and the man has not seen Randy in two or three years. Henry Akers has sent an officer down to that area to follow up that lead. I just find it hard to believe that Randy is roaming around the park for four days without contacting anyone—unless he has amnesia!"

"I tend to agree, Tim," I answer thoughtfully. "All the evidence we have located thus far seems to point a different way, but if it proves to be true, that would be awesome. In the meantime, we'll keep our foot on the gas. Dad is working like crazy to get through the thumb drive password. I really hope Jonah or Dad can break through soon so we get a new clue."

"You know it," Tim replies. "We keep chasing down our leads and just support the Larimer County/Park Service team with what they need. Cuda is still on the sidelines and the Search and Rescue Team continues to look for those missing hikers on the western edge of the park. We'll just take pressure off them as much as we can. Bob has done great research to this point; we just need another break—like finding that helicopter or getting Billy Fulton to agree to an interview with our investigator. I'm fielding phone calls from our District Attorney a few times a day. This whole situation throws the upcoming trial into turmoil, as nobody quite knows what to make of the star expert witness vanishing," Tim tails off.

"You're so right. We do need a break. Leda is such a great tool, but we need to know where to point her. At least Dad has ruled out the storm water retention projects and the freshwater mussel activist as sources for trouble. He would be hard-pressed to make it up the Lawn Lake Trail with a busted leg." Michael grins over at me and I smile back. We're both imagining his wife chucking a bottle of aspirin at his head right about now.

Tim continues, "On top of all that, the principals of the company planning the upcoming IPO for the international water purification units have been calling Randy's boss Glen Gerard daily, wanting to get their technical report. Randy had apparently told them he had it essentially completed and ready to send out. The planned initial public offering date is fast approaching with broker orders looking to hit astronomical levels, but the final technical report needed at the end of the preliminary prospectus quiet period is due to the SEC very soon. Whew!! I think I got all that financial stuff right. Anyway, it's a project with millions on the line and they can't reach their scientist. Glen is in the unenviable position of trying to explain to them that Randy's actual computer directory at Water Analytical Solutions cannot be accessed by anyone except Randy at present.

"The two principals of Agua Pura Ahora, S.A., Matt Hunter and Elicio Cuaron, have been pressing Glen to pull the final report off the system to send to the regulators, but typically that is not the way the company works. Each partner at Water Analytical Solutions does their own work. And, of course, that extra password structure put in place by Randy has proven difficult for Glen's IT guys. They can't get into the directory yet for anything. The stress and worry about his friend are beginning to get to Glen. He told me today he's started smoking again after quitting seven years ago."

"Oh no," I murmur. "That's a shame. The poor guy. He's getting pushed from all sides. Michael and I will get back to Dad's and brainstorm for ideas. We can go through all my gear and have my truck packed in case Leda is needed to run anything down."

"Sounds good, Veronica. I'll be in touch. The girls wanted me to remind you that you still have to pick a dog breed for them. I think it's still a split decision 2-2 for Golden Retriever versus German Shorthaired Pointer, so good luck with refereeing this one," Tim laughs. "Sylvia and I are staying totally out of this."

"You chickens! Tell the girls I'm giving it a lot of thought. Going with a hunting breed is a solid choice and it would be nice for them to have a larger dog to accompany them on hikes and runs. Plus, less yapping with a big dog, typically. Do not tell them yet, but I'm thinking about an English Pointer, also just known as a Pointer. The short coat is easier to keep clean, they don't shed or bark a lot, and they are great companions outdoors or on the couch. And they can have very showy markings. They love Cocoa's spots and speckles, so a Pointer could be just as striking looking."

"Okay, I'll keep mum. But I have to let Sylvia know at least. I honestly think she's just as excited as the girls. She had a blast with you and Leda yesterday."

"It's a deal. Only tell Sylvia about the Pointer though. She did a great job during the Stuffed Mountain Lion Caper. We'll get back to Dad and find something new. Fingers crossed."

CHAPTER 59

Michael turns to me after Tim hangs up and asks what a Pointer looks like. I hand him my cell phone and tell him to search away. He scans through the pictures with rapt attention. "Wow," he exclaims. "That is a cool-looking breed. I have never seen one of those before. Probably not a typical city dog, huh?"

"Usually not so much, but they are popular with pheasant and quail hunters due to their zest, and with families due to their companionable nature. They are pretty common in the South because they tolerate heat better than other breeds. By the way, how is the house training going with Cocoa? Dad said he gave you the basic rundown on how to accomplish that successfully."

"She's doing really good. I take her out a ton and praise her when she potties. She hasn't had any accidents in the apartment and she has looked at me a couple of times when she wanted to go out. It seems like she knows to ask if she needs a bathroom break."

"Great," I reply. "It's going smoothly now because you have been outside a good deal of the time with her anyway for various reasons, so she could potty any time. You just have to remember to keep a close eye on her when she's inside with you. At least, she's not a tiny puppy so she should be picking it up fast. And one of the joys of dog ownership that you can't escape—dogs have to go out no matter how bad the weather. Good thing we just got you all that gear at the surplus store."

Michael laughs and turns to look at his bags of loot in the back seat. "I think I'm prepared for any kind of weather after this shopping trip," he replies.

"Yes indeed, and now Dad can bug YOU about wearing the appropriate outdoor gear every time you leave the house. That should take 50% of the pressure off me!"

We arrive back home, click open and then close the tall, barred gate across the drive and head up the hill flanked by trees until we reach the first of the buildings—the dog training center. We unload all of Michael's shopping bags out of the SUV and into the apartment. It makes me smile approvingly to see him hurry over to greet Cocoa in her kennel run first, even before unpacking his new gear. She presses up against the door of the run whining quietly but firmly until he releases her. Cocoa throws herself down for a tummy rub and wags her tail back and forth slowly. They seem to be bonding well and every day finds her less scared. Michael clicks her new collar into place around her neck and she looks so darn cute. I make a mental note to get her dog license very soon.

We let Gemma and the Springer Spaniels out and stroll outside into the crisp fall air and bright sunshine. The breeze blows at a moderate clip today and sings through the tall trees edging the property. Dad has clearly seen us arrive out his window, as Ripley and Leda come running down to join us a few moments later. Leda dashes up to me in raptures of delight at our reunion. She leaps up in the air and spins a couple of quick circles. "Geez, girl. I'm happy to see you too. I can only imagine what kind of greeting I would get if I was gone for any longer!" Ripley follows more sedately, as befitting his status as the senior dog, but he is soon enticed by Gemma to take a galloping lap around the training yard chasing leaves. The three younger dogs run about checking out scents and leaping on each other. Cocoa is surprisingly not afraid of the boisterous puppies. I watch her closely, in case she thinks she is under attack, but their exuberance actually seems to reassure her. Once all the dogs have gotten out their excess energy, we troop up to Dad's cabin with the whole pack and the bag of sandwiches we picked up on the way back. Leda walks just beside my left leg shoving her head into my hand—just in case I don't know she's right next to me. I ruffle her ears and we jog to the cabin. As usual, I'm famished.

CHAPTER 60

Dad is actually standing and gazing out toward the Flatirons while trying to loosen up his back; he looks very solemn, which is not common for him. He has notepad pages with scrawled writing all over his desk and balled up pages spilling out of his trash basket. Clearly, he has been working hard on the password problem. "Hi, Dad. We brought food for a late lunch. Are you ready for a break?"

"You know it. My back feels like it was growing into the chair. I might have pulled a rib loose when I got up," he jokes. "I did take Leda and Ripley for a quick spin up the Marshall Mesa Trail while you guys were gone shopping for clothes. My brain needed an energy boost. You might be interested to learn the Open Space ranger was working that trail today and checked the dogs on their voice control. I got a lot of compliments on the fast recall I got from both dogs. She said they were the only two dogs that passed the test this week. I told her you train dogs for a living, so they better behave! She laughed and took a couple of your business cards that I had in my wallet. Then I started worrying about Randy again so we hightailed it back to the ranch. Anyway, thank heavens, rifle season for elk opens next week. I need to get my time in the woods."

"Ugh. I'm sorry that getting into those blasted thumb drive files is taking so long," I reply sympathetically. "We'll get Randy found and then you can head out to the high country for a week to recharge. For now, you keep walking and stretching out, I'll get the food and drinks on the table.

Michael can get the Springers into the soft-sided crates so we can eat with less ruckus." Dad likes this plan and wanders around swinging his arms back and forth and overhead while I get the sandwiches, chips, and pickles on the table alongside a pitcher of cold pink lemonade. He stops by his computer when he hears it give an alert tone generated by the outdoor surveillance system and he looks at his screens until he confirms it was just the mail carrier leaving our mail in the box at the bottom of the drive. Michael puts Butter and Scotch in their crates and puts Cocoa in a Down Stay near him where he can correct her if necessary. The three older dogs flop down for naps; watching humans eat is boring to them. (Training tip: this is how you can tell dogs who never get people food.) We fill Dad in on the extensive shopping trip as we engulf the specialty sandwiches of roast turkey with sliced apple and cheddar on sourdough bread. Not surprisingly, Dad comments at length on the necessity of wearing the right gear when you venture out into Nature. Michael smiles at him amiably and agrees. Wise choice.

As we polish off the last few kettle-cooked chips and sit back in our chairs, I ask, "Have you had any luck at all breaking that password on the last few files on the thumb drive, Dad?"

"No luck yet, but the program runs through dozens, if not hundreds, of combos in an hour. But it is certainly not National Security Agency-level code breaking. I really hope that Jonah can get the problem solved so we can review these files and figure out what may have prompted Randy's disappearance. I did take a look at one of the other accessible files on the thumb drive. Randy was working with a new company that helps farmers know exactly when and where to water their crops. The company makes solar-powered soil testers, which show how much water is in the soil. Then the irrigation system adjusts its settings based on that data, which reduces unnecessary water usage and improves crop yields. The product is just in its infancy and I can't find any reason it would be objectionable to anyone. So that file is ruled out. Tim also wanted you to know that the man spotted in Granby by a former workmate of Randy was found to be definitively not Randy.

"However, in the meantime, another clue came in via Tim about the helicopter pilot. Justin, the mechanic at the airfield near Walden, phoned the command team number he was given to call if he remembered anything else about the pilot, the helicopter, or the two men who picked the pilot up after repairs were arranged for. He suddenly recalled that when the pilot was counting off cash to pay the helicopter repair bill, he took a real estate agent's card out of his wallet and set it on the counter to get at his money more easily. It was one of those fancy business cards with a photo of the agent and the name of the real estate company and agent in big, bold font."

Leda gets up and sidles over to my chair when she sees we are done eating and are clearly going to be talking incessantly, like owners are wont to do. She puts her brown head in my lap and gazes up at me with her best serious expression. I rub her head and scratch under her chin. She closes her eyes blissfully. I smile down at her. No wonder owning a pet has been proven to lower people's blood pressure.

Dad continues, "The mechanic said he wasn't trying to be nosy, but he glanced a second time at the card because the female real estate agent was so attractive—long blond hair and blue eyes. Justin saw she worked for Your Home in the Mountains Realty out of Estes Park. He was relatively confident her name was Cindy Payson. The officer who got Justin's call then talked to Cindy at the realty company and she did recall a man with a military-style haircut and veteran's patch on his camo jacket stopping in her office over a month ago. That's an interesting point because that implies this pilot with the ex-military background has been in the Larimer County area for much longer than the last few days. He never specifically told her he was a pilot, however. He said his name was Stan Robinson. When questioned, she stated that to the best of her recollection, the guy had requested a print-out of listings she had for secluded hunting type cabins or camps in the county under $95,000. Stan made some vague comments about getting his buddies from the service together for annual reunions or hunting trips, and putting sweat equity into fixing up a place. He told her he had been stationed at Fort Carson in Colorado Springs.

"Cindy said she did not necessarily get a bad vibe from Stan, but he seemed very reserved. 'Didn't offer a lot of extra information' is how she put it. Since basic property listings are available on the website of every realty company in the United States, she did not see any problem with running him a short list of properties that fit his criteria. I received a copy of the listings Cindy provided to this Stan from Tim's contact on the investigative team. The investigative team officers are going to check those nine properties for any suspicious activity. With the permission of Tim, I called Cindy to question her further about her interaction with Stan. When we were chatting, she remembered one last detail. She also told Stan as an afterthought that she would be getting three more properties in a remote area to list for the sale of the building material *only*, in a week or so, and he could look them up on the website himself very soon. Cindy mentioned that she was thinking Stan might find it cool to buy a portion of this historic lumber and incorporate it into any renovations he and his buddies did later on a hunting camp. He pressed her for specific locations, but she could only offer what she knew since buyers were not to go and personally view them anyway. However, there's a kicker. And I have a theory if you will hear me out..."

CHAPTER 61

"The three properties are actually line cabins owned by the Forest Service in the Roosevelt National Forest east of the spot in the Comanche Peak Wilderness where you saw the helicopter. I did some research and discovered the Forest Service inherited the cabins when the national forest began as part of the Medicine Bow Forest Reserve in 1902 (later renamed in honor of Teddy Roosevelt). They were apparently constructed in the 1880s by a family of opportunistic miners who were convinced they were going to strike it rich by finding gold along several tributaries of Miller Fork to the northeast of Bulwark Ridge. The Forest Service has a legal obligation to make sure any structures left standing in the national forest don't pose a threat to the safety of people coming across them. But the National Historic Preservation Act also requires that an independent assessment be made to determine if the structures have historic significance prior to their removal. These cabins were deemed not worthy of saving, but the initial report recommended allowing citizens the option to purchase any original wood components at auction. This was to be an innovative way of repurposing the historic wood, making money for the Forest Service, and getting the decrepit cabins out of the woods. The three cabins were listed with the realty company so individuals could view photos online and then bid at an auction scheduled for the winter. The cabins would be dismantled next spring when the Forest Service crews could get in there past the snow and the wood transported out to Estes Park for the new owners to collect.

"In the time since Stan visited Cindy Payson and she told him to check the website, the Forest Service changed their mind and decided against the public sale. It's the government, so Cindy wasn't too surprised when they changed their mind arbitrarily without giving any real explanation. So… I'm thinking what if Stan now knows where these cabins are. If he was in the military, he would have had wilderness training and would know his way around the woods. He had several weeks to find the cabins. Maybe that's where they took Randy. It tracks with the direction the helicopter was spotted flying Friday by a number of my social media posting hikers. I have been plotting the sightings on this map tacked next to my desk. I even have another photo showing the tail number beginning with HC. It's fortuitous for us that this younger generation of hikers thinks it's vital to document every moment of their hikes, including minutiae like what type of socks they are wearing or what kind of snacks they eat during a break. I'm starting to feel like a dinosaur," he comments wryly.

"Get this—hikers on both the Signal Mountain Trail and the Indian Trail noted the blue helicopter with silver nose cone traveling overhead and continuing northeast across the Donner Pass Trail just as dusk was encroaching on Friday. Of course, this is air space where air travel is not prohibited, unlike the national park. When I plot the sightings, it all tracks with it heading toward one particular ridge. The listing on the realty company website gave approximate locations of the ancient cabins for informational purposes, but no exact coordinates because the prospective buyers were not to visit the cabins, simply bid on the raw historical materials based on the photos posted online. Even Cindy was unaware of where the three cabins exactly stand except for northeast of Bulwark Ridge, but she helped me as much as she could. She gave me the number for her contact person at the Forest Service. Just our luck, that person is on vacation diving in Indonesia for the next week and no one else in the office could provide me with a more detailed location.

"I finally decided to check online on the university's map archive and, lo and behold, I found one with an overlay for historic mining sites all around Larimer County—many so small they only included three or four miners' claims, and some about half as vast as Lulu City over in neighboring Grand County."

"Have you been able to pinpoint exactly where these cabins are yet, Dad?" I inquire. "Nobody can go blindly wading through the backcountry hoping to run across them. That's like looking for three needles in an 800,000-acre haystack."

"Glad you asked, daughter. Here's how I narrowed it down to this one ridge. I checked the information from the realty company indicating the general vicinity in the Roosevelt National Forest where they are located, cross-referenced with the archived map of mining sites from the university, skimmed a history of the national park and surroundings by a former ranger, and extrapolated coordinates from one topographical map for the watercourses in question. The former park ranger's book recounted a tale in which three brothers each put a cabin along an unnamed ridge, at the ends of three separate streams—which run north/south like the three spears of Neptune's trident.

"So, to make a long story short, I believe I have identified a ridge northeast of Bulwark Ridge where these cabins should be found. From the realty photos, two sites look more plausible as a place a helicopter could set down—clearer top story, adjacent meadows, and less pines. Tim and I were discussing why Randy was apparently abducted and it occurred to us that his pursuers must want something from him—maybe whatever material is secured on the thumb drive. Otherwise, they could have just killed him when they caught up with him in the moraine meadow to which Leda tracked him. It would make sense that they might take him to a secluded location until they get what they want. It may be a stretch, but we need something to pursue.

"Cindy sent me copies of the pictures from when the cabins were briefly listed on their website. They look like squat Lincoln Log boxes in the pictures—maybe eight rough-hewn logs from the ground to a flat roof and a single window with four panes on either side. Hard to imagine more than four people jamming into one of these abodes at night. It's probable they're spread along a four-mile swath of ridge overlooking the three Miller Fork tributaries. The cabins certainly were not much in the way of creature comforts, but they would keep the miners out of the worst of the weather. Just think how smoky it was if any type of fire was lit inside. Anyway, you can see crumbling rot on the crossed logs at the corners, decay between the logs, and the cabins settling into the ground with the weathering of the last 100 years impacting the structural integrity. One looks like a swaybacked, old, brown nag, aging and sinking closer to the Earth. A blown-up photo shows clumps of red Indian Paintbrush growing out of the crevices between logs. It looks like the wall is shooting off a line of magenta fireworks."

Michael, who has been listening intently, raises his hand like he was in a school classroom. A younger person who knows how to listen, rather than just talk all the time—he is going to be a phenomenal K-9 handler. And Dad is great at weaving together a story. Dad looks at Michael over the top of his reading glasses and beams.

"No need to raise your hand, son. Feel free to stop me any time. I do get carried away when I've been researching. Just ask Veronica."

"I grew up in Colorado," Michael begins with a grin, "but I never heard of Lulu City. Where the heck was that?" By this point, we have lulled all the dogs to sleep. Cocoa has her head on Michael's feet, Leda is snoring like a lumberjack, and the Springers are upside down on their backs in doggy dreamland.

"A number of miners moved into the region in the 1870s and 1880s convinced they were going to hit the mother lode of gold or silver along the North Fork of the Colorado River. Two Fort Collins businessmen founded Lulu City, naming it after one of their daughters, based on the hope of

216

silver strikes and processing tons of mineral-rich ore. They even organized a company with the fancy name of Middle Park and Grand River Mining and Land Improvement Company. It included a town site of 100 blocks, complete with streets, avenues, and platted lots. Now it lies disintegrating in the northwest section of RMNP.

"As many as 500 miners moved in, living in tents and newly built cabins. All the businesses necessary to support the miners moved in as well, including barbers, butchers, saloons, hardware stores, hotels, a general store, saw mills, even a dairy when 20 cows were brought in from Denver. Grandiose newspaper articles made promises of high yields of mineral wealth and a booming economy. The ore, in actuality, turned out to be low yielding and a smelter was never built to process what the miners were pulling out of the ground. Lulu City started the bust part of the cycle within a few short years, with the mines being abandoned by 1885. Coincidentally, the decaying cabins still present at the Lulu City site are very similar in age and condition to the ones which were listed for sale by Cindy's realty company in the Roosevelt National Forest. Picture a town being carved out of the wilderness, bustling and humming for four short years, and then just disintegrating as everyone essentially walked away from it. But that same scenario played out over and over across the West.

"The U.S. Forest Service in Colorado has been reviewing structures on its acreage statewide. Just a few years ago, they reviewed the status of six mining cabins in Aspen's backcountry, for example. They made a number of different decisions on those structures based on whether alterations, destruction, or removal of artifacts affected the cabins' historical value. One abode in Conundrum Valley was dismantled and the remaining wood distributed across the location. One cabin at Snowmass Ski Area was torn down with an original rock wall being scattered on site. And one cabin at a mill site in the ghost town of Ruby had partial walls left in situ. The historic assessment on the three cabins Cindy told me about deemed them not worthy of preservation. They were not part of a formal mining site and only housed members of the same small family for such a short period of years before they gave up and moved on. Over time, wilderness has reclaimed much of the area surrounding the cabin sites and not many people, except the rangers, even know they exist. At present, it seems they will most likely recommend knocking these cabins down and dispersing the wood components on site."

CHAPTER 62

I ponder all this new information and then question Dad, "So with all that background in mind, how do you feel about Leda and me going to check out these cabins, while you continue working on the thumb drive issue? When you crack it, you need to review those files posthaste. Michael can take care of all the dogs for us. It may be a wild goose chase, but it is a loose end which ought to be checked."

Dad considers my request for a moment and answers a bit hesitantly, "Well, I am reluctant to send you by yourself. In an effort to shake loose anything that might help us, Tim has started to run standard background checks on the relatives of the incarcerated murderer in the Virginia case, the owners and employees of Agua Pura Ahora, S.A., and Billy Fulton's friends and defense attorneys, after the sensationalized interviews about Chardonnay's character they've been giving to the media. Unfortunately, he texted me that he got called to a violent assault case in Niwot, so he won't be available to accompany you on this cabin reconnaissance. I want you to be safe. And Michael isn't in the kind of shape yet where we can send him haring across the mountainside."

He glances at his computer screen. "The program has checked 2,460 possible passwords so far. How many more permutations of Randy's favorite sports teams and childhood street name can there be?" he groans in disgust. "Why don't you and Michael take the dogs out and do a short obedience session and I'll consider the advisability of you checking out this lead and how safe it would be."

"Okay, Dad, we'll go work with the dogs, but remember, searching is what Bruce trained Leda and me for. He even had me do searches on my own to cover just this eventuality. I'm in great physical shape now and can handle this. I'll just check out the cabins from a distance with Leda; you taught me how to move through the woods unobserved. One thing to consider though is hunting season. It will be tough to safely go incognito in the woods with hunters dispersed throughout the wilderness. What big game seasons are open now in that Game Management Unit?"

Dad responds thoughtfully, "I've actually thought of that and I reviewed the open seasons online again to confirm what I was remembering. There's actually a three-day window where no game seasons are open there, starting tomorrow. It seems quite fortuitous. The state put a few gaps in the hunting seasons this year due to the loss of game populations from the various forest fires we've had in the past two years. If you're going to go, now is the safest time."

"Of course you already thought of that," I chuckle. "I should go, Dad. I'll even agree to take the long-range spy binoculars." We both laugh, but his laughter sounds a bit forced to me. He's probably thinking about what happened in Ohio and if he can bring himself to send me on this search. It's a balancing act for him between keeping me safe and wanting me to be confident and successful in my new profession. I know what he's thinking because the exact same thoughts are running through my mind. This search needs to happen though. Randy's life could be hanging in the balance.

CHAPTER 63

Michael and I leave Dad to consider the possible mission and stroll down to the training building. The afternoon is waning quietly and peacefully, with a soft breeze and that lovely golden light which comes only in autumn. "Are you sure you want to go by yourself to check out the cabins tomorrow? I wish I could go with you. Be useful, you know." Michael asks me softly as we get training collars on the Springers.

"You will be useful, Michael. It takes a load off my mind when I know you will be in charge of the dogs in my absence. This is exactly what I need from you. And Dad can focus on the encryption. Bruce Macklin trained us to handle all sorts of scenarios, and I spent loads of time in the woods with my father growing up. Last but not least, I have Leda as backup. She's pretty formidable, you know. Once we're done with this case, we'll get you going on the obstacle course training and hiking." He looks somewhat unconvinced still, so I distract him from his worries by conducting brisk lessons with the Springers and then Gemma and Cocoa.

With two of us, the work moves along efficiently but not totally smoothly. Butter has decided to forget his Down command completely and ricochets off the walls with uncontained energy—an occupational hazard when working with young dogs. He really is the cutest boy, even when he's defiant. Butter loves heeling so we work on that with treats and praise. He burns off a smidgen of that excess energy and settles down eventually. Then we go back to the Down command and work him through it from the very starting position. Butter wants to please, so he finally gets a solid Down—for today.

"You know Michael, the Springers are actually doing really well for beginning obedience. You can't expect dog training to always go smoothly. Patience and repetition are the primary resources of a good trainer. The next command we will start to train is the Stand Stay, which is useful for examination visits to the vet."

The boarding dogs go back in their runs to relax before dinner and Michael helps me stow my supplies in a bigger backpack. We go through each piece carefully and check for damage to any items, including Leda's harness, the long line, and the water bottles. He grabs extra water purification tablets from the storage area, as well as six green glow sticks for evening use, a massive pack of gauze (useful for staunching bleeding, as I do have a tendency to get scraped up), several 4" x 6" adhesive bandages, and my favorite human treat, chocolate chip granola bars. Michael rummages through sample size bags of Leda's dog food and places five in the backpack. Overstocking is good. That trait comes directly from my parent.

We search through the tubs of supplies the twins had created after sorting through the miscellaneous gear living in the apartment before Michael came along. A camouflage neck gaiter is hiding in here somewhere. It's perfect for pulling up over my face to keep my skin covered to stay better hidden. I pull it out triumphantly and wave it around my head wildly in looping circles. "Success. It had to be in here somewhere!"

Michael starts smiling. "That seems like a massive overreaction to finding a piece of fabric. Is it like the Cloak of Invisibility?" A Harry Potter fan. I'm liking this kid better and better every day.

"Ha. Very funny," I reply. "No magical properties, but it can help hide me. God forbid." I show Michael how it pulls up from being scrunched down around my neck to cover my whole neck and face. "Hard to see the face of a person laying low in the foliage, right?" I ask him and he nods. "If I have learned nothing else in this world from my dad, the one thing I'll pass on to you is that you can never be too prepared for heading out into the wilderness. Plan ahead and it just may save your life one day."

Michael looks at me seriously. "All this preparation makes me think that you *are* planning on going tomorrow…" he tails off.

"I have got to go, Michael. The puzzling helicopter is the thread *we're* following in this narrative, while the police investigators check so many other details. We have to follow our own trail in life." He feeds the boarding dogs in their kennel runs while I finish packing my gear into my SUV. I pull out a George Thorogood CD from the glove box and load it in the player ready for driving. It feels like time for a hit of *I Drink Alone* and *One Bourbon, One Scotch, One Beer*—which is kind of hilarious since I don't drink.

Our friendly neighborhood pine squirrel chitters his way back and forth across the acre behind the dog yard intent on extremely important rodent business. His tail stands up like a paintbrush dipped in rust-colored paint. His antics bring a smile to my face. "You won't be this bold when the dogs are out here, bucko!" Quick texts to Heather Porter and the Duncans are tapped out with updates on their dogs' training, and then I get ready to plead my case for going on a cabin search to Dad.

CHAPTER 64

Back at the cabin, Dad looks like he's deep in thought, so I grab a hairbrush and start dragging it through my tangle of curls. Might as well do something productive while waiting for him to speak first. Geez. It's like a rat's nest in there today.

Dad finally starts talking, "Ronnie, you have convinced me that you and Leda can get this done safely. I'm not totally thrilled, but I have faith in your abilities—if you promise to be very, very careful. While you were gone, I programmed the three likely cabin sites into this handheld GPS. Remember this is product review week for GPS units, so I had a bunch to pick from. This one has the viewing screen which is easiest to read, can upload topographical maps, and can store up to 100 marked locations. And, even under thick tree cover or down in the canyons, it has excellent satellite connectivity.

"Unfortunately, you cannot approach starting at the southern terminus of the Miller Fork Trail due to the closure of the first mile and a half of the trail by the Forest Service. This past spring's flood in that section created a massive washout area. So, I plotted a slightly circuitous course for you to take from the Bulwark Ridge Trail, to the Indian Trail, to the Miller Fork Trail—north of the washout—then to the Donner Pass Trail until you cut cross country to the east to find the ridge in question. Once you leave the trail, it is unclear how long travel will take, but the cabins each appear to be spaced about a half mile to a mile apart along the ridgeline.

"Then you can return the way you came to the Donner Pass Trail. A couple of hours of steady hiking and you should be able to ease in, surveil the locations, and slide back out. It should be fairly obvious even from your vantage point in the tree line if any activity has been occurring at each cabin, or if it looks like a helicopter has set down in the meadow. These are not permanent abodes, so smoke or lights will be a dead giveaway. The high-resolution binoculars they sent me last week to be reviewed are going with you as well. These are lightweight, but will give you an expansive field of view and razor-sharp images at eight times magnification up to 300 yards away from the target. These retail for $2600, by the way. Good thing they gave me a demo pair for free! I will download the Cairn app on your cell phone, which shows through crowdsourcing where other hikers on these trails have been able to get cell coverage in case you need any assistance. It will also show me real-time location tracking so I can follow your progress. Your trails will be inputted on the map in the application and it is set to send me text alerts as you hit the various checkpoints."

I start laughing but don't even get the word "Overkill" out before Dad continues on. "Before you say anything, I will go to any lengths to use modern technology to protect my only child. Also, I've pulled a pile of medium weight camouflage gear out of the closet for you. Leda is brown so she'll blend right in. Don't put her Working Dog vest on. You don't want to look official if anyone sees you, just like a day hiker. If you see anything at all, retreat to a safe area with cell service, and we'll get the forest rangers in there. They are tied up with that lightning fire over near West White Pine Mountain right at the moment, but if you spot suspicious activity, they or the Larimer County Sheriff will get assistance to you. I am worried about the outlook for Randy if we don't find him soon. He has been missing without a trace for four days now. But if Randy is there, Leda will smell him."

I cast an amused look over at Dad. "Well, kudos to you for figuring out a way to force a GPS unit *and* a new cell phone app on me. Why do I feel like this hike is about to become part of a product review article? You know I'm more of a map and compass kind of girl."

Dad answers smugly, "I anticipated this response and have also marked a trail route and the three probable cabin locations on a laminated hiker's map for you. If you prefer, you can go about this the old-school way. But at least take the GPS. Better to be overprepared. And I rustled up a can of bear spray for you to clip to your pack."

"Well, I'm all for multiple resources. It must run in the family." I say consideringly. "It's too late in the afternoon for me to drive up past Glen Haven and start hiking from the Bulwark Ridge Trail today, so it will be best to get there bright and early tomorrow morning. It looks like I'm going to be racking up the miles tomorrow. But it should be a nice day to take a jaunt through the woods. Show me what you've got programmed into this fancy GPS."

Dad and I look at the course plotted on the GPS and then we lay the map on the table and he shows me the marked route to the ridge. It is always easier for me to visualize where I am going in the wilderness when I have seen it laid out on a physical map. My brain absorbs the information and retains a picture of where I am headed much better than blindly following the step by step turns of a GPS. Luckily, I do have a wonderful sense of direction, which helps keep me from getting turned around in the wilderness very often. My childhood friends in Ohio used to call me the Human Compass because when it was time to head home for supper, I always knew which way to aim to get us out of the woods. Sometimes we went right through a swamp, but as the crow flies, I took us straight out of there.

Sylvia texts me to say she won't make it to yoga tomorrow. She is helping victims in a major sex trafficking case prepare their victim impact statements for the trial of the notorious trafficker who lured them away from their homes via a false persona created on the Internet, and then abducted and sold them. Sylvia is the best at her job and never gives any client less than her full attention. I text her back: "No worries. Kick butt in court. Will be gone myself tomorrow and am getting ready tonight. Fill you in later." Smiley face emoji with heart eyes. Dad's love for the emojis is definitely rubbing off on me.

Tomorrow is going to bring with it a lot of tough hiking, but hopefully answers to the mysteries we've been investigating. Gazing outside over to the Flatirons, I admire the calmness of their immobile faces. I wish I felt that calm about my trip tomorrow, but can't shake a little shadow of foreboding. Something serious has happened to Randy and it feels like we have eliminated lots of possibilities without actually pinpointing the cause of his disappearance. Whoever has him has the advantage over us. This feeling of seeking in the dark is not reassuring. I wander into the bathroom to use the mirror, with Leda padding along behind me. She follows me everywhere. It took a little getting used to. At times, I forget and turn around so fast to go get something that I almost flip over her. She'll look at me in disbelief. *Why can the human not remember this routine?* I pat her neck, while leaning on the wooden window sill. I slowly pull the brush through the ends of my hair; it feels much more controlled at long last and I twist it up in a bun and shove clips around the base to secure it. I rest my forehead against the window pane as the loneliness of life weighs on me for a moment.

Thoughtfully, I take out my cell phone and do something I haven't done in months. Scrolling through my folder of photos of Zach, I flip over to my favorite. Zach is smiling with his arm around Leda, dressed in his camo gear and ready to meet my dad to go grouse hunting. His brown eyes are so sincere and warm. You wouldn't even have to know him to feel the force of his personality shining through in this photo. He was one of the truly good people in this world—no rage or hostility, just a kind, supportive, fair, even-keeled guy who loved his family, me, Leda, and his Cleveland Cavaliers. Dead for nothing because of a spiteful man who was just his opposite. Tears fill my eyes and the pain hits me like an arrow under the ribs. I feel a sudden fierce longing for my murdered love, but then gradually, a sense of calm starts to envelop me. I know he is sending me the strength to go search for Randy. He seems to whisper in my ear. "You have the skills, Ronnie. Have faith in Leda and yourself. Randy needs your help."

CHAPTER 65

Feeling partially composed, I return to the living room to study the hiking map and my target area in the national forest. I notice that an expansive swath of private land, or inholdings, is located to the south of the three parallel tributaries Dad has identified as places of interest. An inholding is privately owned land inside the boundary of public lands, that has been privately held since a time prior to the formation of the public lands entity. Of course, a number of the national forests were established over 100 years ago, but certain private lands may have been owned by the same family for even longer and were not available for purchase by the government when the public lands were "created."

Further review of the topo map indicates that my elevation gain should be around 2000 feet. That's a good, steady uphill climb, but not too brutal. Leda and I practiced with Bruce on one eight-hour search that had an elevation gain in excess of 6000 feet—twice. My legs were tired to the point of shaking after that one, but that was before yoga and snowshoeing came into my life. After my first snowshoe up an iced-over waterfall near Nederland, absorbing the sun and cold and silence, I was hooked forever. The view over the frosty upper reaches of the canyon and the gigantic pines with ice crystal-bejeweled limbs, and continuing down the snowy valley was incredible. The stillness was complete. It's a great way to enjoy the out-doors in the winter, and get up into the high country by gliding over the top of the snow, rather than breaking trail with just your boots. It also burns a bunch of calories, so guilt-free hot chocolate and donuts later, of course.

Michael has collected the dogs and lined them up next to each other on the big, braided rag rug in the living room. He places them in Down Stays. I watch with interest from my vantage point leaning over the desk where I'm studying the map. Dad is in the kitchen gathering his provisions together to start food prep. He's pulled out tilapia and red potatoes to throw on the grill. Michael gets full points for taking the initiative to work with the canines. Leda gazes over from her position reclining against the back of my thighs (where else) and also waits to see what activities are going to engage the rest of the pack. Michael has gotten a handful of hot dog treats from the fridge where a bag is always stashed. Scotch starts to half rise from his Down, but Michael is watching out of the corner of his eye and gives him the command again immediately. Scotch sinks back down and whines. "No. Hush," Michael reinforces. Scotch subsides and looks woefully upward fighting against the severe pangs of hunger wracking his body. I'm being facetious.

Michael places a treat about six inches in front of each dog and tells him or her to Leave It. Ripley and Gemma know how this works and set their heads on their paws in resignation. The younger dogs stare at their treats with intense focus, but stay put. One at a time Michael moves down the line and gives each dog their release word. Finally, hot dogs. He trains the command an additional two times then releases and praises the dogs. He really seems to be a natural at this. Just as he's finishing the training session and we sit down on the floor amongst the dogs and distribute Kong toys to them, Tim calls my cell phone.

"Hi stranger. You're on speaker with Dad and Michael too. How is everything going in Niwot?

"Not too bad right this second, as a matter of fact," he begins. "We finally got the statements from all parties involved in this fight at the antique store. Apparently, they believe that since they're in an unincorporated part of Boulder County, they can be uncooperative. We just persuaded the best buddy to give up the initial instigator's current destination. It's believed he lit out for Gold Hill in a truck he swiped from the parking lot, so I'm headed over there now to try to round him up. Two men who ended up in the hospital have been upgraded to good condition at present. I have never before in my life seen a fight start over a load of dang antiques.

"The suspect drove his pickup right through the front door of the antique emporium and started screaming that the owner defrauded him over some Queen Anne tilt-top tea tables. He then started bashing up the emporium's inventory with a crow bar. What is this world coming to? I don't even know what a genuine cabriole leg is, do you? Anyway, by the time the store patrons, the owner's sons, and the crazed driver's passenger got involved and pulled out about 37 open carry and concealed carry weapons, it was like Niwot reverted to its old days as a railroad town. Two guys got shot, one in the butt cheek and the other in the armpit. Thank God these lunatics can't shoot worth a lick. Fifty mirrors were shattered with glass all across the floor, and a cabinet full of bizarre antique dolls with lace dresses out the wazoo was decimated in the cross fire. I'm gonna have a nightmare about that mess for sure.

"The store owner sprayed the passenger with a fire extinguisher while he was busting up a cabinet full of Limoges china with a tire iron, so that dimwit is going to need an appointment at the ophthalmologist— after he gets the dent in his head stitched up from the braining he took from the empty extinguisher. Stuffing from two antique fainting couches was floating through the air like snow. The only things to make it out of the fight unscathed were the damn tea tables and a ventriloquist's dummy scavenged out of someone's curb trash that very morning. Just sitting there in the truck bed as snug as you please. How does the creepy dummy not get wasted in this scenario? I don't even want to think about the insurance claims coming out of this fiasco. We wrote 24 tickets, confiscated 11 guns, and arrested five men and four women. They were ANTIQUING!"

By this point in Tim's narrative, Michael and I are actually rolling on the floor trying to hold in our guffaws, but it's no use. Tim's Irish roots are definitely showing. I literally have tears pouring down my face from laughing and Michael has his hand pressed over his mouth from trying so hard not to crack up—to no avail. Dad, who has been listening from the kitchen breakfast bar, is shaking his head in either amazement or disbelief with a big grin on his face. Being the good guy he is, my dad's first question is to make sure that all the police officers came out of it okay.

"Yep, Bob," Tim reassures us. "Thanks for asking. No bodily injuries, but like I said, it's hard to unsee those decapitated dolls." That does it. Michael and I are hysterical with laughter at this point. There's no reining it in. I realize suddenly that I haven't laughed like this in almost three years. It feels good and another sliver of the ice that Tommy Arnett deposited in my soul melts and evaporates away. Dad looks over at me with an expression on his face that's hard to describe. It's almost relief. I realize how much worry he has held inside over the violence in Ohio and the damage it did to me. I beam at him happily and he looks reassured for the time being.

CHAPTER 66

Tim goes on to tell us that he'll be tied up the next day on this antique emporium mess, and then he'll be going through more background checks on multiple parties related to Randy Jeffers. But he wants to pass on an update. "The D.A. just called me to say that Billy Fulton never showed for his game against the Los Angeles Clippers tonight and his coaching staff can't locate him or the 'Rhodes scholars' he runs with. His coaches didn't worry at first when he didn't get to the arena for early stretching and warm-ups. Billy isn't exactly known for his promptness apparently. The assistant coach who contacted the police after nobody could locate Billy around the hotel said they initially believed it was just part of Billy's usual flakiness. Then he failed to show for the actual game. They sent the strength and conditioning coach to the hotel and the manager let him into Billy's room. His belongings were gone and the room left in disarray as if someone departed in a hurry. The coach had the good idea to check with hotel management on the members of Billy's entourage whom he had brought along, on his dime, of course, to see if they were gone as well. And, sure enough, they're all gone too.

"His defense attorneys claim to have no clue where Billy could be. They indicated that Billy is well aware that he is out on that exorbitant bail amount with the agreement that he stay with his team at all times and engage in basketball activities only. I have no idea why, but the team was allowing him to hang out with his traveling buddies as long as they stayed right in the hotel complex in each city. None of this made the hotel management in the various cities too happy; his friends have been known to trash hotel rooms. Certain people never grow up, I guess. Now the detectives assigned to the murder case are trying to track Billy and his buddies through their cell phones. I'm betting none of them are bright enough to turn them off, which is a bonus. His lead defense attorney, Rod Jaycock, claims Billy is absolutely not fleeing. Billy apparently told Jaycock, and I'm quoting here, he is 'mega stressed out from the Colorado cops trying to question him and harassing his friends over the missing nerd.' Interesting that he doesn't seem to be stressed out by the strange death of his wife less than a year ago, for which he is about to be tried in court. It's a good thing he can play basketball because I literally don't think he could hold another job with that level of intelligence! And now, he's not turned up for basketball."

"Has the judge in the murder case been apprised that Billy skipped town?" I inquire. "His release conditions were very specific and the judge is not going to be happy that Billy is roaming loose with his idiotic friends. Billy did not have prior violence in his past, just stupidity, which is most likely why he set the bail amount at all. Only a pro athlete could have paid a figure as high as that one."

Tim responds, "The judge does know, and livid is the description the District Attorney used. His basketball team assured the judge they would take responsibility for Billy Fulton. No point in putting an ankle monitor on him because it has been shown in many cases that ended in disaster that no one in authority is actually monitoring the monitors. Nothing like a domestic abuser out on bond wearing the ankle monitor while he goes and finishes off his spouse. This job will really get to you sometimes. Regardless, where does a 6'10" pro athlete think he's going to go that nobody will recognize him? He doesn't have a passport. The whole thing is ludicrous. So, that muddies the waters a bit with regard to Randy Jeffers, but as soon as I wind up the case of the Niwot Doll Massacre, I have 20 background checks to get through that could potentially find another lead for us on Randy."

"Okay, Tim," I reply. "We'll let you go and itemize the doll casualties." He snorts in amused exasperation at this waste of his time. "I know Dad mentioned this theory to you on the old cabins in Roosevelt National Forest. I'm going to leave early tomorrow morning and take a hike up there with Leda just to locate them and check them out. Henry Akers told Dad that the deputies discovered no odd activity at the first two properties they checked on from the MLS print-out of nine remote properties which Cindy Payson had given to the pilot, Stan. The deputies will get to the rest of that list as soon as they can. That really only leaves the decaying, and even more remote, Forest Service cabins to be eliminated as a place where Randy might be stashed. The Larimer and Grand County search teams are still looking for those four missing hikers between Mount Bryant and Isolation Peak, and the forest rangers are just getting that fire contained that was started by lightning on West White Pine Mountain. So, we figure we can at least eliminate these cabins for you. Dad has me loaded up with enough gear to rival even James Bond. He's hard at work on the thumb drive and Michael is in charge of canine management." I am definitely trying to downplay the hike so Tim does not feel guilty about being unavailable to accompany me. Tim sounds a bit distracted and his shoulder radio crackles with dialogue in the background.

"You and Leda stay alert. Reconnaissance only, right? And check in with your dad every time you have cell coverage. Anyway, those cabins have to be so decrepit and hard to find that it's a very long shot that our bad guys have any use for them. But it's good to rule them out if possible. I have to go. The D.A. is on the line. Probably about Billy Fulton being on the run. I can only imagine when the national media gets a hold of that tidbit. Be careful!"

CHAPTER 67

"Well, that's a turn of events," my dad offers in a droll understated tone. "I wonder where in the heck Billy and his entourage think they're off to now? I find it somewhat inexplicable. If Billy did arrange for Randy to be taken, what made him get squirrelly and bolt now? Do you think it just dawned on him that it looks vaguely suspicious that the star expert witness for the Prosecution has disappeared into thin air? They do seem like a bunch of guys who never grew up; they do absurd things and worry about the consequences later. But harming Chardonnay and Randy would put them at a whole new level of bad behavior. Have they suddenly realized they're in deep trouble? Okay, I'm just talking to myself," he finishes with a puzzled look on his face as he retreats to the kitchen. Michael rounds up the dogs and heads outside while I go into the kitchen where Dad is chopping up onions into big slices with a vengeance.

"You're right, Dad. This whole disappearance is just really frustrating. Sylvia and I were so thrilled when Leda found the thumb drive at Moraine Park Discovery Center. Now we're stymied again, but we all know the key to unlocking this mystery has got to be on that thumb drive. Otherwise, why hide it? Why don't you try calling Patty Jeffers to find out if she can give you any more key phrases to use in the code breaking program that might lead to Randy's password? Maybe she'll remember something of value. It's disappointing that Jonah hasn't cracked it yet. It's more his area of expertise than yours. We can eat dinner and then you can get back to it while I finish getting ready to leave early in the morning."

He hands me the platter with the potatoes and onions to carry out to the grill, and follows me with the tilapia, paprika in hand. "That's a good plan, Ronnie. I just need to rest my brain and then hit the computer again. You go ahead and set the table and get drinks while I arrange this stuff on the grill." Leda dances over to me, happy that we were only separated for five minutes, and flashes her Chessie smile up at me. Another good thing about having a dog; they are always, always happy to see you. That's a guarantee you don't get with too many other things in life.

Dad grills the food up quickly with his characteristic efficiency and we sit down on the patio while evening settles slowly in the background, a lovely violet tinge to the sky. The dogs take up their positions in a ring around us with Gemma and Cocoa leaning up against each other. The air is only slightly chilly at the moment and carries a refreshing pine scent. Dad and Michael have flannel shirts and I have on one of Zach's Sheriff Department sweatshirts, so we are comfortable enough. There is something so pleasant about eating outside in the fresh air; we drag the season out as long as possible. When we finally abandon the grill and patio for indoor eating, we have accepted that winter is moving in on us inexorably. I ask Michael if he can do just basic training with the dogs tomorrow morning and he readily agrees.

"Oh, by the way, when I get back from this search, we need to go get you a cell phone. That way I can be in touch with you about whatever the dogs may need without running everything through Dad. He is busy too with his articles, so we won't be disturbing him. And Lizzie texted me to say she has printed out the scholarship applications for community college. Their home printer finally cooperated. She will be over tomorrow to fill out those forms with you for submission before the looming deadlines. They have soccer matches tomorrow and school, of course, but she will be here."

Michael looks pleased. "How much will I need to save for a cell phone?"

"You won't need to pay anything for it. It will be a business expense, so we will run it through the company. I need to be able to reach you at any time. All you have to do is pick out which one you want, within reason, and a case for it." He nods happily and applies himself to the massive heaping of vegetables Dad has dished out for him. I have a sneaking suspicion our grocery bill is going to skyrocket. You know what they saying about growing boys.

After a thoroughly enjoyable dinner, I decline Michael's offer to help clean up and he takes the boarding dogs back to the kennel for the evening. He indicates he would like to watch the baseball play-off game tonight, so Dad loads him up with a bag of snacks and several cans of pop for later in the evening. It must be a novelty for Michael to get time and space to himself for the first time since he entered foster care six years ago and he seems to be thoroughly enjoying his own place. Dad and I work together to clear the table and wash the dishes. I sit with Leda on the braided rag rug running a comb through her curly hair and Dad makes a quick phone call to Patty Jeffers. He asks her for any additional phrases Randy might have used for the password on the thumb drive. It's apparent she does indeed have further ideas as Dad grabs his pen and starts writing rapidly for a minute or two. He thanks her and tells her before he hangs up that Leda and I have one lead we will be checking out tomorrow. He turns to me and says, "I didn't want to get her hopes up too much, but she believes in you and your dog."

"No pressure then, right, Dad?" I give him an ironic look. "Leda and I are searching for one lone guy in the middle of hundreds of thousands of acres—if he is even still in the area." He laughs ruefully, "I know. I know. But tomorrow may bring us renewed enthusiasm. Never give up, honey." He's clearly talking about more than just this situation, but I'm too tired to think about it and ready to head to bed.

I give Dad a kiss on the cheek as he sits back down at his computer freshly galvanized to work again, and then give Ripley a scratch around the ears on my way out the door. He licks my chin and looks up at me with his sweet Golden Retriever face before settling down under the desk in his favorite position on Dad's feet. It sure beats the hell out of a chain and a dirt circle and neglect.

Leda and I walk slowly up to the former day spa checking out the stars as we go. I feel vaguely unsettled tonight, so lie down on my living room carpet and do a series of gentle stretching exercises while Leda keeps me company by vigorously chewing her Nylabone. We have work to do tomorrow and need our rest. I get ready for bed, unpin my hair from its bun, and brush my teeth. Leda chews her last biscuit of the night and plops down on her blue-and-green plaid dog bed in the bedroom with a contented sigh. I fall asleep thinking of Zach, and thoughts of him must cast a spell of protection over me, as I sleep dreamlessly and deeply for the first time in ages.

CHAPTER 68

My alarm wakes me early and I jolt awake sure something important has been missed. It takes a moment before I orient myself and my heart stops pounding. An alarm clock has been mostly unnecessary since I left my legal job. It startles the dickens out of me on the few occasions when I have had to use it. Leda stands next to the bed wagging her tail amiably. "Nice to see you so calm, girl. How come that thing doesn't scare the crap out of *you* when it erupts?" She has no idea what I'm saying, of course, but it seems like an opportune time to hop up on the bed and burrow around like a gopher. By the time I'm done laughing at her and she's got her head on my pillow looking ever so innocent, my heart has finally stopped thudding.

Time to face the day, ready for action. She jumps down and gives a shake while I stand up and give a stretch. After Leda goes out for a quick potty break and gets her kibble, I enjoy a brief hot shower and then start to get dressed, while running through all the gear in my head that was packed yesterday. You only want to forget your sunscreen one time before a ten-hour search and you'll never do it again. To say I looked like a tomato at the end of the search would be a gross understatement.

The weather report on my phone looks decent. Sunny with possible high clouds later in the day. Temps in the high 50s, which is perfect for brisk hiking without Leda or me getting too warm. An afternoon thunderstorm at elevation is a distinct possibility almost any day, that's why cautious hikers climbing the big peaks start obscenely early in the morning—so they can get down from the top before any lightning strikes. It is autumn, however, so the chances are somewhat diminished. I pull on the medium weight jeans, short-sleeved T-shirt, and finally long-sleeved T-shirt (all camouflage) that Dad got out of storage. I grab my down vest (also camo) to throw in the car. Sitting at the kitchen counter, I eat a banana and a strawberry yogurt while waiting for my hair to dry enough to use the blow dryer. I'm still hungry, so eat a bagel, too, for good measure. Leda gets bored and sinks to the floor in disgust. She knows through her dog telepathy that we are going off to work—just not quickly enough to satisfy her. Now she's casting mournful eyes up at me. Oh, the guilt trip. I laugh at her as I finish my breakfast and then dry my hair quickly and braid it to keep it out of my face while we're searching. Last but not least, my camo Cleveland Cavaliers hat. Yes, you can buy those. "Now, we're ready to go, Miss Impatient." She surges to her feet and rockets to the door, dancing in circles while I gather my last bits of gear.

We stop off at Dad's as his desk lamp is shining brightly through the window. "Good morning, Ronnie. All ready for the great decrepit cabin search?" I have honestly never seen my dad in a bad mood more than three times in my life. How does he do it? Driving in traffic is enough to make me grouchy for a good half-hour, minimum. Don't get me wrong, he can be dead serious, like during the murder trial, but he is a person who enjoys life and makes the best of everything. I aspire to that state of calm, but realistically, will never get there. However, yoga is helping. Last week, some aging yuppie in a Land Rover tailgated me viciously all the way up Baseline Road, and I kept it down to a single swear word. Dad hands me a go cup of hot chocolate and double-checks with me regarding the gear stowed in my backpack in the SUV.

"I'm ready, Dad. I'll check in with you at the start of the Bulwark Ridge Trail to see if Tim has called with any updates and to let you know when we start hiking. As long as there is service, I'll send you texts once I find the cabins."

"Sounds good. You and Leda take care of each other," he replies. "I'm going to keep working on the password and I'll help Michael with any dog questions." And with that, Leda and I are off. She jumps in the back of the SUV, George Thorogood fills the air with his distinctive voice and guitar, and we start driving north.

Dawn is coming up as we head toward Estes Park, its little tendrils of light edging the dark horizon. The sky lightens moment by moment, as more details emerge on the edges of the road. I sip my hot chocolate and am thrilled to taste nutmeg in there. (He really is an awesome father.) It's early for commuters so we make good time as I sing along to George T. and then the incredible Alison Moyet. Leda takes exception to my rendition of *Invisible* and cuts loose with a howl. As a backup singer, she's not got much to recommend her. On the other hand, she may be trying to drown me out. We swoop down into Estes Park and make our turn behind the Stanley Hotel with its dramatic Lumpy Ridge backdrop and get onto Devils Gulch Road.

Should I ever win the lottery, buying a property on this road will be a priority. It truly is magnificent and magical with stunning views of Longs Pike and the Continental Divide. Randomly distributed colossal rock outcroppings and seasonal streams make it feel almost otherworldly. The rock outcroppings with a tree growing out of the middle of them sure are tenacious! Soon, we swoop down the switchbacks that drop the road dramatically and glide thorough Glen Haven. The mercantile in this tiny hamlet has the most scrumptious cinnamon rolls; I make a mental note to grab a half dozen on my way home from this assignment. It's always good to have a treat to look forward to. Leda looks like a surfer in the back until we get around the first curve, then to my relief, she drops down to the floor of the cargo area for safety. We pick up Dunraven Glade Road and head more slowly toward the trailhead.

Just then, an incoming call comes through. "Hi Dad. Everything okay at the ranch?"

"Ronnie, listen to me. I just got through the password!" The elation, and the exhaustion, are obvious in my father's voice.

"Really? That's great," I exclaim. "What did the trick?"

"Actually, it was your suggestion to talk to Patty Jeffers again last night that worked the magic. I plugged in a few more phrases from her and the program just hit on the right combination about 30 minutes ago. It involved the niece's pet's name, the Nittany Lions, and the first street the Jeffers lived on after they got married. Oh, and a double ampersand at the end. Patty said he always laughs at that word; he thinks it's such a funny word for a bit of punctuation. I had asked her which one he would be likely to use in her opinion. Anyway, I digress. I called Tim first and he is calling Jonah so the investigative team can look at the files too. The D.A. has been apprised and is champing at the bit. Now everyone can get to work reviewing the remaining files and stop worrying about enraged freshwater mussel enthusiasts.

"Tim told me that Henry Akers would like me to peruse the files too, since I've been very helpful to this point, so I'm officially investigating. There are four files in the section of the thumb drive that was password protected. They are entitled Billy Fulton, Idaho drowning, Agua Pura Ahora, S.A., and an odd one, Chad E. I pulled up the Billy Fulton one first and it is a stupendous amount of data. So, I need to get reviewing, but we may have a chance now to get a solid lead. Oh, and Michael fed the dogs and is getting ready to do basic training later this morning."

"That's awesome news. If anyone can dig out a clue by researching, it is definitely you, Dad. Good luck and I'll text you when I reach cabin one—the one built by the brother named Mortimer. Poor guy." We say our goodbyes and I tell Leda, "Now we're finally making headway, girl. You and I have to come up with a contribution today." Leda snuffles my braid through the grate and her warm breath wafts across my neck. "Ahh, that tickles, you silly. Cool it," I laugh at her antics and feel a surge of positive energy as we pull into the trailhead.

CHAPTER 69

Climbing out of the driver's seat, I straighten up with a stifled grunt. I must be harboring more inner tension over the puzzling disappearance of Dr. Jeffers than I realized. A few deep knee bends, plus Mountain Pose into Warrior 1 Pose held for several minutes, and my muscles feel a lot looser. Leda waits eagerly in the back of the SUV for me to let her out. I use the quick release button on my belt to swing the tailgate open for a test. It swings up readily and Leda stands with her toes poised on the edge waiting for me to say "Yes!" She leaps down and spins around like a fish on a line while her harness goes on. It would be much easier if she would stand still, but I am careful not to dampen her enthusiasm for working. That is the key to a successful working dog; they need to love it. I leave her Working Dog vest in the car and adjust my backpack on my shoulders. The ones that come with extra padding on the straps are highly preferable. (I really do make out like a bandit when Dad does product reviews for outdoor magazines.) Our water supply looks great. We're good to go. I swipe on my sunscreen and lip balm, and position my neck gaiter loosely around my neck. Leda is attached to an eight-foot lead so she is in compliance with the rules. I text Dad and Tim to say we're heading up the Bulwark Ridge Trail now and get out my GPS and start following directions.

The trail is predictably quite steep and rocky. Luckily for me, I previewed the trail description online last night on a popular hiking website. Therefore, I'm wearing my hiking boots with the best ankle support. A warning sign indicates that a bull moose has taken up residence near the trail, so we follow the diversion to the right marked by blue and white flags. I'm all about avoiding annoyed moose, so we follow the new route until it cuts us back to the original trail. The center of the trail is studded by rocks of intermediate size, which keep me from moving at a very consistent pace, but we plug along as I dodge and clamber. Leda simply strolls along like a leopard making it all look effortless. "If I do one of those DNA tests on you, am I going to find out you are part feline?" I ask her, as we stop for our first water break. She looks around her with avid anticipation. There's no way she knows the word "feline." I'm fairly certain. Right?

We get a good drink and make our diagonal turn, programmed into the GPS, to the northeast on the Indian Trail. Just as we make our turn, I spy three female hikers coming down the Signal Mountain Trail. All three look like teenagers, maybe early 20s, and are happily chattering away with each other. They give me a cheery hello and then continue south at a good clip down the trail I just hiked up.

My research showed that this section of the Indian Trail comprises a mile of steep, zigzagging uphill with about a 500-foot elevation gain. Leda and I settle into the walk, treading carefully, but enjoying the solitude and the golden hues of the aspens rimming the sidewalls around the trail. Swaths of amber leaves turning to red are visible in the distance. What an outstanding day for a walk! It's only mid-morning, but the sun feels energizing on my back. Now we intersect with the Miller Fork Trail and turn north and slightly west. This trail is less rocky and wonderful for Leda as it parallels the stream. She plays in the water and drinks at her leisure. Birds flit back and forth diving from the trees to the water in meandering circles chasing bugs. Wild mint grows along the sloping banks, vibrant with that dusty lavender color reserved for flowers that come at the end of the growing season. Northern Gentian with its five petal lobes delights me with its deep blue flowers as we hike ever upward. And Western Willow Asters crowd the edges of the moisture with pinkish blue flowers. It's as if a crayon box has been dumped upside down and the colors smeared across the terrain in streaks of cornflower, mauve, and prairie rose. We hike onward in serene contentment, not another soul in sight. Then I spy a majestic grove of old-growth ponderosa pine and snap a picture with my phone. Dad needs to see the size of them.

After six-tenths of a mile, our cutover trail appears, bearing slightly southeast now to take us over to the Donner Pass Trail. So far, the GPS has been relatively easy to use, but I'm not planning on giving Dad too much satisfaction. The paper map in my pocket is imprinted in my head and so far, we're doing just fine. Another half-mile of hiking, and losing a portion of the elevation we worked hard to gain, brings us to the Donner Pass Trail and we move northward. The trail is intermittently difficult to find in spots, but prior hikers have considerately placed rock cairns at confusing junctures. Leda is stepping out happily sniffing the breezes. The multitude of aspens here is overwhelming. Their gold and burnished copper hues against the brilliant blue skies would lift the spirits of even the most jaded hiker. I find myself soaking in the peace and it feels like Zach is walking with us up the trail. He would love this day, this view, and this tranquility.

We stop for a moment on a rock ledge overlooking a particularly magnificent grove of aspens. Perching above them, the view looking down on their golden crowns is divine. I snap a photo and text it to Dad with a caption: "Hard at Work on Donner Pass Trail." My phone shows one bar of cell phone service so it looks like it transmitted. Leda lies patiently at my feet, tongue lolling out while she watches a beetle traverse the path with interest. I pour a portion of water into her collapsible bowl and she takes 10 or 12 good laps. I swig my water and snag a Berry Blast granola bar out of my backpack. The temperature is perfect; I can climb without sweating and Leda looks fresh.

The trail makes a couple of big, looping turns around rugged topographical features, which is just fine. At certain times going around is much better than going up and over. I check my distance on my GPS, which is actually quite useful. I was to complete a hike of about one mile before reaching the area where we turn due east and start navigating to the ends of three parallel mineral-deficient tributaries—where with any luck, we will find three cabins being reclaimed by the wilderness, and a possible clue to Randy's whereabouts. I pull out my map to check the location of the ridgeline Dad believes he has pinpointed. It's time, and Leda and I duck off the trail.

CHAPTER 70

A t around 9300 feet in elevation, the tree cover here is a mixture of ponderosa pine, limber pine, and Engelmann spruce. Working our way upward, we head east and pass a massive grove of lodgepole pine with Rocky Mountain juniper growing around the edges in rounded columnar shapes. The charred spots scattered around the grove indicate this was likely a previously burned section, perhaps from a lightning strike. I gaze around for confirmation of my supposition, and sure enough, a Rocky Mountain bristlecone pine with the patented scorch marks lies dead ahead. I have seen this phenomenon numerous times while horseback riding in the Bridger Teton National Forest in Wyoming with family friends. These long-lived pines, up to several thousand years old, can grow in rocky soil and are extremely drought tolerant. They have a peculiarly charming, gnarled appearance and will oftentimes bear the scorch marks of passing fires.

The tangled foliage makes it difficult going and I unhook Leda from her lead. She will stay right near me and in the unlikely event we run into a forest ranger, we can simply explain that we are helping the Larimer County Sheriff's Office in a missing person search. We break free of the tree and shrub tangle and start climbing up sloping rock escarpments. None are steep enough to hinder us, although we are steadily gaining elevation. Our course undulates up and down with the topography until a glorious stand of Douglas fir and an area of open space ahead reveal themselves to us.

The GPS indicates I have traveled about half a mile; it seemed like a lot more work than that, probably because I have a scrape on my face and am breathing rather hard. I try to slow my breathing, and beat back the sense of urgency emanating from my core. Haste makes waste—an old adage but a true one. I stop and sip water. Leda is not interested in hers. She seems eager to keep moving, but I pull out my paper map to check my distance to the ridge which should run east/west across the top of the tributaries. I rummage in my pack and then press a piece of gauze against my cheek. Not too bad. I hold the gauze in place with pressure until it stops bleeding as we move forward a little more cautiously through a stand of north-facing Douglas fir. An open space appears and looking laterally east and west, it feels like the elusive ridge has been found. In fact, Leda and I are standing on the spine of it. The ground slopes away gradually on either side toward firs and junipers below and jumbled rocks above.

Pulling my camouflage neck gaiter up over my nose, I motion Leda into a Down position with her hand signal. An arbitrary mental picture of the currently scattered and hilarious Springers learning their hand signals later in class and the antics that will undoubtedly ensue at the beginning makes me smile briefly. I crouch down and pull out my high-resolution binoculars. The meadow where Dad thinks a chopper may be able to set down is between cabins two and three, but I should be very close to cabin one, the one owned by Mortimer Kunkle. His parents must have really disliked him to saddle the poor guy with that moniker. Scanning the ridgeline, I listen closely. The sound of flowing water reaches my ears. Not a gushing, but more like a rippling. The water that held so much initial promise for Mortimer and Francis and Gunther, and then broke their hearts when it gave up nothing but a few piles of low-quality ore. All that work to build three cabins in close proximity, stake the claims, work along the tributaries, only to give up and move to Oregon within a season and a half. Sad but not uncommon in the West. To this day, it can be the land of dreamers and drifters. So much space, so many plans, so many bitter disappointments.

I force myself to crouch calmly and stay still, just like Dad taught me when he took me out in the woods when I was little. It was the best game. See what you can spot in ten minutes of not moving and not talking. Animals, birds, or vegetation. It all counted. Boy, would I get frustrated after proudly naming off 12 things, and he would proceed to show me 20 more in that location. I got better and more patient with maturity, but always felt myself itching for movement. The restlessness abated to a degree after Zach came along. His quiet demeanor kept me grounded. Now I have to do that for myself—so I sit patiently and scan down the ridgeline section from my vantage point with the $2600 binoculars. My patience is rewarded when the outline of one of the squat cabins becomes discernible. The frame is tucked under a gigantic south-facing ponderosa pine with large, reddish, fissured plates on its bark and extraordinarily long needles. I watch carefully for ten minutes and see no smoke or signs of movement or activity, except one gray tinted Abert's squirrel with his comical tufted ears sunning himself on a rock at the edge of the clearing, chewing a seed in business-like fashion. He finishes his meal and darts away. Leda has closed her eyes with her face to the sun.

After scanning the cabin for another moment, it seems safe to stand up. Leda's eyes fly open and she watches my hand for her next signal. I motion her to heel and start working my way down the spine of the ridge keeping under the cover of the trees until we are within 100 yards of the cabin. A further scan reveals nothing. In fact, a gaping hole looms where the front door should be and it looks like the cabin is melting into the ground. Even though my mandate was to simply check the area and not the actual cabin interior itself, I'm here now and I like to be thorough. Leda and I ease up to the side wall with no window, and wait for several minutes. The forest is supremely quiet. Western Tanagers flit around the clearing with their yellow bodies, and dark wings and tails, searching for insects. The majority are males with their distinctive orange heads and chuckling calls. I crouch against the base of the homestead's wall and Leda leans against me, facing outward and looking alert. No doubt my tenseness has

TRACY CARTER

been transmitted to her and she is watching and listening too. She reacts to nothing in the vicinity so it appears we are alone.

Finally, I feel confident enough to stand up and ease around to the front of the cabin. The lintel over the doorframe is splintered and bowing. It feels like one more good winter snow load is going to crater this thing out and do the demolition work for the Forest Service guys. I close my eyes for a moment and then step inside and open them. They adjust fairly quickly to the change from light to dark, but the flashlight from my backpack is still vital for sweeping the cabin thoroughly. It does not take long. The room is at most eight feet by ten feet with a sagging ceiling skimming the top of my ball cap. It smells dank, and mounds of old pine cone segments, probably collected by the American red squirrels which nest in tree cavities throughout this forest, are scattered about. Someone is getting ready for winter. The ubiquitous beer can lies crumpled in the corner. So, you could carry in a full can, but couldn't take the empty one away with you, I think with exasperation. I crush it further and put it in a side pocket of my backpack. Little else remains to be seen, certainly no sign that anyone has been inside this place in a very long time. Leda is standing right behind me, as usual, and pivots around behind me as we exit with alacrity. It is approaching mid-afternoon and we have cabin two to check out.

CHAPTER 71

We vanish back into the tree line cresting the ridge where I check my GPS. The course is set to head slightly south for about another half-mile. I look at my phone and see a text had arrived while I was hiking at a lower elevation. Dad has sent me three emojis. Deranged clown face, a slot machine, and a judge's gavel. Oh, heck no!! Did that genius Billy Fulton really skip out on his team to take his pals to Vegas for one last blow-out before he stands trial? Somewhere, right now, a limo driver is either getting a $500 tip, or maybe he's been hijacked and forced to drive them to the Grand Canyon. Well, those are cryptic clues indeed from my father with his ironic sense of humor. Not surprisingly, no cell service exists at this location with trees blocking a clear shot to the sky. As long as Billy isn't hiking his almost seven-foot-tall frame through the wilderness near me, no need to worry about that emoji string right now.

I shake my head in disbelief and swallow some slightly warm water after pouring a few ounces in Leda's bowl for her. I chew a handful of raisins and offer Leda a biscuit. It's not peanut butter, but she condescends to try an apple and oatmeal dog cookie. *Hmmm. Not too bad. Let's see if the human brought any more of those.* I grin into her intelligent eyes and hand her a second cookie. I tell her softly, "You might enjoy that even more if you actually chewed it on the way down." She smiles and waves her tail at me without a care in the world. We are in complete harmony.

We hike quietly and carefully southeast along the ridgeline until we arrive at another small clearing with slightly less tree cover, but an almost identical cabin. No extravagant changing of the floor plan for the Kunkle brothers. Again, I move to my best vantage point, put Leda in a Down, and scan the area with the binoculars from a kneeling position. If anyone is down there looking at the horizon, they will look for people at head height, not lower. The glasses do give an amazingly sharp picture, but they should for $2600—the price of a good Quarter Horse! No smoke, no lights, no people. All is calm and after waiting for 10 minutes, Leda comes to heel and we slide out to the back and around the side of cabin number two. A forlorn window on this side tilts drunkenly toward the ground, with shattered panes of glass littering the outside periphery. I motion Leda to Down farther back to keep her from getting cut, fish her booties out of my pack and slip them efficiently over her paws. She drops to the ground while keeping a laser focus on me as I duck inside the half shut, and warped wooden door.

I use my flashlight again to scan the inside of the cabin and see only a candy bar wrapper with weeds shooting up around it in disapproval. For real? Was this dessert for the beer drinker? I fold it up and shove it into my back pocket. The framework of this cabin looks more solid than the previous one, but it's no more appealing. I step out the door, go get Leda and walk her around the broken glass, and bear almost due east in search of the meadow where Dad suspected a helicopter could land. We don't go very far before we run across the second tributary, the middle prong of Neptune's trident. It's a pretty watercourse tumbling over rocks and weaving merrily in and out of the roots of trees hanging over the water. Leda gets a drink and lies patiently in the shade while her booties are removed and I look for the meadow Dad flagged as a potential landing site.

Through the pine branches, glimpses of a small valley bottom and an open meadow can be seen. We slide forward carefully using as much cover as possible until we are on the verge of entering the meadow. It ebbs and flows up and down with shimmering waves of grass, rather than being totally flat, but it definitely appears level enough to land a helicopter at certain spots in the two or three acres. All is calm and I scan the center slowly with my binoculars. It occurs to me that I am actually enjoying myself unabashedly on this scouting mission. The move to Colorado was definitely the right call after the tragedy in Ohio. Pay attention, I tell myself. I pass over a flattened area and then swing the glasses back. A definite squashed section catches my eye. Dad may be on to something here. Only one cabin remains to be explored—the former home of Gunther Kunkle.

Leda, who has been heeling right next to me placidly, suddenly goes into serious mode. She stands stiffly and tests the breeze vigorously. She is scooping in vast rafts of scent and her attention has been grabbed. Shoot. I shove the binoculars back into my pack and quickly clip on Leda's long line to ensure her close proximity to me. If she thinks it is time for her to work, I am dying of curiosity.

Leda moves out at a brisk pace scenting the air and the ground in alternating patterns. I press the back track feature on my GPS so we can get back to this spot later if necessary. We find the third creek and she walks in and out of it a dozen times, always emerging on the bank on one side or the other. I am hard-pressed to keep up with her while trying to hop from tumbled stream rocks to the stream bank every 10-15 yards. My terrible balance has been addressed previously. Suddenly, she sticks to the near bank only and surges through the scattered aspens, which populate the fringes of this meadow. "Easy girl, easy," I tell her quietly. Trying to watch her and scan for anything worrisome at the same time is a tall task. This is where a follow person would come in handy, big-time. She bounds forward to the end of her line and alerts to a white object wedged under a tree root. I see it just as she approaches and tell her insistently, "Leda, Hush."

She looks at me in puzzlement, having been prepared to give her three triumphant barks, then sinks down to her haunches and watches me intently. I pull the sealed baggie with Randy Jeffers' T-shirt in it from my backpack, open it, and let Leda sniff. She undoubtedly has his scent locked in her brain after searching for it several times in the past few days, but I need to be sure. She looks up at me very seriously. I whisper to her to Find and she scoots closer to the piece of white rag and sits down emphatically, and with attitude. She is completely disgusted about the interruption of the alert barks, but we can't risk it. Leda loves to bark. A lot. I try to make it up to her by rubbing her face and praising her in happy whispers. She forgets her aggravation almost instantly and shimmies over for a scratch around her rib cage. I am forgiven.

Now the real work begins. Randy was most assuredly here and Leda is the tool with which I am going to pry him loose from this wilderness or the bad guys. I return the baggie to my backpack. The white rag, upon closer examination, is a sleeve torn jaggedly off a T-shirt. Scarlet splashes of blood ominously soak the underside. I bundle it into a separate baggie, with a faint thought that it might be needed for evidence later. Then, I pull my neck gaiter up higher and tell Leda *sotto voce* to Find. And then Hush.

She gazes at me with her bright amber eyes and heads north with her nose in the air. She walks forward strongly as I follow attached by the cord that is like a lifeline between us—a conduit of energy and feeling, if you will. Leda radiates positivity. My job at this moment is mostly to stay out of her way, watch her body language, and try not to slow her down too much. As we head north, this direction change is puzzling. Randy seemed to be heading south down the third and final tributary when we first crossed his scent trail. I remind myself that Randy very well may not know where he is in the wilderness. He started following the water downhill, which is a logical choice, but then clearly changed his mind. Maybe because the logical choice is also the obvious choice if you are being pursued. I scan the ground as closely as possible while working my way up and around gently sloping rock ledges wherever Leda's nose takes us. My breath comes a fraction more rapidly; my adrenaline is flowing after this unexpected turn of events. I focus on quieting my breath by pulling air in and pushing it out mindfully. Our twenty-year-old yoga teacher is habitually late for class, but she definitely knows how to teach a person to calm down.

As Leda and I work our way diagonally up another rocky escarpment, glimpses of scarlet appear, splashes on one or two of the level rocks. Telling Leda to Wait, I bend down for a closer examination. They are almost assuredly blood drops. The coppery smell of blood is evident when I lean close to them, and the drops look spherical as if blood has been dripping from a wound. A prickling sensation tingles at the back of my neck. The danger of this situation has just become very evident. If Randy is badly injured somewhere ahead of us, and still bleeding, this whole scenario is a lot more complicated than I estimated. I straighten up carefully and then quietly tell Leda to Find. She moves forward again with alacrity, but I struggle to keep up with the course changes. Either Randy is injured and staggering along or we've got a drunken sailor on the path ahead of us. I need to locate him as quickly as possible, and unfortunately, the afternoon is already fading away from us in that slow drift from sun to dusk, which seems to accelerate so rapidly as autumn moves toward winter.

Of course, Leda can still smell in the dark, but this terrain is tricky footing and waning light does not help me. We move through another stand of Engelmann spruce with its sharp, triangular needles and mountain chickadees fill the environment with their pert little calls. I see a flash of the black cap on one's head and his compact white-and-gray body before he swoops up under the trees. They can live on as little as 10 calories a day. Unlike me. This would be a fascinating hike, if not for the missing person suffering somewhere in front of us needing our help. And if he is badly hurt, how will I get him aid fast? I halt Leda for a moment and give her a drink of water. She stands panting slightly; probably part of my anxiety has been transmitted up the line to her. I need to calm my racing mind. Bruce trained me for all eventualities and I spent all my formative years in the woods with my dad. We can do this. Sipping water out of my bottle, I rub her sides and tell her repeatedly what a gorgeous girl she is. She drinks a smidgen more water and then looks ahead, ready for action. I look at my compass and see we are headed northeast. Time to get a move on before darkness reaches out and drops its ebony cloak over us.

CHAPTER 72

We walk silently through the spruce and head uphill for another 15 or 20 minutes. I have not encountered any more blood drops, but have been focusing mainly on Leda. She looks animated to me now. Hopefully we are near to finding Randy, but I have no idea when in the last five days he traveled this way. I look at my cell phone, more out of habit than hope. No service. Not shocking as cell phones operate on line of sight to towers and the only thing in my line of sight is rock slopes and big trees. Obviously, no place anywhere near this portion of national forest has been wired for connectivity by the cell providers, which only makes sense, but doesn't lessen my feeling of isolation. If I'm going to keep doing this sort of work, Dad needs to get an outdoor supplier to give him a satellite phone to demo, then pass on to me. However, certain of those phones also require line of sight to the satellite, which would be a tough ask around here.

The going gets tougher, but we persevere onward. The advice on the hikers' website to wear your boots with the best ankle support was prescient. Between the trails and the course changes, I'm getting the full tedious experience of rocks in every size and shape. My talented dog skirts the edge of another aspen grove and heads toward a smallish overhanging cliff face. A massive jumble of blowdown is stacked in front of the cliff. I stand there in disbelief for a moment thinking, "How are we getting through or around this mess?" Suddenly, Leda drags me forward with renewed energy. She pulls into her harness like a sled dog seeking the finish line of the Iditarod.

I remind her to Hush. She roots around on the far edge of the tangle of downed timber until she is almost crawling on her belly. I follow her as best as possible, bent over like a wizened crone with arthritis.

After working her way in about ten feet, Leda turns to look at me very deliberately and sits down in a tiny clear spot on the ground. We are under the curling carapace of the cliff at this point, in between two downed spruces with dead boughs of other fallen trees flung haphazardly on top. I look at her and say "Really?" She gives me back that inscrutable look she conjures up out of those stunning eyes occasionally. I bend down and look past her shoulder. And there, in a torn white T-shirt, missing a sleeve, and disheveled khakis is the unmistakable figure of Dr. Randy Jeffers, lying under a tree trunk with limbs pulled down for further cover. The picture of him that appeared alongside the *Denver Press* article was an excellent likeness; the angular face and dirty blond hair are a match. A burst of elation sweeps over me, followed by a plunge of dismay. His eyes are closed and it is unclear from here if he is breathing. Surely, he can't be dead after all this. So close to helping him. I fight down my negative thoughts and a slight rising tide of panic and reach out to touch his wrist. At which point, he opens his eyes and looks right at me. Stifling a little yelp over that startling turn of events, I say, "Dr. Randy Jeffers, I presume?" I couldn't resist.

Randy closes his eyes again briefly and nods wearily, but the ghost of a smile crosses his lips. "Well, hello there. I'm Veronica and this is Leda." He has purplish bruises fading to green around his face and neck and a nasty-looking black eye. Blood is seeping around the edges of a cloth he has tied around the top of his head like a pirate's bandanna. The sections of his skin that are not battered look extremely pale. I have no idea how long he has been out here or what has happened to him since Friday. I just need to get him out of the middle of the suddenly not so benevolent landscape. I carefully help him crawl out from under the tree trunk, which was a hiding spot my father would have approved of, and into the open area so I can examine him. As we squirm our way out, he is clearly favoring his right knee; this situation will become even more problematic if he does not have decent mobility. I check my cell phone, eager to share the news of Leda's find with my father. The No Service banner looks glibly back at me. Of course.

He slumps down and asks, "Were you really looking for me?"

"Yes indeed. We've been looking for you in Rocky Mountain National Park, and now over here, since Saturday morning when your wife called out the troops. Leda found your trail in RMNP, trailing you until it vanished from the moraine meadow, she found your bracelet and your thumb drive, and now she's found you."

Randy reaches out a hand for Leda to sniff and smiles at the mention of Patty. "Tell me Patty's safe right now."

"She's doing fine. The police are keeping an eye on her and she has been a tremendous help to us in figuring out your movements since you disappeared."

While responding to Randy, I am simultaneously rummaging in my backpack. I drop a packet of acai berry-flavored electrolytes in a bottle of water, shake it up, and hand it to him along with a honey and oat soft granola bar. He engulfs both rapidly and with gratitude. "You look like you might have missed a few meals. Were we correct in assuming you were abducted?" I venture.

Randy replies in between bites of his second granola bar, "What an incredible dog to do all that work and find me way up here days later. You are right; I was taken. And for the first three days, I had no idea why. I work on a certain number of high-profile cases due to my specialty, so it took me a bit of time to piece things together and also listen to my captors when they thought I was asleep or passed out from their treatment of me."

By now, I have gotten the bloody rag off Randy's head and use an alcohol wipe to carefully brush away the crusted and seeping blood for a closer examination. He has a pretty decent cut above one eye running horizontally for three inches. Any boxer will tell you it's tough to stop bleeding in that area. I hold gauze on the area with pressure, smear antibiotic salve on it, press the edges together and apply a butterfly bandage, and lastly, wrap a clean piece of cloth around his head and tie it snugly.

Next, the long open cut on the palm of his hand can be addressed. Blood keeps seeping out in steady drops. It's obvious how the rocks leading up here got painted with blood. I run through the same routine of pressure with gauze, antibiotic salve, and a clean dressing. He continues to sip water with his eyes closed while I roll up his khakis and check out his knee. An immense locus of swelling and discolored tissue surrounds his entire knee. I grab my arnica salve from the side zippered pocket of my pack and rub a big glob into his knee.

"I fell over a rock by the streambed not long after I escaped," he offers. "Once that happened, my ability to move very fast was compromised." I have a million questions for Randy, but it's obvious he is physically and mentally exhausted. He eats and hydrates while I keep checking him over. Leda sidles over and lies down next to us, muzzle on paws while she watches me work.

His pulse feels fairly strong. I tear open a foil packet of over-the-counter painkillers and hand over three for him to swallow. These tablets should help mitigate the effects of the abuse to which he has undeniably been subjected. A wash of pity overtakes me as I consider what torments were visited on this poor guy. A further rummage around in my pack unearths a peanut butter and strawberry jam sandwich my father had stowed in my pack. Awesome. I hand it over to Randy, and he smiles, "Nectar of the gods."

"Yes, indeed," I joke back. "You won't find a tastier sandwich anywhere."

Randy grunts as he makes short work of the delicacy. "At this point, I would eat just about anything." Leda raises her head, cocks it sideways, and gives him an inquiring look. "Present canines excepted." We both laugh and it appears the food and water are having a restorative effect on his system. We talk quietly from just a few feet apart, but I keep my ears open. Several moments later, I hear a disturbance in the distance, which reminds me of the *chop chop chop* noise particular to a helicopter. I cast an eye over to Leda to see if she is reacting to anything alarming. She pricks up her ears too and looks downhill toward the horizon. Oh great, can this day get any better?

"So, Randy, I can't bear the suspense any longer. Were you abducted by a helicopter from that meadow between the Lawn Lake and Black Canyon Trails and were you being held in a cabin near that stream where you injured your knee?"

He nods affirmatively. "Wow, you really have put a lot of information together. Two thugs pursued me up the Lawn Lake Trail. I attempted to cut cross-country to evade them with an idea of heading for the Black Canyon Trail and blasting downhill to the Lumpy Ridge Trailhead to get assistance. Unfortunately, they got close enough to shoot me with a sawed-off riot shotgun that shoots beanbags. It took me down so hard I passed out. One of them must have hidden it down his back covered by his coat. By the time I could try to stand, they had me tied up like a Thanksgiving turkey and they were using some kind of HF/UHF radio to call in the helicopter not much later. I did manage to loosen my bracelet from Mexico and slip it off my wrist and out the open door of the helicopter before they blindfolded me and knocked me out again. I'm going to need a test for concussion syndrome, for sure, with the number of times I got pistol whipped in the head." I wince and feel my resolve harden like concrete. This man did nothing to deserve their treatment of him.

"When I came to, I was in a hundred-year-old Forest Service cabin, which initially belonged to one of the Kunkle brothers, if the lowlifes who took me can be believed."

"Oh yes," I assure him. "Three brothers, Mortimer, Francis, and Gunther each built a cabin at the end of a separate tributary in the late 1880s, hoping to strike it rich. They learned the hard way that the ore they could access was low in mineral content and difficult to get out of there and they abandoned hope within 18 months. You must have been in the third cabin. I searched the other two places first."

Randy answers, "I heard the thug they left with me the majority of the time say the name Gunther, so your assumption would appear to be solid. The pilot is the one to watch out for in that bunch. He's ex-military and vicious."

"How long ago did you escape?" I ask curiously.

"It was only just this morning. The pilot and thug number two flew off in the helicopter last evening. I could not tell if they got a mission that needed to be accomplished right then, or if they were going to search further for the computer thumb drive. I managed to work one of my hands free from the bindings over the night and when thug number one nodded off, I got my hands loose altogether and bashed *him* over the head with a shovel that was leaning against the wall. I assume they planned on using that shovel later to bury me. I took a great deal of satisfaction from evening the score a little bit," he chuckles ruefully.

"Rightfully so," I reassure him. "Anybody would!" I check over Leda briskly and pull a burr off the back of her leg. Otherwise, she's in fine fettle. She chows down on a few biscuits with obvious enjoyment. Randy continues his narrative slowly, but his color looks better. "I tied him up and slipped out the door. The helicopter was nowhere in sight and my first thought was to head south down the stream toward civilization. I was weak from no food and limited water and I struggled downhill through those rocky areas. Then after I fell and got bashed up a bit, I figured I would try to outwit them and double back north—keeping in mind that I really have no idea where I am. I must have passed out a few times because I would come to and have no remembrance of having been walking anywhere with purpose. Luckily, no one caught up to me when I was helpless."

I look at him and break the bad news to him reluctantly, "If you can walk at all, we need to move east until we're past those cabins and then cut due south to go get help. We will take it slow and steady and use our cover, but we can't go west to the established trails as that's probably where they'll start looking for you, if they haven't already started."

Randy looks disheartened but he musters up his courage. "Let's try to make a bit of progress before it gets dark and then we can hole up somewhere hidden." Gathering up the detritus from our makeshift first aid session, I'm already feeling the pressure of knowing that people may still be hunting Randy. Shrugging off my long-sleeved camouflage T-shirt, I help Randy on with it to cover his white T-shirt. I unroll my down vest from the spot where it is tied on the bottom of my pack and pull it on.

A multitude of questions are swirling around my mind—namely who perpetrated this assault on Randy, but we have to move right now. I clip Leda's line to my belt, look at my compass for a moment to get my bearings, and assist Randy as he climbs painfully to his feet. He straightens up a trifle and gives me a nod.

"Let's try it. I don't want to fall into their hands again."

I smile at him encouragingly and state, "Now is a good time to move. I think I heard the chopper returning. If so, they'll know soon that you're gone and the stakes have just been raised." It dawns on me as I cast around for a good branch for Randy to use as a crutch that it might be easier said than done. "Why is there never a deciduous tree when you need one in Colorado?" I exclaim in exasperation. "This would take me ten seconds in Ohio." Randy guffaws at that minor bit of comedy and an encouraging feeling buoys me. We forage around until we have an adequate, but not spectacular, branch, and we walk eastward as the light fades behind us.

CHAPTER 73

Randy and I move downhill as I try to calculate how far east we have to go to get clear of the tributaries and meadow where the bad guys have taken up residence. A cut south as quickly as possible is imperative, so we can get proper medical treatment for Randy. He is managing a slow walk while leaning on the crutch moderately, so I feel the tiniest bit more hopeful. The food seems to have given him a bit of energy. It is unclear just how long his adrenaline will fuel him, however. The insistent voice in the back of my head that's calling out "hurry, hurry, hurry" needs to knock it off, because Randy clearly is not going to be able to hurry. We're lucky he's upright at this point. Leda ranges back and forth ahead of us as we make our halting progress down the undulating rock faces interspersed with groves of trees. She sees better in the dim light and picks out a clearer path for us. I help Randy with a hand under his elbow when we come to any trickier landscape features to negotiate. His hand begins dripping a bit of blood from beneath the bandage, but there's no time to stop and attend to it now.

It is imperative that we make headway down these slopes before nightfall envelops us. "Are those painkillers helping at all?" I inquire. He answers in the affirmative and our haphazard descent continues. The light is failing, but we are able to just make out the terrain's contours. The ground has a dusky purple color that throws off our depth perception just enough to keep us from moving out with confidence. By now, the other two perpetrators had to have found Randy missing. With the pilot being ex-military, I have a real fear that he will be able to track us down before we can get help. I'm not sure which is a worse feeling—me trying to hide in an alley while a murderer tried to shoot me at point-blank range, or hobbling slowly away from a trained killer while every nerve in my body screams to dash pell-mell down the mountain.

I look at my phone hopefully. No service yet. I typically appreciate, and heartily endorse, the solitude of the backcountry, but right about now, a wireless communication site would come in really handy. Yellowstone's visitors can actually access spillover signals throughout a majority of its 3500 wilderness acres. But in this location in Roosevelt National Forest, I've got nothing. Well, I'm always telling my dad I prefer to do things old school, so I need to get us out of this predicament using smarts, not technology.

Our slow, silent progress is interrupted by an echoing bugling noise ringing around the valley we are traversing. It's dusk in autumn, so that makes perfect sense. The bull elk are busy trumpeting for mates this time of year. A look to my right finds a big male with an impressive rack working his way through his territory. Leda glances in his direction, but pays no attention. She smelled him long before we saw him. As long as he stays on his side of the meadow, she has no interest. Randy pauses for a moment and wipes sweat off his brow. This has to be tough going for a person who had limited food and water for almost a week and was beaten up and tortured. "Are you okay to walk a little further?" I inquire quietly. Just as Randy nods, a sliding, clattering noise reverberates from a cliff high above us. A rock breaks loose and somersaults through the air crazily before coming to rest off to the side of us. I scan the skyline above us in alarm before finally making out the form of a cow elk. She has her own mission in the valley and it involves either avoiding or crossing paths with the lusty bull elk that has been busy making his presence known. Dad would love to see this spectacle, I think, right before acknowledging how much I wish he were here right now.

We pick our way out into a bigger meadow ringed 360 degrees by lovely papery-barked aspens whose golden leaves glow softly around the treetops like fairy-tale halos. Their leaves tremble ever so gently in the slight breeze with a musical, tinkling noise. I want nothing more than to be folded inside their serenity, but this is no time to be fanciful. I can discern rock ledges to my left at the end of this meadow, which we need to traverse while the waning light still allows us partial visibility. It is a calculated risk to head across the open meadow, but time is not on our side at the moment. I remove my backpack and sling it over my arm intending to dig out the binoculars for a rapid scan of the terrain ahead of us. Unbelievably, just then, as we leave the cover of the guardian trees and start to wade through the river of ankle-deep browning grass flowing through the meadow, the dreaded sound I've been straining *not* to hear kicks up—a helicopter and it's close. A frisson of paralyzing fear hits me, and then determination kicks in as Randy tries valiantly to speed up. The chopper is coming from the west and coming fast.

I clamp the backpack against my stomach and encourage Randy as he hobbles using his crutch to steady him in the rolling waves of thick grass. We are nearly back into the safety of the trees on the east side of the meadow when the helicopter shoots up in the air above the aspens on the far side of the meadow and heads right at us. The trees are so close with their protective arms reaching out, ready to give us succor and survival. Camouflage gear is very useful when you're surrounded by vegetation— not so much when you're a sitting duck in the middle of an open area. Randy is panting hard, but game. He's no quitter and Leda and I won't quit on him. I yell at her over the noise of the rotors, "Leda, GO," and swing my free arm toward the inky haven of the trees with the wide sweeping motion that tells her in an obedience trial to run out to the end of the ring. For a moment, she hesitates. I know she is reluctant to leave me, but she is well-trained and she obeys.

Just as we enter the cover of the trees, the sounds of multiple distinct rifle shots pierce the dusk. They had to have come from that blasted helicopter. I hear a succession of deafening thuds behind me as the guardian trees absorb the impact of bullets. Immediately thereafter, I feel a sharp stinging sensation around my hip and then a vicious jab into my shoulder. The good one. "Son of a bitch," I holler while still trying to keep low and help Randy into the salvation of the trees. "Excuse my French, Randy," I blurt out as we hustle deeper into our hiding place.

"No worries Veronica. I was thinking of a word starting with F myself!" Did those shots hit you anywhere?" he inquires as we press forward into the center of the grove.

"Not directly," I reply. "A glancing blow or a ricochet maybe." An ironic thought flashes through my mind while calculating our next move. I have some experience with this, having been shot before. I was really hoping NOT to be shot in Colorado. My breathing rattles in and out in harsh, ragged gasps as the realization sinks in that, once again, I have been the target of another human's malice. Poor Randy. How did he survive being held by these bastards for five days? Leda presses insistently against my leg whining and looking fierce. She is on high alert; her person is under attack and she's not happy. "Easy girl," I soothe her. I feel myself calm down slightly as my hand rests on her head.

"Randy, let's keep moving through the trees and work our way to the bottom of this open country. We can exit out the far side and get into those rock ledges I saw earlier when we were higher up. Darkness is going to be our best friend in about 15 minutes." Randy straightens up from where he was sucking in oxygen with his hands on his good knee and picks up his disintegrating pine bough crutch.

I peek out laterally into the meadow as we slink along and my heart sinks as the helicopter lands in the meadow. It's difficult to see clearly amongst the clumps of trees and the silvery shadows of dusk, but it appears that one man has dropped into the meadow grass and is moving in our direction with determination. A scan of the meadow with my high-resolution binoculars confirms one man on the ground headed our way, and sure enough, he has a rifle. Bruce trained me well, but we never envisioned a scenario where hired gunmen in a helicopter were pursuing my "found person" and me across the hinterlands of Colorado. I know what my dad would tell me now though. Stay calm and work through each problem as it comes. I force myself to think about our best plan of action as I pull my backpack on hastily—while steadfastly trying to ignore the pain emanating from my hip and shoulder.

We have a slight lead on him, but we need to get into the rock ledges fast and let the helpful night make him blind. His eye in the sky won't be able to assist him then either. We just need to get under the protection of a natural feature substantial enough to hide us. Randy is moving along at a decent clip for somebody so banged up. Perhaps the movement has helped loosen up his muscles. His gait still looks pained to me though and this jolting and jarring is most likely excruciating. Leda trots just ahead of us and her ears prick up each time some foreign sound catches her attention. She does not know exactly from which direction the danger is coming, but she feels its presence permeating this place.

CHAPTER 74

My hip feels like it has been scored by a flaming hot knife and that is definitely blood on the back of my shoulder, wet against my camo T-shirt and vest. Not sure I brought enough bandages for all the damage we're sustaining. Randy and I follow Leda as she winds through the ghostly, welcoming trees and at long last we come out at the bottom of the meadow. I angle us further eastward in an effort to locate the rock features my trusty map had shown me earlier. The ground becomes more barren and sloping as we move silently though the woods. Every sound of a forest creature scurrying out on its evening affairs is amplified and alarm-inducing. I take deep breaths in and out as we shuffle down one rock ledge after another for the next 20 minutes. One of the green glow sticks held down low by my knee illuminates the terrain ever so slightly. We hear the helicopter lift off and fly away to the south, but we have no way of knowing how many pursuers have floated down in our wake.

A jagged promontory juts out about 200 hundred yards away from us and I have an inkling that if we can just make it there, we will possibly be safe for the night. Leda ranges out farther ahead of me now scouting the terrain. A steady breeze blows across the top of the cliff, directly into our faces. We start carefully skirting the final slant leading up to the outcropping, on the edge of a rocky path with treacherous and steep drop-offs on either side. Just as we round the corner on the side hill, Leda turns back toward me, nose in the air, having caught a scent. Looking swiftly over my shoulder, I am shocked to see a figure looming up behind us, shapeless yet terrifying, in the abruptness of its appearance. I have no time to think, to formulate a plan, to withdraw. Instead, I attack.

Dropping Randy's forearm, and wrenching the bear spray off its clip on my belt, I pivot to the back. Please don't let this spray blast back on us now, I pray. I lunge forward screaming at the top of my lungs and spraying the red pepper oil in the proximate location of the monster's head, while simultaneously averting my face. He flinches backward in apparent shock at the female banshee, and then almost immediately begins coughing and spitting. Fabulous. Distraction accomplished. Time for part two.

"Leda, get him," I tell her forcefully. From around the corner of the rocky slice of land perched high on the side hill, Leda continues galloping back toward me at top speed. Our tormentor, eyes streaming tears and mucus pouring from his nose, tries desperately to swing his rifle up to get off a shot, but she closes the ground between them too fast. Leda flies upward, true as a bullet herself, and slams her entire weight into his chest, snapping her teeth savagely an inch away from his jugular. He grunts with the unexpected shock of it and then teeters wildly on the edge of the out-cropping trying to regain his balance. For a worrisome moment, it appears that he will salvage his balance, but Leda is not finished. She drops to the ground like a leopard oozing out of a tree in front of its prey, and lunges against his knees with a perfect takedown tackle.

He windmills his arms wildly at that second blow and then loses the battle to gravity dramatically. Our pursuer falls backward off the cliff face in a tangle of flailing arms and legs. Seconds later, we hear the sickening thud 60 feet below us as his fragile body contacts the rock ledges waiting to pierce him with their punishing backbone. Leda stands peering over the edge growling under her breath menacingly, daring the monster to rise up again and assault her person. I walk over to her slowly. "Good girl. It's okay. Take it easy now."

Looking over the side of the abrasive outcropping into the gathering gloom, I risk a quick pass with my flashlight across the bottom ground. The crumpled figure of the man lies broken below us, his neck at a devastating angle, the rifle caught awkwardly under his mangled body. There is no coming back from that fall. My anger fades away gradually as I consider what could possibly be so important that these hard men are showing such total disregard for the lives of others, and themselves. I feel sorrow over this outcome, but not shame. In this life, you are a victim only if you allow yourself to be one. And I am determined—NEVER again.

CHAPTER 75

R andy hobbles over and looks at me inquiringly. "He's done for," I say simply and quietly.

"Thanks to Leda," he replies. "That guy is the one who gave me this black eye and likes to kick people in the ribs over and over when they're tied up and helpless. He was serving a life sentence, five to ten years at a time, before he got out this last time due to prison overcrowding. Good riddance! He must have still been trying to take me alive for information on the thumb drive location. Otherwise, he could have just shot us as he started to catch up to us. We better find a safe spot to hole up for the night. It's getting too dangerous to travel in this territory in the pitch dark."

"You're right," I give myself a mental shake and approach him. "The bear spray served some kind of purpose. Let's hope we don't run into any **actual** bears before we get out of this mess. At least, Dad found out the infrared in their chopper is not operational, so that gives us one huge break." I vigorously slosh water over Leda's paws to be sure no bear spray transferred onto her. Fortunately, she seems completely unaffected by any of the last five minutes' worth of action.

We inch forward on the rocky ridge of path below the massive rock bluff hovering above us and I shine my flashlight carefully to my left. Just as I was hoping, a deep space is carved back under the stony cap. We force our way through a pair of conical junipers blocking the cleft and glide in under the overhang. This hideout seems heaven-sent at this point in our headlong but unsteady flight to safety. We have almost enough room to stand upright. But instead, we both sink tiredly to the ground with pained relief. The surge of adrenaline that carried us through to this point has definitely evaporated in a hurry. Randy looks white-faced and strained. My hands quiver involuntarily on the snaps of my backpack. This day, after the joy of finding Randy, has been a blur of breathless flight and enervating fear. I pray we are safe here because debilitation has sunk its claws deep into us now.

Finally rousing myself enough to gingerly shrug out of my backpack, I hand Randy a water bottle and a packet of electrolytes. I pour a few inches of water into Leda's bowl and she slakes her thirst. I wince my painful way out of my vest and hand Randy the flashlight. A shudder of fear riots through my whole body as I finally allow myself to consider that we were in the crosshairs of rifles capable of doing a lot of damage to us. I ask him to scan my back and shoulder for the source of the wetness permeating my camo shirt. He runs the flashlight over my side and then back again.

"Well, I'll be darned," he exclaims.

"What?" I call out.

"Just a minute, Veronica. Still checking," Randy replies calmly. The suspense is killing me. He finishes his methodical perusal. "It looks like a bullet slammed off a tree and then smashed the GPS unit and pulverized your cell phone on your hip. Also, another bullet ricocheted up and ripped across the back of your shoulder. You're probably going to have a spectacular bruise on your hip. The shoulder is oozing blood, but not too badly. We're going to be quite the pair when we finally get off this mountain."

It's promising that he said "when" we get off the mountain, and not "if." But I'm definitely feeling a little out of sorts. "Man, this is just great. I'll never hear the end of this from my dad. The GPS saved your life. Blah blah blah. And my cell phone is trashed right when we need help. Good thing I have a physical compass to use instead. On top of all that, I'm going to have scars on **both** shoulders now." I hear myself sounding kind of whiny, but Randy takes it in stride and starts grinning at me—until I cave in and grimace ruefully back at him. "You're right. We could be worse off. I need food. Like pizza or French fries. Or both." By then, we are both snorting weakly with laughter while Leda tilts her head and looks back and forth between the silly humans.

Leda watches intently as one of her sample size bags of dog food pours into her collapsible bowl and she sets to with gusto. We wrap and tape a secure dressing around Randy's palm and it stops leaking like a sieve. The gash on his head looks better and he massages more arnica into his knee while I search my backpack for additional supplies. "We could use a whole M*A*S*H unit out here at this point," I grumble to Randy.

"I agree, but they would never get to us in this wild terrain."

I pull my T-shirt completely off over my head and Randy swabs the bullet graze with antiseptic, slathers on an antibiotic salve, and tapes a thickly padded gauze and bandage dressing over it. "That's quite the scar on your other shoulder," Randy says in subdued tones. "You'll have to tell me about that at a later date." I am grateful he doesn't press the issue because that ugly ridge of damaged tissue has served as a haunting reminder of my prior close call for nearly three years. I cannot permit myself to dredge up any of that barely healed psychic wound from my past. I have to hold it together to survive this situation right here and right now.

My sports bra has soaked up a lot of blood, but it's drying already in the low humidity mountain air. I hand Randy my vest for warmth over his protests, then show him the Cleveland Cavaliers hoodie stuffed at the bottom of my bag before I carefully pull it on. Now that we have stopped fleeing like rabbits before a stoat, we both feel chilled. We each swallow a three pack of painkillers with the last of the water I brought along. However, I hear a flowing tinkle of sound outside the opening of the cleft in the rock and creep carefully outside to check. Hallelujah. A rivulet of mountain water flows down the side of the bluff. I hasten inside and grab an empty one-liter water bottle from my pack, return to the steady trickle of water outside, and fill it up by the greenish glimmer of a glow stick. These glow sticks are perfect for a light source of a lower wattage. The flashlight puts out a little too much light when trying to be surreptitious. Randy smiles broadly as he sees the water purification tablets come out of a side pocket of my pack. He reaches for them with a pleased expression and plops them in the spring water.

"You're making the water expert very happy," he jokes.

"You can thank my father, aka Mr. Safety," I rejoin. "He never lets me leave home unprepared. Even for a trip to the library!"

Roughly five minutes later, Randy tightens down the lid on the water bottle and shakes it up. We will have to guess at the next 35-minute processing period for the water since neither of us is wearing a watch. One last foray into my backpack unearths a parcel of food my dad had secreted in there, just in case. How does he know? Randy and I split another scrumptious peanut butter and strawberry jam sandwich, and then consume a bag of trail mix.

"Your dad is a prince among men."

"You're not kidding. Wait until you've tried his buttermilk pancakes with genuine Geauga County maple syrup." My voice starts to shake a bit as I contemplate the fact that I may never see my father again. He has been the only constant person in my life through all my travails, and his help would be so useful right about now. He will be extremely worried about me as time ticks by and I don't contact him. But realistically, once he and Tim start to piece together where I might be, based on my final cell phone tracking data from the new app, help probably won't be available until tomorrow. Our job is to stay alive until then. Bending my head to hide my tearful face, I burrow around in my bag of supplies. An orange is tucked in the toe of the bag and I hand it and my knife over to Randy. He cuts into its dimpled orange hide and separates out the succulent sections for us to divide. The cool juice feels restorative to my dry throat.

The sheer terror of being shot at, again, has left my whole system feeling somehow desiccated. I put my head on my knees and try to calm my racing thoughts. I can almost hear Zach telling me, "Baby, hang tough." Soon, a funny, rasping noise reaches my ears. My heart leaps in my chest for a moment thinking we have been discovered. My eyes fly open as I look to my left. Leda is rolling around on her back against the rigid floor scratching a nagging itch and grunting with pleasure. She gets up, shakes energetically, turns around twice, and then passes out on her side across the entrance to our hidey-hole. Even in sleep, that nose is turned on. If she smells or senses anything at all, we'll know about it. I am so proud of the beautiful and dependable dog she has become, and she has served as my steadfast anchor in the stormy seas churned up by Tommy Arnett. Her fortitude and bravery were the lodestar for the beginnings of my healing. However, my healing could be in serious jeopardy right now, and I cling desperately to the strengths I have—Leda, Randy's intelligence, and my training. It's all I have to weather this unforeseen tumult.

I unclip the shattered GPS from my belt and chuck the decimated cell phone to the side. How were they even still hanging on? Randy and I both sink into a state of utmost exhaustion. Nevertheless, he looks less pale after sustenance and water. He's got to be tougher than these felons counted on. I pull out my paper map and estimate roughly where we are, based on the terrain we tore through moving downhill prior to the arrival of the helicopter. I show Randy by the dappled light emanating from the flashlight and bouncing off the jagged rock walls that we can cut directly south in the morning, as early as possible. My plan is for us to head right into the heart of the massive inholding that sits to the south of the three dilapidated cabins. At that point, I am hopeful that we can get out to the road and then find an occupied dwelling somewhere along the primitive Lambeth Lane. All we have to do is make our way there undetected before any more of the bad guys find us. And that brings me to the crux of the matter. I turn to Randy and it's time for some long-delayed answers.

CHAPTER 76

"Randy, surely this assault by helicopter and hired guns is pretty hard-core for someone like Billy Fulton. I'm finding it increasingly hard to believe that he or his merry band of idiots have anything to do with your abduction."

Randy nods at me vigorously. "You're going to want to hold on to your hat for this one, Veronica, but not only did Billy Fulton *not* arrange my little soiree in the wilderness, but I just finalized my third review of the data pertaining to Chardonnay's drowning and Billy is completely innocent."

"What!" I squeak, belatedly trying to keep my voice down. "Oh boy. The District Attorney is going to be awfully surprised."

Randy chuckles back at me. "Well, I'm sure part of him will be highly relieved. He doesn't have to put a popular sports star on trial and he certainly doesn't want to prosecute an innocent man. I was finalizing my report to forward to him for review when all this kicked off. Now, mind you, Billy doesn't know I'm going to exonerate him, but this kind of endeavor is way better planned and conceived than anything Billy's crew could come up with. And… I've identified the cause of all this uproar by process of elimination and the information I gleaned from the hired muscle when they thought I was unconscious." The flashlight flickers around the corners of the implacable shelter and I lean forward like a child listening to fearsome ghost stories by a wavering campfire.

"Okay," I put my hand up to slow him down. "I want to hear all about that. But let's back up for just a second. What happened to poor Chardonnay? She did drown, correct?"

"Correct, but it was actually a medical phenomenon known as post-immersion syndrome, sometimes called 'dry drowning' by lay people. Chardonnay had gone swimming at a friend's pool earlier in the day. Her friend, Donna, went from the indoor pool house into the kitchen to get them a platter of cheese, crackers, and fresh fruit. When she returned, Chardonnay was on the side of the pool gasping. She had not realized that the pool got sharply deeper at one end, and not being the most confident swimmer, had plunged under abruptly and scared herself. It's human nature then to gulp down a little bit of water in a state of panic. Because she was able to get herself to the edge and out of the water, her friend assumed the worst was over. Unfortunately, after taking in that pool water, the muscles in her windpipe became constrained to protect the lungs or a spasm occurred in the airway causing it to close up later. I questioned Chardonnay's friend, and she confirmed that Chardonnay seemed inordinately tired and was coughing a bit before she headed directly home after the incident. Billy Fulton claimed in his interrogation that, in retrospect, she seemed to be breathing in shorter, shallow breaths before he left the house for his private workout session and was going to take a bath at his suggestion to calm herself after her unplanned dunk under the deep pool water.

"It seems counterintuitive, but she loved that tub apparently and he thought it would relax her. He turned on the music for her and filled up the hot water before leaving in a hurry, because he is habitually late to meet his personal trainer. She was sitting on the edge of the spa tub in her yoga gear looking at her plethora of bubble baths when he kissed her and left. Billy assumed she would just take her soak and calm down, but when he returned home three hours later, she was face down in the tub, her temple bruised, and still dressed. The police found no sign of forced entry to the house and the security company could show that the alarm system had been set—which ruled out intruders—causing the focus to turn to Billy as the perpetrator.

"But, after reviewing all the data and interpreting the results of the second autopsy, I ascertained that she had died from this post-immersion syndrome, or 'dry drowning' on the side of the tub and then fallen fully clothed into the water. She had no bath water in her lungs. She simply couldn't breathe properly past the closed-up airway and nobody was around then to realize what was happening. This is an extremely rare occurrence in adults; it's overwhelmingly more common in children. Billy was known to be home before she died and they had been arguing sporadically in the weeks before her death. This is a perfect example of initial appearances not revealing the true facts."

"Wow, that's great work, Randy. You are going to make a lot of loyal sports fans happy. Poor Chardonnay though; what a way to go. It had to be so horrible. And she was all alone. I must confess I'm rather glad myself that he didn't harm her. He has always seemed more goofy than violent."

"Yes, it is difficult to equate the ringleader of the famous ice cream truck caper with cold-blooded murder, but spouses have snapped before for no discernible reason," he agrees. My fear abates ever so slowly as Randy and I methodically talk through the details of the circumstances surrounding his disappearance.

"So," I continue. "Dad reviewed the accessible files on your thumb drive and we ruled out the freshwater mussel conservationist, the rainwater retention groups, and the defendant in the Virginia drowning murder. With hints from Patty, Dad broke the password on the last four files right when I was driving up here to search the cabins. You tell me it's not Billy's case. We have eliminated essentially all of your other projects except the three files entitled Agua Pura Ahora, S.A., Idaho Drowning and Chad E., which you encrypted, so I'm going to take a wild guess and say this has something to do with one of those three files."

"Patty actually guessed my password?" Randy inquires in surprise.

"More like she gave Dad key phrases from your life together and he crunched them through a code-breaking program," I clarify.

He grins. "That's my girl. I can't keep you in suspense any longer and it's important that someone other than me knows the villainy at the heart of this whole ordeal. The Idaho drowning case is one on which I was recently asked to consult. It involves the nighttime drowning in the Snake River of the 20-something mistress of a State Representative, so the local Prosecuting Attorney wants my involvement to remain unadvertised for the moment. He fears the political fall-out if it looks like he is conducting a witch hunt against this long-time politician.

"Chad E. actually stands for eastern Chad, the landlocked country slightly north of center in Africa. I have been there three times over the years. Do you know it has over 200 ethnic and linguistic groups? Talk about a melting pot. But it is bordered by crazy Libya and dangerous Sudan on two sides and has an incredibly corrupt regime. People are poor and water is hard to come by in the desert to the north and in the arid swathe through the center of the country. Hundreds of thousands of refugees from Sudan live lives of despair and devastation at camps in eastern Chad.

"An international charity group is interested in building a water purification plant near Lake Fitri to process and provide clean water to surrounding residents and refugees. I was tasked with reviewing the mechanics of the entire system. Water-borne diseases can be substantially reduced in this manner. They knew of my work in Kenya helping the 300,000 family farms sitting in the highlands around the Tana River watershed to the north of Nairobi. We used nature-based improvements to help solve the 30% shortfall between water supply and water demand in the urban area. Small measures like planting bamboo buffers between farm fields and rivers trap silt and keep the water clean, for example. The most successful measure I have helped an international conservancy group implement is the water pans—hand-dug retention ponds lined with heavy-duty plastic that each hold 6,000-26,000 gallons of rainwater. The farmers have water to tap for their crops in the periods between the rains and can avoid drawing from local waterways in the dry spells that run from December to March. We have also assisted them in terracing steep fields prone to run off and in the planting of Napier grass, which serves the dual purpose of halting soil erosion, and feeding their animals."

The light of near fervor burns in Randy's eyes. His passion is clean water and providing it to the masses, especially in some of the world's unloved regions. He gives himself a little shake and finishes up, "Sorry. I can launch into a lecture just about anywhere apparently. The funding for the Chad project has to come through the World Bank and negotiations are at a sensitive phase right now due to regional tensions arising out of the civil war in the Central African Republic. The Board of Governors does not want to make the World Bank a target in the region before it is even clear if this process will move forward. I protected that file simply due to the delicate nature of the negotiations."

CHAPTER 77

"And then there was one," I say to him.

"Exactly. All of this trouble and strife is related to the upcoming initial public offering for a different water purification project—in the Americas and Africa for Agua Pura Ahora, S.A. When it comes right down to it, it has the basest of reasons. The oldest reason in the book. Money. You may know I was engaged to prepare the technical report on the reverse osmosis system to be manufactured by Agua Pura Ahora, S.A. for worldwide operations. The company was already up and running, apparently successfully in Central America, and was looking to expand exponentially. I had no input in their product development until the IPO process was initiated in the U.S.

"My technical report was to be completed right after the preliminary prospectus, or red herring prospectus. Celebrities and citizens of all stripes in North and South America had shown extreme interest in investing in this much-needed, but also feel-good, product. I really expected the data review to support earlier findings regarding the efficacy of their proprietary synthetic membrane under tested pressures. I won't bore you with all the scientific details, but at higher pressures, these membranes were going to fail—most likely within a year. Of course, I eventually realized this was of no concern to at least one of the principal investors who put up the initial capital.

"The IPO is scheduled very shortly after my technical report is due. Shares of the company will be sold to institutional and individual investors, creating a publicly held company from a privately owned company. The public offering should raise new equity capital for the company and increase public awareness of the product even more. But, and here's the key point, Veronica, it can convert the investments of private stockholders like the company founders or private equity investors into a substantial source of revenue. The shares will be listed on stock exchanges and can be traded in the open market after the IPO. When I pieced together all the facts after turning over my projects in my mind, and wove in the snippets I picked up from the mercenaries, it almost broke my heart. It was truly a passion project for me. This plan to produce clean water in vast quantities is desperately needed in specific regions in the countries of Central and South America, and of course, Africa, and it has been turned into a grubby cash grab unworthy of its sincere intent to help people. I believe it is just one investor, but all he wants is to get an obscene profit for his initial investment, while also laundering his drug money through the stock market. When the systems fail and children and the elderly get sick and die in a year or two, he will be long gone with his undeserved profit."

"Wait, hang on!" I burst out at Randy. "I was following you until you got to the drugs part. The mastermind of all this is in a drug cartel?" Inside I'm thinking: Hell no. This day **did** just get worse.

"Yes, it's true and I'm nearly certain that this investor/drug lord, Juan Toledo, convinced or coerced one or both of the owners of Agua Pura Ahora, S.A. to recommend the new IT guy at my company to Glen Gerard. It is the only thing that makes sense. He was placed there to hack into my database and make sure everything was proceeding on schedule for the IPO. They may have even known before I got the data that the membranes are flawed. I'm not sure.

"But let me start at the beginning, when I first began getting suspicious. These two shifty looking characters came to my attention in the parking lot by work. At that point, I thought they were more than likely paparazzi looking for a scoop on the Billy Fulton murder trial. Last week, I had realized there were issues with the mid-pressure reverse osmosis system and needed to think through the technical report and any modifications we could make to salvage the system. I knew the IPO date would be blown, but the project could still be revamped and good could be done. Also, I had my expert's report to write on the Fulton case, which will be shocking, to say the least. I copied my files to my thumb drive so I could work on my laptop and drove up to Estes Park. I was worried about hackers and security given the high-profile nature of this star athlete's trial so put a security measure in place on the four most sensitive files. After eating brunch in Estes, I called Patty and mentioned that I had glimpsed two guys who looked very similar to the ones I had previously seen in my building's parking lot. But I shook it off, and headed into RMNP as planned.

"I stopped at Moraine Park Discovery Center to look at their ecosystem exhibits, my favorite, before I took my customary hike up Lawn Lake Trail to clear my head. It was quiet and deserted at that time in the building. From the upstairs balcony at the visitor center, I looked out and saw these same two characters. I was nearly sure. A momentary flash of alarm, panic almost, shook me and I wondered if they had nefarious motives. Before I even knew what I was doing, I dragged a chair over underneath the taxidermy mountain lion and wedged the thumb drive behind his leg while no one else was in the room. It was an inexplicable urge, but I did it for a reason I still don't quite understand."

"Women call that intuition, Randy. A lot of times, it saves lives. Crossing the street at night if someone makes the hair stand up on the back of your neck, the impulse to check your baby in his crib even though you just looked in on him, the urge to take your dog outside for a walk five minutes before a deranged gunman kills everyone in your office." By now, my eyes are filling up with tears. I am just tired and exceedingly anxious about our chances for survival. The shocking news of a drug cartel's involvement is not very confidence-inspiring for our future chances of survival either. Randy looks at me sadly and with sympathy.

He stares glumly at the cave floor and begins his tale again, "Well, I didn't trust my hunch shortly after the hiding of the thumb drive because when I left out the back door of the visitor center and cut around to my vehicle, the two guys appeared to be with a pair of women. They were joking around and taking photos of the mule deer. I started thinking I was being ridiculous. These two men—who may not have even been the same ones I had seen previously—are on vacation with their spouses and I'm acting like a spy evading capture. I know what you're going to say, Veronica. I should have listened to my intuition. I drove away and parked at the Lawn Lake Trailhead, telling myself to calm down; this was not a James Bond movie and I was just working too hard. Then, a couple of miles up the trail, I glanced back over my shoulder and could see a spiraling section of path winding around below me due to the switchbacks. Sure enough, here come the same two men again. And they weren't just taking a leisurely hike.

"By now, I have no idea what's going on, but I don't like it. I hightail it up the trail. I'm in decent shape so decided to cut across the thicketed area between the Lawn Lake Trail and the Black Canyon Trail and basically run carefully down to the Lumpy Ridge Trailhead and seek assistance or a ride to the rangers. This whole time cell service was non-existent so I needed to lose them. They don't look fit but they came uphill at a good clip. All that working out in prison on the taxpayers' dime."

"Geez," I say. "This gets better and better. Here we go with two ex-cons charging into the mix." By this point, I'm rocking back and forth in my spot trying to calculate how we're going to get out of this mess tomorrow.

"And you know what happened next. They shot me with the beanbag riot gun, tied me up, took my cell phone, and radioed in the pilot and helicopter. At the time it seemed quite odd they just happened to have a helicopter handy and this expensive radio used in mountainous terrain, but I came to find out later that they have been running heroin through

Fort Collins up into Wyoming and over to the Dakotas. Literal peddlers of death.

"The pilot is a mercenary on the payroll of this drug lord and he found a couple of secluded cabins from which he can run the drugs. When Juan Toledo's planted IT guy at Water Analytical Solutions saw my preliminary report and informed Toledo, he got really nervous that the expected profits from the IPO might be in jeopardy. I believe the plan was to kill me and have the new IT guy plant a fake favorable report on my computer database at work to allow the IPO to move forward. What they didn't bargain for was the fact that I had made a thumb drive copy of all my projects and left work. Once their mole discovered that problem, they needed to get that drive back and destroy my negative report which detailed unfavorable results. Hence the abduction, holding me at the line cabin, and the beatings. They let slip a lot of this information about the drugs and people's names because they never intended for me to get out of there alive.

"The crazy thing is—at the very beginning—I had no idea who they worked for or which case this kidnapping was even about. My abductors knew the focus of any investigation and the world would be on the high-profile murder case, and they used it as a smokescreen. If I gave in to their beatings and told them where the thumb drive was located, I was a dead man. Later, I overheard them saying they had given my vehicle a cursory search at the Lawn Lake Trailhead. When they did not find the thumb drive they had seen inserted in my laptop at the diner in Estes, they started their pursuit of me up the trail. Once I was a captive, being unconscious for long stretches of time, and also just pretending to be, bought me some time. They kept leaving, at the insistence of their boss, to try to find and handle one of their dealers who was ripping them off. I also know they went to wherever my car was and searched it again for the thumb drive as well.

"Finally, I pieced together enough information from what I knew and overheard to deduce what this was all about. Then, I got away and you and Leda found me. I think that brings us up to date," he concludes with a long pause. The chilling details of the case swirl through my mind as I dig out the Mylar blanket packet and tear it open. Randy tries to protest when I hand it over to him. "You take it, Veronica. I'm not that cold."

I insist, "Hey, you have been through enough up to this point. You need to be in the best shape possible for whatever comes tomorrow. I won't be cold. Leda is like a little furnace right next to me. I promise." He reluctantly concedes and wraps himself up in the blanket gratefully. A night bird screeches outside on the lonesome slopes and we both jump a foot in the air. Randy pours a portion of the newly clean water into an empty bottle for me and we both sit and rehydrate and think dark, internal thoughts about our precarious plight.

CHAPTER 78

The terrors of the day eventually overtake us and we both doze fitfully under the shelter of the midnight sky and our rocky overhang. Our plan is to wake before the day dawns; we must be prepared to move south as rapidly as possible when the merest glimmer of morning light exists to illuminate our way. Waking at one point from my troubled sleep, I creep out with a muffled glow stick to the tiny trickle of water to refill our one-liter bottle. Leda accompanies me and stands stock-still testing the scent-laden night breezes. We crawl back inside and I drop the water purification tablets in the bottle and go through the shaking routine five minutes later. At least, we will have it ready to go with us when we leave our cover early.

My brown dog curls up tight against my side again and the shared warmth is most welcome. My shoulder has stiffened up as the night progresses and my hip does indeed have the beginnings of a spectacular bruise. The array of purple, black, and green will spread across my hip like a neap tide until subsiding to a sickly yellow shade in a week or two—assuming we survive that long. Randy is finally sleeping deeply it seems. The rest should strengthen him for the second leg of our dash to safety tomorrow. I can only recline on one side without pain jabbing at me insistently, so I lie awake, fretting over what fresh tribulations might befall us tomorrow. I eventually nod off, curled around my watchful dog.

Leda helps awaken us early in the morning when she rises up like a brown wraith from the floor of our refuge and eases out the opening of the cave. She inspects whatever caught her attention outside and glides back in to greet me after two or three minutes of snuffling around outside. Randy and I spend a little time creaking to our feet, asking about each other's injuries, and rotating our arms around to get our circulation going. My shoulder has stiffened up like a rusty latch needing a good oiling. A tranquil yoga class was originally on the schedule for this morning. This pursuit is the furthest thing in the world from a peaceful, refreshing stretch surrounded by my classmates and Sylvia, I think regretfully. It appears we are both feeling dispirited this morning, but through an unspoken agreement, neither of us immediately voices our worries.

I give Leda a small portion of food, so she won't be running on a full stomach, and watch it vanish in five seconds. Meanwhile, Randy and I each gnaw on a cinnamon crunch granola bar. Hard to believe, but I am actually getting tired of them. Apparently, there *is* a limit to how many granola bars I can eat. Peering out between the junipers standing sentry duty at the opening to our little cave, I observe the sky has a lighter hue to it. We should be able to vacate our hiding spot in a few short minutes. The swelling on Randy's knee has subsided a modicum, so perhaps we can make better time.

Using the high-resolution binoculars, I cautiously scan the escarpment's enveloping edges, but have no way of knowing if anyone is lurking just around the corner watching and waiting. Thinking logically, it is unlikely that any of our remaining pursuers made their way here in the obscure dark of night. The helicopter pilot took off before Leda muscled his passenger off the cliff edge. And then we found our sanctuary out of sight. As far as I could tell, only one man was chasing us up close yesterday evening, but I don't want to bet our lives on it. We're going to have to be on high alert moving through the backcountry today. I have an inkling that the pilot will be back and he'll prove to be a more perilous foe than the man lying crumpled at the bottom of the precipice ever was.

Randy picks up his trusty crutch and gives me a sturdy grin, "Let's blow this popsicle stand." A bubble of amusement rises up in me for a transitory moment. Then I struggle gamely into my backpack with his help, cursing my one stiff arm. We drift silently out to the rocky path and follow its studded curves for 250 yards or so before dropping down into another impressive grove of ponderosa pine. The slope faces southeast toward the sun, which is just beginning a shy peek over the horizon. Morning dew glistens like Christmas tree tinsel on the long needles bundled in twos and threes that decorate the pines. Wet, silvery ribbons of mist steam upward away from the stoic trees, as a pink flush creeps into the sky. A dusky flycatcher emerges from the open brushy area to our right and darts after a smallish swarm of insects venturing forth into the warming open space. His tail looks inordinately long compared to his body with its grayish olive back and pale yellow belly.

It seems such a travesty that sickening worry stains the beauty of this languorous locale. I would love to be sitting on a rock watching the birds flit about as the day begins, but this is not destined to be one of those priceless occasions. It dampens my enthusiasm for watching the perky flycatcher. Leda, on the other hand, is full of vim and vigor this sparkling morning. She trots ahead with animation and even makes an abbreviated dash after a red squirrel that wanders across her line of travel. She knows she is not permitted to chase animals, but this rodent was impudent enough to pop up right under her nose. The nerve! I call her softly, "Leda, Here." She wheels around and comes closer looking benignly innocent. "Good girl. Stay close." Randy smiles briefly at her and runs his hand down her curly back. She tolerates his petting now that she knows he is one of our trusted friends.

I worry about Randy; he is looking gaunt and weary through the stubble on his face. We have a good deal of ground to cover today—all while attempting to remain undiscovered. I pull out my map, orient myself to our current position, and compass in hand plot our southward direction. Boy, am I glad I wasn't just relying on the compass in the non-operational GPS or in my pulverized cell phone. One moment of terror occurs as Randy starts sliding crossways down a rock shelf on the diagonal and can't get enough pressure on his bad leg to stop the skid. I hasten forward and grab his arm to slow the slide while Leda stands like a statue in front of him and blocks his legs. We halt for a moment letting our pulse rates return to normal and Randy tests his knee with a few tentative steps. It looks like he's going to persevere. I expect nothing less now that I've seen him in action.

Randy asks, as he limps along next to me, "How many miles as the crow flies until we get to the inholding lands?"

"I'm estimating about three or four miles, but the ground will probably be rough. That will add to our time for sure. Good thing we started this morning as soon as the dark was lifting. Did you tweak your knee very much on that last slip?"

"Not too badly. Let me pop a few more painkillers and let's hit it."

Randy swallows the pills down and grins at me with determination. The insistent voice in the back of my mind urges me to make haste, but I tamp it down. Only a certain pace is achievable based on Randy's sore knee and the weak early blush of the morning sun. We both move grimly and resolutely forward turning over in our minds the sudden potential for attack looming over us. It is just a matter of time.

CHAPTER 79

"We should try to anticipate what the next move of these guys might be," Randy ventures quietly. "Thinking about it logistically, they are going to use our directional heading, which they observed yesterday, to try to intercept us today."

I ponder this comment while fiddling with my backpack strap where it is chafing the scar tissue on my shoulder. "Unfortunately, I have to agree with that assessment, Randy. When I was looking at the map this morning, it seems to make sense that they are going to hike east from the Donner Pass Trail and try to cut our trail as we head south. Or they may put the helicopter down in the open meadow the map shows about a half-mile short of our goal of the inholding lands and Lambeth Lane, the primitive road. By now, my dad will have called out the troops and help will be headed our way; we'll just have to evade these guys until then. We need to stay in cover as much as possible where it exists and look and listen sharply. Leda will let me know if she smells anything that alarms her. I don't want us to be in the middle of a spotting scope on a high-powered rifle again."

"Me neither," he replies fervently. "Okay, eyes peeled then."

We walk noiselessly among the hush of sturdy ponderosa pines from grove to grove, as they pass us into the safety of their brethren in a long, oscillating chain down the mountain. Shafts of sunlight perforate the spaces between these solemn stewards and shine down on mounds of ancient pine cones, motes of dust gyrating mid-air in the piercing light.

The scent from the trees is divine, not just pine, but freshness and earth and peace. I endeavor to soak in the solitude and absorb the venerable strength imparted from the forest to mankind from time immemorial. Anything to hold the blanketing feeling of dread at bay. We hit desolate rock shelves, which alternate with the asylum granted by the savior trees, and scurry across the barren and open stretches of ground with hunched backs and prickling between our shoulder blades. Just as I start to relax minutely, the unmistakable thrum of helicopter rotors approaching us from the west can be heard. Fortuitously, miraculously, we are within yards of a giant grove of ponderosa pine, and assorted ground shrubs, and roughly force our jagged way into the middle of the clutch of foliage.

"Randy, get down on the ground in a crouch under the long branches and keep your face turned down. We don't want anything white to catch their eye. The camo gear will make us blend right in." He complies instantly as I pull my camo gaiter over my face and roll under the limbs of a neighboring tree. Leda crawls in next to me as my hand flashes out the signal for her Down command. She is chocolate brown and blends in well with the heap of needles and cones. The chopper flies incessantly overhead in what I have to assume are quartering search patterns. The relentless noise goes on for what feels like hours, but is probably more like 15 minutes. I know what the fox feels like now, terror singing through his veins, as the hounds bay in close proximity, never ceasing the chase. My heart feels like thunder in my chest, but I rely on my training and stay snug in place. I am confident in our hiding spot, but my pulse continues to race wildly regardless.

After what seems like eons, we hear the chopper bear away and I peek up enough to see it vanish over the horizon. The helicopter's engine sounds like it's sputtering intermittently to me, but that may just be wishful thinking—since I know about the prior fuel system issues. Or maybe they're running out of fuel; we could use a lucky break right about now. "We'll stay put for a bit," I tell Randy. "We need to make sure they aren't trying to trick us into breaking cover." I reckon that we had covered a solid mile in our morning travels before the interruption of the helicopter, and we will begin our approach to another locus of possible alarm shortly. After staying crouched for another good 15 minutes, the three of us move out as carefully as possible. Randy and I skirt downhill on our grim forced march toward safety, both of us breathing hard while we paradoxically try to stay calm. The trees persist and we cling close to their edges in the event of another series of flyover maneuvers by our pursuers. I force myself to concentrate on the map in my head. Soon, we should run across an intermittent watercourse. Ominously for us, however, a vast meadow hugs up against it and it's hard to envision a more perfect spot to set down a helicopter and wait for the mice to blunder in front of the pouncing cat. We have one advantage over the cat, however. A big, brave, yellow-eyed dog.

Randy and I talk quietly as we traverse the final few rock ledges before we expect to run across the seasonal watercourse we plan to follow directly onto Lambeth Lane. It's an ancient primitive road that allows access to the owners of cabins on the private land, or inholdings, within the national forest. It stands to reason that we will find an occupied dwelling or a ride out if we can just make our way closer down to civilization. If nothing else, maybe a better place to hide will present itself.

We discuss the likelihood that the helicopter or the bad guys may now be planning to ambush us at the sizable meadow that sits adjacent to the watercourse we want to follow as our lifeline. The chopper has not been seen or heard since it flew off 35-40 minutes ago, but they may be putting Plan B into effect stealthily. Randy suggests bearing slightly more east to transect the water on its far bank, further away from the meadow even though the territory looks more taxing.

"That's your call," I offer thoughtfully. "I like the idea of keeping our distance from any chokepoint, but how is your knee holding up? Time wise, I don't think it will hurt us substantially, as we'll just strike the road a bit more to the south."

"At this point, I need to tough it out. I will go as fast as I can, but undoubtedly we're going to be a lot safer as far away from that meadow as possible."

I look at him with admiration. This is the man that Billy Fulton's friends called a "nerd." They would all be bawling like babies, curled up in the fetal position right about now, if they had to endure any of what Randy has gone through for close to a week. He deserves to survive this and he is entitled to respect.

"Okay, that's our plan. Let me check the compass." Following our new bearing, we adjust course, and pick our way down rock slopes with full, terrifying exposure, alternating with cover-providing Douglas fir and towering blue spruce, the favorite of Christmas tree growers, as we drop below 8000 feet of elevation. Generally, being in the mountains is a highlight in my life, but right now I cannot wait to see the back of them.

Leda scouts directly ahead of us and seems unperturbed at the moment. Every so often, as Randy negotiates a section of outcropping that slows him a bit, I scan the edges of the horizon and patches of distant cover with the binoculars looking for anything alarming. This action is performed more out of nervousness than complete confidence. If the pilot is ex-military and on the ground, the chances of us spotting him again before he kills us are probably not terrific. I push that worry down deep, however. Randy is plugging away on our route with determination and I need to match his stoic bravery.

CHAPTER 80

Amazingly, I have calculated our course very accurately using my "archaic" map and orienteering skills, and we breathlessly emerge near the end of the capricious creek, our guide to the inholding land and primitive road. Typical of a lot of water ways located in mountainous areas—it is strong and flowing when heavy rains persist or snow melt runs. In drier times, it is harder to locate and has much less flow. Luck may finally be smiling upon us. Enough water burbles down its stony channel that honing in on it is easy. Leda stands in a deeper pool drinking water happily and splashing waves up around her damp face with a long, extended pawing of her foreleg. She has had this silly habit from the first time she ventured in the water after I adopted her. All I need now is for her to stick her whole head underwater and come up with a rock in her mouth, which is another of her patented moves. I prompt her gently, "Leda, Watch," so she is reminded to pay attention to her surroundings. It really was not necessary; she scans our perimeter constantly for any threat or anomaly. She is not sure exactly what is going on, but she is attuned to my tension and knows to take heed of anything unusual.

Randy and I stick to our plan and work our way gingerly down the eastern bank of the stream, which proves to be a lucky choice for us. This decision keeps us further from the massive alpine meadow adjoining the western periphery of the water, which we both fear will be used by our pursuers as a staging area of some kind. And as it turns out, although the footing is tricky, this edge is bordered by a downhill rolling wall of jade green conifers, which gives us cover and throws out a shadow façade to mask our movement. The October sun climbs higher in the turquoise sky; the air is crisp and cool with the promise of a glorious day—if only we can survive it.

Focusing on sticking to the shade and concentrating on not falling over, we bushwhack ever downward. The water we move parallel to vacillates in and out of truly flowing, but it is audible enough to keep using it as our personal route to freedom—with any luck. We have covered approximately a mile of rugged ground when the anticipated, and much dreaded, sound of a helicopter churns out of the west a second time, and the chopper descends at a point behind us and uphill from our current location. Randy glances over his shoulder, even though we are too far to see or be seen at present. "Well, we calculated that correctly with their utilization of the chopper. We need to hustle down to the road you showed me on the map. Then we can go south to get help." Nodding my head vigorously in agreement, I take a quick scan with the binoculars. So far, all is clear. We pick up our pace as much as we can while still staying upright. Randy winces as his foot rolls over a rock and his knee twists laterally.

"Are you okay?" I call to him worriedly.

"I'm fine," he replies. "Just took a bad step." If these guys catch us, it certainly won't be because Randy gave up and capitulated. He soldiers on gamely. A dull headache throbs low at the base of my skull—probably a combination of terror, worry, and slight dehydration due to our clumsy dash through the countryside. I motion Randy to halt and we drink sips of water hurriedly. I figure we have traveled at least a mile down the intermittent stream and that road awaits us like a mirage glimmering on a distant horizon.

One additional scan with the binoculars suddenly reveals the presence of a dreaded stalker, high on the slopes above us and a good half-mile or more behind us. Dad is going to be able to write a bang-up review on these glasses, if I live to tell him the tale. The man following us looks unsure of his agility on the jumbled terrain also, so doesn't appear to be gaining on us much at the moment. I endeavor to quell the nagging internal voice demanding more speed, as my common sense tells me that could very well be a recipe for calamity. Randy has worked out a system of hobbling and leaning on the crutch that gets him down the side of the streambed in an awkward fashion, but he is making it work. Leda is aware of the man trailing us now and she stops alongside us a handful of times sampling the breezes. She will know him if she runs across him again. That won't work to his benefit.

Finally, amazingly, we pop out of a tiny patch of blue spruce and stumble right across the road. It's dirt and not terribly well-maintained, but it looks like the yellow brick road right now. I motion Randy to the left with my hand and we start heading southwest, navigating the curves of the road at a quicker clip. Randy gestures vigorously at a weathered cabin tucked in the woods and set back a few hundred yards off the road. Now the real fun is about to start, I think to myself fiercely. I am proud of myself for feeling more mad than scared right now! A telephone pole, with an adjoining line looping slackly from its top, heads from the dirt road down the lane toward the cabin. I start praying to the gods of archaic technology for a landline as Randy and I hasten into the sun-drenched clearing that outlines the snug little abode with bright light.

The cabin is locked up tight and clearly nobody is around, but we just need the bolthole now while we wait for reinforcements. Randy scouts around in the yard and pulls an axe from a chopping stump at the side of the building while I try desperately to remember Tim's cell phone number. Of course, it is safely stored in my defunct cell phone. What the heck is it? Randy hauls back and clouts the barred front door with tremendous force. Geez, it looks like Randy frequents the gym in between working and testifying at trials. I'm sure he has a plan, so I don't waste any time wondering why he's blatantly destroying the front door.

Randy pummels the locked barrier into submission and I dash inside looking wildly for a telephone. Miracle of miracles, a rotary dial phone sits on the kitchen counter in all its avocado-colored loveliness. I start dialing the phone number for Tim while praying I have dredged it correctly out of my memory. Tim answers, "Sergeant Donovan," as our phones connect.

"Tim, oh thank God."

"Veronica, where are you girl?" He sounds just shy of frantic.

"I have Randy. We are on Lambeth Lane at the cabin owned by the Burchells. (Got to love those carved wooden vanity signs above the front doors of vacation homes. Sorry Burchell family.) We have at least one, but possibly two, armed gunmen in pursuit and they are using that helicopter as well. Please get us help as fast as possible. They aren't far behind. If they get us, this is all because of Juan Toledo, an investor in the water IPO."

"What a relief to talk to you at last. I'm here with Henry Akers and we're scrambling everyone. You two do what you have to do to survive. The cavalry is on the way." Tim's voice is cutting out and I know the reception must be poor wherever he is. The last thing I hear before the call sputters out is Tim saying, "Your dad and Michael are in Estes Park. I'm calling him now." And the line goes dead—of course.

CHAPTER 81

Randy leans on the axe just inside the cabin, catching his breath after his success in battering down the door. That had to have hurt his banged-up ribs. We can both hear the enemy as he storms down the road toward the cabin. He made up time on us once Randy decided to emulate Paul Bunyan. I feel relatively calm despite this turn of events because there is no way in the world Randy and I cannot outwit this runaway train of rage. He calls me over to him, pulls the binoculars out of the top of my pack and steps deep into the concealing shade of the front porch to observe the approaching man. "Perfect. I only see one right now. That's the one I bashed with the shovel. He's an idiot, so we still have a chance."

Randy looks delighted. He is apparently very motivated by being abducted and tortured by these goons for days. Randy steps back inside and orients himself in the great room of the cabin as his eyes adjust to the difference in light from the outside to the inside. Randy sets the front door blatantly ajar and slides a sturdy chest of drawers from the little dining area to a spot parallel to the front door. It dawns on me that we're not just trying to outlast this guy until the police show up. We're setting a trap for him. Well, okay then. I'm definitely on board with this decision. Randy motions for me to shift a bookcase from a nearby wall to a spot parallel to the other side of the front door.

A ha. We're making a cattle chute. If he enters, he won't have a lot of space to move around in initially. Randy is pretty good at tactics. Penny, my instructor in self-defense, would most assuredly approve. "Veronica, put Leda in a safe spot where she'll be protected if he starts shooting."

"I know she won't leave me though; that's the only problem."

"You don't have to lock her up. Just get her under cover. She needs to be able to get to you if this works." Nodding vigorously, I move Leda into the kitchen and put her into a Down Stay behind the kitchen island. She sinks down and looks at me woefully with her enigmatic golden eyes. She is not keen on this position, but she stays. I rub the top of her head and reinforce the command before returning to Randy. She's down, but she's poised to erupt. Randy has shifted the curtain on the front window enough to spy the man steaming right toward us from the road and up the lane to the cabin. He has clearly seen the open door.

"Show time. Let me have Leda's long line please." Randy hands me the snap end of her line and then heads behind the chest of drawers and crouches on one side of the front door while holding the remainder of the line bunched in his hand. His plan is simple but brilliant; I dart behind the bookcase rapidly on his signal holding the snap of the long line in my hand. We both keep the line flat on the floor across the bottom of the doorway. I really hope our pursuer is as stupid as he sounds right now.

Our relentless stalker is yelling outside the cabin in a frenzy of rage and bluster. He must not have enjoyed chasing us down the ankle-busting mountain so much today. Too bad, buddy. I am done being shot. And Randy is done being kicked in the ribs. Randy's face gleams faintly on the other side of the doorway, and I can attest to the fact that Randy is smiling now. Revenge is sweet. Thug number two bashes the door of the cabin further open with the butt of his rifle and starts to plunge through the doorway. Bad use of your gun, idiot, I think to myself. The dim light in the cabin temporarily disorients him after being out in the sunshine. Randy yells "Now," and we both pull the long line up six inches from the floor just as he barrels into the room. I ardently wish we had slow-motion video replay because it works like a charm. He trips over the taut rope and flips into the room like a stuntman falling off a two-story building. Milliseconds later, he lands heavily with a thud that audibly flattens the air from his lungs.

As the man woozily attempts to flounder up and grab for his rifle, I yell for Leda. "Leda, Get Him." She erupts from behind her protection and covers the space to him in three long bounds. She sails through the air in a magnificent rush and latches onto his arm just as he rolls over with the rifle in his hand. Our assailant is exceedingly strong, but Leda hangs on and weathers his desperate efforts to kick and punch her as I rise out of my crouch on the floor. Poor battered Randy emerges from his hiding spot, axe in hand, and proceeds to bash him with the flat end right across the forehead while Leda holds his gun arm in a vice grip. Our pursuer groans deeply and keels over satisfyingly like a felled tree. Randy and I stand and catch our breath. He is pressing his hand to his rib cage with a grimace. Leda gives the bad guy one last growl and shake before dropping his wrist, and then runs over to me when I pant out her name.

"I wanted to get him down before we tried to take him out. He's crazy strong. I can't believe he's even here after I clubbed him in the head with the shovel at the other cabin. Having Leda with us to grab his arm leveled the playing field," Randy explains as he uses the long line to wrap up the bad guy's hands and then feet behind his body. Those look like nautical grade knots so he's clearly not getting out of that. I give Randy a big hug and we both stand in the cabin in a state of shock, realizing that with Leda's invaluable help yesterday and today, we outwitted the two ex-cons. We stand together panting and drained from the last two days, but smiling nonetheless.

However, our jubilation is short-lived as the unmistakable noise of bullets slamming into the outer wall of the log cabin saturates our awareness and glass shatters wildly as one bullet penetrates a window to our right. Randy and I dive as nimbly as we can behind the kitchen island. Leda comes over in response to my hand signal and lies down next to me. She looks very alert and is watching the front door closely. I am frantically trying to figure out how she can help us without getting shot if the pilot comes through that door. It appears that being continually stymied by Randy, and maybe using too much of his own product, have triggered a complete loss of rational thinking in the pilot, our final shadow. He's thrown all caution to the wind with that hail of bullets. Blood seeps down the middle of my back and I'm aware my dive to the floor probably opened up the bullet score across my shoulder. No time to worry about that now.

"Looks like that crazy pilot caught up to us finally," Randy offers.

"I know and we're running out of options here. We really need the police," I say plaintively. "We could try to trade the trussed-up one for our freedom, and use his gun to keep the pilot off us as long as possible," I continue.

"I don't think he cares whether that guy lives or dies. He's just hired muscle," Randy replies disconsolately.

"Well, there is one option still available to hopefully buy us a little time," I tell Randy, as I start sliding on my stomach around the side of the kitchen island. "Leda, Stay." Time seems to be frozen in place as I creep my way across the dusty floor, only raising my head mere inches during my commando crawl toward the fallen bad guy's AR-15.

"Stay low, Veronica," Randy urges me while peering cautiously around the edge of the wood-clad island. Another wild barrage of shots pounds into the cabin's outer wall only feet above my head. So far, the sturdy construction of the cabin is acting as our bulletproof shield, but the uncovered windows loom overhead as a far too tempting target to our pursuer. And sure enough, he totally shatters the window directly above me as I hurriedly turn my face downward to avoid the shower of slicing, clattering glass. My searching hand finally lands on the gun as I take a quick lateral peek at the trussed-up enemy. Still out like a light. An axe to the head will do that to a person.

I would definitely not call myself a gun enthusiast, especially after being shot not once, but now twice, but I am the daughter of a hunter and was the fiancée of a deputy. I know my way around a gun, if needs must. This is a "need a gun" situation. From the placement and trajectory of the two rounds of shots, I've figured out the rough location of the shooter. I can only pray our last villain is not moving up on us too fast, but I do know how to slow him down. Pulling the detachable (illegal but immaterial right now) magazine from the base of the AR-15, I can see this particular magazine is roughly half-full. That gives me approximately 10-12 rounds to cause this creep some consternation. Delay until the cavalry gets here. It's our best hope.

Taking a deep breath, I roll over, lever myself to my knees, and venture a lightning quick scan over the windowsill. Spotting a figure hovering near a tree 150 yards away, I thrust the barrel of the gun through the denuded window and squeeze off several shots before dropping flat to the floor again. Leda gets reinforced with the Stay hand signal and I roll rapidly over to the adjoining window, all the while feeling blood coursing down the middle of my back. Rolling on glass is not a great feeling; take my word on that. Randy's anxious eyes watch me from the corner of his cover position. Our final pursuer starts screaming obscenities and pumps return fire into the cabin wall again near the spot I just vacated. It doesn't appear he is thrilled about being shot at. Join the club, jerk.

I inch the barrel of the rifle through the second window and send another blast of six shots in his direction, and then keep rolling at an angle away from the windows. Not many rounds remain in my borrowed weapon and I want to save a few rounds in case he makes it to the door. I crawl my way back toward Randy and Leda. "I'm saving the last few rounds in case he ventures down here. I'll have one more chance to take him out if that does happen." Randy nods soberly and we both wait with bated breath to see what the pilot throws at us next. And here it comes, another volley of shots tearing into the outer frame of our hiding spot. Clearly, he has a large supply of ammunition—unfortunately for us.

Just as our spirits are plummeting downward, a low-pitched voice from outside penetrates the ringing in my ears from the last fusillade of gunshots, and Leda starts to rise up from her crouch cautiously. I call her back down and we duck behind the kitchen counters while trying to ascertain what threat faces us now. Tentatively, I glance up at the kitchen window over the sink and see an eye and a thatch of red hair framed in the opening. It dawns on me with a surge of bursting hope that the person positioned at the other side of the cabin is calling my name rapidly through a broken windowpane. "Veronica, it's Deputy Bryan Campbell. Are you alright?"

It's the officer I met with Tim previously at the Lawn Lake Trailhead. "Yes, Bryan, thank you so much for coming. We took out the guy in here."

He continues speaking rapidly in a hushed tone, "Good job. I can see that. Tim sent me here when you called. Luckily, I was actually turning on to Lambeth Lane to start searching for you this morning, when you called Tim. I eased in through the woods and saw that guy come in after you. The second guy—the one who was just shooting—is circling up to the cabin through the woods on the far side as we speak. He's spotted in my rifle scope. Can you guys get down as flat as possible on the floor? When he moves out of the woods to come for you, I'll take him out."

"Will do. Be careful," I reply gratefully. Randy and I are pressed to the floor behind furniture now and a very disgruntled Leda is repositioned in her spot behind the kitchen island again. "That definitely has to be the pilot," I murmur to Randy. "Wonder what took him so long to get down here..."

Long fraught moments tick by and just when I cannot stand the tension any longer, Bryan calls out firmly, "Larimer County Sheriff. Drop your weapon now." A split-second later, a single rifle shot rings out. Oh no. I pray Bryan is okay. We wait and look at each other nervously for another 90 heart-stopping seconds. "All clear Veronica. You and Randy can come out. He's down."

Bryan gets on his radio and calls for an ambulance, followed swiftly by the blessed music of law enforcement sirens screaming up the winding, rutted road to assist us. Randy and I walk out into the sun and collapse in a heap on the front steps of the porch. Bryan has collected the long gun the pilot was using to hunt us and stands guard over him while he waits for paramedics. I carefully point the muzzle of the AR-15 away from us and gratefully hand it over to the next deputy on scene. The pilot is hollering ferociously to the heavens; I can't quite make it all out. Something about his boss delaying him at the helicopter with a complaining radio call. Boo hoo.

Oh, the irony. Even mercenaries have bosses who act like nitwits. However it happened, it slowed the pilot down just enough for us to take out thug number two and for Deputy Campbell to sneak up to our perimeter. From my vantage point on the porch, it looks like the deputy shot him right in the meat of the shoulder and dropped him to the ground. Good. We'll see how you like it, I think viciously to myself. I'm tired, I'm hungry, I'm heartily sick of granola bars, my hair is matted to my head, and I really need a scalding hot shower.

Leda sits at attention on the porch above me watching over my shoulder like my guardian angel. Soon the entire grove is filled with a cacophony of sounds—police officers hurrying about, ambulances arriving, and a multitude of calls being sent over official radios. Randy and I lean against the porch railings on either side of the steps and take in all this activity in a kind of daze. Leda watches all the frenzy mutely, but remains on high alert. She grumbles under her breath as two officers carry the hog-tied bad guy out of the cabin, get cuffs on him, and chain him to a stretcher. He is still only semi-conscious, with blood dripping steadily from his forehead, so they are able to get him secured before he can come around and wreak any havoc. The paramedics check him out and carry him away in an ambulance. Two more paramedics get the bleeding stopped temporarily on the pilot's shoulder, while he spews vile curses in the direction of all of us. This guy is so clearly a menace. It's astounding Randy is still alive. Eventually, the demented pilot is secured in the back of a second ambulance and carted away with two armed deputies escorting him in the back of the vehicle. Deputy Campbell joins us at the porch where we thank him fervently for getting to us so quickly.

"No problem. Just doing my job. I was in the right spot this morning thanks to your dad, Veronica. Law enforcement started getting calls late yesterday evening from a few scattered hikers in the national forest who thought poachers were using a helicopter to shoot at game animals. You had been out of contact for a while by that point. He realized what could be happening and calculated where you might head, based on the last data received from the app on your cell phone, and on your own training. Your father is damn good; he was pretty much spot on. I'm thankful it worked out the way it did. That pilot is a real piece of work. He was just hollering about the faulty fuel line on his piece of crap chopper and had a few choice words for you two. It seems like that guy wasn't too happy about being outwitted by a gosh darn girl and a fricking scientist for the past two days. I'm paraphrasing all the expletives." Randy and I both snicker over that comment and he leans over gingerly for a high five from the deputy. Randy really needs to get those ribs checked out.

At long last, Leda leaves her sentry position when Tim drives up the lane in his patrol vehicle in a flurry of dust and disgorges my father and Michael like torpedoes from the back seat. Leda dashes over to them wagging her tail furiously as they praise her and thump her sides. I straighten up slowly and turn back to Randy with my hand outstretched. "Come meet the man who loaded up my bag with all that food—and the water purification tablets!" Randy laughs and gets carefully to his feet with my help. We walk stiffly out into the middle of the clean-up operation and head over to greet the greatest support staff a girl could ever have.

CHAPTER 82

Dad and Michael envelop me in a big, squishy bear hug, with all three of us laughing and talking at the same time. An overwhelming sense of relief to be safe and back with my family floods through me. In just a week, it has become apparent that Michael is well and truly a part of our family now and it's wonderful to see them. After a few moments, Dad lowers me back to the ground and turns to Randy to shake hands.

"Dr. Jeffers, thank you so much for being there for my daughter."

Randy chuckles and says, "First of all, it's Randy, please. And it was more like she and Leda were there for me. You trained her well. They found me injured in the middle of the wilderness. Then she outmaneuvered all three of those killers, using a map and compass no less, and Leda brought the muscle." Leda hears her name mentioned and heads over to Randy for a pat. She really is expanding her universe of people little by little, and I'm proud of her too. Despite her abusive upbringing, she is learning to trust select people.

A third pair of paramedics hurry over to Randy ready to check him out now that the obviously bleeding people have been removed from the vicinity. I can't imagine there are any other available paramedics on duty in Larimer County right now. I hope nobody else needs help. Randy tries to insist that they look at my bullet wound first and my dad's face creases up in dismay.

"Dad, it's okay. Just a graze really. Not like before," I hasten to reassure him. Based on the instant look of concentrated rage on his normally good-natured features, it's an awfully good thing for the sake of the bad guys that they have already been removed from his vicinity. Tim, who has been coordinating all the frenetic activity on the site, sees my father's anger as well and pulls him aside to talk to him calmly for a few moments. If Dad had gotten to us before Deputy Campbell, my father would not have been aiming for the pilot's shoulder. I can tell he's worried about what happened to Randy and me, and now he will fret about me being shot again, and having to testify in court again, and how all that stress will affect my psyche.

The paramedics start an IV to get additional fluids into Randy after hearing about his ordeal since his abduction and Tim talks to each of us for our initial statements. Dad calms down a little when he sees the wound on my shoulder is indeed more of a rip and not another blast through my shoulder, but he is obviously unhappy. Michael takes Leda to the side of the yard for me and gives her a packet of her food and a drink of water. He checks her over thoroughly for injuries and gives her lots of praise before sending her back to me. I'm starting to get really very tired right now and all I want to do is go home and fall into my bed. I unbraid my hair slowly and the result feels like it's not so pretty. Man, do I need a long, leisurely shower, or better yet, a soak in my tub. With bubble bath.

Just as the operation is winding up at the Burchell cabin, a Boulder Police car arrives with Patty Jeffers. I get choked up as she leaps out of the car and comes running over joyfully to throw her arms around her husband with total disregard for the IV bag or anything else in her path. Randy hugs her back tightly with one arm and smiles over at me while Patty thanks us all over and over for our help. I lean down and kiss Leda on the top of her head. "You did good, girl. Really, really good."

CHAPTER 83

About ten days later, everyone involved in this crazy abduction case is invited to a cookout at the Dogged Pursuit property. Tim and Sylvia's girls come over to my house early and help me clean and get the place looking presentable. I spent almost three solid days passed out recuperating after my return, so it can really use a good freshening. Elli and Mari wash dishes and clean the kitchen while Lizzie and Jane clean the bathroom, vacuum, and set out vases of fresh flowers their mother sent over with them. The cool autumn breeze wafts gently through the open windows and the welcome sun throws vast oblongs of bright light around the interior.

Tim and Sylvia arrive bearing shopping bags full of meat for the grill, plus potato salad and macaroni salad. Michael puts together one of his patented green salads with chopped up fruit and vegetables. The array of colors is stunning. Even I am tempted by the obvious healthiness of this salad after the pile of granola bars consumed while Randy and I were running for our lives. Patty and Randy Jeffers appear with two home-made apple pies on which they collaborated—filling from her, crust from Randy—and they look delicious. I promptly forget all about the salad.

Dad shows up and starts grilling the food with Michael's able assistance. He tells me that he has just finished writing the product review of the high-resolution binoculars that were of such great use to Randy and me. And it's a doozy. I can't wait to read this one. Not every product can truthfully claim to have literally saved lives.

We add a table to the end of the big farmhouse table so we can all eat together, and everyone digs into the bounty of food we are blessed to share with such good friends. Randy and I report, in response to everyone's solicitous inquiries, that our injuries are healing just fine and we're suffering no lingering ill-effects. I am happy to realize that statement is mostly true. I have been sleeping pretty well, perhaps just out of sheer exhaustion, and am not feeling the same sense of devastation that haunted me after the incident in Ohio. That is most likely because the three of us survived, but I am proud to have made myself stronger, physically and mentally. Leda and I were able to fight back furiously this time and make a difference.

The girls reveal that Michael has gotten two of the three scholarships for which they helped him apply. He now will have $5000 available to pay for his beginning courses in Criminal Justice. Michael smiles shyly while everyone gives him a round of applause. He and Tim set a date to go run through the police obstacle course. Dad asks Michael if he would like to have the Garcias and their four children out to the property for a meal next weekend and Michael's ear-to-ear grin makes an answer unnecessary. Sylvia and Tim tell the girls that I have selected a dog breed for their family and the girls start screeching at the top of their lungs and calling out guesses. We get them calmed down enough to tell them it's going to be a Pointer and they can't stop smiling.

Once we have decimated the mountains of food before us, the teens offer to let all the younger dogs out of the kennel to play in the yard. We send them down to Michael's with one of the pies and a gallon of vanilla ice cream to share once they have exercised the dogs. The adults all get slices of pie and sit around on the sun porch basking in the peaceful fall Sunday with no work and no worries. Ripley and Leda curl up together in a sunny patch in the middle of the floor and Ripley starts a soft snoring a few minutes later. Tim comments, "I'll be relieved when all the national media leaves town. You would think they were actually here for Billy Fulton's murder trial, not just reporting on the fact that he was exonerated by the District Attorney's expert witness and all charges were dropped."

My father scoops another huge helping of ice cream into my bowl, "They had all that trial coverage planned and budgeted for; they must be wringing every last bit of drama out of him being an innocent man."

Randy offers his contribution, "And then they're all going to come back to Colorado again when the trial starts for the pilot, the one living ex-con who took that axe to the head, and the IT expert that Juan Toledo planted at my company." We all groan at the thought of even more media coverage, but it's what they do.

Randy and I learn from everyone involved in the case, that all sorts of discoveries were being made while he and I were fleeing for our lives from the mercenaries. Dad had broken the password and Jonah had been notified so everyone could start document review in hopes of finding the key to unlock the case. Dad gives us more detail now, "I blazed through the thumb drive data on the defective membrane in the reverse osmosis system and located Randy's draft of an unfavorable technical report that would scuttle the initial public offering. Oddly enough, when I reported this to Glen Gerard, he indicated that the report on Randy's just unlocked database at work was a completely favorable technical review. However, when he investigated it further, he found that the report did not contain Randy's digital signature.

"Apparently, the planted IT guy had broken through to Randy's database already, unbeknownst to Glen, and uploaded the fake report. Glen instantly had the police look further into the background of the bright young IT guy, Julio, who had come highly recommended to Water Analytical Solutions by one of the owners of Agua Pura Ahora, S.A. Then Tim found a link between the IT guy and one of the principal investors in the reverse osmosis system, Juan Toledo. When he ran checks on this Toledo individual, it threw up a red flag to the DEA, who were watching him closely due to his suspected involvement in establishing the drug-running route to areas north of Colorado. When Tim conveyed his suspicions to the DEA and they learned of the helicopter's involvement, the police starting putting together the reason for the abduction and figured out how Toledo was moving drugs."

Tim picks up the story, "Randy's belief that Juan Toledo refused to accept a delay in the IPO was absolutely correct. He was pressed for money, having overextended his credit with a major drug cartel in Columbia and he needed the profit from the IPO to make things right. Toledo, who was just a South American businessman as far as the owners of Agua Pura Ahora, S.A. knew, asked them to recommend the new IT guy to Glen Gerard. Glen was willing to interview the kid because a client highly recommended him and Water Analytical Solutions did need the help. Randy stymied the plan to kill him in a staged accident and plant a fake report when he disappeared with a thumb drive copy of the negative data in hand. Toledo was desperate to get the drive back. Then Randy would have just been a liability. What Toledo did not fully understand is that the SEC is ever vigilant in its efforts to unmask fraudulent research reports with regard to IPOs. It would have caught up to Toledo eventually."

Tim continues, "The pilot was hired, through a periodical well-known in the world of mercenaries, to work for Toledo moving the drug shipments. He brought the two ex-cons aboard to deal with Randy, but neither of them fared too well in the wilderness or when dealing with Leda. His boss chewing him out on the radio for not catching their quarry sooner, combined with the helicopter's mechanical issues, did, in fact, delay the pilot in joining the violent pursuit of Randy and Veronica down the last stretch of the mountain. You have to love the irony. That wasted time allowed Deputy Campbell to locate you two and get the drop on the pilot. Thankfully. The DEA is in the process of dismantling Toledo's entire drug network and has tracked him to a country that actually does have an extradition treaty with the United States. We're confident he'll come back to stand trial for setting this whole abduction in motion. The pilot and the remaining hired gun will face charges of felony kidnapping and attempted murder based on the testimony of you two. On a side note, Billy Fulton went to the hospital and offered to pay off the medical bills for the both of you when he learned what you went through to survive, consequently getting the word of his innocence out there. Now that he is no longer a suspect in the death of his wife, he seems to be genuinely grieving her loss."

Randy and I both smile at the thought of Billy in the hospital with his pen and checkbook and he says, "Maybe I'll take Patty to a basketball game in Omaha and we can sit courtside sometime this year. I guess we'll have to buy a new car first though." Everyone smiles sympathetically; the final mystery of the case remains unsolved and his missing car has never turned up. Tim thinks it sits at the bottom of a lake in Rocky Mountain National Park—courtesy of the hired guns, frustrated in their search for a thumb drive.

Once we finish talking about the many facets of the convoluted case, we all sit in total relaxation happy to be safe and in the company of good friends. The kids can be heard through the open windows playing with the dogs in the yard and it occurs to me that training needs to recommence tomorrow. Michael has really helped me out in my absence. It is almost time to take Gemma to Florida so she can protect the Duncans' orange groves, and Butter and Scotch will go home to be reunited and trained with their parents. I contacted Ricardo Cruz after returning home from the successful search for Randy Jeffers and we set a fast-approaching time to start working with his Doberman, Jinx, on obedience and protection. We both lingered on the phone just a fraction longer than probably was warranted to simply set an appointment. He really does have the nicest voice.

The work will just keep coming, I think. But right now, it's wonderful to sit on the couch and chat lazily as the day winds down with my devoted dog at my feet, knowing I survived against very tough odds and I responded well under pressure. My previous life is dead and gone, but this new life is starting to give me hope again.

EPILOGUE

Three weeks later, my father calls me over to his cabin, saying he wants to talk to me about something important. Leda and I have just finished a gorgeous hike and we head over and bounce our way inside. My father is sitting frozen at his desk staring vacantly out toward the Flatirons. His odd demeanor slows me in my tracks and my heart plummets to the ground. "Dad, what's wrong? Are you feeling okay?"

Then I notice he is holding an envelope in his hand. As I approach, I see it is from the Prosecutor's Office in my home county in Ohio. And my face freezes. Only one person could cause them to have a reason to contact us here in Colorado. "Tell me what he's done," I demand.

Dad turns to me reluctantly, "The letter states that prison authorities became aware that Tommy Arnett saw media coverage of your involvement in the disappearance and recovery of Randy Jeffers in Colorado, and the dismantling of a major drug pipeline. Once Arnett knew where you have been living, he attempted to exploit a weakness in the security of the computers in the prison library to contact a gang member who is scheduled to be paroled soon from prison down in Canon City. Arnett's efforts to contact this gang member, which *were* intercepted by authorities, revealed that he was soliciting this individual to kill you. The current Prosecutor wants you to be aware of this issue, but also to know that Arnett has been transferred to Level 5A of the Ohio State Penitentiary, the highest security prison in Ohio, and with absolutely no privileges allowed. I'm so sorry about this, sweetheart."

I sink wordlessly down to the floor and hug Leda tightly to my chest as I process this unwelcome information. Will the echoes of that past tragedy ever release me to live in peace?

ACKNOWLEDGEMENTS

Irst and foremost this book is dedicated to my late father, Paul R. Carter. He was a wonderful writer, public relations guru, outdoorsman, and all around great Dad. My enthusiasm for writing and nature comes directly from him—lost too soon due to the dreadful disease ALS. His article 'Finding the Spots,' which appears in the November 1999 issue of *Pennsylvania Game News*, is the inspiration for the article written by Veronica's father about hunting the benches.

Thank you so much to all of my friends who encouraged me to write the book and each read a draft (or three)—Kathy, Stephanie, Jamie, Robin, Helen, Cindy, and especially Leslie, who talked through every plot point with me on our daily hikes with our dogs and read every single draft of the manuscript. (And extra thanks to our terrific neighbors, Julie & Rob, who have kindly let us hike their woods for years.)

Much appreciation to my husband, Arthur, who believes in this book and my writing, and cooks me excellent dinners as fuel for the journey!

The wonderful author of the Kate Hamilton mystery series, Connie Berry, has been nothing but generosity itself to me throughout this whole process. If you have not had a chance to read her phenomenal books set in the British Isles, I promise you will love them.

Rick Porrello, author of *To Kill the Irishman* and a number of other great reads, has earned my undying gratitude for his support and willingness to answer questions about the publishing process.

Many thanks to Tudy Morris of Summit Search and Rescue Dogs, who let me hide as a "missing person" during group training exercises, read my manuscript, and kindly answered tons of questions about search and rescue. Any mistakes which remain (or dramatic license taken) are my own.

To Charlie Williams, I appreciate you so much for the invaluable support you gave me while I wrote this book and the multitude of questions you let me ask you—no matter how random! You truly are a great friend.

Thank you to my home library, Geauga West, and to all my friends on the staff who encouraged me every step of the way in the writing of this book: Cindy, Rebecca, Linda, Jan, Gloria, and Lee. You're the best!

Profound gratitude goes to Jeff Zamaiko, racetrack photographer extraordinaire for decades at Thistledown and Northfield, who so adeptly took my ideas and created the gorgeous cover of *Dogged Pursuit*. (Fellow Nancy Drew fans might be interested to know that the idea for the silhouette came from the dark blue silhouette of Nancy with a magnifying glass that appears on the blue tweed editions.)

I have taken minor liberties with certain locales in furtherance of the story. All details related to hiking trails, fire closures, dog restrictions, and hunting seasons around Boulder and Rocky Mountain National Park, should be verified for up-to-date information.

Thanks also to Richard DiMarco and Bill Allen who have trained so many of us in the Chagrin Valley how to train our dogs. Those obedience lessons really work.

Just a note: Chesapeake Bay Retrievers are a wonderful breed, but probably not a good fit for a first time dog owner.

Last, but not least, to the dogs, many of whom were rescues and had very tough starts to their lives:

Scotch (the Brittany who started it all), Ripley and Alex (the Golden Retrievers), Leda and Dusty (the Chessies), Shawnee, Cody, and Ranger (the German Shepherds), Gemma (the Flat-Coated Retriever), and Cocoa (the Llewellin Setter)

Our lives have been immeasurably enriched by your love and personalities.